My Way or God's Way?

Neo-Gnosticism and
Neo-Pelagianism in Interdisciplinary Perspective

My Way or God's Way?

Neo-Gnosticism and
Neo-Pelagianism in Interdisciplinary Perspective

Editors

Francis Gonsalves SJ, Arjen Tete SJ,
Dinesh Braganza SJ

Jnana-Deepa Vidyapeeth
2018

My Way or God's Way? *Neo-Gnosticism and Neo-Pelagianism in Interdisciplinary Perspective*—Jointly published by the Rev. Dr. Ashish Amos of the Indian Society for Promoting Christian Knowledge (ISPCK), Post Box 1585, 1654, Madarsa Road, Kashmere Gate, Delhi-110006 and Jnana-Deepa Vidyapeeth (JDV), Pune.

Online Order: http://ispck.org.in/book.php

Also available on amazon.in

ISBN: 978-81-8465-671-8

Cover credit: Internet sources

Laser typeset by

ISPCK, Post Box 1585, 1654, Madarsa Road, Kashmere Gate, Delhi-110006
• *Tel:* 23866323/22

e-mail: ashish@ispck.org.in • ella@ispck.org.in
website: www.ispck.org.in

Contents

Preface

'My Way or God's Way?' is the title of an interdisciplinary symposium conducted by the Jnana-Deepa Vidyapeeth (hereafter abbreviated as JDV), Pune, on November 3 and November 4, 2017. The symposium attracted academics and scholars from India and abroad to reflect upon two phenomena—neo-gnosticism and neo-pelagiansim—that are cause of current concern in church circles. The seeds of this symposium were sown with a letter dated December 6, 2016, of Cardinal Gerhard Müller, the then-Perfect of the Congregation for the Doctrine of Faith (CDF), Vatican City. Taking cue from Pope Francis's concern about neo-gnosticism and neo-pelagianism, Cardinal Müller expressed the CDF's desire to: "Ask some renowned Universities to organize symposiums pertaining to one or another aspect of these themes for the purpose of studying the possible (neo)gnostic and (neo)pelagian contemporary trends, their impact on the life of the church, and the pastoral remedies for a response."

The CDF's request led to the setting up of an organizing committee that soon set about reflecting upon the theme and finding possible ways and means of conducting a symposium. A 'concept note' was sent to all the faculties of theology and philosophy in India, as well as to a few international scholars. The response was overwhelming. Since the CDF's request was to see how these two trends of thought had repercussions and ramifications in the larger life of Church and Society, presenters were chosen from diverse disciplines so as to ensure the interdisciplinary character of the symposium. It was also decided that these two trends of thought be examined not as some archeological construct of the past, but in terms of their current avatars, which Pope Francis and many others are apprehensive about. The papers are presented in this book, in more or less the same order in which they were presented during the symposium.

In '*Recovering the Original Freshness of the Gospel*' Archbishop Thomas Menamparampil dwells at some length on Pope Francis's apprehension about traces of Gnosticism and Pelagianism in society, today, expressed in his 2013 Apostolic Exhortation *Evangelii Gaudium*. Quoting extensively from this document, he echoes the pope's caution about the gnostic 'dangers of a sterile intellectualism' and 'unrooted and unrealistic ideas' and stresses instead the dire need for insightful thinkers who faithfully keep studying and interpreting the diverse dimensions of Jesus' 'good news' in our own historical and cultural contexts, and who invite others to think and personalize that message. Mission and ministry must always be an overflow of: "An authentic faith – which is never comfortable or completely personal – [that] always involves a deep desire to change the world, to transmit values, to leave this earth somehow better than we found it." (*EG* 183).

In his paper '*Adoration of God or Adoration of the Self? Certain Aspects of Seeking Psychological Security*', Bishop Thomas Tharayil sees neo-gnosticism and neo-pelagianism as motivated by psychological insecurities and immaturities that could lead to the cultivation of ultra-conservative attitudes. Such persons lock themselves within a world of self-centeredness, which results in an 'adoration of the self', so to say. A pathological personality might utilise certain ideologies to protect oneself from possible threats. Moreover, the performance of certain rites and rituals might not be directed towards God's glory but aimed at seeking security. As an antidote to this, one ought to seek self-transcendence and direct one's energies towards the worship of God.

In a 4-part pictorial presentation entitled '*Neo-Gnosticism and Neo-Pelagianism: Responses of the Church through the Eucharist*,' Norman Tanner traces the history of the Mass and shows how the threats of Gnosticism and Pelagianism were warded off by the teaching and devotional life of the Church. The first part looks at the first millennium AD, beginning with a painting from around 190 AD, the oldest known Christian illustration of any kind. The second part focuses on developments in the Catholic Church during the five centuries between the start of the East-West schism in 1054 and the beginning of the Reformation in 1517. The third part examines the Reformation and Counter-Reformation: criticisms of Catholic practices on the part of the Reformers as well as their own teachings and practices; and developments within the Catholic Church, partly in response to these criticisms. A final part traces the developments in the four ecumenical councils: Nicea I (325), Lateran IV (1215), Trent (1545-63) and Vatican II (1962-5).

In his paper '*Hominization of the Word: A Challenge to Neo-Gnosticism and Neo-Pelagianism*,' Jacob Parappally argues that the core Christian revelation, namely, the "Word was made flesh" (Jn 1:14) is the exact antithesis of any gnostic assertion while also subverting the sureties of Pelagianism and its offshoots. This 'hominization of the Word' reaffirms the basic goodness of humans and their world despite attempts by some to thwart God's plan for humans and their welfare. Jesus' birth-life-death reveal the vulnerability of humans, while his rising from the dead affirms the possibility of the transformation of humans and their world. Thus, any ideology like Gnosticism and Pelagianism—and their various neo-avatars—that, on the one hand, devalue the human body or abuse it, and, on the other hand, deny the working of God's grace for salvation, go counter to the Christian gospel.

Michael Amaladoss provides insights into the Asian/Indian aspects of the theme by arguing that the dualisms of the Greek tradition between God and the world, spirit and matter, mind and body, etc., are not stressed in the Indian tradition. God is not merely transcendent, but also immanent. One does not go beyond the world to discover God, but one experiences God as the centre of the universe, embracing and integrating everything. The spiritual path, therefore, is a search for depth. The human ego itself is rooted in the Atman. It is not independent of and opposed to the Atman as in Pelagianism. The Asian/Indian vision is therefore holistic: Gnosis is integrated with

Agape. One can even go further and say that Gnosis and Agape are merged with living Reality.

Providing a feminist perspective to the neo-gnosticism and neo-pelagianism debate, D.J. Margaret argues that the moral mire created by the former often persuades or pressurises us to a relentless bodily hedonism. The implicit devaluation of the body and over-evaluation of the mind has been a major problem in history. One of the impacts of the dualistic view of the human body has been equating it solely with the activity of sexuality, which was considered evil. However, embodiment theology or incarnation theology has challenged this outmoded perception and suggested that the human body is an integral and holistic part of the human experience rather than being regarded simply as an instrument of sexual activity. First, exposing the situation of society and women therein, she then highlights challenges of neo-gnosticism and neo-pelagianism in the development of an embodied spirituality. Finally, she stresses the need for an embodied spirituality, which seeks solidarity with others in the spiritual transformation of self, community, and world.

Three papers give Biblical insights into the theme. In "*Neo-gnosticism and Neo-pelagianism: Biblical Understanding and Present Challenges*," Selva Rathinam provides an overview of the origins, development and challenges of these two phenomena. He then cautions about a religion-less Christianity, which is a new form of gnosticism, today; and proposes a back-to-the-Bible approach to counter the dangerous dualism of gnosticism and the boasts of neo-pelagianism. Next, using the Book of Deuteronomy as base, Thomas Karimundackal shows that human will (i.e., the collective will of Israel) has been enabled by the grace of God to respond to the divine choice and election. As Israel's will is animated by God's grace, it has the propensity and ability to make decisions in conformity to God's will. Human will cannot really respond to God's initiatives apart from his enlightening grace. This vision rebuffs Pelagius's view of the total freedom of human will. Finally, M. Paul Raj points out that, under the influence of neo-gnostic and neo-pelagian ideas, practitioners of Christian theology fail to uphold the 'gifted' nature of human existence and redemption; they are confused or confuse others by advocating ideologies and attitudes that render grace fruitless and ineffective. Considering 2 Cor 12:9-10 as a basic text which describes the 'necessity' and the 'sufficiency' of divine grace, he reflects on how Paul presents the central role of grace in human redemption, thereby contradicting the tenets of Gnosticism and Pelagianism.

In his paper *'Grace is God's Ennobling and Enabling Gift to You and Me,'* Joseph Mattam delves deeper into the nature of grace, defining it as "the self-gift of God, as *the love-ability* which constitutes our being as creatures and children of God." He argues that the most important proof of "God loves us" is our *love-ability*, which is a share in God's love. When does this self-gift of God as love take place in our lives? The classical Catholic position is that it is communicated at baptism, making us God's sons/daughters. This would mean that the non-baptized are *essentially different human beings* as they are not God's sons/daughters. This obviously does not make sense. Critiquing Pelagius who denied the need for divine grace, claiming that humans can discipline themselves so effectively that they could be saved by their own free will, Mattam opines that the flaw in Pelagius's thinking was that he did not attribute the goodness in human beings to a gift of God at creation itself. Humans are good because they are sharers in God's life. This goodness is a free gift; it is not due to the human nature in itself. His paper then reflects briefly on creation as the foundation for understanding divine grace.

Distinguishing between 'Gnostic-Pelagian Ethics' and the 'Ethics of Mercy' in Pope Francis's *Amoris Laetitia*, moral theologian Shaji George Kochuthara argues that, in the Christian understanding, law is not the basis of moral life or the starting point of moral theology; rather, God's grace—manifested in God's compassion, love and forgiveness—is the bedrock of morality. In this regard, Pope Francis's *Amoris Laetitia* firmly follows a moral methodology that rejects neo-gnostic-pelagian ethics, seen in legalism, elitism, pharisaic mentality, subjective and relative morality, while upholding morality rooted in mercy, a profound awareness of human fragility and trust in God's grace. In another paper on moral theology entitled: "*Formation of Conscience as the Core of Christian Ethics*," Paulachan Kochappilly describes the following of Christ as the essence of Christian morality, which is facilitated and accelerated by listening to the voice of God that echoes in the depth of one's being, to love God, to serve neighbour, and to care for nature. This implies conversations with the people of God and a consequent conversion of heart leading to communion with God, the goal of human life. The formation of a right conscience is essential to respond to the demands of love.

A dichotomized view of life and reality promoted by neo-gnosticism poses problems in priestly formation, which, due to such dichotomization, comes to be seen as gradual initiation into secret knowledge. George Karuvelil argues that such formation has had disastrous consequences as it split the academic formation of the priest from ministerial life, not as a moral flaw or personal human failing but as an institutional or systemic flaw. After pointing out some manifestations of this split, he turns to the neo-Scholastic response of the Church in dealing with this conflict, which was abandoned by VC II. The impact of VC II on theological formation is discussed, especially the vigorous attempts made in the second half of the 20th century to democratize the so-called secret knowledge and make it public.

In his essay '*The God-Jesus' Psyche as Continuing Phenomenon*', Konrad Noronha offers insights into Jesus' psyche, with keen consciousness of his sonship in the light of his profound relationship with his Abba-Father-God. From establishing this relationship as the source and sustenance of all Jesus' words and works, he shows how Jesus can be a model for human beings who are also called to be children of God. Jesus' teaching of the reign of God pervade his words and actions, and even today have great pertinence in overturning entrenched worldviews, replacing them with others consonant with his ideals. Jesus' life gives us a glimpse of a world that stands opposed to and in judgment over the realities of today's world. This includes the need of dependence on God. Whichever way one looks at Jesus, Christians must be absorbed into the wondrous life-changing joy of the Gospel and not just become experimenters through new age therapies, neo-gnosticism or neo-pelagianism, in understanding their life and God's action in the world.

More than any other community, the lifestyles and worldviews of the subaltern communities of India stand as a critique against the false dichotomies and hollow pretensions held by the so-called 'higher' castes and 'upper' classes. In his study on subalterns entitled: '*The Earthiness of Subaltern Religious Imagination: A Critical Exploration into the Phenomenon of Pilgrimage to Velankanni*,' A. Maria Arul Raja probes into the victimhood, subjecthood, and community-hood of subaltern communities in their engagement with Our Lady of Velankanni. Studying the stages of this pilgrimage—the preparation, performance, and completion of the process of pilgrimage—he notes how the subaltern discourse underscores the significance of the needs of the poor who have to be served by the divine aspects (instrumentalization of the divine for affirming the marginalized). He also demonstrates how subaltern celebrations, rites and rituals perform the prophetic task of the removal of untouchability, annihilation of casteism, eradication of patriarchy, while militating against the culture of communalism, corruption and consumerism.

Kuruvilla Pandikattu's paper '*Mastery versus Mystery on the Path to Progress*' deals with the dynamic tension between mastery and mystery. The scientific quest to control and dominate with the aim of acquiring 'mastery' is a noble human venture, provided we also acknowledge its limitations. Pandikattu raises basic questions on our views of progress: is there real progress in technology, science, philosophy and religion? Assuming that there is real progress, a disputed issue, we take up the directionality or teleology of this progress. If there is a progress, what is the role of human beings, especially their scientific and religious pursuits? As against neo-pelagian trends, the paper tries to show that while our attempts to master the universe have been successful, the mastery over our own selves is much more a complex phenomenon than we normally imagine. Nonetheless, we need to retain a sense of healthy mystery, which alone can free us from the neuroticism of absolute certainty. Finally, the paper takes up issues related to the directionality of the collective human progress in terms of even human extinction—the so-called 'doomsday arguments'—and argues that we need a rediscover a healthy spirituality, acknowledging the tension between mystery and mastery, the bodily and spiritual, unlike the Pelagian and Gnostic attempts at seeking a clear-cut and guaranteed solution to the complex human destiny.

In the final paper entitled '*Pseudo-Spirituality: Eclipse of God and Neighbour—Neo-gnosticism and Neo-pelagianism in the Light of Evangelii Gaudium*', taking cue from Pope Francis, Joseph A. D'Mello first critiques these two phenomena as manifestations of 'spiritual worldliness'. He then discusses the characteristics of a true Christian spirituality which can never be divorced from the love of God and love of one's neighbour. What is needed, opines D'Mello, is: "A spirituality that is integrated [and] will uphold the relationship with God, with others and with the material universe [against neo-gnosticism]; it will treat God as absolute and all the rest as relative [against neo-pelagianism]."

From the academic menu spread out during the Symposium, one will see that a broad spectrum of academics, scholars, students of theology/philosophy and committed Christians contributed creatively by way of presenting papers, speaking as panelists and actively participating in the discussions. Presented in the pages of this volume is a modest 'work-in-progress'. Happily, as this work goes to the press, two Pope-Francis inspired documents have seen the light of day: (a) *Placuit Deo*,[1] and, (b) *Gaudete et Exsultate*.[2] Both these documents dwell in greater depth on the perils of neo-gnosticism and neo-pelagianism. One would do well to read them and reflect upon them.

The letter received from the CDF, Rome, which was inspirational in getting the Symposium to a swift start and a successful end, read: "This Dicastery has understood the necessity to expand the study, by also involving other institutions." We, at JDV, have got the ball rolling. We hope and pray that many others—individuals, communities, and institutions—join in the discussions and discernment so as to unfailing and everywhere choose God's way, not ours. Therein lies our happiness and hope for a better humanity, a better world.

Prof. Dr Francis Gonsalves, SJ **Dr Arjen Tete, SJ** **Dr Dinesh Braganza, SJ**

fragons@gmail.com   arjensj@gmail.com dineshbsj@gmail.com

Jnana-Deepa Vidayapeeth, Pune

Feast of St Joseph the Worker

May 1, 2018

Endnotes

[1] This document addressed to: "The Bishops of the Catholic Church on Certain Aspects of Christian Salvation," was published from the Offices of the Congregation for the Doctrine of the Faith, Rome, on February 22, 2018.

[2] Pope Francis's Apostolic Exhortation *Gaudete et Exsultate* – "On the Call to Holiness in Today's World" was given on March 19, 2018.

1

Recovering "The Original Freshness of the Gospel" (EG 11)

Archbishop Thomas Menamparampil

1. The Mission of Inviting Thought

It used to be said some time ago, "What Bengal thinks today, India thinks tomorrow." There was some truth in that statement at least in those days, as Bengal had an early start in modern education. Similarly, it would be right to say, "What universities think today, society thinks tomorrow." We remember with pride that Takshasila with 10,500 students and Nalanda with 10,000 students, our civilization made the entire Eastern World think more profoundly. In similar fashion, it would not be far wrong to say, "What Christian intellectuals think today, Christian society as a whole comes to think tomorrow."

In other words, we need insightful thinkers who continuously keep studying and interpreting the diverse dimensions of the Good News that the Lord has given to us in their own historical and cultural contexts, and who invite others to think and personalize that Message. This is what the Fathers and Doctors of the Church did in their own times, and what theologians are doing in our days inspired also by the Magisterium. Thus, I begin by paying respects to the 'thinking element' within the Church, who invite thought within the Christian fold and beyond.

Meanwhile, we cannot close our eyes to the serious threat posed by 'cultural nationalists' in our country to intelligent and independent thinking, enlightened self-expression, and well-informed social criticism. The recent assassination of Gauri Lankesh in Bengaluru following digital threats that preceded it, is one of the many shocking murders that have already taken place. The same forces are bent on glorifying our warrior heroes like Prithviraj Chauhan and Chhatrapatti Shivaji—with a ₹ 4,000-crore monument and statue being built in the Arabian Sea off the coast of Mumbai—rather than leaders in thought like philosophers or scientists that inspired our society, which would have been more in the Indian tradition. This is placing muscle power before brain power.

Similarly, when national or regional heroes and heroines are raised above the status of citizens, and are lionized and divinized, blind followers lower themselves, and seem to renounce their capacity to think. Again, cult leaders and godmen like the now-imprisoned Ram Rahim guide and misguide devotees using mob psychology rather than 'thought power'. So, we see a continuous effort to weaken the 'thinking power' of people in our society. Thus it happens that the quality of 'Public Reasoning' about which Amartya Sen speaks at length in his *The Argumentative Indian* has come down. Little wonder that ex-President of India, Pranab Mukherjee passionately called for better quality of debates in the legislatures.

2.   The Danger of Sterile Intellectualism

While, therefore, reaffirming the value of intelligent thinking, we must pay attention to Pope Francis's warning against a so-called 'sterile intellectualism'. He calls it an expression of 'worldliness' with ostentatious preoccupation with doctrinal formulations, which have little relevance for the concerns of today. He links it with authoritarian elitism, search for prestige, and hasty evaluation of others; with an eagerness to inspect and verify, classify and judge. It manifests itself in an over-concern for the Church as an institution, with too little anxiety about the people in difficult situations and eagerness to open out the doors of grace to them. Persons who have moved ahead along these lines are more in search of self-fulfilment, trapped amidst meetings and events, remaining far from the multitudes that thirst for Christ. Those, further, who are absorbed in the personal experience of "purely subjective faith" and the consolation it offers, may not be far from the one-sidedness that is usually described as '*Gnosticism*' (See *Evangelii Gaudium*, 94-95).[1]

Similarly, in the area of social analysis, the Pope notices a 'diagnostic overload', and not enough realistic approaches to heal the imbalances in the situation. What is really required, he says, is an 'evangelical discernment' which is "nourished by the light and strength of the Holy Spirit" (EG 50). He is not afraid to say, "We should not be concerned simply about falling into doctrinal error, but about remaining faithful to this light-filled path of life and wisdom" (EG 194). "The Church and theology exist to evangelize, and not be content with a desk-bound theology" (EG 133).

In today's context, for example, it is right that we reflect on the consequences of the emergence of Extreme Right-Wing Nationalism on the world scene, with the rise of Vladimir Putin, Recep Tayyip Erdogan, Rodrigo Duterte, Donald Trump, Narendra Modi and others. With dangerous slogans like 'America First', the hawkish and arrogant vocabulary that the world leaders use during elections or while warning neighbouring nations, is a worrying phenomenon. Here is an area where intelligent thought ought to be made relevant. Theologians who were used to addressing Left-Wing exaggerations are still to do some creative thinking about how to address Right-Wing exaggerations: to understand why they have arisen in the first place, and how they may be addressed rather than merely identifying where they are wrong.

3.   Un-rooted and Unrealistic Ideas

Pope Francis notices "a constant tension between ideas and realities. Realities simply are, whereas ideas are worked out." There must be continuous dialogue between the two. Detached ideas have limitations. In fact, some ideas mask reality, garbing it in empty rhetoric, unrealistic ideals, ethical systems bereft of kindness, intellectual discourse bereft of wisdom. Making our abode permanently in the realm of words, images, and rhetoric is dangerous. "Realities are greater than ideas," he says (EG 231). A clear example is the contrast between India's ambition to become a world power and the reality that she has the largest number of 'out-of-school children' in the world, or that eight and a half lakhs under-5 children die every year.

Disagreement over ideas can lead to *tensions*. The Pope laments, "How many wars take place within the people of God and in our different communities! In our neighbourhoods and in the workplace, how many wars are caused by envy and jealousy, even among Christians! Spiritual worldliness leads some Christians to war with other Christians...," some creating an 'inner circle', different and special (EG 98). This is not Christian.

After all, ideas are for communication, understanding, and consequent action. Disconnected from realities, they lead to ineffectual idealism, with no subsequent action. That is why it happens that many politicians and religious leaders with clear and logical proposals do not have followers, because they remain at the theoretical level, their politics and faith are empty rhetoric. On the one hand we must make sure that we are not 'reinventing' the Gospel; on the other, that God's Message comes into *actual life situations*, that it reflects on justice and charity, and not end in self-centred *Gnosticism* (EG 232-233).

It should be our consistent effort to express truths in *'abiding newness'* in this age of vast and rapid cultural changes. An over-concern for 'Orthodox language' can reduce something from the authentic Gospel, especially when it differs greatly from the language people use (EG 41). Thus what takes place is a "disjointed transmission of a multitude of doctrines." On the contrary, a genuine *'missionary style'* while not excluding any of the traditional doctrines, "concentrates on the essentials": what is most beautiful, grand, appealing, and necessary (EG 35).

The Pope refers to the meaningless contentions that often rise over ideas. What are the issues over which Indian society is divided today? Unfortunately, over trifles: beef-eating, love *jihad*, abolition of

Urdu, renaming of roads, ignoring of the Mughals, special deference to *Vandemataram*, personal law. On the contrary, concern for safe train journey, sufficient food supply (3000 farmers committed suicide in 2016), adequate healthcare (2000 children die in Gorakhpur Hospital annually), quality education, and other social needs would have united the nation. We need to unify over core human concerns and discover a new vocabulary that can unite us in a common effort.

4. Reaching Out to the Fringes to "Recover the Original Freshness of the Gospel"

We "recover the original freshness of the Gospel" precisely in seeking to address the anxieties of the people in society today. Experienced missionaries will vouch for the profundity of the following statement: "Nothing is more solid, profound, secure, meaningful and wisdom-filled than that *first proclamation*" (EG 165). To make our basic sharing meaningful we need to continuously discover new signs and symbols, even unconventional ones, to give new flesh to the Word in different cultural settings to make them attractive to people in diverse situations (EG 167).

The pedagogy that Pope Francis suggests is something quite unexpected: he invites us to go to the *'fringes of humanity,'* evidently to help, but also to learn. It really equips us when we gradually come to understand the distress and the discourse of those at the 'periphery'. Their helplessness may not always be in the economic field, it could also be in the psychological, social, cultural, intellectual or spiritual fields. When we remain close to them, listening to them at length, and responding to their need (EG 46), we discover that the *helping process is also a learning process.*

For, the most helpless are also the most motivated in society to transform the painful situation they face. Often, they are stridently eloquent: the landless, the homeless, the foodless, and the healthless... due to uneven distribution of wealth or to absolute wastefulness in a consumer society (EG 191). They constitute the 'driving force' in history. To them we bring not the formulae provided by ideologies, but the *'intelligence of the Gospel'* that enables them to see deeper, wider and further into the historic processes, and sustains their hope and their energy.

It is in our power to make our message meaningful to the poor, the sick, the despised, the overlooked, and those who "cannot repay you" (Lk 14:14), so that we rediscover "the original freshness of the Gospel" (EG 48). They teach us how to express our *faith in the midst of suffering*. "We need to be evangelized by them" so that our lives may be faith-filled. New Evangelization is precisely this: to recognize "the saving power at work in their lives" and embrace their mysterious wisdom (EG 198).

We keep listening to people, taking note of their aspirations, limitations, ways of praying, their language, signs and symbols; answering their questions; linking ourselves with their human situation. It is this *'spiritual sensitivity'* that enables us to read God's message in events (*Pastores Dabo Vobis* 42, 1992). In our interactions with people in diverse situations, we discover the core anxieties of humanity and the language we need to use to address them. Too often shall we find that their dominating sentiment is not one of class-anger, but of *spiritual hunger*. When we attend to these needs we shall rediscover the 'freshness of the Gospel' and develop the right skills for presenting its core content.

In the immediate context we know what our people are worried about: rising prices, food and water shortages, growing violence, communal threats. We also hear of domestic violence and dowry deaths. The statistics are frightening: in 2015 about 7,634 women died in domestic violence: 21 a day, 1 every hour. Every day about 2000 girl-children are aborted or killed soon after birth. There is a *'beti bachao'* campaign. Custodial deaths are on the increase. Kidnapping and rape cases continue. Dalit anger keeps simmering. Creativity expresses itself in developing 'beef detection kits' rather than in malaria eradication strategies. India's image at the international level has suffered a great deal with its 'anti-cow-slaughter laws' (imprisonment, death penalty, lynchings) just what 'anti-blasphemy laws' did for Pakistan. Amazingly, in pain arises also prayerfulness. Those who are closest to pain breathe forth the vibrancy of the Gospel.

5. Lay Initiatives Multiply, as Though to Balance Excessive Clerical Intellectualism

In this entire exercise what comes through is the very reverse of *clericalism* (EG 102). There is no room here for excessive legalism, authoritarianism, dogmatism and intellectualism. It calls for deep faith to see God in the villages, streets, squares, work places, private interactions, and public gatherings. We are in the midst of people to foster solidarity, fraternity, desire for goodness, truth and justice. And all too soon shall we realize "God does not hide himself from those who seek him with a sincere heart" (EG 71).

Once such an atmosphere is created, the entire community begins to evangelize, young people taking the lead. Once again, the Pope takes us by surprise by asking us to listen to the *elderly* and the *young* people in studying the signs of the times, one representing the memory and wisdom of age and experience to avoid mistakes, the other representing the new direction society seeks in order to move ahead and build a sure future (EG 108). Their vision is not distorted by vested interests as in the case of the present-day decision-makers.

Of late, there has been a new development. In seeking to respond to growing secularization, a good section of the *clergy* have moved on to serve in the *secular areas* of life, emphasizing secular interests, and adopting a secular tone. We do not deny that it is a legitimate move, but there can be exaggerations. There have been too, at least in the perception of the laity. As though in compensation, a section of the laity has taken upon themselves specifically religious ministries: of preaching, leading public prayers and offering spiritual counselling.

'Ecclesial movements' have been gathering strength and lay initiatives are multiplying. Words like Evangelization and Miraculous Healings are more in the mouth of the laity than of the clergy. They take to active volunteer work, form service groups, and launch missionary initiatives, as "street preachers, joyfully bringing Jesus to every street, every town

square and every corner of the earth!" (EG 106). However, a word of caution may be in place. An excess of zeal can lead people into fundamentalist styles, despising other religions or disturbing public life. In a country like ours, such activities are carefully watched today; and their indiscretions can invite harassments upon other members of the Christian community as well. Nevertheless, we need to admit that natural missionary zeal is a positive energy to be wisely tapped for the service of the Gospel.

Let us place our evangelical commitment today in the socio-political world. Is democracy slipping from our hands? Is the new economy going to silence dissenting voices? Social observers worldwide warn of the great danger of *economic and political forces* uniting to control global affairs, leaving most of humanity as mere observers and over a period of time as absolute victims.

In India, things are moving faster, and the concentration of power seems to be moving in the direction of something more rigid and all-embracing: 1. Bringing the legislative under the executive, with only *one* leader to decide on all issues. 2. Controlling the judiciary through selective appointment and interferences. 3. Staffing universities with personnel compliant to Hindutva ideology, rewriting textbooks with a skewed presentation of facts and a biased re-interpretation of history. 4. Making the media toe the Ruling Party Line, and silencing/ eliminating dissenting voices through violence-trained volunteers. 5. Enlisting the support of *gurus,* godmen and *babas* for garnering votes, investing money at tax-havens, and to serve as parallel administration in promoting Hindutva causes. When spiritual cronyism combines with business cronyism and political cronyism, it is one step ahead of the forms dictatorship that we have so far seen anywhere. It combines *religious Theocracy with secular Totalitarianism.*

Add to all that, 6. Training and using of anti-social elements and illiterates from lower classes to get the dirty work done: for rabble rousing, chaotic protests, street violence, elimination of the opponents, anonymous murders. It was reported in *The Times of India* (September 16, 2017) that two lakhs Bajrang Dals would be trained to become '*Dharam Yodhas*' (religious warriors) in Uttar Pradesh to defend Hindu temples, protect cows, prevent love *jihad* and so on. Whatever name they are given (Anti-Romeo Squad, *Nari Suraksha Bal, Hindu Yuva Vahini,* Operation Durga, cow vigilantes) they are the foot-soldiers of the Saffron Squad, the *Sangh Parivar.* Ultimately, things end up in mob rule. No crime can be traced, no assassin identified. The strategy of anonymity is taken to perfection. 7. Another strategy is, Dividing communities (Hindu-Muslim, Nepali-Bengali in West Bengal, tribal-nontribal in Tripura) to build up the strength of the upper-caste-supremists. Using the disgruntled elements among minority communities or dissenting groups to undermine them, filing cases against their agencies, their properties, accounting systems, to exhaust their resources. 8. Distracting public attention with tension at borders, visits of dignitaries, PM's performance at the international level, launching of spacecraft by the ISRO, and similar issues.... when 31 farmers are committing suicide every day.

In this complex situation we have the mission "to stand erect, hold our heads high," because we are certain that our liberation is at hand. If we do that, that itself has a message.

6.   Popular Religiosity is not to be Despised. It is 'People's Mysticism'

Bishops of Latin America called popular spirituality '*people's mysticism*', "a spirituality incarnated in the culture of the lowly" (*Aparecida Document*, 2007). Its content is expressed in symbols, and in an act of faith of being part of the Church and of being missionaries. The faithful go on pilgrimages, visit shrines, take children or invite others, in an "evangelizing gesture." "Let us not stifle or presume to control this missionary power!" (EG 124).

Popular religiosity in fact is faith incarnate in culture, which expresses one's relationship with Christ, with Mary, and the saints (EG 90). It builds up a connective network among those who share a "common imagination and dreams about life," and leads to mutually stimulating interactions amidst urban violence: between different religious and ethnic groups, settlers, migrants and 'non-citizens' (EG 74), where a *sense of non-belonging* prevails. Popular religiosity ought to come alive especially in order to create a culture of dialogue. It offers healing in a variety of circumstances, like family conflicts, alcoholism, fatalism, and superstition (EG 69). At the same time, it needs to be guided, lest it verges on superstition.

Increasing erosion of cultural values has led to the weakening of social bonds: of families and communities (EG 66). As though in compensation, *solidarity* has grown among new communities that have come into existence, like prayer-groups and lay associations. They offer assistance to vulnerable individuals and groups, broken families, women in difficulties, including those who have gone through the painful experience of abortion, exclusion, extreme poverty (EG 213-214). If the members of lay groups have had the advantage of undergoing a period of formation, they can do amazing things.

In the same way, liturgy can be made to relate to human needs. It is not merely a moment of celebration, but also of formation to apostolate. That this may happen, *the* missionary "must *know the heart of his community,*" their desire for God, and where they have failed (EG 137).

7.   Confronting Challenges Itself is a Form of Sharing the Gospel

One of the most stirring statements in *Evangelii Gaudium* is this: "We also evangelize when we attempt to confront various challenges which can arise" (EG 61). Theorizing alone will not help, addressing the problem adequately will take history forward. And *new challenges* are continuously arising: e.g., restrictions imposed limiting religious freedom, instances of persecution, hatred, violence. And even in ordinary situations, while development is bringing better health-care, education, communication closer, the vast majority are unable to take advantage of these possibilities. In fact, big sections of society hardly have sufficient means to keep themselves alive; diseases are spreading, fear for the future keeps growing. For them, desperation is around the corner.

While new economic possibilities keep rising, deepening inequality keeps them out of reach for ordinary people. Hence the mounting anger of the *Aam Aadmi*, the common citizen, especially when economic disadvantages are combined with lack of respect for his or her dignity. Absolutely speaking, science and technology, have opened out new vistas for humanity, but in concrete reality their advance has fallen into the hands of a privileged few, which has resulted in the emergence of "new and often *anonymous kinds of power*" (EG 52). Glorifying *Yoga* and insisting on *Surynamaskar* are no solutions.

"An authentic faith…always involves a deep desire to change the world, to transmit values, to leave this earth somehow better than we found it" (EG 183). To accomplish this, God's people must be a "*leaven* in the midst of humanity" that often goes astray (EG 114). For example, we must admit that "*Business* is... a *noble vocation...*" if the chief actors search for the common good while strengthening production (EG 203). On the contrary, an "economy of exclusion and inequality," only alienates and kills (EG 53). "Money must serve, not rule!" The rich must help, respect and promote the poor, encourage solidarity (EG 58).

It is not easy to rouse this sense of responsibility in the well-to-do for the welfare of their fellow citizens. Statistics show that about 6000 Indian millionaires shifted overseas in 2016; 4000 had done so in 2015. But do the 264,00 millionaires and 95 billionaires who remain on in India show a sense of responsibility? Very few have succeeded to stimulate generosity in such people as Mother Teresa did.

8.   Structural Violence Is Strengthening Itself in Society

In his exhaustive study entitled: '*Capital in the Twenty-First Century*'— which has sold 2.2 million copies in three years—Thomas Piketty cautions us against the possible return of the 19th century situation of gross inequality in the present century. From the 1970s, income *inequality* has been visibly *rising* (Piketty 15); after the fall of the Soviet Bloc the contrast is even sharper. According to Piketty, the Marxist principle *of infinite accumulation* remains a danger in the 21ˢᵗ century, and it can lead to 'destabilization' (Piketty 10), by which he means outbreak of violence.

He points to gross imbalances like, "Top managers by and large have the power to set their own *remuneration,* in some cases *without limit,*" even without any relation to their contribution to productivity and profit (Piketty 24). Thus, the earnings of business leaders keep growing exponentially and their gap with those at the lower levels keep widening. Moreover, a new form of tyranny comes into existence, "invisible and often virtual". Corruption and tax-evasion take on worldwide dimensions, bringing in their wake damages to environment. And "a deified market" becomes the ultimate rule in everything (EG 56).

Furthermore, in today's globalized world "...every country is to a large extent owned by other countries" making *small countries vulnerable* (Piketty 193). Inequality within the same country can be a greater cause for anxiety. The biggest danger Piketty sees is that of the possibility of rich countries coming to be owned by their own billionaires, and the world by the world's billionaires (Piketty 463).

"Inequality eventually engenders violence..." the Pope himself admits (EG 60). In India, the poor in their helplessness turn not so much against others in a Revolution, as against themselves in suicide. Every year about 3000 farmers commit suicide for inability to repay loans due to nature failure or market failure. Christians ought to seek to heal such wounds, help build bridges, and assist people to bear their burdens with courage (Gal 6:2) (EG 67).

The right steps to prevent an endless inegalitarian spiral that Piketty suggests are *progressive capital tax* and a high level of international financial transparency (Piketty 515). But that would call for a coordinated international effort. Difficult as this is likely to be, it is still required if we wish to prevent redistribution by force of arms (Piketty 538), by which he means a repetition of the Russian or Chinese Revolutions.

India has gone through difficult days but has not gone for a Revolution. But as though in compensation, we have become specialized in the 'politics of protest'. Before he relinquished office, on the one hand, ex-President of India, Pranab Mukherjee, spoke strongly against this *'culture of unrest'*, and, on the other, he encouraged a culture of free debate and independent thought. 'Politics of Disruption' may not be the best way of addressing economic problems: constant socio-political unrest, *dharna,* rally, *bandh,* blockade, turmoil, effigy burning. The danger of taking to the street too frequently is that it weakens the economy, saps civic energies, distracts from analytical and responsible study, and marginalizes healthy and intelligent debates. Piketty is inviting precisely intelligent discussion on economic issues.

9. Acting as Committed and Responsible Citizens

People enhance the social dimension of their lives "by acting as committed and responsible citizens," not as thoughtless mobs. Pope Francis says, "Let us not forget that responsible citizenship is a virtue, and participation in political life is a moral obligation." To achieve that end, people should create a "peaceful and multifaceted culture of encounter" (EG 220). We need "politicians capable of sincere and effective dialogue aimed at healing the deepest roots" of problems not merely appearances. *"Politics,* thus, though often denigrated, remains a *lofty vocation* and one of the highest forms of charity" when it seeks the common good (EG 205).

Today there are countries where democratic structures are in position, but where democratic values are missing, where structures of accountability are manipulated, of participation are made ineffective. What really matters is that self-questioning habits and motivating reasons are planted into the heart of a society, and that it keeps challenging its unbalanced structures and reworking them at every stage. Theologians can help Christian thinking in this respect exploring "how best to bring the Gospel message to different cultural contexts and groups" (EG 133) and address diverse needs. An alert Christian community too keeps studying issues in a holistic manner, proposing correctives, and offering cooperative support. Merely criticizing the government is inadequate (EG 207).

Besides human rights there are also *rights of peoples*, of ethnic minorities and disadvantaged communities. But we must remember that "even *human rights* can be used as a justification for an inordinate defence of individual rights or the rights of the richer peoples" (EG 190).

What is central in all these matters is not finding economic solutions alone but ensuring human dignity. Christian politics, therefore, defends the *dignity of the powerless*, while working for the restoration of justice and equitable distribution of goods, and while striving for global solidarity and ethics that will find wide acceptance. In pursuing these goals, citizens must go beyond mere rhetoric and token gestures. It is imperative to create a *'new mindset'* that brings a new world into existence (EG 188). Such an ambitious project seems far beyond our reach today. But we can *set* in motion *processes*, like initiating reflection and launching institutions of education (EG 223). If this is done in faith, the results are bound to be enormously fruitful.

10.   Populism has its Limits

One should remember that patriotism is not nationalism, much less the *ultra-nationalism* of the present day. Albert Einstein called nationalism "an infantile disease. It is the measles of mankind." With increased mobility of people, and with immigrants threatening the cultural identity of indigenous communities and reducing their job opportunities, Right-Wing politics has gathered strength in several countries including the US, Russia, France, India, European nations close to the Middle East. With rising indigenous anger, emotions run high, populist vocabulary finds welcome, bluster and *histrionics* seem to pay, and hate-words find acceptance. Thus, elections are marred and nations are shocked with the results. Excessive nationalism isolates nations, and an 'India first' formula will soon turn out to be 'me first'. In the same way, making India 'great' will turn out to be 'making India hate.'

The same fervour is imitated at the regional level, some leaders playing the wizard with regional pride. They indulge in populist policies, which become ready channel for siphoning off funds for private ends with little regard for the economy, thus damaging the long-term interests of their own people. Actor-politicians remain actors all the time mesmerizing the mobs with Hitlerite oratorical skills, and never becoming actual performers. They command the collective psyche of communities and use it for their own purposes, accumulating wealth beyond the royalty. They expect *adulation* verging on adoration and almost become demigods like Kim Jong-un of North Korea (the 'Eternal Leader'), who can say anything and do anything, with no legal boundaries. So, despite having Indians like Mahatma Gandhi and Rabindranath Tagore who 'held their heads high' before imperious British powers, we now see many grovelling before petty politicians and self-proclaimed divinities. We also hear of political leaders with swollen heads beating up airport personnel and humiliating towering intellectuals. Alert citizens are shocked that their constituencies support such behaviour.

Today, while those in power cater to regional pride, caste superiority, majority arrogance, religious exclusivism, national pretensions, etc., what is most needed for society never gets done. Yogi Adityanath won the UP election with the slogan 'development for all'; but, the very first thing he did after election was to introduce cow-protection measures, mostly calculated to impoverish the Muslims. This was followed by witch-hunting, moral policing, anti-Romeo squads, *gau rakshaks*, ransacking of business houses, theatres, imposed self-defined patriotism, violence to artists, writers, critics and so on.

Yogi Adityanath is a 5-time MP from Gorakhpur, a city that remains one of the dirtiest in the country, along with 52 others in UP considered the untidiest. Could he not do something to clear up all that filth? He is proud of the achievements of his co-religionists in history (like Prithviraj and Rana Pratap), while down-grading the Mughal Taj Mahal. However, he forgets that they have the *lowest educational levels* among religions, the largest *gender gap*, and the highest *internal inequality*, according to Pew Research Centre.

Yogi spoke disparagingly of Mother Teresa. Yet, if she were alive and told that 1296 children had died in Gorakhpur Hospital since January, she would have rushed there to help. Para-military forces were called to keep away protesters around the hospital. Some *2000 children die* there every year, and 10,000 have died there during the last ten years. Are their lives less precious than the starving cows of UP? Meanwhile, people perish in railway accidents, inter-caste clashes and political violence. These are matters of no concern for Yogiji. Child labour continues, human trafficking intensifies. The CM is happy if you cry out: *"Jai Shri Ram!"*

What is most worrying of all is the *political use of the Judiciary.* Twenty-four years after the Babri Masjid demolition, the Supreme Court revived charges against L.K. Advani just when it was being whispered that his name would be proposed for Presidency. It seems that cases in court are not being taken up on their own merit but are kept there as political weapons for timely use against the opponents of the regime. The case against Shashikala came up when she was being proposed as Chief Minister. Many other cases can be exposed in similar fashion.

These are issues that are too weighty for a minority community to address, but every intelligent citizen plays a role for the smooth functioning of democracy. Every *perceptive word* counts.

11. Bringing Healing to Situations of Hurt, to Historic Memories

It becomes evident that "a rigid programme of evangelization" is not what is relevant to such complex realities. For example, how bewilderingly diverse are problems like human trafficking, narcotic trade, abuse of minors, neglect of the elderly and the sick; increasingly diverse forms of corruption; growing isolation and mutual distrust in a developed and a sophisticated society (EG 75). Add to these the suppression or delimitation of the freedom to choose or express one's religion or affirm one's cultural identity (EG 255). Think, further, of clandestine warehouses, rings of prostitution, children used for begging, undocumented labour and the harassments they suffer; growing diversity and networks of crime. '*Silent complicity*' makes every citizen a partaker in these evils in some manner (EG 211). This thought alone should arouse a sense of responsibility in every sensitive person.

Unfortunately, what emerges today is a world divided by wars, violence, selfishness and resentments based on old divisions. The annual expenditure on arms is estimated to be $ 1.6 trillion a year. The Indian defence budget is one of the highest. Christians must make every effort to bring healing to damaged relationships and forgiveness and reconciliation to historic injuries. But the pain may linger and call for ongoing attention (EG 99-100). There are people who seek to keep alive negative memories in society. When India called its ballistic missile *Prithviraj* in memory of the Hindu warrior who defeated the Muslims, Pakistan named its missile *Ghori* to honour the Muslim general who defeated the Hindus. By contrast, Obama and Abe sought to heal the old memories by visiting Hiroshima and Pearl Harbour together.

There is no doubt that the *rejection of the transcendent* has weakened the ethical consciousness and the sense of personal and collective sin in society; it has led to disorientation among youth (EG 64). Added to all these is the anxiety that our production-consumption culture is leading to '*desertification of the soil*', extinction of species, destruction of the earth and devastation of nature for future generations (EG 215).

These are areas where we need to join hands with people of every religion, and even with those who reject religion altogether, as long as they recognise truth, goodness and beauty. We accept them as our "precious allies in the commitment to defending human dignity, in building peaceful coexistence between peoples and in protecting creation". The New Areopagi that are arising at the world level are contexts for discussing ethics, art, science, peace, and the search for transcendence (EG 257), and encounters where faith, *reason and sciences* can converse (EG 132-133). These are contexts in which one discovers the "original freshness of the Gospel." The Vatican itself has remained dynamic and exemplary in this respect. Last year, Stephen Hawking addressed the Pontifical Academy of Sciences about the origin of the world and met Pope Francis.

12. The Fire of the Holy Spirit Burns in Our Hearts (EG 261)

When one studies carefully the problems enumerated above, one feels a sense of helplessness. This is the moment when one must remember that "God's word is unpredictable in its power." Once sown, it keeps growing by itself while the farmer goes to sleep (Mk 4:26-29). It accomplishes what "surpass our calculations and ways of thinking" (EG 22). So, Pope Francis says, "...be guided by the Holy Spirit, renouncing the attempt to plan and control everything to the last detail." Allow him to enlighten, guide, and direct us, leading us wherever he wills. "This is what it means to be *mysteriously fruitful*" (EG 280). By contrast, it is a great mistake to trust in our own powers, especially if it leads to a feeling of superiority to others because we keep some rubrics and norms or are fiercely faithful to some archaic religious forms and traditions. This may be called expressions of *Neo-Pelagianism* (EG 94). We need to trust in God's initiative and look to the Holy Spirit for guidance (Rom 8:26; EG 280). He is with us in our evangelical discernment (EG 154). What we need to do is to "keep silence and allow him to speak" (EG 143). He is active and creative; we are his instruments (Rom 12:1; EG 145). We are not masters but "heralds and servants" (EN 78, 1975).

13. "Life Grows by Being Given Away" (EG 10)

"Spirit-filled evangelizers are evangelizers who pray and work." Neither abstract notions alone nor dissertations or social and pastoral practices without spirituality will change hearts nor transform society. Incomplete proposals will not go beyond a few groups. Without adoration, encounter with the word, conversation with the Lord, work becomes meaningless, a loss of energy, weariness, and full of difficulties (EG 262).

"Evangelization consists mostly of patience and disregard for constraints of time." It is taken forward through *apostolic endurance*. It cares for the grain but is not impatient of the weeds; it does not grumble or overreact. Fruit may be slow in coming and may be imperfect and incomplete when it actually comes. But then it bears fruit. Its goal is not to make enemies, even if it means paying the last price (EG 24). "Life grows by being given away, and it weakens in isolation and comfort. Indeed, those who enjoy life most are those who leave security on the shore and become excited about the mission of communicating life to others" (*Aparecida Document* 2007, 5th Latin American Conferences; EG 10). These are contexts when Jesus' message becomes fully alive and we re-discover the "Original Freshness of the Gospel" (EG 11).

Endnote

[1] Pope Francis's Apostolic Exhortation Evangelii Gaudium, The Joy of the Gospel, was issued in Rome on November 24, 2013, on the solemnity of Christ the King. This document will hereafter be abbreviated as EG.

References

Aparecida Document, 5th Latin American Conferences, 2007.

Pope Paul VI, *Evangelii Nuntiandi*, Rome, 1975.

Pope John Paul II, *Pastores Dabo Vobis*, Rome, 1992.

Pope Francis, *Evangelii Gaudium*, Rome, 2013.

Piketty, Thomas. *Capital in the Twenty-First Century*, The Belknap-Harvard University Press, 2014.

2

Adoration of God or
Adoration of the Self:

Certain Aspects
of Seeking Psychological Security

Bishop Thomas Tharayil

Introduction

Given the different interpretations and various systems of spiritual life, arriving at a definition of genuine spirituality is a complex process. Different people from different moral and social settings claim to be spiritual. In India, brand new gurus are sprouting up with a special hallow of anointment who claim that all spirituality is their patrimony. But it is a reality that what we understand as devotion to God can sometimes be a disguised devotion to oneself. Instead of adoring God, I might be adoring myself. Here, discernment is the only way out. Discernment of the motives behind our acts of faith and our doctrinal dispositions may enlighten us regarding the underlying factors, spiritual as well as psychological, whether they really lead us to God or keep us obsessed with ourselves. The discussion about neo-pelagianism and neo-gnosticism must also include an analysis of such factors so that our understanding becomes precise and real.

1.   Faith: Self-Actualisation versus Self-Transcendence

According to Franco Imoda, as the human reality does not contain in itself the reason of its being, the human person needs to transcend the self in order to discover it. That means, to be human is to transcend one's self towards the other and naturally towards the Ultimate Other, God. Since the human person is a mystery, one contains in oneself a fundamental exigency for transcendence which incites one to a total gift to another and openness to the Ultimate Other (Imoda, 1998). It is this capacity and fundamental exigency for transcendence that leads a person to God. As long as we hold that being human basically means relating and being directed to something other than oneself (Frankl, 1978), then self-transcendence is the only way to actualise the human potential.

For many who consider self-actualisation as the goal of human development, God is also an instrument for the actualisation of self. I believe in God to actualise myself – this will be their motto. When faith is conceived as an act of self-actualisation, God becomes a shield for fulfilling many of the overt or covert desires of a person that can never lead that person to happy living. If made the goal of one's development, self-actualisation drives us to dissatisfaction and anxiety since one can never fully actualise oneself unless one seeks it through transcending one's self towards the other. Faith is an act of self-transcendence.

According to Viktor Frankl (1969), self-actualisation cannot be considered as one's ultimate destination, not even one's primary intention. If self-actualisation is made the primary goal of human development, it contradicts the self-transcendent quality of human existence. When "the self-transcendence of existence is denied, existence itself is distorted. It is reified. Being is reduced to a mere thing. Being human is de-personalised. And, what is more important, the subject is made into an object" (Frankl, 1978, p.53). The reason is that human survival always depends on the direction to a 'what for' or a 'whom for'.

> I thereby understand the primordial anthropological fact that being human is being always directed, and pointing, to something or someone other than oneself: to a meaning to fulfil or another human being to encounter, a cause to serve or a person to love. Only to the extent that someone is living out this self-transcendence of human existence, is he truly human or does he become his true self…. A healthy eye sees nothing of itself—it is self-transcendent (Frankl, 1978, p.35).

Self-transcendence implies sometimes self-denial or self-sacrifice for the other, but it is not the denial of the true self and its radical exigencies that make love impossible. Here, self-denial, as it is inevitable for fulfilling many of our goals, leads to self-realisation. The notion is that self-actualisation does not mean self-fulfilment in a narcissistic sense of satisfying one's wishes. Fulfilling all one's wishes and possibilities in this can be an "impossible illusion" (Conn, 1998, p.35). "Through self-transcendence, the self is not sacrificed, but realised in its authentic being. But the realisation of the true self in its drive for meaning, truth, value, and love rejects any self-centred striving for happiness through fulfilment, requiring that one empty oneself (even losing one's life) in the loving service of the neighbour" (Conn, ibid.).

Our religiosity needs to be analysed using the categories of self-actualisation and self-transcendence. If one's relationship with God serves the realisation of one's wishes and goals, it becomes a reductionist mode of God experience. Then, one's own whims and fancies can be interpreted as God's will and one's own need for perfection and order can be considered genuine spiritual quest. Here also discernment of one's motives emerges as important.

2.   Security in God or Security in Oneself: Mixed Motivations

One reason why our pursuits of discovering God ends up in plunging in oneself is that our motivations are governed by different elements, both conscious and unconscious. These mixed motivations usually do not let us become pure in our intentions resulting in immature behaviour and thoughts which accommodate even materialism and narcissism disguised as spiritual dispositions.

2.1.   *Spiritual Materialism and Spiritual Narcissism*

In the 1970s, Buddhist guru Chogyam Trungpa coined the term 'spiritual materialism' to denote the tendency to turn spirituality into ego building. He states:

> Ego is able to convert everything to its own use, even spirituality. For example, if you have learned of a particularly beneficial meditation technique of spiritual practice, then ego's attitude is, first to regard it as an object of fascination and, second to examine it...Ego translates everything in terms of its own state of health, its own inherent qualities. It feels a sense of great accomplishment and excitement at having been able to create such a pattern. At last it has created a tangible accomplishment, a confirmation of its own individuality" (Trungpa, 2002, p.21).

A distorted, egocentric version of spirituality is so cleverly disguised that even the strengthening of our egocentricity through spiritual techniques rather than developing a genuine spirituality, eludes our attention. It is this fundamental distortion that Trungpa called 'spiritual materialism' (Trungpa, 2002). For example, if we use some yoga principles with the sole aim of achieving material prosperity, can it really lead us to God? Here, we are using spirituality for material goals. This tendency is evident in many of the New Age spiritual groups and preaching. New Age neo-gnostic modes of spirituality fall into this category.

Another tendency is spiritual narcissism, a kind of unstructured rationalisation that leads people to cherish whatever is most convenient for their self-image at the moment. They tend to believe that they are spiritually advanced and enlightened beings; and consequently, they deserve special love and respect from others. Metaphysics is for them a tool to validate their behaviours, even their sins; and they claim that God alone can sit in judgement when they get caught sinning. They try to justify whatever they think and they do as if they are most righteous people. This is again a tendency of self-adoration instead of adoring God.

2.2.   Conscious-Unconscious Dialectic

What can be behind the seeking of non-spiritual goals through spiritual acts? We need to take into consideration the possibility of the simultaneous existence of different levels of consciousness in us. The psychoanalytic terminology would call this 'conscious-unconscious dialectic'. Even when I intend to do some charity for the other, I might actually be seeking honour for myself. Even when I vehemently fight for certain Christian ideologies openly, I might be, in reality, protecting my own self. Sometimes I desperately need the Church to win, because its failure can actually be a failure of my own personality. This possibility for dichotomy is always there.

The unconscious contains repressed experiences or memories that are traumatic and undesirable, non-utilised psychic energies of the individual, impulses that are not completely integrated or repressed and motivational tendencies or modalities of action habitually used and therefore automatic (Cencini & Manenti, 1986). Powerful unconscious exerts its influences on all activities of the individual by mixing up with the conscious motivations and activities. That is why someone with the best intention of preaching the word of God ends up in establishing one's own personal fame utilising God's name. Instead of feeling secure in one's relationship to God, one might be seeking a temporary solution for oneself through one's apparent spiritual deeds. Here God becomes just a means for someone, not the end. This happens in the realm of our beliefs and ideologies. Extreme ways of holding and propagating certain beliefs and teachings notwithstanding their original message can be an act of guaranteeing one's personal security.

In this way, many of the so-called spiritual activities or dispositions become just a mask for one's insecurities. Masking is a process in which one changes or 'masks' one's natural personality to conform to social pressures, abuse and/or harassment. It can be strongly influenced by environmental factors such as authoritarian parents, rejection, and emotional or physical abuse. Our conscious acts can be a hiding place for us that help us to escape from intensive internal conflicts. In this way, our professions, states of life, charity endeavours, religious aspirations, can be masked. In a strict analysis of our motives, both explicit and implicit, we need to examine whether our ideologies also fulfil the function of masks.

3. Seeking of Security through God

According to the attachment theory, every individual develops a sense of security depending on the availability and responsiveness of the caregivers. Internalised object relations lead to the formation of this state of security that differs according to the healthy or pathological caregiving received in the early childhood. When threatened this security gives rise to various attachment behaviours with the goal of seeking felt security (Tharayil, 2012). The relationship with a caring all-powerful God also can result in better internal secure base.

When security is threatened, attachment behaviours arise which if not properly addressed, get reinforced through certain beliefs or ideologies. God also can be relied upon as an attachment figure who becomes an answer to the calls for security. Whenever one seeks God just as a temporary or shallow shield of one's insecurity, it becomes an immature act of utilising God for one's own needs. Here, one has not spiritually grown in one's relationship with God but is just using God for one's own selfish goals.

At the same time, forming an internal security as a result of one's attachment to God is healthy. Therefore, growing in internal secure base as a result of one's healthy attachment to God, and using God as a solace to one's insecurities, both are quite different in orientation. Here, security is seen as a result of one's spiritual life. Often God is seen as an answer to one's insecurities, but the relationship with God does not foster one's internal secure base. Faith can be defined as one's internal security that God is there for him or her. When this internal security is seriously disrupted either due to situational or due to developmental factors, God becomes a utility and religiosity becomes a mask.

4.   Ideologies as a Mask of One's Insecurities

We can approach neo-pelagianism and neo-gnosticism as two ideologies held by a section of believers. Pelagianism refers to the doctrine of Pelagius and his followers; in particular, the denial of the doctrines of original sin and predestination, and the defence of innate human goodness and free will. As Adam and Eve's sin did not taint human nature, people are still capable of choosing good or evil without the influence of God through the Holy Spirit in the form of divine grace. Sin was just a bad example to follow. According to Pelagianism, the Cross simply becomes an unfortunate accident, and atonement through the blood of Christ is not necessary. One must simply follow Jesus' good example—that's all what is needed for salvation (Brazier, 2013). It is a form of neo-Pelagianism, which 'asserts humanity's right to raise itself up, improve itself, defining whatever it chooses as the good' (Brazier, 2013).

Pope Francis seems to use the term 'neo-pelagians' to characterise the traditionalists in the church who think that just following some doctrines and traditions suffices for salvation. In a September 19, 2013, interview to *America* Jesuit magazine, he said: "If a Christian is a restorationist, a legalist, if s/he wants everything clear and safe, then s/he will find nothing... Those who today always look for disciplinarian solutions, those who long for an exaggerated doctrinal 'security,' those who stubbornly try to recover a past that no longer exists—they have a static and inward-directed view of things. In this way, faith becomes an ideology among other ideologies."

Gnosticism is a compilation of different systems of thought that professed that the material world is created by an emanation of the highest God, trapping the Divine spark within the human body. This Divine spark could be liberated by gnosis of this Divine spark. "Jesus", for the Gnostics, was either a magician or an ascetic. The Gnostics held that there are two kinds of faith: a crude, imperfect faith suited to the masses, which remained at the level of Jesus' flesh and the contemplation of his mysteries; and a deeper, perfect faith reserved to a small circle of initiates who were intellectually capable of rising above the flesh of Jesus towards the mysteries of the unknown divinity" (Cf. Pope Francis's *Lumen Fidei* n.47). Neo-gnostics claim that they have all spiritual solutions for themselves.

The charm of Gnosticism, Pope Francis said, quoting his Apostolic Exhortation *Evangelii Gaudium*, "is that of a faith locked into subjectivism, which affects only 'a certain experience or set of ideas and bits of information which are meant to console and enlighten, but which ultimately keep one imprisoned in his or her own thoughts and feelings'." (n.94) "The difference between Christian transcendence and any form of Gnostic spiritualism is in the mystery of the Incarnation," the Pope added. "Not to put into practice, not to lead the Word into reality, means building on sand, remaining in theoretical ideas and degenerating into intimacies that bear no fruit that make sterile its dynamism." Here, the Pope seems to be referring to the individualist tendencies to make faith according to one's own wishes and fancies. It is also against the transcendent quality of faith.

Right from the origins of the Church, there have been different ideologies which have motivated many people to genuine as well as heretical faith. Why do ideologies play a great role in the lives of certain people? As a motivational force, ideology is very potent. Abstract belief systems were represented in courage, sacrificing their own lives for the sake of abstract belief systems (Jost & Amodio, 2012). That is why, some even qualify human beings as ideological animals. Even a cursory glance at history should convince one that individual crimes committed for selfish motives play quite an insignificant part in human tragedies, compared to the numbers massacred in unselfish loyalty to one's tribe, dynasty, church, or political ideology.

How can certain abstract configuration of ideas so strongly inspire individuals and groups so that they are willing even to sacrifice their own lives? It is a fact that socially shared beliefs, opinions, and values make people more courageous and generous (Jost & Amodio, 2012). Why do these ideologies motivate us? Psychologists opine that uncertainty-reducing function of ideology motivates people. According to Hogg (2007), ideologies "arise under uncertainty and prevail to ward off uncertainty" and they confer existential security. "The purpose of ideology, according to this view, is to cope with anxiety concerning one's own mortality through denial, rationalisation, and other defense mechanisms (Jost & Amodio, ibid).

Another reason for the motivating power of ideology is that socially shared beliefs lead the person to affiliation. Religion is a fraternity that brings people together, giving them an edge over those who lack this social glue (Bloom, 2005) Ideologies serve underlying epistemic, existential, and relational needs. Political and religious ideologies offer certainty, security, and solidarity (Jost & Amodio, ibid). Therefore, social belongingness resulting from holding the same ideology is also an important element of its power.

5.   Conservatism versus liberalism

In a September 2015 radio interview with *Radio Millennium*, Pope Francis said,

> Fundamentalists keep God away from accompanying his people; they divert their minds from him and transform him into an ideology. So, in the name of this ideological god, they kill, they attack, destroy, slander. Practically speaking, they transform that God into a Baal, an idol. … No religion is immune from its own fundamentalisms. In every religion there will be a small group of fundamentalists whose work is to destroy for the sake of an idea, and not reality.

Any ideology that is conservative has negative consequences. In the available psychological research, political liberalism is identified with a balanced mind, while conservatism is identified with rigidity. But when it comes to faith, extremes in both traditionalism and anti-traditionalism need to be considered conservative positions. According to Jost *et al.*, two core dimensions distinguish liberalism and conservatism: (a) advocating versus resisting social change (as opposed to tradition), (b) rejecting versus accepting inequality. Some suggest that individual preferences for these dimensions stem from basic psychological orientations toward uncertainty, threat, and conformity. Scholars like Wilson (1973) opined that "the common basis for all of the various components of the conservative attitude syndrome is a generalised susceptibility to experiencing threat or anxiety in the face of uncertainty" (p.259).

Wherever some range of possible opinions is given, Jost *et al.* hypothesised that conservative ideology should be more appealing to individuals who are either temporarily or chronically high in needs to manage uncertainty and threat, whereas liberal ideology should be more appealing to individuals who are low in such needs. Preserving the status quo allows one to maintain what is familiar and known while rejecting the risky, uncertain prospect of social change (Jost, *et al.*, 2007).

Many studies reported findings that, on the one hand, factors like death anxiety, system instability, fear of threat and loss, dogmatism, intolerance of ambiguity, and personal needs for order, structure and closure were all positively associated with conservatism; while, on the other, openness to new experiences, cognitive complexity, tolerance of uncertainty and self-esteem are positively associated with liberalism. Liberals were seen to exhibit implicit as well as explicit preferences for social change and equality when compared with conservatives (Jost, *et al.*, 2012).

Weber and Federico found that anxious and avoidant (insecure) attachment styles were associated with right-wing authoritarianism and social dominance orientation, respectively. The perception of a dangerous world is consistently related to the endorsement of right-wing ideologies. Some longitudinal studies also gave similar results. Bock and Block (2006) found that 3-year olds who were rated by teachers as fearful, rigid, indecisive, vulnerable and inhibited turned out to be more politically conservative as adults. In contrast, the 3-year olds who were energetic, resilient, self-reliant, expressive, dominating and more prone to developing close relationships became more liberal in adulthood (Jost & Amodio, 2012). Matthews et al. (2009) arrived at a conclusion that those who have perceptions of inter-group threat and anxiety are more associated with system justification and social dominance orientation, i.e., support for the status quo and for group-based hierarchies (Jost & Amodio, ibid.).

Some have found that adherence to conservative ideology was associated with a more prudent but less informative learning strategy. Liberals engage more in exploratory behaviour (Jost & Amodio, ibid.). Some of the studies give conflicting results too. Most of the research studies use a unidimensional approach in studying preferences of people using the liberalism vs conservatism binary. It is true that various social and economic components interact with attitudes of people that might be best conceptualised on a multidimensional approach (Koleva & Rip, 2009).

6.   Personality Styles and Ideologies

Obsessive compulsive persons are liable to develop many rigidities with regard to their thinking. For them, rules and traditions provide a sense of orderliness in their lives as well as a measure of control. They can very well opt for a conservative ideology, though necessarily not. They tend to believe that the world functions best when there is order rather than chaos, and life is gentle and predictable rather than harsh and unpredictable. So their cognitive processes are attenuated and rigid, lacking a sense of playfulness and flexibility. Their image of God is of a task-manager, judge or police officer (Sperry, 2000).

Those suffering from narcissistic personality disorder have a tendency to project their ideas as supreme and tend to subject all others to their views and thoughts. Narcissists rely on themselves rather than on others for the gratification of their needs. For them, it is unsafe to depend on anyone's love or loyalty. Consequently, they pretend to be self-sufficient. In order to compensate for their inner deprivation and emptiness, they become preoccupied with establishing their power, appearance, status, prestige, and superiority. They live with many illusions—for instance, that they have a right to be served, that their own desires are superior to others' and that they deserve special consideration and entitlements in life (Sperry, 2000).

"Because of their self-absorption and self-deceiving tendency, narcissistic ministers must creatively distort the precept to love God and neighbour to fit their pathological perspective. For them, God, and everyone else, exists for one purpose: to love and take care of them. Their basic spiritual deficit is a lack of awareness of grace and an incapacity for gratitude. … they believe God will do exactly as they ask in their prayers, with no regard to the kind of claim God has on them" (ibid., p.18). Their sense of specialness and grandiosity often leads them to stubbornly stick to their beliefs and experiences. When prayers are unanswered, they become narcissistically wounded and deeply rejected. As they lack empathy, they are likely to be insensitive to the sufferings and needs of others. Reactive narcissists have no difficulty in devaluing others to underscore their own superiority (ibid.).

Histrionic personality types can even opt for and adopt a liberal way of thinking, as they try to attract the appreciation of others. They feel a need to please everyone as their worth depends on others, for which they may be ready to compromise their beliefs. They actively seek the attention and approval of others and expect others to take care of them and their needs. Sperry opines that they feel compelled to 'perform' for others (ibid.); their thinking style is characterised as impressionistic, global and unfocused, which is not conducive to a differentiated sense of self. This can lead to cognitive distortions like dichotomous thinking, overgeneralisation and emotional reasoning. Such people need not stick on to a particular code of ethics or reasoning.

Liberalism can sometimes originate from one's aggression to parental figures. For example, a boy who has had a strained relationship with his parents will most probably reject the values of his parents, claiming that he has become progressive and liberal. Detachment from faith and morals of parents can be a detachment towards the parents themselves. Aggression towards one's father might be behind one's negation of traditional values. In patriarchal societies where authority figures are important for people, traditional mindset is often in vogue; but those who deny any kind of parental control, might break away from the values and rules provided by parents.

7.   Faithfulness to Tradition and Conservatism

Pope Francis apparently uses the term 'neo-pelagianism' to denote possible aberrations contained in the assertions of the traditionalists in the Church. He states:

> A supposed soundness of doctrine or discipline leads instead to a narcissistic and authoritarian elitism, whereby instead of evangelizing, one analyzes and classifies others, and instead of opening the door to grace, one exhausts his or her energies in inspecting and verifying. ... Since it is based on carefully cultivated appearances, it is not always linked to outward sin; from without, everything appears as it should be. But if it were to seep into the Church, it would be infinitely more disastrous than any other worldliness which is simply moral (*Evangelii Gaudium*, n.94).

Here, a question arises whether faithfulness to tradition should always be denounced as neo-pelagianism. Faithfulness to traditions can also arise from an esteem about one's social identity, the loss of which would divest one of one's characteristic identity. Individuals generally strive for maintaining or enhancing their self-esteem and self concept through belonging to a group. Social identity may be positive or negative according to the evaluations of those groups that contribute to an individual's social identity. Positively discrepant comparisons between in-group and out-group produce high prestige. Negatively discrepant comparisons between in-group and out-group result in low prestige (Tajfel & Turner, 1985). Positive social identity depends largely on favourable comparison made between the in-group and some relevant out-groups.

If one has internalised group membership and belongingness to the church as an aspect of one's self-concept, one will always prefer to identify with church traditions and practices. Intergroup comparison also brings about an allegiance to the group if positively evaluated. This differentiation sometimes leads to competition, too, based on perceived superiority and inferiority (Tajfel & Turner, ibid.). Proper esteem about the resources of the group leads to a healthy social identity that necessitates no social competition. Those who feel inferior passionately strive to defend themselves by creating an imaginary battlefield. The realistic esteem about one's group leads to faithfulness to one's social traditions and openness to changing circumstances.

One's social identity depends on several elements such as customs, traditions, cuisine, culture, values, beliefs, attitudes, stereotypes, history, norms, ideology, goals, and aspirations, intentions, activities through which one can easily describe the specificity of one's group and the difference of one's group from other groups. This form of identity can also be described as cultural identity (Korostelina, 2007). Applied to the ecclesial traditions, if they are viewed against the background of social identity, faithfulness to traditions simply reflects proper living of one's identity without which no community can survive.

8.   Individualism and Anarchism

In broader terms, individualism stands for personal freedom and achievement. An individualist culture appreciates personal accomplishments and humanitarian achievements that make an individual stand out by awarding these acts with social status. Collectivism, on the contrary, encourages conformity and discourages individuals from dissenting and standing out. The critics of individualism identify behind it the tendencies of self-absorption, narcissism, alienation, atomism, unscrupulous competition, deviance, relativism and nihilism (Walterman, 1984).

Individualism in its extreme manifestation takes the form of unfettered egoism and radical demand for personal autonomy that eventually grows as anarchism. For an anarchist, society is important so much so that it entertains free rein of individual autonomy unrestricted by laws and constitutions. Anarchists claim that the future society must be devoid of laws and constitutions as they necessarily restrict the sovereign autonomy of the individual. Some thinkers opine that an anarchist's commitment to the ego outweighs its variously coloured socialistic veneers (Bookchin, 2014). This sheds light into the fact that extreme individualism behind certain ideologies may end up even in anarchic thought and functioning.

Different visions of self can be seen as the basis of both individualism and collectivism. While the collectivist vision is that self is interdependent, individualism perceives the self as independent that forms its identity only from the inner attributes of the individual that sees one as independent. The individual inner attributes remain significant for defining, regulating, and thus predicting the behaviour of an individual (Markus & Kitayama, 1991). There are many positive as well as negative consequences for this self-concept. People from individualist cultures seem to have a high need for 'self-enhancement' that cannot accept discovering bad traits in oneself as it damages one's self-esteem. There is much more emphasis on individual ability as a cause of success. The need to stand out is seen more in individualists while the need to fit in is more in collectivists (Kim & Markus, 1999). The independent self makes choices autonomously without taking others into account. The individualists see in the personal achievements a confirmation of their exceptional personality traits and talents which they are motivated to discover more and more. In the religious sphere, such individualist tendencies may result in ideologies like neo-gnosticism. In individualist tendencies there is also a great desire to protect the self. In the extreme, a tendency to adore the self, so to say, is very evident. One who follows extreme individualist attitudes in faith may go astray from living Gospel values and end up in following the aspirations of the self.

9.   Conclusion

Our search began with the question whether it is the adoration of God or of the self behind certain extreme ideologies that reign in the hearts of a significant group of Christians. When we see different versions of neo-pelagianism and neo-gnosticism in today's world, we need to understand that certain mindsets push persons towards specific ideological frameworks. Those who feel extreme insecurity in their inner selves always try to defend themselves through certain thinking patterns which take the shape of conservatism or individualism. One's developmental experiences of insecurity can form a conservative mindset in some people, while aggression towards paternal figures can incite anti-traditionalist attitudes. Certain personality styles like obsessive-compulsive or narcissist contain in themselves authoritarianism and rigidity of mind while histrionic or dependent styles mould individuals to please others by not taking any particular position. Extreme individualism can even stimulate anarchist tendencies that negate all tradition and authority.

Whether or not we can decipher the different mental dispositions bolstering these extreme positions of neo-pelagianism and neo-gnosticism, we can probably identify an irresistible tendency to protect the self which is a kind of 'self-absorption'. In other words, both these ideologies lead the faithful towards adoration of their 'selves' rather than adoration of God. We need to discern the motives—both conscious as well as unconscious—in order to purify our dispositions to the living God who liberates and sanctifies.

Bibliography

Bookchin, M. *Anarchism as Individualism*, from http://new-compass.net/articles/anarchism-individualism, August 5, 2014. Retrieved March 23, 2018.

Brazier, P. *C.S. Lewis: On the Christ of a Religious Economy*. Eugene, O.R: Pickwick Publications, 2013.

Cencini, A., and A. Manenti. *Psychology and Formation. Structures and Dynamics*. Mumbai: Pauline Publications, 1986.

Conn, W. *The Desiring Self*. New Jersey: Paulist Press, 1998.

Francis, Pope. *Evangelii Gaudium: Apostolic Exhortation on the Proclamation of the Gospel in Today's World*. November 24, 2013.

Frankl, Viktor. *The Will to Meaning*. New York: The World Publishing Co., 1969
_____ . *The Unheard Cry for Meaning*. New York: Simon and Schuster, Inc., 1978.

Hogg, M. "Uncertainty-identity Theory." *Advances in Experimental Social Psychology* 39 (2007), pp.69-126.

Imoda, Franco. *Human Development. Psychology and Mystery*. Leuven: Peeters, 1998.

Jost, J. "Elective Affinities: On the Psychological Biases of Left-right Ideological Differences." *Psychological Inquiry* 20 (2009), pp.129-141.

Jost, J. T., and D. M. Amodio. "Political Ideology as Motivated Social Cognition: Behavioural and Neuroscientific Evidence." *Motiv Emot* 36 (2012), pp.55-64.

Jost, J., J. Napier, H. Thorisdottir, S. Gosling, T. Palfai, and B. Ostafin. "Are Needs to Manage Uncertainty and Threat Associated with Political Conservatism or Ideological Extremity? *Personality and Social Psychology Bulletin* 33 (2007), pp.989-1007.

Kim, H. and H. Markus. "Deviance or Uniqueness, Harmony or Conformity? A Cultural Analysis." *Journal of Personality and Social Psychology* 77 (1999), pp.785-800.

Koleva, S., and B. Rip. "Attachment Style and Political Ideology: A Review of Contradictory Findings." *Social Justice Research* 22 (2009), pp.241-258.

Korostelina, K. *Social Identity and Conflict: Structures, Dynamics, and Implications.* New York: Palgrave Macmillan, 2007.

Markus, H., and S. Kitayama. "Culture and the Self: Implications for Cognition, Emotion, and Motivation." *Psychological Review* 98/2 (1991), pp.224-253.

Sperry, L. *Ministry and Community.* Minnesota: The Liturgical Press, 2000.

Tajfel, H., and J. Turner. *Social Identity Theory of Intergroup Behaviour.* In *Psychology of Intergroup Relations,* ed. S. Worchel and W. Austin. Chicago: Nelson Hall, 1985, pp. 7-24.

Tharayil, Thomas. *Beyond Secure Attachment.* New Delhi: Media House, 2012.

Trungpa, C. *Materialism, Cutting through Spiritual.* London: Shambhala Publications, Inc., 2002.

Walterman, A. *The Psychology of Individualism.* New York: Praeger, 1984.

Wilson, G. *The Psychology of Conservatism.* London: Academic Press, 1973.

3

Neo-Gnosticism and Neo-Pelagianism: Responses of the Church through the Mass / Eucharist

Norman Tanner, SJ

Introduction: Historical Overview in Pictures

Rather than provide a historical overview in textual form of how the heresies of Gnosticism and Pelagianism were warded off by the Church's teaching and devotional practices, I will do so with a pictorial presentation, divided into four parts. Since the Mass/Eucharist[1] is central to our Christian life, I shall specifically highlight the history of the Mass to show how the gnostic and pelagian threats were countered by this central Christian practice. The first part looks at the first millennium AD, beginning with a painting from around 190 AD, the oldest known Christian illustration of any kind. This first millennium is the common heritage of the Catholic and Orthodox churches and, for the most part, of churches associated with the Reformation: a welcome dimension, therefore, of ecumenism. The second part focuses on developments in the Catholic Church during the five centuries between the start of the East-West schism in 1054 and the beginning of the Reformation in 1517. Eucharistic teaching and devotions developed considerably within the Catholic Church during this time; developments that indicate deep piety, it is argued, but which were to be severely criticized during the Reformation. The third part examines Reformation and Counter-Reformation: criticisms of Catholic practices on the part of the Reformers as well as their own teachings and practices; and developments within the Catholic Church, partly in response to these criticisms. A concluding part looks at the role of four ecumenical councils in these developments: Nicea I (325), Lateran IV (1215), Trent (1545-63) and Vatican II (1962-5). The last council and its aftermath have brought healing to many difficulties as well as hopeful signs for the future; yet divisions remain which impede full communion between the churches.

1.   Early Church

The first picture is the oldest known Christian illustration.[2] It comes from the catacomb of Saint Callistus in Rome and is usually dated to about 190 AD.

In the full painting there are two fish, one on the left carrying five loaves of bread, and facing it, another fish (pictured here) carrying beakers of red wine. The two paintings are amazingly well preserved. It seems likely that the place within the catacomb where they are to be found was a space in which the Eucharist was celebrated. The Greek for fish is ἰχθυς and these letters can be expanded to ᾽Ιησους χριστος θεου Υοις Σωτηρ (Jesus Christ Son of God Saviour). Accordingly, a fish was quite a common representation for Christ in the early Church; indicating, too, that Greek was understood in Rome, the capital of the mainly Latin-speaking western half of the Roman empire.

This interpretation of the fish would be hidden from non-Christians: a sensible precaution in times of persecution. One may note, too, that the picture fits well with the story of the feeding of the five thousand (Jn 6:9-11), when two fish and five loaves of bread are multiplied to feed the people. In the catacomb picture we see the fish (Jesus) carrying us (the contents of the two baskets) willingly – even joyfully – yet, as quite a burden. We are difficult people!

The following three illustrations bring us to the eastern half of the Roman empire in the second half of the sixth century. By this time the western half of the empire had been conquered by tribes coming from outside: Lombards in Italy, Franks in France, Visigoths in Spain, Angles and Saxons in Britain. All these tribes converted to Christianity and would provide the backbone of western Christendom in the Middle Ages; but in the meantime, they seemed to bring an end to Roman civilization. It was, rather, the Greek-speaking eastern half of the Empire, with its capital Constantinople (later called Byzantium), which successfully resisted these tribal invasions and was better able to preserve the traditions of the ancient Roman empire; although this eastern empire was itself increasingly threatened from another direction - the rise of Islam - from the late seventh century onwards.

The first picture shows the chalice thought to come from Antioch in modern Turkey and now preserved in the Cloisters Museum in New York.

At the centre, Christ welcomes us with outstretched arms. Other individuals can be seen within the vine, representing perhaps apostles and people who come to the Eucharist. Altogether the scene is joyful and fruitful, very positive in tone. Even after the first three centuries of intermittent persecutions, life was hard for most Christians: many were slaves or living in harsh circumstances and difficult employment. Christians, therefore, didn't want all these difficult features to be rubbed in on Sunday, the day of resurrection. At least on that day, rather, the joyful, fruitful and everlasting results of the resurrection should be emphasized. These are my thoughts.

The next picture is of a paten, also from the second half of the sixth century and coming from the Greek-speaking eastern half of the Empire.

This paten, too, was made of expensive material, silver, so we shouldn't exaggerate the poverty of the early Church: though objects made of precious metals are, of course, more likely to have survived than those made of wood or other more perishable materials. This paten, usually called the "Riha" paten, which is now part of the Dumbarton Oaks Collection in Washington DC, USA, carries an appropriate quotation in Greek around the edge. To the left, Christ gives the bread to six apostles, with a paten underneath to indicate bread; and a more heavenly figure on the right offers wine – indicated by the jug underneath – to the other six apostles, while one of them, presumably Judas, looks uneasy.

Our last illustration from the first millennium AD comes from the Rossano Gospels: a book comprising the four gospels together with some illustrations, which is thought to have been composed in Syria in the late sixth century and is now preserved in the cathedral library of the diocese of Rossano in Italy. In the top-left we see Jesus with the twelve apostles at the last Supper, with Judas Iscariot stretching out his hand towards Jesus – the sign of his forthcoming betrayal – and the relevant passage in John's gospel (13:26) above. On the right, Jesus washes the feet of the apostles and the relevant gospel passage (Jn 13:5). Underneath are four passages from the old Testament pointing to these events: three from the Psalms,

indicated by the crowned figure of David, and one from the prophet Zephaniah. Altogether it is a brilliant depiction, which is supported by two more illustrated pages depicting the Last Supper with Christ giving bread and wine to the apostles. In this case, too, the materials are costly: gold and silver on purple vellum.

Gnosticism and Pelagianism – *foci* of this Symposium – are not cited directly in the pictures we have seen. But their indirect influence, principally through the Church's desire to counter them, is likely. For, throughout this period the teachings of Gnosticism were influential as were, for most of the time, those associated with Pelagius (+ after 418). Against Gnosticism, we can see the reality of Christ's humanity – he is no mere phantasm – especially in the left-hand figure on the Riha paten and in the paintings of the Rossano gospels. Against Pelagianism, the importance of God's initiative in our good works is evident in all the illustrations; the fish carries us; Christ on the chalice welcomes and invites us; Christ on the paten offers bread and wine to the apostles; and Jesus takes the initiative in the three illustrations in the Rossano gospels. We have a role, surely, but it is to respond to God's invitations rather than to try to work on our own.

2.   Middle Ages

The next picture comes from the Middle Ages: after the beginning of the split between the western church centred on Rome and the eastern church centred on Constantinople, which is usually dated to the exchange of excommunications by the papal legate and the patriarch of Constantinople in 1054; and before the schism within the western church initiated by Martin Luther's protest in 1517. The first point to note is that the Mass / Eucharist was not among the disputed issues causing the East-West schism of 1054 and it has not been contested by the two churches subsequently. This is very consoling. It means the two churches are in communion regarding this central mystery of Christianity. Moreover, Gnosticism and Pelagianism were not among the issues in dispute between the two churches.

However, this same period – 1054 to 1517 – saw the western Church develop increasingly on its own, without the support or correction of its partner in the East. Developments in the western Church regarding in the Eucharist, moreover, were to become central to the controversies between Catholics and Protestants[3] at the Reformation.

The picture shows a Corpus Christi procession in Italy around 1485. It is attributed to Attavante degli Attavanti and forms part of

the Gradual book of the Camaldolese Benedictines, which is now kept
in the Biblioteca Mediceo-Laurentiana in Florence.

The feast of Corpus Christi had been established by pope Urban IV
in 1264 and soon a central feature of the celebration was a procession
through the neighbourhood, with the host carried in a monstrance by
the local bishop or parish priest, surrounded by clergy and laity. Our
picture is a fine example of this, with the monstrance carried by the
bishop. Reformers would soon criticize these processions, alongside
other Catholic developments, for removing the Eucharist from its
proper context. We can appreciate, however, the devotion of those
taking part in the procession.

Such piety is revealed, too, in our second illustration from the
late Middle Ages: the Despenser reredos in Norwich cathedral in
England, which was likely placed above a side-altar in the cathedral,
to help the devotion of both the priest saying Mass there and the
congregation. Five scenes are depicted with great sensitivity. Mary,
mother of Jesus, is depicted (in blue) both at the crucifixion and, on
the right, during Christ's ascension into heaven. Around the four sides
are the emblems of those who sponsored the work: prominent East
Anglian personalities, including Henry Despenser, bishop of Norwich
(1370-96). The reredos hardly suggests a decadent Church in need
of radical reform.

3. Reformation and Counter-Reformation

The altar-piece painted by Lucas Cranach the Elder in 1539, for the parish church of Wittenberg, provides the best illustration of Lutheran teaching on the Eucharist. The date was five years before Martin Luther's death in 1544 and Wittenberg was the town in which – according to tradition – he had posted his 95 theses in 1517, thereby ushering in the Reformation. For most leaders of the early Reformation there were just two sacraments – baptism and the eucharist – because only they were instituted by Christ. The right-hand panel illustrates the first sacrament with the baptism of a child. The other three panels concern the Eucharist.

The large central panel provides an idealized picture of the last Supper, underlying the point that the Eucharist was central to the reformer's beliefs. The other two panels focus on preaching: for Luther and most other Reformers the sermon formed an integral part of the Eucharist. To the left we see Martin Luther beside a pulpit. Underneath is the pastor preaching to a congregation. Notice that he is preaching Christ crucified. This highlights an important point.

It is only the second picture of the crucifixion in this presentation. As already mentioned, iconography in the early Church focused on the joyful and fruitful results of Christ's passion rather than on his sufferings as such. This approach remained influential into the Middle Ages, with Christ's sufferings represented in a noticeably sensitive manner. Emphasis upon the brutality of these sufferings enters much more with the Reformation (though not especially in this picture), while Catholics – perhaps not to be outdone by Protestants – rather followed suit during the Counter-Reformation and later; an epoch in which the Society of Jesus played a central role. So, what we may take almost for granted today – the crucifix at the centre of the church and indeed dominating it and much of Catholic spirituality – is a somewhat recent development. Important, too, is that Luther and all the other Reformers charged the Catholic church with placing too much emphasis upon our free will, not enough upon the gratuitous nature of God's choice: a subtle form of neo-Pelagianism, contrary to "justification by faith alone" as taught by the Reformers.

Our next picture comes from the Counter-Reformation, the Catholic response to the Protestant Reformation. It was painted by Peter Paul Rubens, from Catholic Flanders, and is now to be found in the Prado gallery in Madrid: Flanders (in modern Belgium) then formed part of the Spanish empire and, as a result, many Flemish paintings came to Spain and are now kept in the Prado. By 1625, the date of the painting, the Counter-Reformation was gaining momentum and Catholic forces held the upper hand in the Thirty Years War (1618-48). The painting reveals well this renewed confidence as well as an unpleasant aggressive streak, which Catholics today must face in relation to their past. The woman in the chariot represents the Church, with the papal tiara above her head. She carries aloft the host inside a

monstrance, thus indicating the centrality of the Eucharist within the Reformation controversies. The chariot, drawn by horses, is moving ahead confidently, while the man run over represents Protestantism, which is now in crisis. At the foot of the painting, in the centre, is another papal emblem: an orb representing the universal authority of the pope over the worldwide Church.

4. Councils and Conclusion

You may have noticed that so far in this presentation there has been no mention of the church's ecumenical councils, a topic on which I am rarely silent. The main reason lies in the consoling observation already made, that the Eucharist was not one of the issues in dispute between the churches of East and West – Orthodox and Catholic –

during the first millennium AD, nor has it become an issue between the two churches since then. However, many of the heresies within the Christian community during this first millennium, particularly those regarding Christ's divinity and humanity, had major implications for eucharistic teaching, even if they were not expressed in these terms. One of them – often described as the primordial Christian heresy inasmuch as so many other difficulties are rooted in it – was Arianism. If Christ is not fully divine, as Arius was condemned for teaching, the implications for the Eucharist are great. The next picture, accordingly, shows the first council of Nicea in 325, at which Arius was condemned for teaching a diminished divinity in Christ.

At the top of the picture, standing in a pavilion, is the young Christ. Some men – most of them representing bishops at the council – are looking at him, others are talking to each other about him. In the lower half of the picture we have senior bishops at the council – maybe they can be identified individually – with the crowned emperor Constantine at the centre. He had convoked the council and presided: Pope Sylvester I (314-37) was not present but, importantly, he was represented by two legates. Lying on the floor underneath, partly cut off in this photo, is the condemned Arius.

The picture, dating from the ninth century and painted onto the iconostasis of St Catherine's monastery in the Sinai Peninsula in Egypt, is the earliest and best representation of the council known to survive.

The next picture brings us to an important council in the Middle Ages. It is a miniature from the mid-fourteenth century copy of Matthew Paris's *Chronicon Maior* – written in the mid-thirteenth century – which is now kept in the Courtauld Museum in London.

It represents the summoning of the fourth Lateran council of 1215. The young pope Innocent III, carrying a pastoral staff, is surrounded by members of the Roman curia. He extends his hand to summon bishops to the council. Some of them are not eager to come but their leading figure raises his hand in a gesture of acceptance for the whole group. The Latin text in red, translated into English, reads: "The council celebrated under pope Innocent in the Lateran church" – the Lateran church, not the more famous St Peter's, is the cathedral church of the diocese of Rome. This council, which came to be included in the Catholic church's list of ecumenical councils,[4] is very important for the history of the Eucharist because it was the first such council to use the word "transubstantiation" (decree 1).

The protracted and very important council of Trent is our next port-of-call. Altogether the council lasted through nineteen years, from 1545 to 1563: three periods when the council was in session – 1545-9, 1551-2 and 1562-3 – interwoven with the years 1549-51 and 1552-62 when it remained suspended. The city of Trent

(in northern Italy) was chosen because it was acceptable to both Pope Paul III and Emperor Charles V, the principal ruler in Germany where the Reformation had begun with Martin Luther's protest in 1517. Although lying outside the papal states in central Italy, Trent formed an enclave of territory belonging to the papacy; the area was German-speaking and the emperor hoped the council might lead to the healing of the Reformation schism.

The picture, painted by Titian, shows Pope Paul III (1534-49), who called the council, and on the right the city of Trent with its cathedral in the middle. Among many topics covered by the council, the Mass was treated very fully. This is not surprising inasmuch as the Mass is so central to Christianity and because it was a key issue in the clash between Catholics and Protestants. The latter were divided in their understanding of the Eucharist, but all of them rejected the teaching on transubstantiation – that following the priest's words of consecration, the bread and wine are changed "in substance" into the body and blood of Jesus Christ, so that the bread and wine remain only "accidentally" or in appearance – as contrary to both Scripture and common sense. Though the word "transubstantiation" had been used by Lateran IV in 1215, Trent developed the teaching more fully in chapter 4 and canon 2 of its decree on the Eucharist (session 13

on 11 October 1551). However, though transubstantiation remained
for long the favoured term for Catholics to express the mystery of
the Eucharist, Trent in no way excluded other traditional expressions
of Christ's presence: real, mystical or sacramental presence or simply
"presence".

Another key topic covered by the council of Trent – and linked
to the Mass – was justification. As mentioned, the Catholic church
was accused by Protestants of teaching what amounted to a Pelagian
emphasis on the role of our own efforts in our justification. Trent
responded to this charge by its lengthy 'decree on justification':

> Justification in adults takes its origins from a predisposing grace of
> God through Jesus Christ, that is from his invitation which calls
> them, with no existing merits on their side. Thus, those who have
> been turned away from God by sins are predisposed by God's grace
> inciting and helping them, to turn towards their own justification by
> giving free assent to and cooperating with this same grace … So
> those justified in this way and made friends and members of God's
> household … grow in that very justness they have received through
> the grace of Christ, by faith united to good works. (Session 6 on
> 13 January 1547).

Thus, we see Trent listening to Protestants regarding their insistence
that the initiative in our justification comes wholly from God, but
insisting too that our cooperation is essential: therefore, good works
as well as faith, not faith alone. We may note, too, that while neo-
Gnosticism was not an immediate issue at the time, the council began
its doctrinal decrees (session 3 on 4 February 1546) by quoting in full,
in Latin translation, the Nicene creed. This creed had been drawn up
by the councils of Nicea I (325) and Constantinople I (381) at a time
when Gnosticism was a serious threat to the Church: it can be seen,
in part, as a response to this threat.

The final picture shows Vatican II in progress in St Peter's church
in Rome. To the left and right, in tiered seating, are the bishops and
other members of the council, with the high altar at the far end.
This council did not produce any document specifically dedicated

to the Mass, but it resulted in much improved relations between the Catholic church and the churches of the Reformation – especially the Anglican and Lutheran churches – which, in turn, resulted in healing some of the wounds – though surely not all of them – regarding the understanding and celebration of the Eucharist. Altogether there was a new atmosphere.

During the following half-century until today, further difficulties have emerged and inter-communion has not been permitted, except in special circumstances, by the authorities of the Catholic church. Even so, Vatican Council II represents a milestone in the history of the Eucharist and it forms a fitting conclusion to this presentation. The council, too, may be considered the culmination – so far – of all the previous ecumenical councils, including therefore their stances against both Gnosticism and Pelagianism.

Endnotes

[1] The words 'Mass' and 'Eucharist' are used inter-changeably in this article, though 'Mass' more frequently when referring to the Catholic sacrament.

[2] There is one slightly older surviving picture, also in a Roman catacomb, which mockingly portrays the crucified Christ as a donkey; so, it is better described as anti-Christian than as Christian.

[3] 'Protestants' and 'Reformers' and allied words are used in this article for the sake of convenience, while recognising that wide differences existed among those described in this way.

[4] The list comprises twenty-one councils from Nicea I in 325 to Vatican Council II in 1962-5. The word 'ecumenical' derives from the Greek *oikoumenike* and means literally "where there are houses", and so by extension "of the inhabited world" and then "of the whole world".

4

Hominization of the Word: A Challenge to Neo-Gnosticism and Neo-Pelagianism

Jacob Parappally, MSFS

Any extreme position on any subject is dangerous as it is situated precariously. It is obvious that an overemphasis of any dimension of truth can take away the essential content of truth. This is also true with regard to the revelation of God in Jesus Christ. The Christological controversies that emerged in the first century after the death and resurrection of Jesus continued throughout the centuries and still continue even today in one form or another. The fundamental Christian faith-affirmation that this human reality of Jesus is God or Jesus Christ is God become human was a difficult proposition for some who had a dualistic worldview. In this dualistic worldview, there is an unbridgeable gap between spirit and matter, divine and human, absolute and relative, eternal and temporal, heavenly and earthly, soul and body and all such possible polarities that denote the separation between trans-historical and historical. The Fathers of the Church like Ignatius of Antioch and Irenaeus, and great theologians like Tertullian, Origen and others tried to overcome this false teaching because it undermines the foundational Christian faith in God who became human. However, there is a serious doubt whether Christian theology and Christian spirituality have adequately overcome this serious problem of dichotomizing and polarizing the two dimensions of reality. Such polarization can affect the true meaning of God become human in Jesus Christ.

Against the backdrop of the dangers of dualism, certain questions arise: How does the reality of Jesus Christ challenge the extreme negation of the material world and devaluation of human body by the Gnostic teachers of the Post-NT times and to some extent affect the Christian spirituality even today? How does our faith in Jesus Christ, both human and divine, challenge any form of spiritual elitism that claims to have special experiences that are valid but only available to a few who claim salvation only for those whom they judge to be strict and meticulous in their following the laws and the spiritual disciplines of the Church? How does the reality of God becoming human subvert all philosophies and doctrines that claim absolute autonomy for humans to chart their course of obtaining salvation or wholeness without any recourse to God, the author of creation and salvation? The emerging neo-gnosticism and neo-pelagianism devalue the dignity and sacredness of human beings and their God-given freedom revealed through Jesus Christ, the Word became human.

Jesus Christ is both the revelation of the mystery of humans as well as the revelation of the mystery of freedom in history. There was never a human who existed in the world before him or after him as he was the most unfolded or the most evolved human being. In him human freedom regained its original purity by being united with God's will and freedom which makes humans authentically free. It reaffirms the paradox that by submitting oneself to infinite love and freedom humans become truly free. Both Pelagianism and neo-Pelagianism tried to understand and articulate human freedom independent of its source, God. In our times, such thinking gains popularity as it resonates with the sentiments of the people of today, especially the youth, who think that their freedom is absolute. By idolizing human freedom to the extent that it is separated from its source, the Trinitarian God, human freedom loses not only its sacredness and dignity but reduces it to a brute force that has the potentiality to destroy other humans and the world. In fact, in the criminal history of the world, we have many instances of such misuse of human freedom that destroyed the lives of millions of people and have done irreparable damage to nature.

Jesus lived and showed that God-encounter is not the privilege of a select few but the privilege of every child of God. It is a privilege that is gratuitously granted by God. So, the restlessness of humans to reach out to God is created by God. No system or structure, no law or regulation, no rules of purity or impurity prevent humans from encountering God. Jesus revealed that humans become truly free to be themselves only in submitting themselves to the power of God who through his favourable justice and grace reaches out to humans and enables them to respond to him. Humans come to themselves when they abandon themselves to God. In Jesus Christ humans' God-given capacity to go beyond themselves reaches its maximum possible expression when God's self-communication or God's Word chose to be united with humanity which has the God-given capacity to reach out to God.

1. Jesus the Answer to Spirit and Matter Dichotomy

Philosophical thinking—both in the Hellenistic world and in the Indian sub-continent even before Christ—was confronted with the problem of the relationship between spirit and matter as well as assigning a comparative value to each. Obviously, the spirit dimension of reality was considered far superior to the material dimension of reality. The Vedantic system of philosophy assigned absolute value to the Spirit dimension of Reality to the extent that it considered that it is the only Absolute Reality and matter as nothing compared to it. What is of relative value is only an appearance in comparison with the really real, *satysyasatyam* and tried to overcome the duality of spirit and matter, the absolute and the relative by the philosophy of non-dualism. The Stoics of the Hellenistic world resolved the dichotomy of spirit and matter by their philosophy of logos. According to their teaching the logos is present in the matter thus making it a pantheistic philosophy. For Plato, matter or body is subordinate to spirit as the matter exists not in the ideal world but only in its reflection. But the Gnostic philosophy not only emphasized the dichotomy of matter and spirit but also polarized them to such an extent that they became irreconcilable as good and evil. For the Gnostics matter is evil and the spirit is good. Humans are good spirits caught up in the prison-house of the body.

The classical gnostic Christianity denies the fundamental Christian faith that God has become really and truly human in Jesus Christ. Saturninus and Basilides, the better-known Gnostics claim that there are a number of Christs who are lesser and lesser in degree and that the last one touches matter and is born in the world. Even this Christ is caught up in the evil matter. The apocryphal book, the Gospel of Judas,[1] labels Judas Iscariot as the 'Saviour of the Saviour' because by his betrayal he got Jesus killed and thus he saved or liberated Jesus Christ from his evil body! In his dialogue with Judas, Jesus tells him, "You will exceed all of them, for you will sacrifice the man that clothes me." This variety of Gnosticism denied not only the hominization of the Word but also true salvation through it and through the death and resurrection of Jesus. For the Gnostics in general, salvation is achieved through one's own effort with the help of a guide who is able to help those who seek salvation by leading them through true knowledge or gnosis that they are caught up in the evil matter. This salvation according to the Gnostics can be achieved only by those who are spiritually elite and cannot be attained by the *hoi polloi* ordinary people or so-called people at the margins of society or religion.

Gnosticism and its offshoot Docetism, which teach that Jesus only 'appears' to be human and is not really human continue to influence all sections of the Church including some of those in the ecclesiastical hierarchy. It is easy for people to believe that Jesus Christ was truly God. They will even confess that Jesus was truly human. But they would find it very difficult to accept that Jesus was a human being like any other human! According to their philosophy and worldview, God could not become truly and fully human!

Ignatius of Antioch (d.110 AD) defended the foundational Christian faith that Jesus Christ was truly human by his martyrdom offering up his body as a sacrifice. Irenaeus (d.202 AD), the bishop of Lyons, was the first Christian theologian who developed a systematic theology against Gnosticism which devalued human body as evil and denied the true humanity of Christ. Irenaeus says: "If the flesh were not in a position to be saved, the Word of God would certainly not have become flesh. And if the blood of the righteous were not to be sought after, the Lord would certainly not have had blood."[2] In his book, *Adversus Haereses* or *Against Heresies* he argued that whatever God had created is good. God created everything with both his hands, the Logos and the Pneuma, or the Word and the Spirit. Humans are not created perfect but created for perfection; and therefore, they are given the capacity to become perfect through the assistance of God. Because of the original mistake of Adam and Eve the image of God in them, namely, reason and will were weakened and their likeness of God that is their friendship with God was lost. So, God becomes human in order to make humans perfectly human and thus divine. Even if there was no original mistake, God would have become human to lead humans to their perfection. It is by using their God-given freedom that humans can become truly humans. In the hominized Word, Jesus Christ, the full realization of human as human and the full expression of human freedom in surrendering to God have been achieved. It is in Jesus, the human being, that both the human reality and human freedom find fulfillment according to God's plan for humans.

Against all types of Gnosticism, the Fathers of the Church and the early theologians of the Church affirmed the goodness of everything that had been created as well as the reality of the humanity of Christ and salvation brought to the world through the hominization of the Word, his life, death and resurrection. They also affirmed that the salvation or wholeness brought about by Jesus Christ is offered to all without any differentiation and discrimination. First of all, nobody can claim salvation and nobody can be excluded from God's gratuitous gift of salvation. Gnosticism with its perverted worldview and false doctrines were not just a threat to true Christian faith in the first centuries of the Christian era but continued its influence on the Church throughout the history either by creating classes of Christian believers, namely, those who take a flight from this evil world (*fuga mundi*) to devote themselves to prayer and ascetical practices and others who are involved in the evil world and follow the ordinary life of faith in the Church. Those who followed the ascetical practices and disciplines undertook severe penances to suppress the body as if it were the most evil burden the good and holy soul has to bear and constantly struggle with. In the 16th and 17th centuries, saints like Ignatius of Loyola invited Christian believers to see God in all things, and Francis de Sales insisted that God's call to holiness is not limited to any elite group but is a call addressed to all and is to be freely responded to by everyone following their state of life.

In our times Gnosticism has received another mutation called 'neo-gnosticism' because it is practised by those Christian believers who consider themselves an elite group separated from the rest of the believers though their vision of the Church as an exclusive society which needs to practice its laws and regulations with certain rigidity. They would not let God to exercise his mercy and compassion to those who are at the margins of society like LGBT who are excluded also from the Church. They refuse to consider these marginalized humans as humans or their right to be treated with dignity. Every human being is an image and likeness of God, the Trinity, or absolute communion as well as objectively redeemed by the hominization of the Word. When the Logos assumed humanity, or when God became human, the entire humanity was included in him. Jesus Christ is an inclusive personality or a corporate personality in whom all before him, all after him and all contemporaneous with him are included according to Pauline theology. But it becomes operative only when one accepts it in faith or total self-surrender in freedom which itself is a gift from God. Therefore, any theology that excludes humans from communion is not faithful to the fundamental Christian experience of God in Jesus Christ who is the Logos become human, or the hominization of the Word.

Our vision of the Church depends on our vision of Christ or our ecclesiology depends on our Christology. If Christ is the Alpha and the Omega, the all-embracing reality of God, the Church, the sacrament of Christ cannot be a society of a privileged few but a communion of every human being of good will. The neo-gnosticism of today wants to separate the Church from the reality of the world and safeguard its divine dimension without its human dimension. The mystery of the Church is that it is the sacrament of the *totus Christus*, the entire Christ, the Word became Human, both divine and human, historical and trans-historical. It is the human dimension of Christ that is manifested in the Church when it welcomes and is hospitable to every human-being, both righteous and unrighteous, law-abiding and law-breakers, strong and weak, obedient and rebellious, faithful ones and the prodigal ones. The neo-gnosticism of those Christian believers both among the hierarchy and other faithful exclude people and devalue the sacramentality of the body and the material world. By their eagerness to be faithful to the tradition of the Church, they become so rigid in their understanding of laws and regulations in all matters of Christian life and worship that they reduce and distort the very meaning and purpose of the hominization of the Word.

2. God's Hominization a Challenge to Neo-Pelagianism

The reality of Jesus Christ, the hominization of the Logos, is the fulfillment of the God-given capacity of humans to transcend and reach out to God as well as the fullness of God's self-revelation in history. It affirms the essential nature of humans to go beyond themselves and the existential expression of it in human freedom. Since human nature of transcendence and its existential expression in freedom have their source in the infinite goodness and generosity of God human freedom is not absolute. To discover the true meaning of human existence we must refer back to its origin and end, or its source and goal in God, and true human freedom must refer back to its source, the infinite love of God that lets humans to exercise their freedom and become truly what they are called to become, namely, unfolded humans like Jesus the human.

From the history of theology, we know that Pelagius (AD 354-425 or 440) was a British or Irish monk who denied the effect of the original sin of the first parents affecting the entire humanity as well as affirmed that untainted by original sin humans' will can choose good and avoid evil. While affirming that God created human beings with a free will, which has sufficient capacity to live a sinless life, Pelagius is believed to have taught that divine assistance of grace was needed to do any good work or a good moral life. The followers of Pelagius who made Pelagianism a heretical doctrine affirmed the complete autonomy of humans and claimed that they could attain salvation by their own efforts. Pelagianism was condemned in the Council of Ephesus in 431.

Pelagius was probably reacting to the extreme position of St Augustine, that by original sin humans were "vitiated, corrupted, lost and dead" which seemed to have influenced Christian theology throughout the ages. According to this view, there is no goodness left in humans after the original fall of the first parents and the original sin is transmitted to all of humankind. In order to stress the gratuitous grace of God, based on Pauline theology, Augustine stressed the miserable situation of humans after the fall. So, he could not see anything good in humans created in the image and likeness of God before baptism in which justification is affected by love of God, which itself is a gift of God. Pelagius opposed Augustine's negative anthropology but Pelagianism went to the extreme of denying any assistance of God's grace as necessary for exercising human freedom. Semi-Pelagianism acknowledged the need for the cooperation of God and humans for salvation but the initiative of seeking God originates from free will of humans to which God responds. The implication of this way of thinking is that humans can control God's way of acting on them. Neo-pelagianism of today emphasizes human freedom and blindly follows self-transforming doctrines and techniques based on one's own capabilities of transformation without any recourse to divine assistance or grace.

Even more than a decade before his election Pope Francis spoke against the new forms of Pelagianism appearing in the Church. Already in 2001, as a Cardinal he affirmed that that authentic Christian morality has nothing to do "with the Pelagianism so fashionable today in its different, sophisticated manifestations. Pelagianism, underneath it all, is a remake of the Tower of Babel. … Grace always comes first, and then comes all the rest."[3] As the Pope, addressing the priests said, "it is not in soul-searching or constant introspection that we encounter the Lord: Self-help courses can be useful in life, but to live our priestly life going from one course to another, from one method to another, leads us to become Pelagians and to minimize the power of grace, which comes alive and flourishes to the extent that we, in faith, go out and give ourselves and the Gospel to others." Later he said that there are dour Christians who confuse "solidity and firmness with rigidity," adding that "today's Pelagians … are convinced that 'salvation is the way I do things'."[4] While addressing the Latin American bishops, Pope Francis observed, that "there are different ways in which the Gospel is reduced to an ideology." One of them is the "Pelagian solution. This basically appears as a form of restorationism. In dealing with the Church's problems, a purely disciplinary solution is sought, through the restoration of outdated manners and forms which, even on the cultural level, are no longer meaningful."[5]

In his encyclical, *Evangelii Gaudium* or *The Joy of the Gospel,* he *warns* against a "spiritual worldliness". He writes:

> This worldliness can be fuelled in two deeply interrelated ways. One is the attraction of Gnosticism, a purely subjective faith whose only interest is a certain experience or a set of ideas and bits of information which are meant to console and enlighten, but which ultimately keep one imprisoned in his or her own thoughts and feelings. The other is the self-absorbed promethean neopelagianism of those who ultimately trust only in their own powers and feel superior to others because they observe certain rules or remain intransigently faithful to a particular Catholic style from the past.[6]

According to Pope Francis both neo-gnosticism and neo-pelagianism are dangerous for Christian life as they deny the working of God's grace in hearts of the faithful leading them to ever new ways of encountering God by recognizing the impact of the Gospel in the lives of the people and the concrete needs of the present time. A supposed soundness of doctrine or discipline leads to a narcissistic and authoritarian elitism, whereby instead of evangelizing, one analyses and classifies others and instead of opening the door to grace, one exhausts his or her energies in inspecting and verifying. In neither case is one really concerned about Jesus Christ or others. These are manifestations of an anthropocentric immanentism.[7]

According to St Augustine we are created for God and are restless till we rest in God. This restlessness cannot be stilled by any human efforts however ingenious the psychospiritual methods may be. It can be stilled only by the One who created that restlessness in humans, knowing well that humans become truly human only in the process of responding to the grace of becoming by using their God-given freedom. By nature, humans are not autonomous beings or they are not a law unto themselves. But they can choose to become autonomous, seeking independence from their ultimate source, God, and start living a life of destruction and self-dehumanization. In this process, they destroy others and their world. The emerging neo-pelagianism insists on human freedom and autonomy independent of their ultimate source, God, who through his grace reaches out to humans and empowers them through the Holy Spirit to respond to God's invitation to become what they are called to become, namely, the glory of God!

How does neo-pelagianism affect the life of the Church? According to Pope Francis "In some people we see an ostentatious preoccupation for liturgy, and for doctrine and for the Church's prestige."[8] Some may wonder why such an attitude is wrong. Is it not being faithful to the traditions of the Church? The problem is not in preserving the traditions but the pharisaic attitude of some Christians who through the meticulous following of the rubrics of the liturgy and the faithful repetition of the dogmas of the Church consider themselves to be true Christians and exclude others who do not share their exclusive attitude and follow the discernment of the Spirit who makes everything new and offer new insights about the truth of the Gospel and its actualization in fast-changing situations of the world. If the Church has to feel within itself, "The joys and the hopes, the griefs and the anxieties of the people of this age, especially those who are poor or in any way afflicted, these are the joys and hopes, the griefs and anxieties of the followers of Christ. Indeed, nothing genuinely human fails to raise an echo in their hearts. For theirs is a community composed of human beings. United in Christ, they are led by the Holy Spirit in their journey to the Kingdom of their Father and they have welcomed the news of salvation which is meant for every human being."[9]

The Church preserving its sacred traditions needs to remain open to God's offer of grace through the Holy Spirit to discern and actualize God's offer of wholeness and salvation to all without any discrimination or exclusivism. No dogma or doctrine, no tradition or practice of the Church can prevent the action of God's Spirit in the Church. In a subtle way neo-pelagianism tries to prevent the initiative of God to renew the world according to God's plan by tenaciously clinging on to a static understanding of God's revelation. The uniqueness of the biblical experience of God is that God is a living God and the God of history. Any attempt of humans to limit the understanding of God's action in the continued history of the world and the Church to form such attitudes that prevent the mission of the Church in the world, is an arrogant claim of human autonomy and certainly an affront to God's sovereignty.

Any idolatry is blasphemy. It reduces God to something which can be defined and controlled. When dogmas and doctrines take the form of idols they fail to be symbols that evoke reverence to the infinite mystery of God and become 'dogmalatry'. When laws and regulations become rigid and enslaving, they fail to assist humans to overcome their physical and mental tendencies that make them less human. When human beings begin to understand their freedom as absolute autonomy and exercise it without its relationship to God and other humans it becomes an arrogant affront to God, the source of that freedom and destroys the dignity and sacredness of humans. Neo-gnosticism and neo-pelagianism reappear today in various forms that do not recognize the absolute sovereignty of God or God's gratuitous grace to become what they are called to become revealed through the hominization of the Word, Jesus Christ the way to the real freedom of humans by his exercise of freedom in his total abandonment of his human self to the Father.

By challenging the new trends of neo-gnosticism and neo-pelagianism, Pope Francis is inviting the faithful to an authentic spirituality of Christian discipleship that relies on the grace of God to live Christian life by actualizing authentic freedom that comes from discerning of God's Spirit. What makes one live human like Jesus and promote real unity and harmony in the Church is discerned as the gift of the Spirit. This leads the disciples of Jesus to go out of themselves to reach out to all humans as brothers and sisters and relate with them according to the values of the Gospel.

Conclusion

The problem of both Gnosticism and Pelagianism was that they negated the self-revelation of God in Jesus Christ and tried to promote a philosophical vision that devalued the true humanity of Jesus Christ and the true freedom that he revealed by relying on the power and providence of his Father. Hominization of the Word demolishes not only the demonization of the body and matter and all forms of spiritual imprisonment in ideologies, philosophies, techniques of psychological liberation, obsession with rigid implementation of rules, regulations, blind adherence to traditions which do not serve their purpose in the changed situations of the world any more but also the attempts to pull down the tower of Babel of arrogant exercise of human freedom that does not rely on God's grace communicated through the Holy Spirit. By his intimate union with his Father, by total dependence on him and led by the Holy Spirit, Jesus builds a community that lives the values of God's reign, namely, justice, love, equality, fellowship, peace and reconciliation. Thus, he destroys the evil power of human autonomy that creates injustice, corruption, discrimination, division, war and violence or the power of *objectivated* sin. What is required of us, his disciples, is to subjectively accept Jesus and his values and become human like Jesus and thus authentic manifestations of Christ or Christophanies!

Endnotes

[1] Rodolphe Kasser, Marvin Meyer and Gregor Wurst, eds, *The Gospel of Judas*, 2nd ed. (Washington DC: National Geographic Society Publishing, 2008).

[2] *Adversus Haereses*, 5,14,1; William A. Jurgens, *The Faith of the Early Fathers*, vol. I (Bangalore: Theological Publications in India, 2005), 101.

[3] J.J. Ziegler, "Pope: Ancient Heresy Plagues Modern Church – Today's Pelagians are convinced that 'salvation is the way I do things'," OSV News Weekly, 2 December 2014; Robert Moynihan, *Pray For Me: The Life and Spiritual Vision of Pope Francis* (London: Rider-Random House Publishing, 2013), 172.

[4] Ziegler, ibid.

[5] Ibid.

[6] *Evangelii Gaudium*, n.94.

[7] Ibid.

[8] Ibid., n.95.

[9] *Gaudium et Spes*, n.1.

5

My Way or God's Way:
An Indian Perspective

Michael Amaladoss, SJ

It is customary to compare the gnostic ways focusing on 'salvific knowledge' of the East to the agapeic ways concentrating on the 'redeeming love' of the West.[1] The East, of course, stands for Hinduism, Buddhism and Jainism, while the West stands for Christianity. Gnosticism is considered heretical in the West. Agape is considered insufficient in the East. A deeper analysis, however, would show that both in the East and in the West knowledge and love, gnosis and agape, are complementary, not competitive. While neo-gnosticism is attributed to the Enlightenment in modern times, ancient Gnosticism was attributed to the influence of Eastern thought, especially Buddhism. Alexander came to India in the 4th century before the common era. There must have been commercial and cultural contacts between India and the West before and after Alexander. The influence of Greek art can be seen in the images of the Buddha in north-west India. Historical references in Egypt and Greece speak of the presence of Indian thinkers in Alexandria. Greek thinkers like Pythagoras and Plotinus may have been influenced by Indian thought. St. Clement of Alexandria refers to the Buddha even in the period after Christ.[2] Buddhism was a missionary religion and there is every possibility that some Buddhist monks travelled West—as they travelled East to China. The Buddha himself was honoured as a Christian saint for some time in the Eastern Church. But a careful analysis will show that Gnosticism was a home-grown product, though a misunderstood form of Buddhism and Indian thought in general may have had its influence. I would like to suggest that a dualism between God and the universe, the spirit and the body, reason and the senses has its origin in Greek culture and philosophy and not in Indian thought. Such dualism is also set in a superiority-inferiority framework. It is this dualism that led to Gnosticism in ancient times. Following the Enlightenment, neo-gnosticism further denies God and the spirit and affirms a dualism between mind and matter. My aim here is to show that though a gnostic orientation is present in Indian religious thought, Gnosticism as a system or ideology is not an Indian phenomenon.

Is Buddhism Gnostic?

Aloysius Pieris shows how, in Buddhism, gnosis and agape complement each other to offer an integral experience of liberation. *Prajna* or wisdom leads to gnostic disengagement from the world while *karuna* or loving kindness leads to agapeic involvement in the world. Their mutual dependence can be spelt out in this way: "By *gnosis* a Buddha anticipates here and now the beyond; but, by *agape*, so to say, he transfigures the here and now in terms of the beyond."[3] The Buddha speaks of the eight-fold path: right view, right resolve, right speech, right conduct, right livelihood, right effort, right mindfulness, and right '*samadhi*' (meditative absorption or union). Through a way of knowledge, determination, right living and concentration one becomes free of one's ego. One becomes totally free. But there is no one who becomes free. It is simply an experience of freedom without limits. Since there is no point to which one is attached or limited, one is related to everything. It is not an other-worldly experience. It is an experience of wholeness. It is also emptiness, the absence of all name and form, all particularity, all reference. It is a network of pure relationships. Everything is related and inter-dependent. Everything is moving. As a matter of fact, we cannot really speak about it. We can only experience it. To verbalize the experience is to limit it. But if we cannot talk about it, we can still live it.

There are two schools in Buddhism called the little and the great vehicle. Bhikku Buddhadasa of Thailand, who follows the 'little vehicle', speaks of '*dhammic socialism*'.[4] Everything, everyone is related and mutually responsible. The whole universe is a network. Thich Nhat Hanh of Vietnam adheres to the great vehicle. He speaks of 'inter-being'.[5] To 'be' is to 'inter-be', to 'be in relationship'. It is a community of beings without egos, everyone living for the others, human and non-human—all that lives, including plants. Nirvana or emptiness does not mean simply nothing, but no-thing with a name and a form that makes it stand apart from everything else. Such relationship can be lived by mutual love and service, precisely emptying oneself. This is where *gnosis—prajna* leads to *agape—karuna*. Knowledge and Wisdom lead to Love and Compassion. There is no dualism here between spirit and matter, between body and soul, between this and another (higher) world. There is no knowledge that puffs one up. Though *prajna* and *karuna* are related, they are not the same nor equal. They are different. While *karuna* takes you back to the world, from which one is now detached, it is *prajna* that leads you to the liberating Absolute, the Real. So, the way of the Buddha towards liberation is basically gnostic. But it is a Gnosticism that is experienced in compassion and service. Its detachment denies attachment, not involvement. Being becomes a cosmic experience. I think that this is an experience very different from what Gnosticism or neo-gnosticism stands for. If some form of Buddhism influenced the Gnostics in the past it was not authentic Buddhism, but a corrupt form of it. True Buddhists today are not gnostic.[6]

The Ways of Hinduism
Hinduism speaks of four ways or *margas* of reaching the ultimate goal of life. They are *jñana* or insightful wisdom, *bhakti* or loving devotion, *karma* or committed action and *yoga* or psycho physical discipline.

These are not seen as separate and independent ways. They are inter-dependent and mutually influence each other. One or other way may dominate the practice of an individual. The way of wisdom is normally given pride of place. Its focus is not so much knowledge but awareness, involving not only the intellect, but all the human faculties. The earlier texts like the Upanishads focus rather on *jñana*, while the later ones like the Bhagavad Gita focus on *bhakti*. The focus of *karma* changes from ritual action to action in general. Since the overall focus of the four ways is *jñana*, Hinduism is sometimes said to be gnostic. But a look at the texts and the praxis will show that the Indian way is an integral way involving all the different elements. Such integration avoids the dualisms and dichotomies of western Gnosticism. This will be true of most modern gurus. Let us now look at some texts.

The *Chandogya* Upanishad tells us the story of Svetaketu. When he comes back home after following a traditional school teaching him the Vedas, his father introduces him to a deeper knowledge. He asks him to bring a fruit of a banyan tree, break it open to find the seeds and break further a seed to find that there is nothing. The lesson then follows: "My son, from the very essence in the seed which you cannot see comes in truth this vast banyan tree. Believe me, my son, an invisible and subtle essence is the Spirit of the whole universe. That is Reality. That is Atman. Thou art That."[7]

In the *Brihadaranyaka* Upanishad, the sage Yajnavalkya instructs the king Janaka. Starting with the question 'What is the light of man?', the king is led to go deeper from the sun to the moon, fire, voice to the Soul or Self or the Spirit. There is no duality in the Spirit, because it is 'the All'. "In the ocean of the Spirit the seer is alone beholding his own immensity'... This is the great Atman, the Spirit never born, the consciousness of life. He dwells in our own hearts as ruler of all, master of all, lord of all... But the Spirit is not this, is not this. He is incomprehensible, for he cannot be comprehended. He is imperishable, for he cannot pass away. He has no bonds of attachment, for he is free; and free from all bonds he is beyond suffering and fear... Who knows this and has found peace, he is the lord of himself, his is a calm endurance, and calm concentration. In himself he sees the Spirit, and he sees the Spirit as all."[8]

The *Katha* Upanishad changes the symbol. "He is the Eternal among thing that pass away, pure Consciousness of conscious beings, the One who fulfils the prayers of many. Only the wise who see him in their souls attain the peace eternal... There the sun shines not, nor the moon, nor the stars; lightnings shine not there and much less earthly fire. From his light all these give light, and his radiance illumines all creation."[9] We can see similar symbols in the *Mundaka* and *Swetasvatara* Upanishads. The *Mundaka* Upanishad actually underlines that it is not just self-effort. "Not through much learning is the Atman reached, not through the intellect or sacred teaching. He is reached by the chosen of him. To his chosen the Atman reveals his glory."[10] The small *Isa* Upanishad offers a summary. "Behold the universe in the glory of God: and all that lives and moves on earth. Leaving the transient, find joy in the eternal... Who sees all beings in his own Self and his own Self in all beings, loses all fear."[11]

From the Upanishads to the Bhagavad Gita

As the Hindu tradition moves from the period of philosophical reflection documented for us in the Upanishads to the period of the epics like the Ramayana and Mahabharata, the holistic vision is not lost. But the Atman becomes personal and even takes historical forms in avatars like Rama and Krishna. The truth of the Upanishads becomes personalized in the *Bhagavad Gita*. Krishna favours Arjuna with a vision of his cosmic being: "I will give thee divine sight. Behold my wonder and glory."[12] Arjuna sees and exclaims:

> I see in thee all the gods, O my God; and the infinity of the beings of thy creation...
> I see the splendour of an infinite beauty which illumines the whole universe...
> Thou God from the beginning, God in man since man was.
> Thou Treasure supreme of this vast universe.
> Thou the One to be known and the Knower, the final resting place.
> Thou infinite Presence in whom all things are.

God of the winds and the waters, of fire and death!
Lord of the solitary moon, the Creator, the Ancestor of all!
Adoration unto thee, a thousand adorations; and again and again
unto thee adoration.
Adoration unto thee who are before me and behind me;
Adoration unto thee who are on all sides, God of all.
All powerful God of immeasurable might.
Thou art the consummation of all: thou art all.[13]

After this vision Krishna assures Arjuna:

Not by the Vedas, or an austere life, or gifts to the poor, or ritual
offerings can I be seen as thou hast seen me.

Only by love can men see me, and know me, and come unto me.

He who works for me, who loves me, whose End Supreme I am,
free from attachment to all things, and with love for all creation, he
in truth comes unto me.[14]

So, Krishna can invite and promise Arjuna in his concluding words:

God dwells in the heart of all beings, Arjuna: thy God dwells in
thy heart... Give thy mind to me and give me thy heart, and thy
sacrifice, and thy adoration. This is my Word of promise: thou shalt
in truth come to me, for thou art dear to me.[15]

Later Bhakti Poets

The Tamil Bhakti poets feel that it is God who possesses them and
leads them rather they trying to reach out to God. Manikka Vachagar,
the Shaivite, sings:

That day Thou owned me, that very day, O Lord, firm as a rock!
Hast Thou not made Thine own, my life, body and all?
Is there any misery for me today, my Lord?
Thou might cause pleasure or pain! Am I to question Thee?[16]

Appar has the same sentiment.

I cannot say, I will approach Him and compel Him to dwell in me.
He himself comes, with yearning for me,

And dwells in my body and mingles with my life.
Is it possible for Him now to leave me?[17]

Nammalvar, the leading poet of the South Indian Vaishnavite tradition, has a similar experience and celebrates it in song. It is not the saint who tries to reach out to God through his own efforts. It is God who reaches out to him.

> Becoming himself, filling and becoming all worlds, all lives,
> Becoming him who becomes even me,
> Singing himself, becoming for my sake,
> Honey, milk, sugarcane, ambrosia,
> Becoming the lord of gardens too,
> He stands there consuming me.[18]

> My Lord, who swept me away forever into joy that day,
> Made me over into himself and sang in Tamil
> His own songs through me:
> What shall I say to the first of things, flame standing there,
> What shall say to stop?[19]

Allama Prabhu laughs at people who trust in their own efforts.

> With your alchemies, you achieve metals, but no essence.
> With all your manifold yogas, you achieve a body, but no spirit.
> With your speeches and arguments you build chains of words
> But cannot define the spirit.
> If you say, you and I are one, you were me, but I was not
> you.[20]

Devara Dasimayya suggests that *jñana* and *karma* should go together, of course in the context of *bhakti*.

> Fire can burn, but cannot move.
> Wind can move, but cannot burn.
> Till fire joins wind, it cannot take a step.
> Do men know it's like that with knowing and doing?[21]

He also has a unified vision of reality.

> Whatever It was that made this earth the base, the world its life,
> The wind its pillar, arranged the lotus and the moon

And covered it all with folds of sky,
With Itself inside,
To that Mystery, indifferent to differences, to It I pray, O Ramanatha.[22]

The human is not only a microcosm of cosmic reality, but something alive. Sings Basavanna:

The rich make temples for Siva.
What shall I, a poor man, do?
My legs are pillars, the body the shrine,
The head a cupola of gold.
Listen, O Lord of the meeting rivers,
Things standing shall fall, but the moving ever shall stay.[23]

Rabindranath Tagore also has similar joyful cosmic visions.

Let all the strains of joy mingle in my last song – the joy that makes the earth flow over in the riotous excess of the grass, the joy that sets the twin brothers, life and death, dancing over the wide world, the joy that sweeps in with the tempest, shaking and waking all life with laughter, the joy that sits still with its tears on the open red lotus of pain, and the joy that throws everything it has upon the dust, and knows not a word.[24]

No wonder, then, that such a vision invites him to involvement in the world with people.

Deliverance is not for me in renunciation. I feel the embrace of freedom in a thousand bonds of delight.
Thou ever pourest for me the fresh draught of thy wine of various colours and fragrance, filling this earthen vessel to the brim.
My world will light it hundred different lamps with thy flame and place them before the altar of thy temple.
No, I will never shut the doors of my senses. The delights of sight and hearing and touch will bear thy delight.
Yes, all my illusions will burn into illumination of joy, and all my desires ripen into fruits of love.[25]

Is the Hindu Tradition Gnostic?

Looking superficially at its insistence on *jñana*, one might rather hastily conclude that it is gnostic. But we have seen how, while yoga is used by all spiritual traditions as a psycho-physical preparation, the other three *margas* are integrated, while *jñana* or *bhakti* may predominate according to a given tradition; all methods of *sadhana* lead to experiential insight, which is not purely rational-intellectual. It will be similar to the contemplative traditions of Christianity. Secondly, while a certain hierarchy of beings in the world is recognized, it is not discriminatory. God or the Absolute is at the centre of everything and integrates everything. The hierarchical order is not bottom-up, becoming more and more refined and rarefied in intellectual terms, but rather top-down, going down to the centre where one experiences the Ultimate that holds everything together. It gives a value to everything which becomes the icon or symbol of the Absolute within. So, *sadhana* becomes a descent into one's own inner being rather than an ascent to some abstract realm leaving behind the inferior material world. Integration in terms of *advaita* or non-duality avoids the dualisms and dichotomies of Gnosticism. The modern Enlightenment philosophies are not even dualistic since they deny anything beyond the sensible, material world.

My Way or God's Way?

The title of the symposium 'My Way or God's Way', seems to refer more to the Pelagian heresy. The Pelagians denied original sin and affirmed that people can achieve the goal of their lives through their own efforts without any need of God's assistance. It was a heresy in a Christian context. But I wonder whether we can simply apply that term to Indian systems of *sadhana* that do not explicitly evoke the divine power. Indian religious traditions do not either have the concept of original sin, though everyone will be reborn with the good and evil karma of previous existences.

Among the Indian ways to reach the goal of human life, some do not believe in God. Buddhism and Jainism do not speak about God though they do have a moral sense of right and wrong. They do not pretend that we are born pure without any human or moral tendencies, good or evil. But they do not speak of a law-giver. Yoga is a psycho-physical method that other ways like *Jñana* and *Bhakti* can also use as a preparatory method of self-discipline. I have spoken of

Buddhism earlier. Though it does not speak about an Absolute Being called God it projects an Absolute inter-dependent Reality. I think that it is impersonal, inter-dependent Absolute with an agapeic element, which involves right and wrong, justice and injustice. Thus, it is not an egoistic enterprise as Pelagianism seems to be.

The Yoga

The system of Yoga seems to be a system of personal discipline. Many of the modern gurus seem to use it as such to promote a sense of equanimity and peace. The first two steps or *angas* of the yoga spell out moral demands. The first step *Yama* asks for non-violence, truthfulness, non-stealing, right use of energy (*brahmacharya*) and non-greed. The second step *Niyama* insists on cleanliness, contentment, discipline, self-study, and surrender to a higher power (*Ishwarapranidna*). This last element indicates a religious element, but without any elaboration in terms of a formula or ritual. Used in a religious context, Yoga can be a religious exercise. The concentrated meditation at the final steps of the yoga can focus on a particular divinity. Yoga can take its place as one of the four *margas* or ways of *sadhana* if its focus is on experiential insight integrating the body and the mind. Otherwise it can remain a psycho-physical exercise, beneficial for the body and the mind. But in so far as it does not formally deny any divine influence in the way of attaining spiritual experience, it need not be considered pelagian.

Other Hindu Traditions

The Hindu tradition, in all its forms, is basically *advaitic*: I and the Absolute are not two, neither one, but not-two: *a-dvaita*.[26] So when someone speaks of what s/he is doing in the area of *sadhana*, s/he is not talking of what his/her little self is doing, but what the Self or the Absolute is doing in and through him/her. S/he is quite aware that s/he cannot do anything on his/her own. S/he has to collaborate with the Absolute active in him/her. The collaboration is not at a level of equals. But one does not speak always of this double identity. One may not even be always aware of it. But it is the reality. In such a situation one cannot speak of my way and God's way. There is only one way.

Of course, it is possible that one can separate oneself and isolate oneself. In the Hindu tradition, one may forget one's dependence. One may be ignorant. But one will never consciously deny it. Besides, as I have said earlier with reference to Buddhism, there may be a sense of karma, about which one does not really know much. But there is no sense of being born in sin in the Christian sense, actually bearing the guilt of someone else.

Conclusion

In the Indian philosophical tradition, the principle of *advaita* or non-duality protects it from any sort of Gnosticism and Pelagianism, old or new. It is Greek dualism opposing God and the human, the human and the world, spirit and matter, soul and body, reason and emotion that leads to value the former and downgrade the latter. Modern Enlightenment in Europe has not only affirmed this dualism, but even denied whatever is not directly accessible to the human sense experience. It is, on the one hand, godlessness and, on the other, the proclaimed incapacity of the senses and reason of the humans to reach beyond matter that lead to neo-gnosticism and neo-pelagianism. But this is a Euro-American, not an Indian or Asian, problem. The Indian advaitic vision of reality and its holistic approach to sadhana save us from these European heresies. Symbols and symbolic actions are still valued here. The thriving popular religiosity in India in all religions is a concrete manifestation of the anti-gnostic spirit. This is one more occasion to realize that our world and Church and our theology and spirituality need not be Euro-American centred.

Endnotes

[1] See Aloysius Pieris, *Love Meets Wisdom: A Christian Experience of Buddhism* (New York: Orbis, 1988), 75, 85.

[2] Ibid., 23-26.

[3] Ibid., 75.

[4] Bhikku Buddhadasa, *Dhammic Socialism* (Bangkok: Thai Inter-Religious Commission for Development, 1988).

[5] Thich Nhat Hanh, *Interbeing* (Berkeley: Parallax Press, 1987).

[6] For this short section on Buddhism see Aloysius Pieris, ibid., 85-86, 111-118.1s

[7] Juan Mascaro, trans., *The Upanishads* (Penguin Books, 1965), 117.

[8] Ibid., 135-143.

[9] Ibid., 64.

[10] Ibid., 81. See also 60.

[11] Ibid., 49.

[12] Juan Mascaro, trans., *The Bhagavad Gita* (Penguin Books India, 1994), 89.

[13] Ibid., 90 and 93.

[14] Ibid., 95.

[15] Ibid.,120-121.

[16] A.J. Appasamy, ed., *The Temple Bells* (Calcutta: YMCA, n.d.), 64.

[17] Ibid., 110.

[18] A.K. Ramanujan, trans., *Hymns for the Drowning. Poems for Vishnu by Nammalvar* (Penguin Books India, 1993), 77.

[19] Ibid., 85.

[20] A.K. Ramanujan, trans., *Speaking of Siva* (Penguin Books, 1973), 147.

[21] Ibid., 108.

[22] Ibid., 103.

[23] Ibid., 19.

[24] Rabindranath Tagore, *Gitanjali* (Macmillan India, 1981), 38.

[25] Ibid., 49.

[26] Here I am talking of *advaita* in a general way, not in its particular interpretation by Sankara.

6

Reflections on Neo-Gnosticism and Neo-Pelagianism:

A Feminist Perspective

D. J. Margaret, FMA

1. Introduction: Dangers of Dualistic Thinking

The dualism seen in some forms of early Christianity was offshoot of the Greek philosophical tradition and has characterized western culture for long. Gnosticism promoted the division between spirit and knowledge, on the one hand, and emotion, action and ritual, on the other. This division was also seen as male-female dualism. Christianity, in general, has often retained this dualistic view of the human person, which has had widespread effects. One of these effects has been the traditional perception that the body is evil and earthly; and, consequently, all that is related to bodily experience is considered sinful. The spirit and knowledge are good and are the possessions of a few elites. Within this dualistic perspective, various ideologies and heresies arose within the Church, such as Pelagianism and Gnosticism. These ideologies and heresies endorsed a dualistic view of earthly life, biased vision of grace and salvation, and ambiguous knowledge of God's will and human efforts.

Neo-Pelagianism focuses purely on human effort and excludes the necessity of grace for salvation, the need to depend on God, and experience of God's mercy and compassion, while Neo-Gnosticism radicalizes the dualistic view of the human person. With the Enlightenment, the spirit/intellect side is further reduced since any transcendence is denied. So now the battle in neo-Gnosticism is the human mind and intellect against the body, emotion and action. The male-female dualism continues; the female is subordinated and exploited. Male is considered as intelligent, thus, superior, while the female is equated with the body therefore considered inferior. There is no place for transcendence. When transcendence is denied, the focus on the intellect becomes merely humanistic. It is intellectual knowledge against love (emotion) and action (service).

Today, as pointed out by Pope Francis,[1] we can witness various effects of neo-Gnosticism and neo-Pelagianism on people's dualistic views on various issues of life and belief systems. There are a number of binaries which reveal people's understanding of the human person, human body, human life, beliefs and practices: like holy and unholy; superior and inferior; intelligent and ignorant; ascetics and hedonists; heavenly and earthly; God's grace and human ability; mysteries and knowledge; immanent and transcendent; mystics and gnostics; soul and body; faith and reason, and so on.

Though it is Gnosticism that pays exclusive attention to the soul and negates the body, it is post-Enlightenment neo-Gnosticism that has created the moral mire we perceive all around us that often persuades or even pressurises us on a relentless bodily hedonism. The implicit devaluation of the body and over-evaluation of the mind has been a major problem in human history. Indeed, it encourages that rationalism which insists on splitting off absolute from relative, objective from subjective, reason from emotion, human efforts from grace, and reason from sense. All this dovetails with other dichotomies such as sacred and secular, body and soul, grace and nature.

One of the impacts of the dualistic view of the human body has been equating the human body with the activity of sexuality, which was considered evil. By contrast, the literature of embodiment theology or incarnation theology has challenged this traditional perception and has argued that the human body is an integral and holistic part of the human experience rather than for the sexual activity. It is the source of our capacity for relationship, for emotional and spiritual connection, for intimacy and for transcendence. The human body stands as an embodiment of holistic human expression, of human existence and experience.[2] In this paper I present my reflections on the effects or impacts of neo-Gnosticism and neo-Pelagianism from a feminist perspective. The first part of the paper presents a very brief context of our society and women; the second part highlights a few important aspects in the development of an embodied and holistic spirituality.

2.   A Brief Contextual Reality of Our Society and Women

Rapid global mass communications and connectivity, massive changes in human lifestyles and technology, fast development of the arts and sciences, easy international travels and tours, constant rise in cultural and religious upheavals, widespread multinational corporate companies and business centres, search for happiness and fulfilment from humanist philosophies, political ideologies and hedonistic lifestyles are increasingly and swiftly exposing contradictions and limitations in traditional beliefs and value systems. Our busy business centred lifestyles and the prevalence of use and throw culture seemingly indicate that authentic and effective relationships are impossible. Inept or even reluctant to live by the demands of Christian dogmas, doctrines, and traditions many people have left the church and some have even abandoned systems of morality, resorting to explicit amorality. Hypocritical behaviour by spiritual and political leaders, rampant dishonesty and injustice in every sphere, and the obscurity of urban, modern and postmodern life further encourage the rejection of God and God's ways.

At the same time today, life offers enormous freedom and possibilities that enforce increasingly various, difficult and far-reaching choices on our lives at all levels and at every stage. We can even modify genes, manufacture life and will soon create artificial intelligence.[3] The best possible living is made absolute and successful; social interactions have become an integral part of our thriving lives. The human search for wisdom has become universal and diverse. Traditional religions flourish and new spiritualities proliferate. While billions are persuaded by one or another claim to wisdom, cynics continue to sneer and seekers still search. Contemporary scientific naturalism tries to explain religion without God, meaning without genuine purpose, perversity without evil, and hope without transcendence.[4]

People would like to live a different type of spirituality in line with new trend of life. They affirm that they are not becoming 'less religious'; rather they are becoming 'differently religious'. Tony Jones calls this significant paradigm shift as a 'tectonic shift, seismic or tsunami shift'.[5] The changes in lifestyles and worldviews, in ideologies and in convictions, in the profession of faith and in the propagation of one's religion, in living and giving expression to one's spirituality and religiosity are shaking the earth beneath our feet.

Within this context, ever since his election, Pope Francis repeatedly keeps cautioning the Church about the new dangers that Pelagianism[6] and Gnosticism[7] pose. In his apostolic exhortation *Evangelii Gaudium,* he presents the great danger of consumerism, the desolation and anguish born of a complacent yet covetous heart, the feverish pursuit of frivolous pleasures, and a blunted conscience. A postmodern mindset is trapped among two extremes: neo-Gnosticism and neo-Pelagianism, wherein traditional Catholics are becoming more traditionalistic instead of being and becoming more merciful and compassionate.[8] Therefore, the Church is invited to fight against materialism that emphasizes meritocracy over the community of postmodern culture; against sheer obesity and decadence over vitality of life from within; against dualism that emphasises heavenly over earthly, soul over body.[9] Since neo-Pelagianism is but an added view of Gnosticism, let us define Gnosticism before we reflect on the challenges of neo-Gnosticism and neo-Pelagianism from a feminist perspective.

2.1. Gnosticism

Gnosticism is the theory of salvation by knowledge. Already in the first century of the Christian era there were Gnostics who claimed to know the mysteries of the universe. They were disciples of the various pantheistic sects that existed before Christ. The Gnostics borrowed what suited their purpose from the Gospels, wrote new gospels of their own, and in general proposed a dualistic system of belief. Matter was said to be hostile to spirit, and the universe was held to be a depravation of the Deity. Although extinct as an organized religion, Gnosticism is the invariable element in every major Christian heresy, by its denial of an objective revelation that was completed in the apostolic age and its disclaimer that Christ established in the Church a teaching authority to interpret decisively the meaning of the revealed word of God.[10]

There is no single, uniform Gnostic system. However, there are some of the common ideas to justify a general characterization of Gnosticism: preoccupation with the problem of evil; sense of alienation from the world; desire for special and intimate knowledge of the secrets of the universe (knowledge as salvation); dualism; cosmology/the pleroma or divine world; anthropology; eschatology; ethical implication (for some Gnostics this meant libertinism for others it was asceticism).[11]

2.2. Neo-Gnosticism and Neo-Pelagianism from a Feminist Perspective

Gnosticism is the teaching based on *gnosis*, the knowledge of transcendence arrived at by way of interior, intuitive means. It expresses a specific religious experience, an experience that does not lend itself to the language of theology or philosophy, but which is instead closely affinitized to, and expresses itself through, the medium of myth.[12] Because the Gnostics held that God is beyond good and evil, and beyond being, they could not identify God with any one form, i.e., either good or evil, or male or female, body or soul. Hence, in their writings God had to be inclusive of both male and female, father and mother, while transcending both.[13] When transcendence is denied, the emphasis on the intellect becomes merely humanistic. It is intellectual knowing against love/emotion (Deut 10:12-19; Jn 15:13; Mt 23:6-8;

Rom 13:10; 1 Cor 13:4-8; Eph 4:2; 1 Pet 4:8; 1 Jn 4:7) and action/ service (Mt 25:35-43; Lk 10:25-37; Jn 12:26; Mt 23:11; Mk 10:45; Gal 5:13; Heb 6:10; 1 Pet 1:12).

The status of women today is progressively changing. A range of factors has affected the change: political freedom, social reform, economic emancipation, religious-cultural awakening, information and technological development. History, literature, religion and politics abound with examples of women who have transformed society. We can see the move towards an egalitarian society wherein women have become protagonists in building up a new humanity through various movements and groups. However, the position of women continues to be one of subjugation. Women have become victims of the patriarchal culture, social ethos, political domination, religious rituals and customs. Women are facing a situation in which poverty is their lot, exploitation of the body is their slot, and deprivation is their common fate. The body, a recurrent theme in a variety of recent interdisciplinary studies, figures as the material or symbolic basis for much feminist embodied spirituality, in contrast to the fiction of disembodied subjectivity that marks mainstream modern epistemology. In today's complex and multi-religious context women are called to value sacredness of the body and contribute for the development of a holistic embodied spirituality of life. The following could be some of the reflections on neo-Gnosticism and neo-Pelagianism from feministic perspective.

The implications of the Gnostic beliefs influenced some Christians who literally beat their bodies into submission and lived such ascetic lives that they never allowed themselves the enjoyment of bodily pleasures. Others went to the other extreme and permitted their physical passions to run unbridled upon whatever course they chose. Unfortunately, traces of Gnostic thought continue to permeate the thinking of many Christians today in so-called neo-agnosticism. For example, some Christians think that only two things will last into eternity: God's Word and the souls of men and women—an emphasis on the spiritual and an exclusion of the physical. The Bible explicitly teaches that not only will these two last unto eternity but so will our bodies, in a glorified state (Jn 5:28-29; 1 Cor 15:42-44). Both body and spirit have equal importance and value in God's eyes. Paul said, "Whether you eat or drink or whatever you do, do all to the glory of God" (1 Cor 10:31). Therefore, we are invited to glorify God by upholding physical and spiritual, bodily and spiritual as important and significant.[14]

3.   Evolution of the Embodied Spirituality

Differing from Gnosticism or neo-Gnosticism, Pelagianism or neo-Pelagianism embodied spirituality views all human dimensions—body, soul or spirit, heart, mind, and consciousness—as equal partners in bringing self, community, and the world into a fuller alignment with the Divine Mystery out of which everything arises. A fully embodied spirituality emerges from the creative interplay of both immanent and transcendent spiritual energies in individuals who embrace the fullness of human experience while remaining firmly grounded in body and on earth.[15] A truly embodied spirituality is an integrated spirituality of the entire human person. It is an integration of human life, action and contemplation. The following are some of the important features of an embodied spirituality.

3.1. Embodied Spirituality as Conscientious Integration of the Person

Neo-gnostic view of the human person is observed to be deeply dualistic separating men from women, from each other and from the world. It divides the experience of the body, work and matter from that of the spirit. For centuries, many of the writings on Christian spirituality have exalted the spirit over the world and have cautioned us of the threats of being immersed in worldly things to the detriment of one's 'soul'.[16] Our focus on an embodied spirituality is to be holistic in approach and in affirmation of the human persons and the entire cosmos. It discards any kind of dualism: male and female, body and spirit, earth and heaven, humanity and creation. In an embodied spirituality, every experience takes place within the framework of integration and wholeness of the human person.

In this process of being and becoming whole or integrated persons, embodied spirituality creates new consciousness and a sense of identity, leading to a critical re-examination of the past forms of spirituality that separates body and soul. It provides new possibilities for an integrated spiritual quest and for spiritual transformation. For instance, embodied spirituality facilitates to overcome gender divisive forces and focuses on the spirituality of equality and equity. Traditionally, women are associated with subjectivity and emotion, body and inferiority, while men are regarded by themselves as the objective, rational and therefore, more legitimate thinkers and superior. Rejecting this position, embodied spirituality takes up a mission against such chauvinist and dualistic thinking. It does not patronize meekness and gentleness of women as weaknesses, kindness and friendliness as superficiality, love and truth as limitations, compassion and care as upshot. Rather, these are divine qualities embodied in integrated human persons.[17] Embodied spirituality not only connects body and mind, but also empowers both men and women.

An integrated spirituality will break through comfortable illusions of self-satisfaction, self-obsessions, and irreproachability. It challenges and comforts; respects human autonomy and agency; fosters the human flourishing of both women and men; leads to fullness of life in and through the full acceptance and experience of graced human condition.[18] Thus, an embodied spirituality invites us to reconnect all human potentials in an integrated way. It assists one to develop self-reflective consciousness of the heart and mind, body and soul; to re-appropriate and integrate the various instinctive dimensions of human nature into a fully embodied spiritual life. It is a call to an embodiment of wholeness and holiness witnessing to the fundamental values of the Gospel (Jn 10:10). It is an integral part of divine presence, saving grace and healing transformation.

3.2. Embodied Spirituality as Dynamic Praxis-Centred

Socio-economic and religious-political problems lead to the dehumanization of human persons, destabilization of families and communities, and destruction of the earth. Embodied spirituality emerges from very different social, cultural, economic, religious and political situations. It is to discover the essential aspects of human experience of God.[19] It is spirituality of life and for life—the life of women and men, young and old, rich and poor, saint and sinner. An embodied spirituality is based on an experiential life of the person in the Spirit. The experience of the Spirit cannot be separated from positive action.[20] For example, within the context of oppression of whatever kind, people begin to discover that they are subjects, not objects (e.g., Latin American Liberation Movement, Women's Movement). Jesus' announcement of his mission is a clear example of how the Spirit calls believers to action (Lk 4:18-19). Every divine action is in the Spirit and it makes all things new.[21]

An embodied dynamic spirituality is not based on ascetics or ritual or orthodoxy or devotional practices. It is centred on actions or oriented in orthopraxis. It consists in loving as Jesus loved, even to the extent of loving one's enemies (Lk 23:34) and giving oneself in service to the least (Lk 10:25-37). It consists primarily in seeing God, the world and human beings as Jesus did, and responding to life with confidence in God (Mt 6:25-34), forgiving love towards one's neighbours (Mt 18:15-35), and readiness to share one's gifts with those who have less (Mt 25:31-46).

A spirituality of orthopraxis calls for unconditional love (Mt 5:43-48) in action (Lk 15:1-32) and ever willing service of the least (Jn 13:1-15), the weak and the marginalized (Lk 15:25-37). In the parable of the Last Judgement (Mt 25:31-46), the one criterion on which people are commended or condemned at the end of their life is their willingness to share what they have with those in need. What is most important is living one's spirituality not religious ritual or orthodoxy, but orthopraxis, active love for those in need, who could be even one's enemy. "Go and do likewise" (Lk 10:37) is an exhortation that does not need any explanation in ortho-praxis.

A dynamic spirituality of orthopraxis for women is encountering the mystery of God in daily life and action. For many women, the practice of spirituality is a force for survival, a power to inspire, struggle and resistance. The struggle for life can also be interpreted quite literally as women's immense labour and their ever renewed pain in bringing life into this world and nurturing its growth so that it can develop into a fuller and more abundant life (Jn 10:10).[22] For example, in my research done on the role of spirituality among women living with HIV/AIDS (WLHA), 65 % of them said that spirituality encouraged them to live and work in solidarity with others living with HIV/AIDS. The following examples highlight the solidarity of WLHA with others suffering with the disease.

"I know what it means to be living with this illness. When I undergo pain and weakness I always think of people living with this illness. I pray and ask God to take care of me and all those who are becoming victims of this illness"; "Helping out around here, in the care-centre, gives me the feeling that I am worth and I am able to do something for others"; "I enjoy working with others who care for the WLHA. I experience some kind of fulfilment in working for and with them"; "I would always talk to WLHA with kindness and enquire them of how they are doing with the consequences of this illness. I would teach them how to manage with illness. I would kindle in them optimism and hope. I would pray for them".[23] If the practise of any spirituality is not life-oriented, action-centred it is meaningless and it will face slow death. "If a brother or sister is naked and lacks daily food, and one of you says to them, 'Go in peace: keep warm and eat your fill,' and yet you do not supply their bodily needs, what is the good of that?" (Jas 2:15-16). Therefore, an embodied spirituality has to respond to the needs of the people and to the signs of the times.

3.3. Embodied Spirituality as Experiential Contemplation

Unlike the neo-gnostic view, matter is not something opposed to spirit, but suffused with God's presence. We need to view material reality in a new way - as the theatre of God's action, revealing God to us in wonderful ways. Rakoczy defines spirituality as an approach which seeks and finds God in all the circumstances of life, affirms life and growth in others, work with other to bring a greater fullness of life, wholeness and right relationships into every situation and structure, of culture and society, including the church. [24]

In an embodied spirituality, contemplation is one way of experiencing the divine, a loving and simple gaze with our attention enraptured and seized by God's goodness. Contemplation is more experiential than theoretical and therefore defies any easy categorization. It is the highest expression of intellectual and spiritual life. It is spiritual wonder—awe at the sacredness of life, gratitude for life. It is a vivid realization that this life flows from an abundant Source. In contemplation, women and men became aware of that Source, with a certainty that goes beyond the mind, in a kind of spiritual vision.

In an embodied spirituality, contemplation stands for a conscientious and a vivid awareness of God; so, contemplatives speak of being "touched by God." This awareness leads us to understand that life is much more than activity. We need to discover not only things outside, but also things inside us. The quality of our actions matters much more than the amount of activity. At times the most necessary and most difficult thing to do is stop acting and just *be*. An emphasis on contemplation as a fundamental feature of an embodied spirituality is the satisfaction and fulfilment one experiences in the engagement with others in "transcendent" spiritual enterprises and mysticism (as with Teresa of Avila).[25]

An authentic spirituality fosters both commitment and fidelity to living in conscious relationship with God. It fosters the deepening of soul's search for interiority, for reflection and contemplation. It widens enough to encompass more than one way of praying (Lk 18:9-14) and more than one way of living interiority (Lk 19:1-10). A truly contemplative spirituality fosters the organic growth of all the virtues. It is as concerned with relationships and the active loving of others as with the more interior aspects of their lives. It integrates the love for God and the love for neighbour.

3.4. Role of the Body in an Embodied Spirituality

Although we are not in favour of a disembodied spirit or mind, yet in an embodiment, priority is given to the mind or spirit, not to the body. In order to value the devalued status of the body, here we shall focus on some significant aspects of the body in the evolution of an embodied spirituality. An embodied spirituality regards the body as subject, as the habitat of the human being, as a source of spiritual enlightenment, as a miniature of the cosmic world, a progressive integration of matter and consciousness, immanent and transcendent spiritual energies. Let us now explore a few intricacies of the human body in the process of developing an embodied spirituality.

3.4.1. Body as Locus of an Embodied Spiritual Integration

Neo-Gnosticism looks at the body, particularly female bodies, with suspicion. This negative attitude is being transferred to created reality. To perceive the human body as a locus of integration means to value it as an embodiment of all humanness. Bodily pleasure and grief, joy and sorrow, relaxation and tension, yearning and desisting, companionship and isolation are some of the indications through which the body communicates to us. To view the body as locus or centre of an embodied spiritual integration implies the promotion of the harmonious blending of all human faculties and attributes in the spiritual conduit without stress and tension, dichotomy and dissociation. Without neglecting the spiritual significance of the human body, we need to move towards an integral transformation of the human person that entails the spiritual configuration of all human dimensions and connectedness. In this context, John N. Ferrer states that by any measure, the body is not an 'It' to be objectified and used for the goals or even spiritual ecstasies of the conscious mind, but a 'Thou', an intimate partner with whom the other human dimensions can collaborate in the pursuit of ever-increasing forms of liberating wisdom.[26]

3.4.2. Body as a Habitat for Spiritual Awakening

Both literally and metaphorically, we can say that the body is our habitat of human autonomy in the course of our earthly life. This view calls for an awakening to overcome the dualistic view of matter and spirit, body and soul. Here, body can no longer be considered as a "prison of the soul" or even as a "temple of the Spirit" (1 Cor 3:16-17; 6:19-20). For the mystery of the Incarnation does not teach us the entry of Spirit into the body, but to its becoming flesh: "In the beginning was the Word, and the Word was God . . . And the Word became flesh" (Jn 1:1,14). The mystery of incarnation (Jn 3:16) will awaken in us a spirit of union of body and soul, human and divine. Perhaps paradoxically, this spiritual awakening of the mystery of incarnation teaches not only the mystery of life in the body/habitat but also of a peaceful detachment of life and death (1 Cor 15:12-28) from this habitat. The body/habitat must journey from this material existence with a profound sense of fulfilment because this is one of the most accomplished essential purposes of being born into the world. In my research done with women living with HIV/AIDS, the women were asked whether the spiritual beliefs and practices helped them to overcome the fear of death and its consequences, nearly half (47.7 %) of the respondents responded positively, 37.1 % of them responded negatively while 15.2 % of them remained neutral. One of the respondents said, "When I think of my children, I want to live. I am praying to God to spare my life, until I settle my children and I keep fighting with Him."[27] The permeability of the body to immanent and transcendent spiritual energies leads to its gradual awakening, or rather conscious awakening of every part of human habitat.

3.4.3. *Body as a Springboard of Embodied Spiritual Transformation and Integration*

The body as a God-given source searches for spiritual understanding, enlightenment, and wisdom. Body also becomes the genuine source of spiritual knowledge. For instance, bodily sensations, emotions, feelings, and growth can become basic springboards in the embodied transformation of Spirit's creative energies in each human life. In the dearth of crucial obstruction or connectivity of life, these creative energies can lead the body to acquire spiritual insights or enlightenment, spiritual visions, and, ultimately, contemplation. As the Buddha said,

"Everything that arises in the mind starts flowing with a sensation in the body." In addition, in listening and responding to the deepest needs of the body (Rom 12:1-2) we realize that the human body can be a genuine source of spiritual transformation (e.g., Zen schools). The ultimate meaning of human life is not only something to be discerned by the intellect or mind, but also to be felt in the depths of our body/flesh. In a context of embodied spiritual aspiration, sensuous happiness becomes indispensable to rescue the dignity and spiritual significance of body. The recognition of the spiritual significance of the body can bridge or integrate the gap between sensuous love (*eros*) and spiritual love (*agape*). This integration or transformation will promote the emergence of genuinely human love into an unconditional love that is concurrently embodied and spiritual.

3.4.4. *Body as a Miniature of the Cosmic World*

All religious traditions unanimously agree that there is deep resonance among human beings and the cosmic world. The Bible teaches that human beings are created in the image and likeness of God/*imago Dei* (Gen 1:26-27). Hindu understanding of the body as (*Atman*) entails the belief that the divine dwells physically within the human body.[28] The Jesuit palaeontologist, Teilhard de Chardin, wrote: "My matter is not a part of the universe that I possess totally, but the totality of the universe that I possess partially."[29] All these perceptions portray an image of the human body as mirroring and containing the innermost structure of both the entire universe and the ultimate creative principle. Nevertheless, this does not mean that the body is to be valued only because it represents or can affect 'larger' or 'higher' realities. Embodied spirituality recognizes the human body as a pinnacle of the Spirit's creative manifestation and, consequently, as overflowing with intrinsic spiritual meaning.

We are born on the earth. It is here in our home—earth and body—that we can develop fully as complete human beings without needing to 'escape' anywhere to find our essential identity or feel whole (Ps 139). When the body is felt as our home, the natural world can be reclaimed as our homeland as well. This 'double grounding' in body and nature not only heals at its root the estrangement of the modern self from nature, but also overcomes the spiritual alienation. In other words, having recognized the physical world as real, and being in contact with immanent spiritual life, a complete human being discerns nature as an organic embodiment of the Mystery. To sense our physical surroundings as the Spirit's body offers natural resources for an ecologically grounded spiritual life.[30]

3.4.5. Body as a Symbol of Wholeness

Today every person aspires for wholeness. Wholeness or holistic lifestyle is a way of living or being, that allows one to be healthy, happy, and whole.[31] Being whole is an ongoing, positive approach to life that includes all the dimensions of the human person. Wholeness of the body or life entails treating the body as a whole, and the environment, too, as a home for all to live. Wholeness of the body or life, invites us to respect body, heal relationships, care for the environment, show love for all humankind and live life with a purpose.

The wholeness of the body or of the person is one which perceives how the need for unity applies on every level of our lives and interactions. It is an attempt to look beyond notions of duality and see the underlying wholeness and interrelatedness of all things. In a word, it is the continuation of that prayer which Jesus himself prayed: "May they all be one, Father; may they be one in us as you are in me and I am in you" (Jn 17:21). Wholeness of the body mirrors the wholeness of the spirit which perceives the world around and all that is in the world are connected spiritually. It implies that we are all one with Spirit/God/the universe, with each other, with the earth and all of its creatures, and with the cosmos itself.

3.4.6. Body's Call for Social Engagement

One can speak of 'body' both as individual and as group/community. A transformed human being recognizes that, in a fundamental way, we are our relationships with both the human and nonhuman world, and this recognition is inevitably linked with a commitment to social transformation. To be sure, this commitment can take many different forms, from more direct active social or political action in the world (e.g., through social service, spiritually grounded political criticism, or environmental activism) to more subtle types of social activism involving distant prayer, collective meditation, or ritual. Given our current global crisis, an embodied spirituality cannot be divorced from a commitment to social, political, and ecological transformation—whatever form this may take.

By focusing more on the various aspects of the human body, one can contest the depreciation of the body and the feminine in Gnosticism. I also think that human experiences are embodied and women seem to achieve this better than men because of their rootedness in bodily experiences. The above reflections highlight that women are not only sex and body, but also have mind and spirit. Like women, men also have bodies which they cannot neglect, if they want to be really and fully human.

4. Conclusion

This paper is a humble attempt to reflect on neo-Gnosticism from a feministic perspective. The first part of the paper presented a very brief context of our society and women; the second part focused a few impacts or challenges of neo-Gnosticism in the development of an embodied spirituality. It has highlighted some of the significant aspects of the embodied spirituality as conscious integration of the person; as dynamic praxis-centred; as experiential contemplation. It also presented the human body as locus of an embodied spiritual integration: body as a habitat for spiritual awakening; body as a springboard of embodied spiritual transformation and integration; body as a miniature of the cosmic world; body as a symbol of wholeness; and body's call for social engagement.

An embodied spirituality is not simply a struggle for life but also a spirituality of life whereby people are nourished and strengthened by the experience of the processes of life itself, its great energies for renewal, sustenance, new birth and further growth. By strongly trusting life, through faith and hope in the powers of God's Spirit, acting in and through all the experiences of daily life, we are strengthened and grow to experience a vision of the dignity, beauty and fullness of life—a vision we can share and transmit to empower others in today's world.[32] Women's perspective on spirituality affirms their bodily experience, their creative human power and their spiritual depth. It is a reclaiming of female power beginning with the likeness of women to the Divine, the rehabilitation of the bodily as the very locus of that divine likeness, and the right of women to participate in the shaping of religion and culture.[33]

In this paper I have tried to explore an embodied spiritual life that can emerge today from our participatory engagement with both the energy of consciousness and the sensuous energies of the body. Ultimately, an embodied spirituality seeks to catalyse the emergence of human beings—beings who, while remaining rooted in their bodies, earth, and immanent spiritual life, have made all their attributes possible to transcendent spiritual energies, and who can cooperate in solidarity with others in the spiritual transformation of self, community, and world. In short, as Ruth says, "a human being/body is firmly grounded in Spirit-Within, fully open to Spirit-Beyond, and in transformative communion with Spirit In-Between."[34]

An embodied spirituality can access many spiritually significant revelations of self and world, some of which have been described by the world contemplative traditions, and others whose novel quality may require a more creative engagement to be brought forth.[35] When Paul says that God will be 'all in all' he means that it is the body, not just the soul, the mind or the spirit, which is God's temple. The body is meant for God, he says, and the Lord for the body.[36] The Sacred can be known and experienced in the body and the body can embody the Sacred. I conclude with the words of C.S. Lewis, "Believe in Christianity as I believe that the Sun has risen, not only because I see it, but because by it I see everything else." We too can behold the Divine not only within the body but also in and through the body.

Endnotes

[1] Pope Francis critiques it by calling it: "the self-absorbed Promethean neo-Pelagianism". Its adherents rely on human powers and consider being superior because of their observance of certain rules or remain dogmatically faithful to a particular Catholic style from the past. He continues saying that such an apparently sound doctrine or discipline leads them to a narcissistic and authoritarian elitism. They exhaust their energies in inspecting and verifying others. In the bargain they forget about their concern for Jesus Christ or others (See *Evangelii Gaudium,* nn. 93-94); hereafter abbreviated as EG.

[2] See Martha J. Horn, Ralph L. Piedmont, Geraldine M. Fialkowski, Robert J. Wicks and Mary E. Hunt, "Sexuality and Spirituality: The Embodied Spirituality Scale," *Theology & Sexuality* 12/1 (2005): 82-83.

[3] See internet article of Peter Voss, "True Morality-Rational Principles for Optimal Living," https://medium.com/@petervoss/true-morality-rational-principles-for-optimal-living-3d1541933182, (accessed October 2, 2017).

[4] See internet article of John W. Cooper, "The Image of God, Religion, and the Meaning of Life: Toward a Christian Philosophical Anthropology," http://www.cslewis.org/journal/the-image-of-god-religion-and-the-meaning-of-life-toward-a-christian-philosophical-anthropology/, (accessed October 1, 2017).

[5] Tony Jones, *The New Christians: Dispatches from the Emergent Frontier* (San Francisco: Jossey-Bass, 2008), 2; see also Jeremy Bouma, "Pagitt and Pelagius: An Examination of an Emerging Neo-Pelagianism—Introduction 1," http://www.jeremybouma.com/pagitt-and-pelagius-an-examination-of-an-emerging-neo-pelagianism-1/, (accessed July 30, 2017).

[6] Pelagianism was a philosophy developed by a monk, supposedly, who taught that human beings could achieve salvation through asceticism, good works and personal discipline. Jesus is significant, not so much for his sacrifice, but for his role as a moral teacher. See Catholic Sensibility, "The Myth of Neo-Pelagianism," https://catholicsensibility.wordpress.com/2006/11/15/the-myth-of-neo-pelagianism/, (accessed June 25, 2017).

[7] "Gnosticism is often defined as a "cult" of "secret knowledge" or to quote, "these gospels emphasize knowledge that initiates have and others do not." See Lewis Loflin, "An Overview of Gnosticism and the Bible," http://www.sullivan-county.com/id2/gnosticism.htm, (accessed October 2, 2017).

[8] See EG nn. 93-97.

[9] Shaun Kenney, "Pope Francis and Neopelagian Crisis," https://thejeffersoniad.com/blog/tag/neopelagianism/.

[10] http://www.therealpresence.org/cgi-bin/getdefinition.pl, (accessed July 26, 2017).

[11] "Church History Study Helps: Characteristic Features of Gnosticism," accessed on October 1, 2017, at the weblink http://www.theologywebsite.com/history/gnosischarac.shtml.

[12] Stephan A. Hoeller, "The Gnostic World View: A Brief Summary of Gnosticism," http://gnosis.org/gnintro.html, accessed on October 1, 2017.

[13] R.J. Rushdoony, "Gnosticism," (Chalcedon Position Paper n. 74), https://chalcedon.edu/magazine/gnosticism, accessed on October 1, 2017.

[14] Derrick G. Jeter, "Mind over Matter: The Heresy of Gnosticism both Then and Now," internet article, accessed on at https://www.insight.org/resources/article-library/individual/mind-over-matter-the-heresy-of-gnosticism-both-then-and-now, on October 1, 2017.

[15] Jorge N. Ferrer, "Embodied Spirituality: Now and Then," http://www.integralworld.net/ferrer2.html.

[16] Susan Rakoczy, "Living Life to the Full: The Spirit and Eco-Feminist Spirituality," *Scriptura* 111/3 (2012): 395-407.

[17] See Pieter G.R de Villiers, "The Rise and Nature of Feminist Spirituality," *HTS* 55/4 (1999): 901, www.hts.org.za/index.php/HTS/article/download/1639/2931, (accessed July 15, 2017).

[18] Janet K. Ruffing, "Look at every Path Closely and Deliberately: What's on Offer?" *The Way Supplement* 84 (Autumn 1995):16.

[19] See Ursula King, "Women's Contributions to Contemporary Spirituality," *The Way Supplement* 84 (Autumn 1995): 26-37.

[20] Jose Comblin, *The Spirit and Liberation,* trans. P. Burns (New York: Orbis Books, 1989), 20.

[21] Denis Edwards, *Breath of Life: A Theology of the Creator Spirit* (New York: Orbis Books, 2004), 118.

[22] See K.C. Abraham and Bernadette Mbuy-Beya, eds., *Spirituality in the Third World* (New York: 1994).

[23] See my *Finding God in Illness and Care-giving* (Chennai: Don Bosco Publication, 2017), 92-93.

[24] S. Rakoczy, *In Her Name: Women Doing Theology* (Pietermaritzburg: Cluster Publication, 2004), 374.

[25] Sally B. Purvis, "Christian Feminist Spirituality," in *Christian Spirituality: Post Reformation and Modern*, ed. Louis Dupre and Don E. Saliers (New York: Crossroad, 1996), 512.

[26] Jorge N. Ferrer, "Embodied Spirituality: Now and Then," http://www.integralworld.net/ferrer2.html.

[27] My *Finding God in Illness*, 127.

[28] Andrew Wilson, "Image of God and Temple of God," in *World Scripture: A Comparative Anthology of Sacred Texts*, ed. Andrew Wilson (New Delhi: Motilal Banarasidass Publishers), 139-143.

[29] Pierre Teilhard de Chardin, *Science and Christ*, trans. Rene Hague (London: Collins, 1965), 13.

[30] Pope Francis, *Laudato Si*, nn.157-162.

[31] 'Wholesome' is defined as the well-being (health) of body and mind of a person. See http://www.merriam-webster.com/dictionary/wholesome, (accessed October 10, 2017).

[32] Theresa King, *The Spiral Path: Explorations in Women's Spirituality* (MN: Saint Paul, 1992), 9.

[33] Sandra M. Schneider, *Women and the Word: The Gender of God in the New Testament and the Spirituality of Women* (New York: Paulist Press, 1986), 30.

[34] Ruth A. Tanyi, "Towards Clarification of the Meaning of Spirituality," *Journal of Advanced Nursing* 39/5 (2002): 506.

[35] Jorge N. Ferrer, "Embodied Spirituality: Now and Then," http://www.integralworld.net/ferrer2.html, (accessed October 1, 2017).

[36] N. T. Wright, "Mind, Spirit, Soul and Body: All for One and One for All Reflections on Paul's Anthropology in his Complex Contexts," http://ntwrightpage.com/2016/07/12/mind-spirit-soul-and-body/, (accessed October 2, 2017).

7

Neo-Gnosticism and Neo-Pelagianism: Biblical Understanding and Current Issues

Selva Rathinam, SJ

Introduction: Neo-gnosticism and Neo-pelagianism as Threats to True Christianity

Gnosticism is a subjective faith in which one is imprisoned in one's own thoughts and feelings, that is, ideas and experiences (*Evangelii Gaudium* 94).[1] In neo-pelagianism one trusts only one's own power and feels superior to others who observe certain Catholic rules and lifestyle from the past. Both are forms of 'anthropocentric immanentism' and are least concerned about Jesus Christ or the other.[2] This worldliness is evident in one's "ostentatious preoccupation for the liturgy, for doctrine and for the Church's prestige, but without any concern that the Gospel have a real impact on God's faithful people and the concrete needs of the present time. In this way, the life of the Church turns into a museum piece" (EG 95). In other words, neo-gnosticism implies 'feel good' Catholicism and neo-pelagianism implies 'self-absorption'.[3] Neo-pelagianism "excludes the necessity of grace for salvation, again it is individualistic, again it excludes a dependence on God, which is at the heart of Francis' preaching on 'mercy'."[4]

In neo-gnosticism one is preoccupied with mystical experiences and 'feelings' and not love in action. In neo-pelagianism one is preoccupied with works only. Pope Francis rightly calls neo-pelagianism 'promethean' (EG 94), which indicates defiance towards the gods as Prometheus was trying to wrest from God fire that belongs to God. Similarly, Pelagius promoted the idea of salvation by mere human effort, denying the role of grace that pertains to God. Thus, neo-gnosticism a religion of mystical experiences and neo-pelagianism a religion of works are opposed to each other, but both together are opposed to an authentic Christianity as both the above are the heretical extremes of the Gospel truth. "The essence of the heresy of Pelagius is an emphasis on the primacy of human effort in salvation, with divine grace providing mere assistance to what man (*sic*) is capable of accompanying on his own, as if his nature were not wounded by Original Sin."[5] Neopelagians are those who think that they can fix things like a plumber fixes a broken toilet.[6]

In this paper we are going to focus our attention on the biblical understanding of neo-gnosticism and neo-pelagianism and their present-day issues in the Catholic Church.

1. A Brief Look at Neo-Gnosticism

1.1. Gnosticism as a School of Thought

Most of what we know of Gnosticism,[7] and the Gnostics, has come from polemics or anti-gnostic writings. It would not be completely unbiased. For example, Epiphanius of Salamis the neighbourhood Bishop writes that the Gnostics are a filthy and promiscuous bunch, holding orgies instead of Church services and eating babies instead of bread and wine for the Eucharist. He is an extreme example. The better way to find out about Gnostics is to read their own texts. We have a large collection of Gnostic texts called Nag Hammadi library, a collection of Christian texts discovered in Egypt in 1940s. Comparing the Nag Hammadi Library along with the polemics of the Church Fathers, scholars have re-constructed stereo-typical Gnostic theology.

First, they believed in a 'dualistic anthropology' that separated the material body from the spiritual realm. They believed in a soul that is transcendent but trapped in a dirty and corrupted body. Their idea of afterlife, therefore, is for the soul to escape from the body and enter into the spiritual realm. Gnostics said spirit is good and matter is evil. In creation a being of pure spirit emanated levels of spirit outward like a series of ripples created by a rock dropped into a pond. The closer the emanation to the source the purer the object is. That is the reason why a variation of Gnosticism known as Docetism said that Christ only appeared human but in actual did not possess a physical body. Yet, Scripture never says matter is evil. God made everything 'good' (Gen 1:31). Anyone who denies that Jesus came in the flesh is not a believer (2 Jn 7). Thus, the early Church rejected Gnosticism. Though our souls are with the Lord at death, we are incomplete without our physical bodies and we look forward to the resurrection of the body on the last day (Dan 12:1-2). Underlying Gnosticism is the dichotomy in anthropology.[8] For *Plato* in Greek Philosophy, the human person is essentially 'a soul,' a non-material entity temporarily housed in a material body. The image of the human person for Plato is charioteer in the chariot, that is, a soul residing in a body.

The above gnostic views are contrary to the *Biblical understanding* of a human person who is an animated body. Here, the human person is the body rooted in the cosmos and related to other human beings (*ha adam*). This understanding is very holistic and the human person is essentially material and communitarian. In such an understanding, the destiny of the human person is neither the salvation of the soul nor the abandoning of the body for a spiritual heaven but it is the resurrection of the body. Thus, salvation is not eternal life in spiritual heaven up there but the transformation of the cosmos into the "new heaven and the new earth" (Rev 21:1-4). Salvation is thus not the negation of human and cosmic history but their fulfillment. While trying to combine both biblical ('animated body') and Greek ('incarnated soul') understanding of the human person, traditional Christian theology held the view that the human person is soul and body like form and matter. Here, the soul (unlike a stone or a tree) is an immortal and substantial form that can exist only in conjunction with matter. Therefore, after death, a soul can exist separated from the body but always maintaining a 'transcendental relation' to it, meaning, relation to matter belongs to the soul's own essence. However, in popular Christian belief there is a reversion to the Greek or Hindu idea of the human person which we have explained above. Here spirituality becomes a matter of saving only the soul! In such an understanding, the main concern would be conversion of people (saving souls and not economic, political and social liberation) and evangelization (converting infidels or turning believers away from sin). By contrast, biblical religiosity is salvation history as we see in the Exodus event; it is this worldly, holistic and communitarian. The Jesus of the gospels was living out such a biblical spirituality in his own struggle for the poor and the oppressed.

Secondly, Gnostics developed a 'dualistic theology'. Since this world is messed up and corrupt, this world must have been created by a messed up and corrupt god. There are two main gods: one higher and perfect god called '*Monad*' (the One) and the other lesser and inferior god called '*demiurge*' the creator of the material universe. The Nag Hammadi text called 'The Apocryphon of John' reinterprets the creation myth that we find in the book of Genesis. It is the *demiurge* who created humanity and trapped them in a corrupted planet while hiding the keys to divine knowledge in the tree of the knowledge of good and evil. But, Jesus Christ is the saviour sent by the Monad to save humanity from the demiurge. He encourages humanity to eat the forbidden fruit to attain the divine knowledge and thereby eternal life.

Finally, gnosis, is secret knowledge. Gnostics believe that salvation came through gnosis ('knowledge', in Greek) and it was Jesus Christ who brought the knowledge into the world as a messenger of the Supreme Being.[9] This contradicts the view of St Paul who preached: "by grace you have been saved through faith" (Eph 2:8). Simon Magus (Acts 8:9-24) was identified as the first Gnostic by early Christian apologists. In the gospel of Judas, only he had the secret knowledge of the special mission of Jesus. The gospel of Thomas begins like this: "These are the obscure sayings that the living Jesus uttered and which…Thomas wrote down. And he [Jesus] said, 'whoever finds the meaning of these sayings will not taste death'. The eternal life itself depends on the secret knowledge here." The Gospel of Truth written by the arch Gnostic Valentine himself has no wicked demiurge, it has practical moral values and he also speaks about earthly Jesus who died and rose again from the dead. But for the Church Fathers like Hiereneus and Ephiphanias, Gnosticism represented heresy. It is called the phenomenon of 'the Naricissism of the minor differences'. When closely related communities are engaged in near constant warfare it is because even the small differences among them can be more threatening for asserting their identities than big differences coming from their distance foes. Such understanding may help us to cut through religious conflicts today.

Thus, Gnostic spirituality is otherworldly spirituality which fosters individualism and attitudes of world negation and social indifference. In our country many traditional Christians have such attitudes partly influenced by some charismatic groups, popular devotions and counseling or retreat centres from within and by Brahmanic Hinduism and Ashram type life from without. Such spirituality puts action groups and apostolic spirituality in conflict. What we must have is a spirituality of liberation. But for Gnostic-oriented people spirituality and liberation do not go together. For them spirituality implies the things of the spirit like prayer, contemplation, interior freedom, detachment and discernment; and liberation implies the things of the world like the price of bread, the finding of a job, etc.

1.2. Biblical Religiosity Devoid of Dualism

In the Old Testament the human being is holistic and there is neither the dichotomy of body and soul nor a trichotomy of body, soul and spirit.[10] Here, the human being is neither a composite of two separable parts nor an incarnated immortal soul, but an animated body.[11] The human being is a unity; and here none is separated and none survives. In Gen 2:7: "The Lord God formed man from the dust of the ground and breathed into his nostrils the breath of life; and the man became a living being." Traditionally the 'living being' (nephesh) was thought of as an immortal soul which will be separated from the body at death. But in actual the 'living *nephesh*' is not 'part' of the human being but the whole of the human being and the mortality of the human being is suggested through the word 'dust.' In fact, in Gen 1 the 'living *nephesh*' is used three times (1:21, 24, 30) denoting animals implying, perhaps, the dignity of animals as companions of human beings. In fact, God gives the 'breath of life' both to human beings and to animals (Gen 7:22) and it meant both animals and human beings depend on God. If *nephesh* in Gen 2:7 refer to human beings' immortal soul, then in Gen 2:19 animals, too, should be considered as having immortal souls.[12] "The frame work of anthropology in the Old Testament is based on the covenant relationship between God and human beings in the sense of humans' dependence on God."[13] Thus, here, life is always life with God. In this sense, life-after-death is possible in relationship with God and by God's grace. Even in Deut 6:5 it is said that we need to love God with all our soul, what means is to love God with one's own entirety of being. The *nephesh* exists so long as the body exists and when the body ceases to exist, the *nephesh* also ceases to exist (Gen 35:18; Job 14:22; Eccl 12:7). No word in the Old Testament like *nephesh*, *basar*, *leb* and *ruah* suggests the immortality of human nature. "…there is an agreement in both Testaments that the human soul, whether it is called, *nephesh* or psyche, is not to be considered immortal but in existing only in relationship with God."[14] The New Testament depicts human beings as a unity of the *psyche* or *pneuma* and *soma* or *sarx*, which are diverse aspects of human beings. Here, too, the possibility of the life-after-death is not intrinsic to the nature of humans but is a divine gift in which, at the resurrection, one can be transformed with a new embodiment in God's grace.[15]

Biblical religiosity is paradoxical and holistic; there is no dualism in it. It locates the sacred in the secular,[16] and encounters God in the marketplace. Here, the human person is an animated body (Gen 2:7) and not a soul in a body and human destiny is the resurrection of the body (1 Cor 15:35-50) and not the salvation of souls. The Bible's approval of material creation does not deflect its focus on nature but on history where it has its foundational God experience (Ex 6:6-7).

This continues in the New Testament in the revelation of God in the history of Jesus. The presence of the sacred in the secular is nowhere so clear as in John 1:14 – "The Word became flesh and dwelt amongst us." Here the word which is creative (Gen 1:1-26), prophetic (Jer 1:9-10), personified (Prov 8:22-31; Wis 7:25-26) and divine (Jn 1:1) enters into the realm of matter ('flesh') and of history ("dwells amongst us"); and thus, the sacred becomes the secular.

The Biblical tradition's encounter of God in the world of matter and in the world of human history are quite opposed to Greek philosophy where matter is opposed to spirit and to Indian philosophy where *vyavaharika* is opposed to *paramarthika* in Vedanta. It is said that the word became flesh (*sarx*) and not body (*soma*). "Flesh" (*basar*) in the Old Testament is that which binds people together (Gen 2:23) and it implies solidarity and interconnectedness of the individual with the community (Gen 6:17; 37:27; Isa 40:4f; 49:26). It is this biblical belief in the oneness of humankind that made Paul argue from the universality of the sin of Adam to the universality of the redemption wrought by Christ (Rom 5:18). Therefore, the word becoming flesh is not merely limited to the individual understanding of Jesus' humanity but it extends to the collective understanding of Jesus' link with the whole of humanity. Thus, from now on we can encounter God in any person and in any history and this makes the human concern so central to the ethical teachings of Jesus Christ (Mt 5:23-24; Mk 2:27; Mt 9:13; Mk 7:9-14). It is this secularization of religion we see in Jesus' creative combining of the love of God with the love of one's neighbour (Mt 22:34-40; 25:31-46).

In view of this nondual biblical vision, any and every neo-gnostic tendency to limit one's seeing of God in *shravana* (listening), *manana* (reflection) and *nidhidhyasana* (silence) should give way to the seeing of God in the privileged locus of human person and history. The use of the word *skenoun* ('to pitch a tent' [*skene*]) instead of *Kaoikein* ('to set up house' [*oikos*]) made Bultmann to interpret Jesus as the 'gnostic redeemer' who visits the world temporarily to set free the scattered particles of the spirit that have been imprisoned in matter.

But John's usage of *menein* ('to remain') to indicate a temporary stay (Jn 1:38f; 2:12; 4:40; 11:6; 19:31) not *skenoun*,[17] which is never used for impermanence does not indicate a temporary stay. Thus, it excludes any sort of avatar type of Gnostic Christianity for the word used for Christ, too, is 'becoming' (*genetai*) and not 'as appearing' (*phainetai*) flesh. If Jesus becomes a Gnostic redeemer or Christian avatar, his divinity may become an alibi for our reluctance to follow him. But in his incarnation—in his self-giving love manifest through his words and deeds—he becomes a challenge and a paradigm for action rather than merely becoming an objection of devotion.

1.3. Challenges of Neo-Gnosticism to Christian Faith

Today, the Catholic Church is challenged by growing liberal factions. Scandals like suicide, murder and sexual abuse perpetrated by the clergy and religious wo/men are either widely publicised or hushed up. These aberrations in priestly and religious life can be understood either as fallout of the sexual revolution or indicative of the spirit of dissent raging within the Church in India. Many formation houses employed councillors trained in systems of 'humanistic psychology' and 'self-actualizing theories' pioneered by liberals like Carl Rogers with great emphasis on the 'self' and little place for God and neighbour. Those who go through formation within this system unconsciously tend to develop problems with those wielding authority. Consequently, they petition Rome to be released from their religious vows as they value only the authority of their inner selves and do not want to be under anyone's authority.

While the LGBT movement is making great strides in terms of political power and cultural acceptance, some issues associated with the LGBT movement under the umbrella of inter-generational sex and relationships in the name of liberalism, like public sex, pornography, paedophilia or eroticism between adults and young people, poses a serious cultural tension. This is what is wrong with the 'feel good spirituality'. "Fastidious about pollution and animal rights, the techno-pagan does not engage in human sacrifices on the solstices, rather he offers human sacrifice daily in test tubes and abortion clinics. Neo-

pagans no longer enslave catamites and prostitutes for their temples
as the ancient pagan cultures once did; instead they publish studies
that discover that incest and "intergenerational sex" is not necessarily
harmful to children. The life issues before modern societies, abortion,
population control, euthanasia, cloning, and genetic modification of
plants, animals and humans brought a seismic shift in our cultural
landscape. If there are no moral laws, no accountability before God
and all things are permitted, then 'right' and 'wrong' is determined
by raw power."[18]

Rationalism abandoned Christian Revelation in favour of a new
god, science. Feuerbach (1804-1872) relegated Christianity to man's
intellectual past and promoted a 'religion of action' focused strictly
on improving the temporal world. Nietzsche's nihilism pronounced
God's death and thus the demise of the moral law; hence, 'all things
are permitted.' The neo-pagan elites of Europe believed passively
that science, not God, would solve humankind's problems. "Dissident
theologians like Fr. Charles Curran of Catholic University led gullible
American Catholics to abandon the Church's moral teachings in favor
of a liberal 'tolerant' lifestyle; contraception, abortion, divorce and
remarriage, pre-marital sex and homosexuality were not sins; failure
to be tolerant of the lives of others was a sin."[19]

Nineteenth century liberal theology was very much influenced by
the radical immanentism of Hegel and the radical subjectivism of
Schleiermacher and even naturalism, which holds that nothing exists
outside the physical universe.[20] This made liberal theologians deny the
miracles of the gospels and the existence of the personal God. Gospel
miracles were given materialistic interpretations. The feeding of the
five thousand, for example, was interpreted as the miracle of sharing
by the crowd convinced by Jesus (Mk 6:30-44). The well-known figure
who belonged to liberalism was Rudolf Bultmann. Completely denying
the apostolic witness like the historicity of the resurrection (1 Cor
15:14), Bultmann said that the New Testament contains a kernel of
historical truth, around which are found myths like the resurrection.
When Bultmann argued that the historicity of the biblical incident is

unimportant and what matters is only the faith of the disciples, he was advocating some kind of mysticism over against biblical faith. If so, how do we know if we are following the same Jesus? "A personal encounter with Jesus is necessary, but we do not believe simply because He 'lives in our heart' (1 Cor 3:16). We believe because He truly came, truly died, and truly rose again."[21] Gnosticism said that salvation is available only to those who possessed the hidden truths of Christ (Col 1:24-25).

In the Hegelian view the relationship between the infinite and the finite has been a complicated and controversial one. According to the theist view, the infinite is pure transcendence, distinct, exterior to, and beyond the finite world.[22] According to the humanist position, the finite cannot know the infinite. But Hegel is critical of both the above positions and postulates an immanent unity of the finite and the infinite. He believes that finite becomes knowable. Hegel argued that to know the finite, one has to transcend it toward the infinite and it becomes possible in such unity. Offering a radically immanentist reading of Hegel, Kojeve identifies Absolute Spirit with the human spirit and argues that for Hegel "Nature is only an abstraction," only "Spirit is real or concrete," because the meaning of the totality of the real is revealed in its historical becoming, through discourse in History.[23] "In radical immanentism, the Absolute would have no reality or content of its own; all content would be determinate, limited, and therefore finite. A radical immanentism would conceive Absolute essence as nothing more than a dialectical law, which operates in the midst of finitude. And the Absolute would have no consciousness or self-consciousness of its ow but be reduced to the finite self-consciousness of the historical dialect."[24]

Schleiermacher (1768-1834) was a German theologian, philosopher and biblical scholar. He attempted to reconcile the criticisms of the Enlightenment with traditional Protestant Christianity. He is often called the 'Father of Modern Theology'.[25] He developed the view that experience is the basis and authority of certainty and he legitimized mysticism in the Christian churches which then extolled the importance of feeling and experience.[26] Schleiermacher claims that the essence of religion is piety and it is a feeling and not knowing or doing for it is a feeling of immediate self-consciousness of absolute dependence on the divine. The Church of Christianity is the pious association of believers. Dogmatics is the verbal expression of piety. Schleiermacher's anthropological approach shifts Christianity's traditional epistemology—in which faith begins with Knowing and accepting divine revelation—to immanence-oriented human subjectivity and self-consciousness (similar to Kant's morality).[27]

In the time of the Enlightenment, which brought about a paradigm shift, humans became autonomous and their reason became the only arbiter of truth. As a result, authoritarian sources like the Church and the Bible faced open challenges. It was "largely secular, scientific, and optimistic in outlook...[and] confronted Christian faith with a challenge of major proportions."[28] However, a reactionary movement known as Romanticism had arisen to challenge the Enlightenment by the 1790s. Schleiermacher was a central figure of these conflicting worldviews. The Enlightenment did not deny all religious belief but accepted naturalist and deistic views. God became Aristotle's unmoved mover and miracles were declared to be a violation of the fixed laws of nature. Jesus was interpreted as a simple Galilean preacher who was made out to be a messianic figure by his followers. Romanticism reacted against it by stressing mystery, imagination and feeling.[29] Romanticism emphasized the immanence of God and sought to reunite the physical with the supernatural, humanity with nature and God and reason with the sensuous. It assumed that our selves are finite expressions of an Absolute self. Schleiermacher was a Romanticist who rejected the Enlightenment and believed in the capacity of the intellect to connect with the divine. To make Christian faith appealing, he proposed that it not depend upon doctrines but by more subjective parameters. For him, "true religion is sense and taste for the infinite" in one's mystical experience.[30] Contextualizing the Christian faith within Romanticism, Schleiermacher saved it from the threat of Enlightenment. But unfortunately, the experiment of Schleiermacher was a failure with regard to the biblically anchored Christian faith. Thus, the uncritical application of neo-gnosticism to the threat of postmodernism will end up harmful to Christian faith today.[31]

2. A Brief Overview of Neo-Pelagianism

2.1. Pelagianism Defined

Pelagians lack simple faith according to St. Augustine. When children were stopped from being led to Jesus, he told the disciples, "Let the little children come to me, and do not stop them; for it is to such as these that the kingdom of God belongs. Truly I tell you, whoever does not receive the kingdom of God as a little child will never enter it" (Lk 18:15-17). Jesus projects the simple faith of children as exemplary. What is this simple faith? In order to understand this, we need to read what comes before this passage and what comes after it. What comes before is the parable of the Pharisee and the tax-collector (Lk 18:9-14) and what comes after is the story of the rich young man (Lk 18:18-30). The dependence of the Pharisee on himself and of the rich young man on his wealth is contrary to the dependence upon God which is what simple faith entails. As children depend upon their parents for their survival, so too do we need to depend upon God.

2.2. Pelagianism Explained

Pelagianism can be explained under five headings: Adam, Christ, human, sin and death.[32] *Adam* committed sin but his sin affected only him and not the whole of humanity. He set a bad example through his sin; *Christ* came into the world to counter the evil example set by Adam through his teaching and good example of virtuous life; We, *humans*, are endowed with the natural powers of doing good that is pleasing to God and thereby to merit heaven; we need not depend upon any other internal grace to do good and in fact, the Law of Moses is as good as the Gospels to give an external guidance to go to heaven. *Sin* is choosing evil over good and it is the misuse of one's free will. This sin is not passed on to posterity and therefore there is no 'original sin'; hence, we do not require baptism for sanctifying grace as we already have capacity to do good. *Death* is natural to any human being and it is not the consequence of Adam's sin and even if Adam had not committed any sin he would have died.

2.3. Pelagianism Countered

Pelagianism was countered deftly by St Augustine and many others like St Jerome. It was ultimately condemned as heretical in 418 in the Synod of Carthage and again in 431 in the Council of Ephesus. Augustine taught that Adam's sin is transmitted by concupiscence affecting the whole of humanity resulting in the enfeeblement of freedom of will (though not destroyed); St. Paul's idea of redemption hinged upon the contrast between the sin of Adam and the death and resurrection of Jesus Christ; We, humans, need sanctifying grace not only for the forgiveness of the past sins but also for the help to avoid future sins. The grace of Christ discloses the knowledge of God's commandments and it also strengthens our will to execute them; even the new-born children should be baptized on account of original sin. The concept of original sin was developed by St Augustine based on Rom 5:12-21; 1 Cor 15:22 and Ps 51:5 although it was first alluded to in the 2nd century by St Irenaeus in his controversy with Gnostics. Death came to Adam not through a physical necessity but through sin.

There are three ways how sin entered or who is responsible for sin in the Bible. Sin entered the world through devil in the form of a snake (Wis 2:24) or through a woman (Sir 25:24) or through a man (Rom 5:12-21). The concept of original sin is developed from the last entry (Rom 5:12-21). As St Paul explains in this passage: as sin came from one man, redemption came from another man. We ratify Adam's sin through our sin and we ratify Jesus' redemption through our faith. While trying to understand this passage Augustine was of the view that sin is handed over by parents to the children through libido (lust) and thus 'concupiscence' (desire, sexual) within us is the essence of original sin which is blotted out by baptism. However, the Council of Trent took up Thomas Aquinas's view more than that of St Augustine. According to which, even after baptism 'concupiscence' remains but the effect of Adam's sin (original sin), that is, death is taken away. Accordingly, we define 'original sin' in the following way: the sin which I commit is the consequence of Adam's sin. Therefore, his (Adam's) act was original sin. My sin has got its origin in him. Such interpretation of original sin is not without problem. The whole of above interpretation treats Adam's story as history. This we reject today. We say it is a 'myth'—etiological. Thus, we need to re-interpret original sin and baptism. When God created, God created a 'good' universe with human being as basically good and there was 'sanctifying grace.' But now, the world seemed to have lost its 'sanctifying grace' and thus we have in this world suffering, death, sickness and weakness which is 'original sin.' Each child is born into this mess and is forced to sin, deprived of God's sanctifying grace. In baptism we become the inheritors of this sanctifying grace. Thus, in Jesus we receive the power to overcome sin, suffering and death. The community takes responsibility for bringing up the child in the Christian faith.

2.4. Challenges of Neo-Pelagianism to Christian Faith

Today, pelagianism has returned to the Church in varied forms;[33] this is why we speak of 'neo-pelagianism'. Nowadays, there is a nonchalant attitude in the Church toward infant baptism with the prevailing mistaken belief (Eph 2:3; Jn 3:5) that babes are innocent and will go to heaven if they die in infancy; therefore, infant baptism is delayed or put off for months or even years. Although the current Code of Canon Law demands that new-born children be baptized within a couple of weeks of birth, many parishes make baptisms available only once a month! Today some hold the view that: "All Scripture is inspired by God" (2 Tim 3:16) literally; and so, any religion is good enough! If so, why do we need or preach the gospels? Today there is a belief that any human being, irrespective of any religion, can do good. If so, why do we need baptism, prayer, breviary, spiritual readings, priests, sacraments and Holy Mass for the needed grace to grow in holiness (1 Cor 13:3)? Such questions lead to scandals and loss of priestly or religious vocations! Today, the sense of sin, the frequency for the sacrament of reconciliation, the belief in the efficacy of the blood of Christ or the New Covenant have greatly diminished! So, they say, "for he knows how we were made; he remembers that we are dust" (Ps 103:14)! Today some hold the view that death is natural to humans as this is what the theory of evolution teaches. If so, why worry about morality or immortality (Gen 2:9)?

Vatican Council II was called to 'update' the Church in line with the modern world. But there are some traditional Catholics who are restorationists of the bygone Catholic civilization. They resemble the 17th century Pelagians who abhorred the company of others (who attend the New Mass after the VC II reforms) and worshipped in their own chapels. One such example is the personal Apostolic Administration of St. John Mary Vianney in Brazil and another one is the Pellagrini of Northern Italy who were known for their elitism and disdain for praying with other faithful. Pope Francis brands such pelagians as 'restorationists' who use 'outmoded' or 'outdated' forms or practices of worship like counting beads or attaching too much of importance to numbers like novenas, the 'forty' days of Lent, recitation of a certain number of rosaries. Numbers can be good if they help one in the path of holiness. But when numbers become an end in themselves, they become ludicrous. One might wonder—what is Pelagian here? It is this: There are some traditional Catholics who believe that because of their resolve to undergo some suffering to attend 'correct Mass,' to observe certain 'numbers' or devotional practices, God owes them salvation and they also hate the idea of mercy being shown to anyone who doesn't also suffer likewise. Pope Francis says it is Pelagianism if you think that by being a traditionalist, you think that you are 'earning' some favour with God. Here, of course, to Pope Francis the post-conciliar Catholic seems to be the standard and those using pre-Vatican forms and expressions seem to be exceptions to be discouraged.

3. Conclusion: Trust in God's Amazing Grace

Gnosticism bloomed in the 2nd century A.D but we hardly know its origin. This 2nd century Gnosticism amalgamated some of Christian ideas within itself and formed a syncretistic movement. The second century Gnostics were condemned as heretics by the early Church. A religion-less Christianity is a new form of Gnosticism today. Ontological dualism of world and spirit in Gnosticism ended up with Docetism denying incarnation. The dualism of the Christ of faith and Jesus of history is the form of gnosis in the Church today. For St Augustine we are a part of fallen human nature. However, in our relationship with Christ we can be purified through his grace, which was denied by Pelagian. In fact, if Christ's grace is taken away from the Church, all sacraments and rituals within the Church make no sense. But, with the grace of Christ, they all become the celebration of faith. In contrast to Pelagianism, faith and grace are so emphasized within the Catholic Church which goes even to the extent of saying that our sacraments can fetch God's saving grace even when they are administered by sinful clergy.

Endnotes

[1] See Pope Francis, Apostolic Exhortation *Evangelii Gaudium* on the Proclamation of the Gospel in Today's World, 24 Nov. 2013. This document will hereafter be abbreviated as EG.

[2] Ibid.

[3] Ray Blake, "Self-absorbed Promethean Neo-pelagianism" in http://marymagdalen.blogspot.in/2013/11/self-absorbed-promethean-neo-pelagianism.html, accessed on 24/10/2017.

[4] Ibid.

[5] Christopher A. Ferrara, "Who are the Real Promethean Neo-Pelagians?" accessed on the following link on Oct 24, 2017 https://remnantnewspaper.com/web/index.php/articles/item/2713-who-are-the-real-promethean-neo-pelagians

[6] Ibid.

[7] What is Gnostic Christians believe? In https://www.youtube.com/watch?v=Iuvk2bLCzwM, accessed on 3/11/2017.

[8] George M. Soares-Prabhu, "The Spirituality of Jesus," in *Biblical Spirituality of Liberative Action, vol. 3*, ed. S. Kuthirakkattel (Pune: Jnana-Deepa Vidyapeeth, 2003), 86-88.

[9] "Gnosticism" in http://www.ligonier.org/learn/devotionals/gnosticism/ accessed on 24/10/2017. I owe to this site for the understanding of "Gnosticism" found in this paragraph.

[10] H.D. Preuss, *Old Testament Theology, vol. 2* (Louisville, Kentucky: Westminster John Knox Press, 1996), 110.

[11] Robinson, *Religious Ideas in the Old Testament* (New York: Charles Scribner Sons, 1915), 83.

[12] Kiseong Shin, *The Concept of Self in Hinduism, Buddhism and Christianity and its Implications for Interfaith Relations* (Oregon: Pickwick Publications, 2017), 95.

[13] Ibid., 95.

[14] Ibid., 103.

[15] Ibid., 107.

[16] George M. Soares-Prabhu, "The Sacred in the Secular," in *A Biblical Theology for India, vol. 2*, ed. S. Kuthirakkattel (Pune: Jnana-Deepa Vidyapeeth, 1999), 201-213. My ideas in this section owe much to this article.

[17] This word is found only five times in the New Testament: Jn 1:14; Rev 7:15; 12:12; 13:6; 21:3.

[18] Mary Jo Anderson, "Neo Gnostics at the End of the Age," internet article accessed on 26/10/2017 in https://www.catholicculture.org/culture/library/view.cfm?recnum=4635.

[19] Ibid.

[20] See http://www.ligonier.org/learn/devotionals/neo-gnosticism/

[21] Ibid.

[22] Zeynep Direk, "Simone de Beauvoir's Relation to Hegel's Absolutes," in *A Companion to Simone de Beauvoir*, ed. L. Hengehold (UK: John Wiley & Sons Ltd., 2017), 203.

[23] Alexandre Kojeve, *Introduction to the Reading of Hegel: Lectures on the Phenomenology of Spirit* (NY: Cornell University Press, 1991), 204.

[24] Ibid.

[25] C.W. Christian, *Fredrich Schleiermacher* (Waco: Word Books, 1979), 12-13.

[26] Gregory A. Thornbury, "A Revelation of the Inward: Schleiermacher's Theology and the Hermeneutics of Interiority," https://pdfs.semanticscholar.org/5eea/6db0ece01aa3a1731b2357aa72db46e7376d.pdf accessed 24/10/17

[27] See Mark C.H. Shan, "Friedrich D.E. Schleiermacher," accessed on the following weblink on November 2, 2017: http://people.bu.edu/wwildman/relexp/reviews/review_schleiermacher01.htm, /

[28] C.W. Christian, ibid., 19-20.

[29] Colin Brown, *Philosophy and the Christian Faith* (London: Tyndale, 1973), 109.

[30] Schleiermacher, *On Religion: Speeches to the Cultured Despisers*, trans. John Oman (New York: Harper Torchbooks, 1958), 39.

[31] S. Alan Corlew, *Schleiermacher and Romanticism: A Failed Experiment and its Implications for Contextualizing Christianity within a Postmodern Paradigm.* This is a thesis available at https://www.researchgate.net accessed on October 24, 2017.

[32] Adfero, "Confused how some Catholics can be labeled "Pelagians"? in https://rorate-caeli.blogspot.com/2013/08/confused-how-traditional-catholics-can.html, accessed on October 26, 2017.

[33] Ibid.

8

Election Theology and the Pelagian Understanding of Human Will

Thomas Karimundackal, SJ

Pelagianism and its many avatars uphold the view that human beings can attain salvation by their own efforts. These heresies—traces of which are seen even today—assume that moral perfection is attainable in this life through human free will, without the help of God's grace. However, Augustine contradicted the Pelagian view by teaching that moral perfection was impossible without divine grace, because human beings are born with a sinful heart and will. In the biblical tradition, the people of Israel cherished the idea of 'divine election'—the belief that Yhwh had specifically chosen them among all the nations out of his gracious love and free will. This paper attempts to analyse the biblical doctrine of election. In so doing, it hopes to provide some insight on how this doctrine is consonant with Augustine's response to Pelagianism.

1.   Pelagian Understanding of Human Will

Pelagianism, popularized by Pelagius and his followers, stressed the essential goodness of human nature and the freedom of the human will.[1] Pelagius interpreted grace as an external aid to human free will, which he, however, considered as a pre-given in human nature.[2] As a result of this, Pelagianism held that human beings have an unimpaired moral ability to choose that which is spiritually good and also possess the free will, ability, and capacity to do that which is spiritually good.[3] This led the Pelagians to think that one could choose to follow God's precepts because one had the power within oneself to do so. Thus, Pelagianism saw revelation as divine grace by which human minds are enlightened or an action of God by which knowledge is imparted to humans.[4]

1.1. Augustine's Response to Pelagius

In his response to Pelagius, Augustine pointed out that human beings could not attain salvation by their own efforts and were totally dependent upon the grace of God. He held that God's grace does not consist only in the disclosure of divine 'institutions,' by which humans would know what to do; but it appears, first of all, as the revelation of God's justice by which sinners are justified gratuitously.[5] According to Augustine, God's grace not only instils love in the human heart, but this grace also changes the inner character of human beings so that they truly love and follow God's commandments.[6] Therefore, Augustine held that a person's salvation comes solely through a free gift, through the efficacious grace of God; and since this was a gracious gift one, had no free choice to accept or refuse.[7] However, a direct intervention of the divine grace in human nature would leave huge space for human freedom of choice.

1.2. The Aim of this Paper

In the context of Pelagianism and Augustine's response to it, this paper examines the concept of election in the First Testament with a special focus on its emphasis in the book of Deuteronomy. An examination of various elements of election in the book of Deuteronomy shows that the human will (i.e., the collective will of Israel) has been enabled by the grace of God to respond to God's choice and election. As the human will is saturated with the grace of God, human beings have the ability to make decisions in favour of divine grace. The human will cannot respond to God's initiatives apart from his enlightening grace. Therefore, the findings of this paper reject Pelagius's understanding of the freedom of the human will, a pre-given gift in human nature, while affirming Augustine's claim that a person's salvation (i.e., Israel's redemption) comes solely through a free gift, the efficacious grace of God.

2.   Election Theology in the First Testament

Election in the First Testament is the conviction of the people of Israel that they have been chosen by God among the peoples/nations (see Ex 19,5-6; Deut 7,6-7; Isa 41,8-9; 51,2; Ezek 20,5; Amos 3,1-2; Hos 11,1; Ps 105,5-10.43). Israel is not chosen because it is better than other nations; rather it is the outpouring of divine grace that makes Israel worthy to be God's treasured people in its weakness and worthlessness (Deut 10,20). When God chose Israel in its weakness and bondage, it is divine grace revealed in human history. God's electing and saving grace are revealed in the election of Israel, as they could not have been a great and powerful people among the nations.

2.1. Election Theology in Deuteronomy

The concept of the election of Israel finds its most articulated form in the Book of Deuteronomy.[8] Election in Deuteronomy is basically a demonstration of Yhwh's exclusive relationship to Israel, i.e., why and how Yhwh chose Israel to be his people and dealt with it as his own. Deuteronomy reveals this unique relationship between Yhwh and Israel by employing various words, metaphors and figurative expressions, such as בהר (4,37; 7,6-7; 10,15; 14,2), לקח (4,20.34), היה לי לעם (4,20; 26,17-19), עם קדוש (7,6; 14,2.21; 26,19; 28,9), עם סגלה (7,6; 14,2; 26,18), נחלה (4,20; 32,9), etc.[9] All these figurative expressions basically denote a special relationship between Yhwh and Israel which is the *raison d'être* of the election itself. We shall consider a few texts which illustrate various characteristics of divine election in Deuteronomy.

2.1.1. Deut 7,6-8: A holy, chosen, treasured people

Deut 7,6-8 give the classical Deuteronomic formulation of election. Deut 7,6-8 appear in the context of Moses' commandment to put the Canaanite nations to the חרם.[10] The command to destroy all the Canaanites, their cultic objects and to refrain from intermarriage with them (v2b-5) is justified on the basis of Israel's special status as Yhwh's chosen people (v.6). An analysis of the election formula in v.6 gives us with the fundamental characteristics of divine election in Deuteronomy.[11]

כי עם קדוש אתה ליהוה אלהיך 6a	For a holy people are you to Yhwh your God
בך בחר יהוה אלהיך 6b	in you chose Yhwh your God
להיות לו לעם סגלה מכל העמים 6c אשר על־פני האדמה 6d	to be to him a people of treasured possession from all the peoples which are upon the face of the earth.

The causal כי at the beginning of v6 shows that the ideas presented in v1-5 are causally connected with what follows in v6, i.e. Yhwh's setting apart of Israel from all the peoples of the earth (מכל העמים אשר על־פני האדמה) is closely related to their holiness (עם קדוש) and election (בחר). Israel's privileged status in v6 is expressed especially by the terms העמים מכל, עם סגלה, בחר, עם קדוש. Yhwh chose (בחר) Israel out of all the peoples (מכל העמים) and set it apart as a holy people (עם קדוש) as his own, bestowing upon it a unique value of possession (עם סגלה).

i. A holy people

The affirmation of Israel's holiness (עם קדוש) in v.6 is linked with the problem of cultic contamination by Canaanite practices (vv.2b-5). The assertion that Israel is a holy people (v.6a) is followed by the claim of Yhwh's choice of Israel (v.6b). Thus, first of all, the claim of Yhwh's choice of Israel suggests that Israel is distinctive: Israel is a holy people (קדוש עם) whom Yhwh chose to be his own people out of all the peoples (see 14,2; 26,19; 28,9).[12] Since they are separated to be a holy people to the Lord, they have to refrain from all the abhorrent practices of the Canaanites (vv.2b-5). Secondly, Since Yhwh sets them apart from all peoples and chooses them to be a people for his own possession, they become עם קדוש, a people dedicated to Yhwh (אתה ליהוה אלהיך עם קדוש). Thus, the term עם קדוש basically defines a relationship between Yhwh and his people[13] and Israel's holiness derives from its chosen status as Yhwh's own people chosen out of all the peoples on earth (מכל העמים אשר על־פני האדמה see 14,2; 26,19; 28,9).

ii.   A chosen people

The concept of Yhwh's election of Israel is closely related to the use of the verb בחר.[14] By and large, בחר denotes a choice of an individual or a group of people[15] out of the totality of peoples (מכל העמים see 7,6-7; 10,15; 14,2; 26,19) for a purpose.[16] In 4,37; 7,6.7; 10,15; 14,2 the object of Yhwh's choosing (בחר) is Israel—a people of his treasured possession. The choice (בחר) always involves a direct relationship between the one who chooses and the chosen, i.e., between Yhwh and Israel.[17] Moreover, the choice is always a deliberate action of Yhwh[18] and a manifestation of his grace (see vv.7-8). The combination of בחר with the terms of "love" (אהב 4,37; 10,15; Isa 41,8; 43,4; Mal 1,2; Ps 47,5; 78,68; חשק 7,7; 10,15; אהב 18,6; Ps 132,13; רהם Isa 14,1; רצה see Isa 42,1; 1 Chr 28,4; חפץ Isa 56,4) further complements the reason for Yhwh's election of Israel.[19]

iii.   A treasured possession

The distinctive phrase עם סגלה in v6 is used to infer that Israel is Yhwh's unique treasure in contrast to the peoples of the earth (מכל העמים).[20] The term עם סגלה appears three times in Deuteronomy (7,6; 14,2; 26,18) and each time it appears in the context of Israel's election (בחר) and Israel's status of holiness (עם קדוש). Israel is viewed as Yhwh's unique possession, a people of treasured possession (עם סגלה)[21] which is set aside from the many choices that Yhwh had (see 32,8-9). Israel has been chosen by Yhwh out of all the nations on the face of the earth (7,6; 14,2; 26,19) and has been made his עם סגלה

(7,6; 14,2; 26,18). Thus, the deuteronomic adaptation of סגלה from its Akkadian (*sikiltum*) and Ugaritic (*sglt*) equivalent shows Yhwh's special affection for Israel and Israel's direct relationship with Yhwh.[22]

iv.   Deut 7,7-8: the foundation of Israel's election

Deut 7,7-8 demonstrate the reasons for Yhwh's choice in 7,6; first, with a negative claim of Yhwh's choice of Israel despite its insignificance (v.7) and then with a positive claim showing Yhwh's love towards them and to their ancestors (v.8). Israel was hardly impressive in size (v.7);[23] however, it is favoured among the nations by reason of Yhwh's incomprehensible "love" (חשק v.7; אהבה v.8) for them and his faithfulness to the promises that he made to their fathers (v8). This is further demonstrated by recalling Yhwh's saving grace (הוציא יהוה אתכם ביד חזקה) and redemptive grace (ויפדך מבית עבדים) towards them. Yhwh's electing grace is emphasized by the repetition of מכל־העמים (2x) in v.7. Israel's special status in v.6 is thus substantiated by five divine actions: Yhwh's love towards them (חשק v.7, אהבה v.8); Yhwh's choice out of all peoples (מכל־העמים [2x] v.7; see v.6); Yhwh's faithfulness to his promises to their ancestors (לאבתיכם אשר נשבע v.8); Yhwh's saving deeds in Egypt (הוציא יהוה אתכם ביד חזקה v.8); Yhwh's redemption of his people (עבדים ויפדך מבית v.8). Therefore, there is nothing significant that made Israel worthier of Yhwh's favour than other nations but only Yhwh's deliberate choice.

Israel's Present Status: (7,6) Yhwh's claim	Israel's Past Status: (7,7) Negative Reasoning for Yhwh's claim	Israel's Redeemed Status with Yhwh: (7,8) Positive Reasoning for Yhwh's claim
For a holy people are you to Yhwh ... Yhwh your God chose you to be to him a people of treasured possession out of all the peoples ...	You were not more in number than any people, that the Lord became attached to you, or chose you, for you were the smallest of all peoples	But because of the love of the Lord towards you, and because he kept the oath ... sworn unto your fathers, the Lord has brought you out ... and redeemed you out of the house of bondage ...

2.1.2. Deut 10,14-15: Yhwh's elective grace upon the 'fathers and their seed after them'.

Against the background of Yhwh's universal sovereignty (v.14), Yhwh's unique love for the patriarchs and his choice of 'their seed after them' is articulated in v.15. Through a series of verbs (בחר ← אהב ← חשק) Moses describes the elective grace of Yhwh in choosing only Israel from all the people at his disposal. Yhwh has drawn to his heart (חשק) loving (לאהבה) the insignificant ancestors (באבתיך) and he has chosen (בחר) their seed (בזרעם) after them. The governing verb חשק indicates Yhwh's conscious decision to love Israel, the object of his love and choice (see 7,6-8).[24] That is to say, Yhwh's attachment of love towards Israel does not emerge from any inherent quality of Israel but from his own deliberate decision. Thus, Yhwh's choice of Israel in v.15 could be seen in a progressive way: He bestows his affection (חשק) on them, he loves (אהב) them, and he chooses (בחר) them.

Yhwh's choice of Israel in 10,15 could be seen as a summation of
Moses' previous assertions (4,37; 7,7-8).

4,37	7,7-8	10,15
וַתַּחַת כִּי אָהַב אֶת־אֲבֹתֶיךָ וַיִּבְחַר בְּזַרְעוֹ אַחֲרָיו וַיּוֹצִאֲךָ בְּפָנָיו בְּכֹחוֹ הַגָּדֹל מִמִּצְרָיִם:	7,7 לֹא מֵרֻבְּכֶם מִכָּל־הָעַמִּים חָשַׁק יהוה בָּכֶם וַיִּבְחַר בָּכֶם כִּי־אַתֶּם הַמְעַט מִכָּל־הָעַמִּים: 7,8 כִּי מֵאַהֲבַת יהוה אֶתְכֶם	רַק בַּאֲבֹתֶיךָ חָשַׁק יהוה לְאַהֲבָה אוֹתָם וַיִּבְחַר בְּזַרְעָם אַחֲרֵיהֶם בָּכֶם מִכָּל־הָעַמִּים כַּיּוֹם הַזֶּה

The terms בחר and אהב of 4,37 are repeated in 10,15 almost in parallel
manner (אהב את־אבתיך; ויבחר בזרעם אחריהם//ויבחר בזרעו אחריו
// לאהבה אותם). The rationale for חשק and בחר in 7,7 (see בחר in
7,6) is explained by the feminine singular construct of אהבה in 7,8,
which is further extended to 10,15 (לאהבה אותם). The negatively
formulated חשק and בחר in 7,7 is positively affirmed in 10,15 and
the construct אהבת of 7,8 is changed into a determinate action (אהב
qal infinitive construct) in 10,15. The twice repeated מכל־העמים in
7,7 to denote the slight significance of Israel among the peoples is
reiterated positively in 10,15 by specifying Yhwh's choice of Israel
from all the peoples (מכל־העמים).[25]

2.1.3. Deut 14,1-2.21: Being Set Apart for Yhwh

Deut 14,2 practically reiterates, word for word, all the characteristic
features of 7,6. Israel, the children of Yhwh (v.1a) are a holy people
(עם קדוש), belong to Yhwh their God (אלהיך ליהוה) whom Yhwh
has chosen (בחר) out of all the peoples on the face of the earth
(אשר על־פני האדמה מכל העמים) to be his own treasured possession
(לעם סגלה). However, the context of the text (v.1; see 14,1-21) adds
more 'elective' significance to these terms, namely Israel should not
get involved in the practices of their gentile neighbours (v.1b; Lev
19,28; 21,5-6; Jer 16,6; 41,5; 47,5) for they are a holy people to the
Lord their God (כי עם קדוש אתה ליהוה אלהיך).

As children of Yhwh (בנים אתם ליהוה אלהיכם v.1a; see 1,31; 8,5;
32,5.19.20; Isa 1,2-4; Mal 2,10; Ps 103,13) Israel should never forget how
distinctive their relationship to the Lord is. Yhwh has chosen Israel and
they have been set apart for Yhwh. Therefore, as a people belonging
to Yhwh, Israel is required to be holy (see Lev 20,26) and to avoid

customs unworthy of that relationship (v.1b). This is illustrated by the parallel construction of v.1a and v.2a. The opening clause, "sons you (pl) are to the Lord your (pl) God" (בנים אתם ליהוה אלהיכם v1a) is in parallel to the opening clause of v.2, "for a people holy you (sg) are to the Lord your (sg) God" (אלהיך כי עם קדוש אתה ליהוה).[26] Thus, the 'elective' status of Israel in v.2 serves as a motivation to the prohibition of v.1b. The repetition of עם קדוש אתה ליהוה אלהיך in 14,21 provides the basis for refraining from the abhorrent pagan practices and the dietary laws in 14,3-21.[27] That is to say, the prohibitions of their Canaanite mourning practices and dietary laws are framed between the statements of Yhwh's relationship to Israel and statements that define what holiness means for Israel (vv.1a.2.21ab). Yhwh's holy people (עם קדוש) must refrain from all the detestable practices of their pagan neighbours and from eating what is unclean in the sight of the Lord. Thus, the restrictions between clean and unclean, what is acceptable and abhorrent indicate the criteria for the separation between Israel and other nations.[28] Therefore, Israel's status of עם קדוש in ch. 14 should be viewed in the context of Yhwh's 'elective' grace and Israel's distinctiveness. It necessarily denotes a relationship between Yhwh and Israel rather than a ritual or ceremonial purity.[29]

The clause, "sons you (pl) are to the Lord your (pl) God" (בנים אתם ליהוה אלהיכם 14,1a) demonstrates Israel's relationship to Yhwh in a unique way, like that of children to their father. In 1,31 and 8,5 Moses has already compared Yhwh's relationship to Israel to that of a father and son (כאשר ייסר איש את־בנו 1,31; ישא־איש את־בנו 8,5). But now in 14,1a Moses strengthens this relationship by using a metaphor[30] rather than a simile: Yhwh not only takes care of Israel like a father cares for a son, he is Israel's father.[31] This intrinsic "father-son" relationship, at this point, intensifies Deuteronomy's view of election (see 7,6), and places Israel as a whole in a close familial relationship with Yhwh.

While the comparison in 1,31 and 8,5 focuses on Yhwh's action for Israel in care and discipline, the metaphor in 14,1 emphasizes the inherent parent-child relationship between Yhwh and Israel. In

32,5.19.20 this metaphor is used negatively to illustrate the faithlessness and perverseness of Israel. The "father-son" relationship in all these instances (1,31; 8,5; 14,1; 32,5.18-20) brings home the implied obligation of Israel to obey Yhwh as a child obeys the parent's will.[32] In short, the image of "father-son" in Deuteronomy is an important metaphor which portrays its election theology.

2.1.4. Deut 26,17-19: Set high above all nations

Deut 26,17-19 is an exposition of how Yhwh and Israel enter into a mutual commitment.[33] In v.17 Yhwh declares (אמר *hiphil*)[34] that he will be Israel's God (לאלהים להיות לך)[35] and spells out what it means for them to enter into a mutual commitment (v.17b). In v.18-19 Israel declares (אמר *hiphil*) that they will keep his commandments and points out what they will receive from the Lord for accepting this commitment (v.18a.19). Israel's willingness to accept the demands of the Lord, such as to walk in his ways (see 5,33; 8,6; 10,12; 11,22), to keep his statutes, his commandments and his ordinances, and to obey his voice (11,13. 27; 12,28; 13,18 [v.17b]), has significant implications for their place in the world (v.18-19): they become the Lord's treasured people (עם סגלה), a people set high above all the nations (כל־הגוים ולתתך עליון על see 28,1) and a people holy to the Lord (עם־קדש ליהוה אלהיך v.19). Thus, the language of vv.17-19 echoes the earlier elective claim of Yhwh in 7,6 and 14,2.

However, there is an important distinction between the previous passages (7,6 and 14,2) and 26,17-19, i.e. if Israel remains faithful to the covenant of Yhwh (v.17b), they will be renowned among other nations (v.19). In 26,18-19 the Lord promises Israel to set them high above all the nations (ולתתך עליון על כל־הגוים v19), whereas in 7,6 and 14,2 the Lord chooses Israel from all the peoples (מכל העמים 7,6; 14,2) of the earth. Thus, in vv.18-19 Israel's privileged status is intensified as Yhwh promises to set them high above all the nations "to praise and to name and to honor" (לתהלה ולשם ולתפארת).[36] In short, Yhwh's choice of Israel as a "treasured people" (עם סגלה) and their distinction of being holy to the Lord (עם־קדש ליהוה אלהיך)

would bring praise, reputation and honor to them (ולשם ולתפארת ולתהלה)above all nations.

2.1.5. Deut 28,9-10: Called by the name of Yhwh

Deut 28,9-10 show how the establishment of Israel as Yhwh's holy people would make all the other peoples of the earth recognize that they are called by the name of Yhwh. V.9 reiterates that the Lord shall establish (יקימך hiphil imperfect) Israel as a holy people (עם קדוש) unto himself (see 7,6; 14,2; 26,19). This would cause the nations to look upon Israel with fear (ירא)[37] for they shall see that "Yhwh's name is called over them" (כי שם יהוה נקרא עליך v.10). The phrase "Yhwh's name is called over them" not only gives a unique identity to Israel but also gives it a distinctive character among the nations. While in 26,17-19 Israel is renowned amongst the nations "in praise and in name and in honour" (לתהלה ולשם ולתפארת), in 28,9-10 the nations will see that "Yhwh's name is called over them". Moreover, as a mark of identity and distinctiveness the phrase "Yhwh's name is called over them" manifests an intrinsic relationship between Yhwh and Israel that is inherent in being chosen from among all nations (see 4,7-8.19-20.32-34.36-38; 7,6-8; 9,26-29; 10,14-15; 14,1-2.21; 26,17-19; 32,7-10; see Ex 19,6). Consequently, the phrase "Yhwh's name is called over them" (see 2 Chr 7,14; Jer 14,9; Isa 63:19; Amos 9,12) basically denotes Yhwh's ownership of Israel and his protection of them.[38]

2.1.6. Deut 4,7-8.32-34.36-38: No people other than you

Yhwh's elective grace upon Israel is made explicit in the rhetorical questions of 4,7-8 and 4,32-34.[39] While 4,7-8 accentuate the incomparability of Israel on account of Yhwh's choice of them, 4,32-34 highlight Yhwh's incomparability on account of his relationship to Israel, manifested in his saving deeds towards them. Israel's greatness and incomparability in vv.7-8 is introduced by two מי questions, showing Israel's relationship to Yhwh in two parallel phrases: they have a God in their midst, a God who is identified as (כ) "Yhwh our God" (כיהוה אלהינו v.7) and the inheritance of statutes and judgments which is identified as (כ) "all this teaching" (ככל התורה הזאת). Thus, the parallelism between v.7and v.8 demonstrates twice Israel's uniqueness and incomparability among the nations.

כיהוה אלהינו	אלהים קרבים אליו	אשר־לו	מי־גוי גדול	V7
ככל התורה הזאת	חקים ומשפטים צדיקם	אשר־לו	ומי גוי גדול	V8

The rhetorical questions in vv.32-34 introduce the uniqueness and incomparability of Yhwh. The rhetorical question in v.32 challenges Israel to ask in time (למן־היום אשר ברא אלהים אדם על־הארץ , since creation of man)[40] and space (ולמקצה השמים ועד־קצה השמים → from one end of the heaven to the other) whether such things ever happened or were heard of. Here, Yhwh's greatness and incomparability is initiated by two ה-questions (הנהיה כדבר הגדול הזה and הנשמע כמהו), which is further intensely illustrated by two other ה-questions in parallel phrases: no other god has let any people hear his voice as (כ) Israel heard it (v.33) and no other god has ever taken a nation for himself as (כ) Yhwh took Israel (v.34).

כיהוה אלהינו	אלהים קרבים אליו	אשר־לו	מי־גוי גדול	V7
ככל התורה הזאת	חקים ומשפטים צדיקם	אשר־לו	ומי גוי גדול	V8

The expected negative answers to these questions affirm Yhwh's exclusive love and choice for them:

V.32b: Whether there has been *any such thing* as this great thing *is*, or has been heard like it?[41]	No
V.33: Has any other people heard the voice of God speaking out of fire, as you have, and lived?[42]	
V.34: Or has a god tried to go to take for himself a nation from within *another* nation by trials, by signs and wonders ... as the Lord your God did for you in Egypt before your eyes?	

No people other than Israel has seen or heard a great event like this before; no people other than Israel has heard the voice of Yhwh from the midst of the fire and lived to tell about it; and no other god has ever tried to take for himself one nation out of another. The crucial point is that only Israel had the chance to be taken from the midst of the nations. The term לקח in 4,34 clearly denotes Yhwh's election of Israel because only Yhwh took for himself one nation out of another nation (מקרב גוי "from within another nation"). Yhwh's taking (לקח) one nation "from within another nation" is an act of election.[43] Thus, through the rhetorical questions in vv.7-8 and vv.32-34 Moses invites Israel to engage in Yhwh's unique relationship with them and Yhwh's redemptive deeds for them.

Vv.36-38 make explicit what is implicit in v.34, i.e., choosing a nation from the midst of the nations.[44] Yhwh's series of saving deeds in v.34 takes a theological turn in v.37 in choosing (בחר) the progeny of the ancestors. The reason for his choice of Israel is none other than his love for their fathers (v.37).[45] Thus, Yhwh's saving deeds in vv.36-38 have an explicit elective purpose: He lets Israel hear his voice (השמיעך v.36) to instruct them (ליסרך v.36), and he lets them see (הראך v.36) his great fire, loves (אהב v.37) their fathers, chooses (בחר v.37) their seed after them, brings (יצא) them out of Egypt to drive out (להוריש v.38) the other nations, and brings them (להביאך v.38) to the land to give it (לתת־לך v.38) to them as inheritance (נחלה).[46] In short, vv.36-38 demonstrate Yhwh's unique love and choice of Israel.

2.1.7. Deut 4,19-20; 9,26-29; 32,7-10: Yhwh's inheritance

Israel is Yhwh's inheritance (נחלה).[47] The phrase עם נחלה (4,20; 9,26.29; 32,8-9) semantically intensifies Yhwh's exclusive relationship to Israel in the sense of his own inheritance/possession. The figurative use of עם נחלה does not emphasize the inheritance of property but expresses a constant, enduring relationship between Yhwh and Israel.[48] Israel's special status as Yhwh's inheritance (נחלה) is highlighted in 4,20 with a contrast to Yhwh's relationship to other peoples in 4,19. While Yhwh allots (חלק) the astral deities to the peoples (v.19b), Yhwh takes (לקח)[49] Israel and brings them forth from the iron furnace (v.20a)

to be his inheritance (v.20b). The hortatory appeal not to bow down
(חוה) and serve (עבד)[50] the astral deities in v.19a remains as a backdrop
for Yhwh's exclusive wish for Israel in v.20b,[51] i.e. Yhwh wants Israel
to remain his inheritance because Israel belongs to Yhwh. Thus, the
allotment of the astral deities to the other peoples is to define the
identity of Israel in terms of their unique relationship to Yhwh. The
successive use of the preposition מן (2x מכור הברזל ממצרים) and
ל (3x להיות לו לעם) in v.20 demonstrates Yhwh's saving deeds "from
where" to "to where", i.e. from the "iron furnace" to "to a people
of inheritance".[52] The narrative development of these verses can be
seen in the contrasting relationship between Yhwh, Israel and the
other people: (Yhwh allots the astral deities to the peoples [v.19b])
→ (Yhwh takes Israel [v.20a]) and (Yhwh warns Israel against idol
worship [v.19a]) → (Yhwh claims Israel as his inheritance [v.20b]).[53]

ופן־תשא ... והשתחוית להם ועבדתם	V19a	
אשר חלק יהוה אלהיך אתם לכל העמים	V19b	
ואתכם לקח יהוה ויוצא אתכם מכור הברזל ממצרים	V20a	
להיות לו לעם נחלה כיום הזה	V20b	

Israel's special status as 'Yhwh's inheritance' is repeated twice in Moses'
prayer in 9,26-29 forming a rhetorical inclusion for the entire prayer.[54]
V.26 and v.29 assume the language of election, "your people and
your inheritance" (עמך ונחלתך) as the backdrop of Yhwh's unique
relationship with them in the past (see 4,20). Moses' entreaty not to
destroy (שחת hiphil)[55] "your people and your inheritance" (v.26a)[56]
is justified by recalling Yhwh's saving deeds in Egypt (v.26bc.29)
and his unique relationship to the patriarchs (v.27a; see 10,15). The
request "not to destroy your people and your inheritance" bears its
own justification as they are Yhwh's people (עמך) and his inheritance
(ונחלתך). The assertion that Israel is "your people and your inheritance"
is further substantiated by Yhwh's redemptive engagement with them:
"whom you have redeemed in your presence" (v.26b) and "whom
you brought out of Egypt with a strong hand" (v.26c). Similarly, the
second request – "remember your servants, Abraham, Isaac, and Jacob"

(v.27a)[57]- presupposes Yhwh's unique relationship with the patriarchs which is considered as a reason for the third request "not to look at the stubbornness of this people or at their wickedness or their sin" (v.27b). Thus, the first three reasons (26b.26c. 27a) invariably affirm Israel's special status with Yhwh.

V.28 continues with the Exodus theme and argues rhetorically that Yhwh's reputation is at stake before Egypt if he does not bring Israel into the land that he has promised. This makes Moses conclude his prayer with a positive foundation by repeating his opening statements in slightly different words: "they are your people and your inheritance, whom you brought out by your mighty power and by your stretched-out arm" (v.29). In short, Moses' prayer demonstrates the very nature of Israel as Yhwh's inheritance whom he has redeemed by his own power and grace. The following request-reason pattern of Moses' prayer may help us to identify its running theme of election of Israel.

v26b	Request + Reason	⇕	"do not destroy your people and your inheritance" (עמך ונחלתך)
v26c	Reason		"whom you have redeemed in your presence" (v26c)
v26d	Reason		"whom you brought (אשר־הוצאת) out of Egypt with a strong hand" (v26d).
v27	Request + Reason	⇕	"remember your servants, Abraham, Isaac, and Jacob" (v27a) "do not look at the stubbornness of this people or at their wickedness or their sin" (v27b).
v28	Reason		Yhwh's reputation before Egypt
v29	Conclusion		"they are your people and your inheritance (עמך ונחלתך) (v29a), whom you brought out (אשר הוצאת) by your mighty power and by your stretched out arm" (v29b).

Deut 32,7-10 further provides us with a clue how Israel became a chosen people starting in primeval times. Israel's unique relationship with Yhwh is highlighted in a mythic setting of vv.8-9.[58] In primeval times (see v.7 שנות דור־ודור ... ימות עולם)[59] when the "Most High" (עליון)[60] gave the nations their inheritance,[61] he kept Israel (יעקב)[62] as his own, making them his inheritance (נחלתו v.9). That is to say, Yhwh chose only Israel when he had other nations as choices.[63] Consequently,

Israel has the privilege of relating to the "Most High" directly, while the other nations relate to the "Most High" through their apportioned gods.[64] V.10 recalls once again the Exodus experience and narrates how עליון has encircled him (יסבבנהו) and instructed him (יבוננהו), guarding him (יצרנהו) "as the apple of his eye" (כאישון עינו).[65] Thus, v.10 illustrates Yhwh's response to a vulnerable group of people whom he has decided to choose as his inheritance. In short, vv.8-10 show Yhwh's election of Israel and his special relationship with them, i.e., the "inheritance" that the "Most High" chose to allot to himself.[66]

3.   Conclusion

The concept of divine election takes on its most concrete form in Deuteronomy: Yhwh chooses (בחר 4,37; 7,6-7; 10,15; 14,2) Israel from all the peoples (מכל העמים 7,6; 10,15; 14,2) bestowing upon it a unique value of possession (עם סגלה 7,6; 14,2; 26,18). He sets them apart as a holy people as his own (עם קדוש 7,6; 14,2.21; 26,19; 28,9) placing them high above all the nations (ולתתך עליון על כל־הגוים 26,19) to praise and to name and to honour (לתהלה ולשם ולתפארת 29,19). Consequently, all the people of the earth recognize that they are called by the name of Yhwh (כי שם יהוה נקרא עליך 28,10). They are Yhwh's inheritance (עם נחלה 4,20; 9,26.29; 32,8-9) because no other god has let any people hear his voice as Israel heard it and no other god has ever taken a nation for himself as Yhwh did with Israel (4,33-34). They have been the object of God's unique love and choice (4,36-38) since the primeval times (32,7-10) because they are his children (1,31; 8,5; 14,1; 32,5.18-20).

The election of Israel is justified as going back to Yhwh's promise to the patriarchs (4,37; 7,8; 10,15), his love for them (חשק 7,7; 10,15; אהב 4,37; 7,8; 10,15), his saving and redeeming grace for them (4,32-38; 7,7-8; 9, 26-29). The reason why Yhwh has chosen Israel is also given in their status to be his "holy people" (עם קדוש 7,6; 14,2.21; 26,19; 28,9), "to be his people" (היה לי לעם 4,20; 26,17-19), his "treasured possession" (עם סגלה 7,6; 14,2; 26,18), his "inheritance" (עם נחלה 4,20; 9,26.29; 32,8-9) and his "children" (בנים אתם ליהוה אלהיכם 14,1; see 1,31; 8,5; 14,1; 32,5.18-20). The 'elective status of Israel directs their past relationship to the existing relationship between Yhwh and Israel. Thus, the election of Israel involves the free act of Yhwh which even has a present binding force.

The examination of the various elements of the election in the book of Deuteronomy shows that the election of Israel is totally out of the will and grace of God. Thus, it rejects the Pelagian emphasis on human will, which claims that through the sustained efforts of human will human beings can achieve salvation. The Pelagian emphasis on the freedom of the human will is essentially a denial of God's grace bestowed upon the election of Israel. In the election of Israel, God's gracious love and free will is revealed rather than Israel's efforts to be God's people.

Endnotes

[1] H. Rondet, "Pelagianism," *Encyclopedia of Theology: A Concise Sacramentum Mundi*, ed. K. Rahner (Wellwood, 1993), 1185.

[2] See M. Mercator, *Patrología Latina* 48 (Turnhout 1995), 598-606.

[3] See B.R. Rees, *The Letters of Pelagius and his Followers* (Woodbridge 1991), 36-37.

[4] J.L.C. Quy, "Revelation, Christology and Grace in Augustine's Anti-Manichean and Anti-Pelagian Controversies," in *Phronema* 28/2 (2013): 148.

[5] Ibid., Revelation, 146.

[6] Ibid., Revelation, 144.

[7] E. Stump – N. Kretzmann, *The Cambridge Companion to Augustine* (Cambridge 2001), 130-135.

[8] The divine election of Israel is one of the major themes of Deuteronomy and some scholars even identify the theology of Deuteronomy as election theology, see C. Vriezen, *Die Erwählung Israels nach dem Alten Testament* (AThANT 24; Zürich 1953), 47.

[9] S.T. Sohn, *The Divine Election of Israel* (Grand Rapids 1991), 10-100, analyzes philologically certain figurative expressions and terms which describe the Yhwh-Israel relationship such as verbal forms and terms which convey the idea of Yhwh's election: הפלה, הבדיל, ידע, היה לי לעם, לקח, בהר etc., and various metaphorical images which describe the Yhwh-Israel relationship: father-son, master-servant, shepherd-sheep, potter-clay, and farmer-vineyard etc. His systematic analysis of these metaphorical terms and expressions

reveal that Yhwh chose Israel not because of their inherent value but because of his grace and purposes and Israel became "conscious of their special relationship with Yahweh through their experiential knowledge of him, and they tried to explain it in their everyday language in terms of typical human relationships", ibid., 10.

[10] For a detailed analysis of the connection between חרם and election in Deut 7, see J.N. Lohr, *Chosen and Unchosen: Conceptions of Election in the Pentateuch and Jewish-Christian Interpretation* (Siphrut 2; Winona Lake 2009), 168-183. See also R.W.L. Moberly, "Toward an Interpretation of the Shema", *Theological Interpretation of Scripture. FS B.S. Childs* (ed. C.R. Seitz) (Grand Rapids 1999):135, no.2.

[11] Deut 7,6 recalls Ex 19,5-6 with a slightly different wording. The difference found in the Exodus narrative, especially גוי קדוש, ממלכת כהנים (v6), suggests the idea of theocracy, i.e., Israel is a holy nation, a nation ruled by God. Note the substitution of עמים in Deuteronomy, for גוי in Exodus. For the semantical difference between גוי and עמים, see D.I. Block, "Nations/Nationality", *NIDOTTE* IV, 966-972. The omission of the phrase ממלכת כהנים in Deuteronomy is in tune with its understanding of the relationship to Yhwh. See the explanation of J.G. McConville, *Deuteronomy* (ApOTC; Illinois 2002), 155, "The idea of priesthood, as a metaphor of dedication to God, apparently did not suit Deuteronomy's idea of the whole people as an integrated entity before God, in which the priest is not set up as the ultimate model of holiness".

[12] The verb קדש is mostly found in the sphere of cultic regulations with the meaning "to sanctify" (see Ex 19,10.14; Josh 7,13; Job 1,5; 1 Sam16,5; Ezek 20,12; 36,23; 37,28). It is Yhwh who sanctifies Israel (אני יהוה מקדשכם see Ex 31,13; Lev 20,8; 21,8.15.23; 22,9.16.32; Ezek 20,12; 37,28). When the verb קדש is used for a man or a group of people, it implies the meaning "to set apart," "to be chosen," or "to be devoted" (see Ex 29,1; 30,30; Num 8,16.17; 1 Sam 16,5; Jer 1,5). See also Sohn, *Election*, 96. The qal form of קדש denotes exclusively cultic holiness with no moral element (see Ex 29,37; 30,29; Lev 6,11.20; Deut 22,9; 1 Sam 21,6). The niphal form, where the subject is always God, denotes the self-representation of Yhwh's holiness (see Ex 29,43; Num 20,13; Isa 5,16; Ezek 20,41; 28,22.25; 36,23; 38,16; 39,27). קדש in piel (see Gen 2,3; Ex 20,11; Jer 17,22.24.27) and hiphil (see Josh 20,7; 1 Chr 23,13; 2 Chr 29,19; 30,17; Num 3,13; 20,12; 27,14; 1 Kings 9,7; Isa 29,23) have a more or less similar semantic meaning: "bring something/someone into the condition of holiness according to the cultic regulations or make holy, consecrate, surrender to God as a possession. The root קדש in hithpael means to bring oneself into the condition of

holiness (see Ex 19,22; Lev 11,44; 20,7; Ezek 38,23; Num 11,18; Josh 3,5; 7,13; 1 Sam 16,5; 2 Chr 31,18). As a predicate of God, קדשׁ takes the meaning of divine, and thus becomes an adjective for God (Isa 5,16; 6,3; Hos 11,9 etc.). See also, O. Procksh, "ἅγιος", *TDNT* I, 90; W. Kornfeld - H. Ringgren, "קדשׁ", *TDOT* XII, 527-528.

[13] Procksh, ἅγιος, 91-92. The concept of Israel's holiness emerges out of their relationship to Yhwh as it is evident from the Holiness Code (Lev 17-26): "You shall be holy, for I the Lord your God am holy" (יהוה אלהיכם אני קדשים תהיו כי קדושׁ Lev19,2); "and you are to be holy to me, for I the Lord am holy" (והייתם לי קדשים כי קדושׁ אני יהוה Lev 20,26). Therefore, Israel has to conform perfectly to the holiness of Yhwh in every aspect of life: in religious life (Lev 20,8), moral life (Lev 21,8.15.23), and in food habits (Lev 22,8-9,16). For a thematic consideration of Israel as a "holy people", see J.B. Wells, *God's Holy People: A Theme in Biblical Theology* (JSOTS 305; Sheffield 2000), 27-129.

[14] As far as the development of the concept of election in the Hebrew Bible is concerned, to Deuteronomy is attributed the first use of בחר for the election of Israel, see G. von Rad, *Old Testament Theology I: The Theology of Israel's Historical Traditions* (trans. D.M.G. Stalker) (London 1989⁶), 178; S.R. Driver, *A Critical and Exegetical Commentary on Deuteronomy* (ICC; Edinburgh ³1902), lxxx; N. MacDonald, *Deuteronomy and the Meaning of "Monotheism"* (FzAT 2; Tübingen 2012²), 152; H. Wildberger, "בחר", *TLOT* I, 215. According to H. Seebass, "בחר", *TDOT* II, 83, "בחר as a technical term for the election of the people of Israel stands under the symbol of universalism". For a history of the concept of election, see H. Wildberger, " Die Neuinterpretation des Erwählungsglaubens Israels in der Krise der Exilszeit", *Wort - Gebot- Glaube. FS W. Eichrodt* (ed. H. Stoebe) (AThANT 69; Zürich 1970), 307-324.

[15] However, בחר has various semantic fields of meaning in the OT, such as choosing an object for use (see 1 Sam 17,40; 1 Kings 18,23.25) or a place to reside in (Gen 13,11; Deut 23,16); to choose men for military service (1 Sam 13,2; 2 Sam 10,4; 17,1), individuals for leadership (Ex 18,25; 1 Sam 8,18; 12,13), friendship (1 Sam 20,30); possible courses of action (2 Sam 15,15) and suffering (2 Sam 24,12); making decisions (Isa 7,15-16; Deut 30,19); choosing the deities—either Yhwh or other gods (Josh 24,15, 22; Judg 5,8; 10,14). בחר is employed theologically when Yhwh is the subject of בחר with both persons and places as objects (see 1 Sam 2,28; 10,24; 16,8-10.12; 2 Sam 6,21; Deut 12,5, 11.13.14.18.21.26; 14,23.24.25; 15,20; 16,2.6.7.11.16; 17,8.10; 18,5.6; 26,2; 31,11; 1 Kings 14,21; Pss 105,26;

132,13). For an analysis of בחר in the OT, see SEEBASS, "בחר", 74-87; G.E. Nicole, "בחר", *NIDOTTE* I, 637-641.

[16] According to Vriezen, *Erwählung*, 109, the choice always contains a mission and only out of this mission can man comprehend the choice of God.

[17] Seebass, בחר, 87, argues that בחר does not signify so much the relationship between Yhwh and his people, but "that which results from this basic relationship".

[18] According to Nicole, בחר, 639, "Almost 100x in the OT (about 60 percent), God is the subject of the verb בחר. These uses are concentrated in Deut (29x), Sam (7x), Kings (12x), Chr (18x), Ps (9x), Isa (11x). They apply to the choice of the place of worship for all Israel (44x), of David and his descendants as kings over Israel (ca. 18x), of Israel as the people of God (ca. 17x), and of the priests or Levites (9x)".

[19] In certain cases בחר is followed by some of the terms for love, such as, אהב, חשק אוה, חמד, רהם, רצה, to supplement the reason for Yhwh's election of Israel. For a detailed analysis of בחר + the terms for love, see Sohn, *Election*, 45-50; G.E. Wright, *The Old Testament Against Its Environment* (SBT 1/2; London 1968), 46 and 49.

[20] M. Weinfeld, "The Covenant of Grant in the Old Testament and in the Ancient Near East", *JAOS* 90 (1970), 195, no.103, suggests that the basic meaning of the root סגל is "to set aside". However, N. Lohfink, "Dt 26, 17-19 und die, Bundesformel", *ZKTh* 91 (1969), 545, suggests that the noun סגלה originally applied to the private property of an individual but later it began to express the subordination of a king or an individual to a god or a great king.

[21] The Akkadian equivalent (*sikiltum*) and Ugaritic equivalent (*sglt*) describe the kings as the special possession of gods. For the meaning of סגלה and its Akkadian equivalent *sikiltum*, see M. Greenberg, "Hebrew Segulla: Akadian sikiltu", *JAOS* 71 (1959),172-174; M. Weinfeld, *Deuteronomy and the Deuteronomic School* (Oxford 1972), 226, no. 2. The term סגלה also occurs in treaty contexts to distinguish the special relationship of the overlord to one of his vassals, see Id., *Deuteronomy1-11* (AncB 5; New York 1991), 368.

[22] See McConville, *Deuteronomy*, 157. The term סגלה appears only 8 times in the OT, of which six refer to the people as a whole, who are called Yhwh's treasured possession (סגלה לי Ex 19,5; לסגלתו Ps 135,4; סגלה Mal 3,17; סגלה מע 7,6; 14,2; 26,18). In the other two instances (1 Chr 29,3 and Eccl 2,8) סגלה is used to denote the private wealth of a king unlike the wealth held in trust for the people.

[23] The idea that Israel is "the smallest among all peoples" is in conformity with their feeling before the nations (see1,28) and their beginnings in Egypt although it contrasts with Yhwh's promise to Abraham (Gen 15,5; see Deut 1,10; 10,22). See also McConville, *Deuteronomy*, 157.

[24] G. Wallis, "חשק", *TDOT* V, 262-263 demonstrates how חשק is theologically used to denote the intrinsic relationship between God and mankind which emerges from a "firm and deliberate attestation of trust" and not from a "sudden surge of emotion". The root חשק has the basic meaning, "adhere to, be attached to or be united", see *HALOT 1*, 362; H.J. Franken, *The Mystical Communion with JHWH in the Book of Psalms* (Leiden 1954), 36. חשק in qal with the preposition ב generally means 'to be attached to, to love somebody' (see Gen 34,8; Deut 21,11→ woman; Ps 91,14 → God; Deut 7,7; 10,15 → God as subject; Sir 51,19 → wisdom) and with the preposition ל with infinitive means 'to desire' (see 1 Kings 9,19; 2Chr 8,6). חשק in niphal means 'devoted' (see Sir 40,19) and in piel and pual it means 'to join together' (piel see Ex 38,28; Pual see Ex 27,17; 38,17). The relationship to Arabic *ʿašiqa* and *ʿasiqa* may suggests the metaphorical meaning "to love passionately", see Wallis, חשק, 261.

[25] For the relationship between 7,6-8 and 10,15, see also N. Lohfink, *Das Hauptgebot. Eine Untersuchung literarischer Einleitungsfragen zu Dtn 5-11* (AnBib 20; Rome 1963), 226,

[26] While the use of the plural 'you' (אתם) in v1 brings home the covenantal responsibility of each member of the community, the singular you (אתם) of v2 reminds Israel of their collective responsibility as an 'elect nation' (7,6; 26,18).

[27] W. Houston, *Purity and Monotheism: Clean and Unclean Animals in Biblical Law* (JSOTS 140; Sheffield 1993), 56. McConville, *Deuteronomy*, 155-156, argues that there is no cultic view of holiness in 14,3-21, although "it echoes Lev 11, and embraces the language of 'cleanliness' and 'uncleanliness' in relation to permissible and impermissible foods".

[28] See Housten, *Purity*, 241-244.

[29] However, we may notice a contrast between the concept of holiness in Deuteronomy and the "priestly parts of the Pentateuch", see G. Braulik, *Deuteronomium 1-16,17* (NEB; Würzburg 1986), 63; Weinfeld, *Deuteronomy*, 61.

30 The basis for the phrase, "sons you are to the Lord your God" (בנים אתם ליהוה אלהיכם) may be Ex 4,22-23, where the "first-born" implies Israel which is in a covenant relationship with Yhwh. According to D.I. Block, *Deuteronomy* (NIVAC; Grand Rapids 2012), 343, this metaphor derives from ancient Near Eastern Political relationships (see 2 Kings 16,7) where

the suzerain's status was referred to as "fathership" and the status of the vassal was referred to as "sonship".

[31] Block, *Deuteronomy*, 343.

[32] The "father-son" motif is relatively rare in the OT. The other instances where we see this motif are Isa 1,2.4; 30,1.9; 43,6; 45,11; Jer 3,14.22; 31,9; Ezek 16,21; Hos 11,1; Mal 1,6; 3,17; Ps 103,13. In these passages Israel as Yhwh's children either speak of their filial duties of honour and loyalty to Yhwh or of their faithlessness and rebellion against Yhwh.

[33] Vv.17-19 form part of the covenant renewal ceremony in the plains of Moab although the ceremony itself is not made explicit here. For its relationship to the covenantal renewal ceremony, see P.C. Craigie, *The Book of Deuteronomy* (NICOT; Grand Rapids 1976), 324; McConville, *Deuteronomy*, 382-383. Authors like Z.W. Falk, *Hebrew Law in Biblical Times* (Jerusalem 1964), 135; M.A. Friedman, "Israel's Response to Hosea 2:17b: 'You Are My Husband", *JBL* 99 (1980), 204, no. 14, suggest that the mutual commitments of vv.16-17 reflect a marriage ceremony between Yhwh and his bride, Israel. G. Braulik, *Deuteronomium II*, (NEB; Würzburg 1992), 198, sees here a close resemblance to the parity treaty formula in the ANE. For a detailed study of this passage, see Lohfink, Bundesformel, 517-553.

[34] The hiphil of אמר, means literally 'cause to say', is unique to this passage as it appears nowhere else in the Hebrew Bible. It seems to indicate a formal declaration of commitment between partners as in the covenant-treaty formula, see CRAIGIE, *Deuteronomy*, 324; E.S. Kalland, "Deuteronomy", *The Expositor's Bible Commentary, Vol. 3: Deuteronomy, Joshua, Judges, Ruth, 1 & 2 Samuel* (ed. E. Frank) (Grand Rapids 1992),158. D.J.A. CLINES, *The Dictionary of Classical Hebrew I* (Sheffield 1993), 325, suggests that hiphil of אמר with the infinitive of "to be" means "to proclaim or vow to do something". S. Wagner, " אמר", *TDOT* I, 329, also suggests that אמר in hiphil is used "in the sense of an official, binding statement". The hiphil of אמר may have a causative (which includes declarative) or intensive meaning, see *GKC* § 53c.d. Both causative and intensive meanings have been suggested by various commentators according to their interest. For example, with a causative hiphil, Driver, *Deuteronomy*, 293, understand v17 as a declaration by Yhwh and v18-19 a declaration by Israel. With an intensive hiphil, Craigie, *Deuteronomy*, 324-325; J.A. Thompson, *Deuteronomy* (TOTC 5; Illinois 2008), 282; D.L. Christensen, *Deuteronomy 21:10-34:12* (WBC; Nashville 2002), 644, understand v.17 as a declaration by Israel and v.18-19 a declaration by Yhwh. I tend to take an intensive sense as the literal rendering of the hiphil of אמר in v.17 ("You have caused the Lord to say …") may make

the syntax of the subsequent portions of v17 awkward as Israel does not cause God to say anything, see Craigie, *Deuteronomy*, 324, no. 3.

[35] The phrase להיות לך לאלהים ("to be to you for a God") is a common phrase in the OT, appears either with the personal pronouns you (sg) or you (pl) or them etc. to express an intrinsic relationship between Yhwh and Israel (see 29,12; 2 Sam 7,24; 1 Chr 17,22; Jer 7,23; 11,4; 24,7; 30,22; 31,33; Zech 8,8; Gen 17,7. 8; Ex 6,7; 29,45; Lev 11,45; 22,33; 25,38; 26,12.45; Num 15,41. Syntactically, the preposition ל plus nouns or pronouns indicates the goal of a process (see *BHRG* § 39.11.I) and therefore the phrase להיות לך לאלהים could be understood as a goal achieved in the covenantal process.

[36] It is possible to interpret the phrase לתהלה ולשם ולתפארת as referring to God and not to Israel. Yhwh's placing of Israel above all nations would result in praise and honour to him because the chosen community would reflect the glory of Yhwh in its distinctiveness of being holy to him (עם־קדש ליהוה אלהיך v19) and consequently their covenantal life. For a similar discussion, see P.D. Miller, *Deuteronomy* (Interpretation; Louisville 1990), 188. Jer 13,11 and 33,9, using the same triplets (תפארת, שם, תהלה; in Jer 13,11 and 33,9 תהלה, שם are reversed), explains that God's purpose in choosing Israel is his glory. For the exegetical implication of the citation of Deut 26,19 in Jer 13,11 and 33,9 see, G. Fischer, *Jeremia 1-25* (HThKAT; Freiburg 2005, 455; Id., *Jeremia 26-52* (HThKAT; Freiburg 2005, 228.

[37] ירא could also mean "awe or reverence", (see H.F. Fuhs, "ירא", *TDOT* VI, 303) which would also be appropriate in this context, i.e., the nations would look upon Israel with amazement and fear.

[38] Driver, *Deuteronomy*, 305; J.H. Tigay, *Deuteronomy* (JPSTC; Philadelphia 1996), 259; I. Cairns, *Deuteronomy: Word and Presence* (ITC; Handsel 1992), 242, show that the phrase שם יהוה נקרא עליך combines the sense of Yhwh's ownership and protection of Israel. MacDonald, *Deuteronomy*, 157 argues that "the content of the nations' recognition is YHWH's ownership of Israel". See also *HALOT II*, 1130. This phrase is also used to call Yhwh's name upon: Jerusalem (Jer 25,29; Dan 9,18-19); the Ark (2Sam 6,2); the temple (1 Kings 8,43; 2Chr 6,33; Jer 7,10.11.14.30; 32,34; 34,15). Fischer, *Jeremia 1-25*, 300, identifies this phrase as a characteristic feature of Jeremiah to show Yhwh's close relationship to the people who come into the temple.

[39] For the rhetorical relationship between vv5-8 and vv32-34, see K. Holter, *Deuteronomy 4 and the Second commandment* (SBL 60; New York 2003), 103-104.

[40] The recurrence of היום in v.32 (למן־היום אשר ברא אלהים אדם על־הארץ) and v.40 (היום אשר אנכי מצוך) may suggest the extension of the historical

span to the present moment, by bracketing all history between the "day of the creation" and the "today" of Moses' renewed appeal for obedience to the commandments of the Lord. For the actualizing function of היום in Deuteronomy, see D. Markl, *Gottes Volk im Deuteronomium* (BZAR 18; Wiesbaden 2012), 70-79.

[41] The question under consideration is not whether an event as great as this happened, but whether a great event like this has happened before, see C.J.H. Wright, *Deuteronomy* (NIBC; Peabody 1996), 55.

[42] For the notion that no one can see God and live as the radiation of God's glory is lethal, see Ex 3,6; 24,10-11; 33,20-23; Judg 6,22-23; 13,22; Isa 6,5.

[43] According to Sohn, *Election*, 15, among the many meanings of לקח, the most significant one is to describe the idea of Yhwh's election of Israel, see 4,34; Ex 6,7; Hag 2,23. Ibid., 11-16, gives the further meanings of לקח and summarizes them as: "לקח carries the meanings 'to capture', 'to select', 'to marry', and 'to adopt'. When it has a person as its object, it establishes a relationship between subject and object. And this term basically carries the meaning of marriage from the perspective of man as the initiator". לקח obviously indicates the idea of choosing: choosing or selecting the tribal leaders from among the people (Deut 21,3; 26,2; see Gen 6,21; 32,13; 47,2; Judg 6,25; 1 Sam 7,9.12; 2 Sam 3,15; 12,4; 1 Kings 18,31; 2 Kings 7,14; Isa 44, 15; Ezek 16,16; 17,15); a man choosing a woman for his wife from among many others according to his own desire (Deut 21,11-12; see Gen 6,2; Judg 21,19-24).

[44] A. Rofé, *Deuteronomy, Issues and Interpretation*, (New York 2002), 19, argues that "the background of this statement is the notion that every people has its own particular god" and he demonstrates it by identifying various national gods in the Semitic world.

[45] See the use of תחת כי in conformity with תחת אשר meaning 'because' in 21,14; 22,29; 28,47. See also Rofé, *Deuteronomy*, 19.

[46] Rhetorically the elective purpose is intensified by a series of infinitive constructs with the preposition ל (לתת, להביאך, להוריש, ליסרך), see Holter, *Deuteronomy*, 105.

[47] נחלה is often derived from the verb נחל which means "to possess". In Deuteronomy נחלה can designate three different objects: a) the people who are Yhwh's inheritance: 4,20; 9,26.29; 32,9; see 1 Kings 8,51.53; 2 Kings 21,14; Isa 47,6; Jer 10,16; Mic 7,14; Pss 33,12; 78,62.71; 94,5,14; 106,5.40; b) the Levites to whom no territory is allotted and whose share is Yhwh 10,9; 12,12; 14,27.29; 18,1.2; see Jos 13,14.33; 14,3; 17,4; 3) the

land which Yhwh gives to his people as their possession 4,21.38; 12,9; 15,4; 19,10.14; 20,16; 21,23; 24,4; 25,19; 26,1; 29,7; see Jos 11,23; 13,6.7; 23,4; 24,28.30.32; 1 Kings 8,36. For the semantic development of נחלה as a biblical term expressing land tenure, see B.A. Levine, "Late Language in the Priestly Source: Some Literary and Historical Observations", *Proceedings of the Eighth World Congress of Jewish Studies, Panel Sessions (Biblical Studies and Hebrew Language*, (ed. D. Krone) (Jerusalem 1983): 69-82.

[48] See C.F. Lipiński, "נחלה", *TDOT* IX, 331.

[49] For the word play on לקח → חלק see G. Braulik, *Die Mittel deuteronomischer Rhetorik erhoben aus* Deuteronomium 4,1- 40 (AnBib 68; Rome 1978), 45; D. Knapp, *Deuteronomium 4. Literarische Analyse und theologische Interpretation* (Göttingen 1987), 74.

[50] In the larger context of Deut 4 the verb pair עבד/חוה serves to interpret the second commandment, see Holter, *Deuteronomy 4*, 81. In Deuteronomy this word pair refers to the worship of gods, see 5,9; 8,19; 11,16; 17,3; 29,25; 30,17.

[51] The issue in v19 is not the worship of the astral deities by the peoples, but by the people of Israel because the worship of the astral deities is permissible for the nations. For more on the notion that worship of the astral deities is permissible for the nations, see N. Lohfink, "Verkündigung des Hauptgebots in der jüngsten Schicht des Deuteronomiums (Dt 4,1- 40)", *Studien zum Deuteronomium und zur deuteronomistischen Literatur 1* (SBAB 8; Stuttgart 1990): 183-184; Olson, *Deuteronomy*, 143-145; M. Fishbane, "Ancient Wisdom and Modern Man with Special Reference to the Hebrew Bible", *CJR* 20/2 (1987): 46.

[52] Braulik, Rhetorik, 45, also shows that the narrative movement of v20 can be seen in the repeated use of prepositions.

[53] Holter, *Deuteronomy 4*, 78-81, proposes a chiastic structure for v19-20 where the outer layer (v19a and v20b) and inner layer (v19b and v20a) are allowed to contrast each other. Although we see a chiastic pattern in terms of its contrasting theme, we do not see a chiastic pattern in terms of its literary features.

[54] For the common vocabulary and content regarding inheritance and redemption in v26b and v29, see Braulik, *Deuteronomium I*, 81. On פדה in Deuteronomy, see Kalland, *Deuteronomy*, 82; Weinfeld, *School*, 326. The other instances of פדה in Deuteronomy are 7,8; 13,6; 15,15; 21,8; 24,18. On Moses as intercessor, see P.D. Miller, "Moses, My servant: A Deuteronomic Portrait of Moses", *Int* 41 (1987): 245-255; S.E. Balentine, *Prayer in the Hebrew Bible: The Drama of Divine - Human Dialogue* (Minneapolis 1993), 135-139.

[55] See 4,31 where שחת is used in hiphil to reassure the people that Yhwh is a compassionate God, who will neither destroy Israel nor forget his covenant with the ancestors. So Moses recalls again here Yhwh's commitment to Israel.

[56] This request looks back to Yhwh's reason for disowning Israel in v12. Now Moses reminds Yhwh that Israel is "your people and your inheritance" and not his.

[57] It is only here in Deuteronomy that the patriarchs are named and called עבדיך. The only other instance is in Ex 32,13. S. Boorer, *The Promise of the Land as Oath: a Key to the Formulation of the Pentateuch* (BZAW 205; W.de Gruyter 1992), 305, argues that v27a is a "blind motif" which presupposes Ex 32,13. The patriarchal remembrance in v27a is also in conformity with 9,5 where another mention of patriarchal promise is made, see G. Seitz, *Redaktionsgesichichtliche Studien zum Deuteronomium* (BWANT 93; Stuttgart 1971), 54. On the appeal to patriarchs in other prayers, see J.G. Plöger, *Literarkritische, formgeschichtliche und stilkritische Untersuchungen zum Deuteronomium* (BBB 26; Bonn 1967), 77.

[58] See R. Nelson, *Deuteronomy* (OTL; Louisvilie 2002), 371; For the Sumerian background of these verses, see Flood Narratives, *ANET*, 43, lines 91-99.

[59] ימות עולם may refer back to the earliest history (as in Amos 9,11; Mic 7,14; 1 Sam 27,8) reaching back to mythic times, see Gen 6,4), see Nelson, *Deuteronomy*, 371. However, A.D.H. Mayes, *Deuteronomy* (NCBC; London 1981), 384, consider that ימות עולם refers particularly to "the period of Israel's formation, from Egypt onwards as vv. 8ff. show"; see also R. Hauri, *Das Moseslied: Deuteronomium 32; Ein Beitrag zur israelitischen Literatur und Religiongeschichte* (Zürich 1917), 22-23. For the various possible meanings of עולם, see G.A. Knight, *The Song of Moses: A Theological quarry* (Michigan 1995), 33-35.

[60] עליון is an honorific epithet for Yhwh in the OT, glorifying him as the one and only Most High God, see Gen 14,18-20; Num 24,16; 2 Sam 22,14; Isa 14,14; Pss 7,17; 9,1-2; 21,7; 46,4.7; 47,2; 78,21; For a detailed discussion of עליון, see A.R. Johnson, *Sacral Kingship in Ancient Israel* (Cardiff 1967²), 48-49; E.E. Elnes - P.D. Miller, "Elyon", *DDD*, 295.

[61] For a legitimate function of the national gods among the ancient peoples, see D.I. Block, *The Gods of the Nation: Studies in Ancient Near Eastern National Theology* (Grand Rapids 2000), 21-25; J.J.M. Roberts, "Zion in the Theology of the Davidic-Solomonic Empire", *Studies in the Period of David and Solomon and Other Essays, Papers Read at the International Symposium*

for Biblical Studies, 5-7 December, 1979 Yamakawa-Shuppansha (ed. T. Ishida) (Tokyo 1982), 97-98.

[62] See Gen 32,29. יעקב is the birth name of the ancestor of "Israel" who inherited their national name from the name that God had given him.

[63] See W. Brueggemann, *Deuteronomy* (AOTC; Nashville 2001), 279.

[64] Driver, *Deuteronomy*, 356, puts it more succinctly: "that the nations were entrusted to the care of subordinate divine beings …, while Jehovah presided over Israel Himself."

[65] See Ps 17,8; Prov 7,2; It is an expression that symbolizes "that which is precious and particularly worthy of protection", see Mayes, *Deuteronomy*, 385.

[66] For Israel's familial relationship to Yhwh in the song of Moses, see vv. 5.6.18.19.20.43. In Deut 32, 6 the people of Israel are said to be Yhwh's possession purchased by Yhwh (קנך הלוא־הוא אביך see Ex 15, 16). As a corollary to this in 28,68 Yhwh warns that he would sell them in the case of their apostasy, see Sohn, *Election*, 78-79.

"My Grace is Sufficient for You" (2 Cor 12:9):

Grace vs Boasting in St Paul

M. Paul Raj

---

1.   The Problematic

Way back in 2001, praising a book by Fr Luigi Giussani (1922-2005), Cardinal Bergoglio—now, Pope Francis—lamented Pelagianism's continuing influence and said, "Pelagianism, underneath it all, is a remake of the Tower of Babel. ... Grace always comes first, then comes all the rest."[1] The Pope's subtle remark concisely encapsulates the most fundamental tenet of Pelagianism, namely, the non-requirement of divine grace for human salvation. If Pelagianism rejects every form of divine assistance for human redemption, Gnosticism with its dualistic understanding of reality twists the Christian understanding of grace and salvation.

Sometimes, under the influence of neo-Gnostic and neo-Pelagian ideas, teachers and students of Christian theology fail to uphold the 'gifted' nature of human existence and redemption. Being confused themselves, they confuse others by advocating ideologies and attitudes which render grace fruitless and ineffective. In the process, anthropocentrism gets absolutized through a misinterpretation of the theology of incarnation and the self-perceived greatness of human beings takes centre-stage. A close and careful scrutiny of such ideologies and attitudes reveals that all these are centred on the axis of human pride. That is why the Pope could confidently say that Pelagianism is a remake of the Tower of Babel.

In this essay, we reflect on how Paul presents the central role of grace in human redemption which contradicts the teachings of Gnosticism and Pelagianism. We do that by considering 2 Cor 12:9-10 as a basic text which describes the 'necessity' and the 'sufficiency' of divine grace. Towards the end of the essay, we shall also quickly take into account a few other related texts from the epistles of Paul, to make the reflection a little more comprehensive. Before we do that, let us clarify a few of the basic tenets of Gnosticism and Pelagianism in order to place ourselves in the context.

2.   A Brief Note on Gnosticism and Pelagianism

To draw any conclusion on whether Paul's writings were influenced by Gnosticism and Pelagianism or not, one must first raise questions about the origin and definition of both.

2.1. *Pelagianism*

We are not interested here in presenting Pelagianism in its fullness. It is enough for us to know some of its basic teachings. Pelagianism was a post-Biblical phenomenon. Pelagius was born around 355 AD and became a monk. He popularized the thinking that human beings could achieve salvation through asceticism, good works and personal discipline. Jesus is significant not so much for his sacrifice as much as for his role as a moral teacher.[2] Pelagius believed that "man could, by the natural power of free will and without the necessary help of God's grace, lead a morally good life."[3] "His followers denied that baptism cleanses the soul from original sin and also denied that the sacrament elevates the baptized into a state of supernatural friendship with God. Pelagius did believe that God wished to make it easier for human beings to lead sinless lives, and so God instructed people through the law of Moses and by Christ's teaching and good example. However, he held that human beings do not need the interior assistance of God's grace to avoid sin and lead holy lives; instead, he believed that holiness is attained through one's unaided free will."[4] Probably Paul was never aware of Pelagius. Anyway, Paul would seriously object to Pelagius's understanding of grace as texts like 2 Cor 12:9 suggest.

2.2. Gnosticism

We are not sure about the pre-Christian origins of Gnosticism, though the discovery of gnostic writings near Nag Hammadi in Egypt (c. 1945), of the *Gospel of Thomas* and of the meditative treatise *Gospel of Truth* are all suggestive of a pre-second century gnostic origin.[5] A comprehensive collection of Gnostic literature is found in the 'Gnostic Bible.'[6] In spite of such a wide range of literature, one still cannot imagine that there were already fully developed systems of thought on Gnosticism and Pelagianism when Paul started writing his epistles. At the same time, we also cannot rule out the possibility that the Pauline epistles were somehow influenced by earlier forms of gnostic ideas and myths. It is even possible that the New Testament traditions consciously opposed gnosticizing views because both of them come from the same heterodox Judaism.[7] Thus, though the New Testament cannot be held to advocate or combat gnostic ideas or systems of the second century, yet the religious currents of both the New Testament and Gnosticism are part of the same horizon within which they have to be interpreted.

As in the case of Pelagianism, it is not possible for us in this essay to track exactly back to the origin and development of the different systems of Gnosticism which would have possibly influenced the writings of the New Testament. For our purposes it is enough that we understand a few of its basic characteristics so that we would be able demonstrate later that Paul through his epistles is not advocating a 'gnostic' form of faith but on the contrary he seems to instruct his readers to beware of ideas and concepts coming from this system.

Etymologically 'Gnosticism' is founded on *gnosis* which means knowledge and thus would include every religion which claims to have and communicate knowledge of God.[8] However, actually the meaning and usage of Gnosticism is much more restricted and narrower than that, though there is no one definition which is universally accepted. Van Baaren makes a list of sixteen characteristics of Gnsoticism from which we can pick up the following more fundamental elements: The *gnosis* of Gnsoticism is not primarily intellectual but based on revelation and those who possess it will attain full salvation. Such a knowledge is higher than *pistis* (faith) and the material world. Matter is inherently evil and there is a radical ontological dualism between the divine and the material world which is the result of ignorance and created by its creator-demiurge. In addition, the transcendent God is distinct from the creator(s) of the world, the latter are identified with the creator God of the biblical narrative. Salvation is possible through the heavenly *salvator salvatus* or *salvandus* (the 'redeemed redeemer') and is different from the human appearance of Jesus of Nazareth. Salvation amounts to a total severing of all ties between the world and the spiritual part of man.[9]

3.   Is Paul a Gnostic?

It is assumed from Paul's presentation of Christianity as a religion of salvation and of Jesus of Nazareth as the redeemer of humanity that he was influenced by a pre-Christian Gnosticism.[10] W Schmithals is more than convinced that Gnosticism is combatted in the two Thessalonian and in the Galatian Epistles.[11] R. Bultmann suggested that Paul's description of Adam's fall and its relationship with the sin of humanity in Rom 5:12-21, his description of baptism into the body of Christ in Rom 6:5, his teaching of the fall of creation in Rom 8:20-23 and his reference to the powers of this age in Rom 8:38-39 are all heavily influenced by Gnostic myths and teaching.[12] One of the texts in Paul—which is in any case considered to have been influenced by at least some incipient form of 'Gnostic' movement—is the so-called '*Colossian Error*'[13] which entailed a false philosophy and an empty deceit (Col 2:8), a human tradition (Col 2:8), elemental spirits of the universe (Col 2:8) and angels (Col 2:18). It demanded observance of food regulations and festivals, new moons, and Sabbath (Col 2:14, 16, 20, 21) and it encouraged ascetic practices.

A few scholars also opine that the Corinthian Epistles are also influenced by Gnosticism,[14] and the opponents against whom Paul argues in his Corinthian Epistles are Gnostics. First of all, there is no unity among the scholars that the opponents of Paul in Corinth were all Gnostics. J. L. Sumney, for example, suggests four groups of people as possible opponents of Paul in Corinth: "advocates of Gentiles adopting circumcision, Sabbath, and food laws from the Torah, Gnostics, "divine men," and Pneumatics.[15] Secondly, it is not proved that Gnosis was a problem in Corinth. Wolfgang Schrage, for example, while approving the position of many scholars who see 'Gnsoticism' as a problem in Corinth as meaningful, insists that we can only speak of a 'pre-Gnosis' or 'proto-Gnosis' or of 'Gnosis in *statu nascendi*.' According to him, what we find in Corinth are merely 'gnosticizing pneumatics or tendencies' because a radical, dualistic view of the world and God supported by a metaphysical antagonism between God and creation which are foundational for Gnosticism, are totally missing in Corinth.[16]

Thus, we realize that neither Paul can be considered a Gnostic nor his writings are mere responses to the influence of Gnostic ideas and beliefs. Yet, there are a number of other texts in the Epistles of Paul which are identified by scholars as combating Gnostic doctrines such as 1 Cor 2:14-15; 14:44-46; Phil 2:6-11; 3:2-3.19; Col 1:18; Eph 1:23; 2:14-16; 1 Tim 4:3; 6:20 and 2 Tim 2:18, though these texts could be interpreted better from a non-Gnostic context. In the second half of this paper we shall spend some time looking at some of these texts. 2 Cor 12:9-10 is one such text which we study now.

4. Study of the Text 2 Cor 12:1-10

4.1. *The Context of 2 Cor 12:9*

The revelatory statement of Paul made here, namely, "My grace is sufficient for you" seems to refute quite a few pelagian and gnostic positions. In this text—which occurs in the context of a "fool's speech"[17] which begins already in 2 Cor 11:1 and extends up to 12:13—Paul is engaged in a polemic against a group of opponents who have probably scorned his apostleship in terms of false or pointless boasting to which his opponents have driven him and through which he claims he could illustrate his apostolic credentials. In fact, four chapters of this epistle, namely 2 Cor 10-13, have as their theme Paul's defense of his apostolic authority. In 2 Cor 10:12-18 he is addressing the issue of the improper boasting of some people who were "boasting of work done in someone else's sphere of action" (v.16). Their boasting consisted of self-promotion (v.12), boasting beyond proper limits (vv.13.15), overstepping the limits (v.14) and self-commendation (v.18). While denouncing the false claims and boasting of such 'intruders' Paul declares: "let anyone who boasts, boast in the Lord" (v.18), and thereby attempts to clarify to the Corinthian Christians that he is the one who had the legitimate authority among them as was willed by God.

In fact, the actual theme and the purpose of this section is to identify self-boasting as foolishness before the Lord and invite every apostle and missionary to boast in the Lord, because it is the Lord who is the origin of the mission and who will lead it to fulfillment. At least in four places in this speech (cf. 11:21.30; 12:5.9), he declares that before the Lord he would boast only of his weaknesses. Having thus clarified the distinction between the legitimate and the illegitimate boasting, Paul himself begins to indulge in some kind of illegitimate boasting in 11:1-12:13, in the so called 'fool's speech.' At this point the reader of this text is confronted with the question as to why on earth Paul is doing this. His consideration could be something similar to the proposal made in Prov 26:4-5: '*Do not answer fools according to their folly, or you will be a fool yourself. Answer fools according to their folly, or they will be wise in their own eyes.*" The juxtaposition of the two apparently contradictory proverbs[18] invites the reader to make a choice between the two. Applied to the context here, this would mean that Paul has to make his choice between the following two possibilities: Either he responds to the claims of the intruders in their own style thereby risking himself to be misunderstood by the Corinthians and playing into the hands of his rivals or he refrains from any such response. If he refrains from any kind of response, then the claims of the intruders might be accepted by the Corinthians as true. In fact, the Corinthian Christians seem to have believed in the claims of the intruders (cf. 2 Cor 11:4-5.20-21). In that case he might lose them to a false Gospel. Being fully aware of the folly of his choice, Paul finally decides in favour of a 'fool's speech' in order to bring the Corinthians to their senses.[19] Indeed, Paul's aim here is to convince the Corinthian Christians of the legitimate boasting, namely, that anyone who boasts should boast about one's weaknesses and not about one's strengths (2 Cor 12:9; cf. 1 Cor 1:31; 3:21; 2 Cor 10:17). The opposite will render everyone as a fool.

The 'fool's speech' can be clearly divided into two main parts: Part I: 11:1-21a which contains a prologue to the speech which actually clarifies the context and then Part II: 11:21b-12:10 which has the speech proper.[20] Each of these two parts can be divided into a number of sub-units on the basis of the arguments contained in them. In the following we try to provide a brief description of these sub-units focusing mainly on how Paul invites the Corinthian Christians not to fall prey to the boastful preaching of the 'super apostles' (cf. 11:5) but to remain grateful to the grace that has been given them.

4.2. Prologue – 11:1-21a

4.2.1. 11:1-4 – An Appeal for Tolerance

Paul has just criticized his opponents for their boasting in 10:12-18 and now he anticipates that he might offend his readers with his own boasting; therefore, he begs their indulgence in advance (*prodiorthosis*, an anticipatory correction). The foolishness of resorting to self-display is affirmed again in the epilogue to his speech in 12:11 (*epidiorthosis*, a subsequent correction of a previous impression).[21] From what we find in 11:16-17, it is clear that the apostle is uneasy in this role of self-display or self-boasting. Still he does it because of the criticism he has received from his opponents. Verse 11:4 provides important information about the identity and the teaching of Paul's opponents. They could either be the members of Corinthian congregation who were supporters of Cephas or others who preached the Gospel after Paul or members of the groups who were following gnostic ideas,[22] the tendencies of Sophia-Theology (liberation through wisdom) and realized eschatology or even to itinerant missionaries who have come from elsewhere (Didache12:1-2).

As these four verses suggest, these people have both, taught the wrong message to the Corinthians as well as advocated an adversary attitude towards Paul. Their false teaching consisted of another Jesus, different spirit and Gospel and an understanding of apostles that was opposed to that of Paul himself. They seem to have insisted that authentic apostles must display power and authority and should be ready to receive financial support from the people. Contrary to that, Paul understood apostleship and ministry as participation in the crucified Lord. In addition, they seem to have enjoyed a certain measure of success in the congregation, while Paul is still struggling to persuade them in both the Epistles.

4.2.2. 11:5-15 – Paul versus the Super-apostles

In this section Paul is comparing himself with the intruders in terms of 'status' and claims that he is in no way inferior to them. There is an opinion that the super-apostles here are not the same as the 'false apostles and deceitful workers who disguise themselves as apostles of Christ' (cf. 11:13) but refer to the twelve or to the three (Peter, James and John).[23] In any case the readers would have exactly known whom Paul is referring to, but we can only deduce it from the context. The context makes it vivid that Paul is here comparing himself with one particular group of people who are indulging in illegitimate boasting about themselves and the different designations found in the whole speech such as 'intruders,' 'super-apostles,' and false apostles' must all refer to the same group. Further, a separation of these different designations as referring to different groups of apostles is not in agreement with the one integrated statement found in vv.5-6. Again, the mention of super-apostles in 12:11 which is the epilogue to the whole speech confirms the view that these are one and the same. In fact, the term super-apostles is used of Paul's missionary rivals in

Corinth because of the exaggerated claims they make about themselves who, far from espousing a world-fleeing or world-denying position, were intent on exalting themselves. They are proud of their Jewish heritage (11:22).

Having claimed equality with the super-apostles, Paul at once makes an admission that in the skills of rhetorical arts he is inferior to them (11:6). His conceding his lack of oratorical eloquence is probably to attack the self-importance of the super-apostles. While he admits that he is weak in speech, he refuses to admit that his knowledge (deep spiritual insight) is also weak. He is thus firmly denying that rhetorical skill can also guarantee the reliability of the content. In proclamation what really mattered was the content and not the mode of communication, though the latter is also important.

In 11:7-11 Paul is pointing to a contradictory behavior between himself and the false apostles in the matter of accepting financial support from the people. While he clearly refused to accept such financial support from the Corinthian Christians in return for proclaiming the Gospel message (cf. 1 Cor 9:3-8), his opponents have done that. The rhetorical question in 11:7 by which Paul is asking whether he has committed some sin by declining to accept financial support from the Corinthian congregation, should be taken as an ironic criticism of the opponents' behavior. Further, Paul denies the opponents the opportunity to compare their ministry to his apostolate and calls them 'false apostles' and 'deceitful workers' who disguise themselves as apostles of Christ and compares their disguise to that of Satan who disguises himself as an angel of light (11:12-15). Thus, Paul strips off the masks of the opponents and reveals their true identity.

4.2.3.   11:16-21a – Second Appeal to Bear with the Foolish Boasting

In 11:16-19 Paul uses once again the fool's mode as a cover for some self-commendation.[24] Though he feels constrained to boast, still he wants to do as little of that as possible. While doing that, he also makes it very clear in v.17 that such boastful confidence is not according to the Lord but done as a fool according to human standards. The phrase 'not as one in the Lord' (*kata Kyrion*) in v.17 is contrasted with the phrase 'according to the flesh' (*kata sarka*) in v.18. As a justification to this repeated appeal Paul begins to describe in v.19 how the Corinthian Christians have accommodated the false apostles, by putting up 'gladly' with them. This again is an ironical statement which heightens the sarcasm. Then, v.20 elaborates the ironic remark of v.19 by delineating the false behavior of these deceitful apostles. They 'enslave' (*katadouloi*). This enslavement, following Gal 2:4, might be considered to refer to bondage to the law. However, the context here demands that we understand this enslavement as the pastoral control of the opponents who were "domineering, grasping, crafty, arrogant and violent."[25] The type of enslavement here referred to becomes more clear in the following four expressions, namely, that they 'prey upon' (*katesthiei*), 'take advantage of' (*lambanei*), 'put on airs' (*epairetai*) and 'slap you in the face' (*eis prosopon derei*).

11:21a concludes this sub-unit by speaking about the weakness of Paul, which he admits in contrast to the brute force exercised by his rivals. He begins this verse by saying 'according to dishonor' (*kata atimian* – translated as 'to my shame' by NRSV). A more correct translation will be: 'It is with shame that I have to confess that I was too weak for that (the kind of behavior of the opponents).'[26] Here it serves as an ironic concession to the claims of his opponents.

4.3. The Speech Proper: 11:21b-12:10

After the lengthy prologue (11:1-21a), Paul now begins his 'foolish' boasting with which he has been so reluctant to get involved. Once again, his self-awareness of the foolishness of the boasting is apparent in v.21b (*I am speaking foolishly*) and in v.23a (*I am out of my mind to speak this way*), yet he feels he has been forced to this tactic by his rivals in Corinth (cf. 12:11). Having argued in 11:6-15 that he is not 'inferior' to the false apostles and now in the speech proper in 11:21b-12:10, he demonstrates, speaking in the disguise of a fool, his equality (by using the expression 'I too' - *kagoo* - cf. 11:21b-22) and his superiority (by using the expression 'I more'- *huper ego* - cf. 11:23a-12:10). The areas of his equality and superiority with the false apostles include his heritage, labors, sufferings and reception of extraordinary visions and revelations which were far greater than those of the false apostles. In doing this, Paul is only countering each of his rivals' claims with those of his own.

4.3.1. 11:21b-29 – Paul's Credentials are far Superior to those of the False Apostles

In this section, Paul still continues to talk like a fool. That is why he begins this section by emphasizing his ethnic, social, and religious significance of being a Jew in v.22 (cf. Rom 11:1; Phil 3:5-6). Then, after staking his claim to superiority as a better minister of Christ (v.23a), he makes a catalogue of hardships (11:23b-29; cf. 4:8-9; 6:4c-5; Rom 8:35; 1 Cor 4:9-13) and continues to offer a long list of sufferings (11:23b-29) over and against the pretentious boasts of those who claim for themselves special apostolic powers and religious insights. Claims of such apostolic powers must have included in addition to their ethnic and religious identity (11:22), personal boldness (10:1-11), missionary achievements (10:12-16), eloquent speeches (11:5-6), ecstatic experiences (5:12-13) and the ability to perform miraculous deeds (12:11-12).

4.3.2. 11:30-33 – The Turning Point

This section provides the turning point in the whole argument. Having boasted of his labours and sufferings, now Paul declares he would rather boast of his weaknesses. It becomes clear, that the necessity of boasting does not make it less foolish. Paul's uneasiness about responding in a foolish way to the claims of others leads him to conclude that he would boast only about his weakness. Moreover the boasting in which he is now engaged concerns only his weaknesses consisting of a long recital of adversities (11:23b.29), of how much he suffered and therefore of his vulnerability. In the following (11:32-12:10) Paul presents two specific cases of his weakness (v 30): first his painful escape from Damascus (11:32-33) and the second the obligation to continue to bear the 'thorn in the flesh' (12:7-9).[27]

4.3.3. 12:1-10 – My Grace is Sufficient for You

This section contains the culmination of the whole of 'fool's speech.' This section is divided into the following sub-units:

12:1-4	Journey to heaven (v.2) or paradise (v.4)
12:5-6	A reflective comment on boasting
12:7	Reception of the thorn in the flesh
12:8	Prayer for the removal of the thorn in the flesh
12:9a	Denial of the request
12:9b-10	Paul's ability to boast of his weakness

Paul begins this unit with a curious account of a journey to paradise which yielded no useful religious knowledge (12:1-4). This journey to the paradise demonstrates that he is no stranger to extraordinary religious experiences. It cannot be proved what he exactly means by the "third heaven" and "paradise." Paul himself refrains from explaining the nature and the content of his experience. Thus, this experience is different from other visionary experiences such as call narratives of the Old Testament prophets (Isa 6:1-13; Jer 1:1-18) and even of Paul himself (Gal 1:11-17) in which an open demand is made for proclamation. Further, by narrating the whole incident in the third person instead of in the first, Paul is making a distinction between Paul the visionary and Paul who is known to the Corinthians. About the heavenly experience itself, Paul makes only the following statement, namely, he "heard things that are not to be told, that no mortal is permitted to repeat" (2 Cor 12:4), thus making a double, or emphatic denial. Both the terms point to a prohibition which renders as nothing such an ecstatic experience which could have become a basis for further self-boasting.

Then Paul narrates another incident which exposes his limitedness and dependency on the Lord, namely, the reception of the thorn in the flesh. He says explicitly that it was given to him 'to keep him from being too elated' (v 7b). That Paul wants to boast of his weakness, that is, the thorn in the flesh, is not due to any masochist tendency. This is clear from the fact that he has already appealed to the Lord three times to remove the "thorn in the flesh" (v 8).[28] In place of the pleaded for physical healing, what is given him is a spiritual healing through the promise "My grace is sufficient for you, for my power is made perfect in weakness" (v 9). The statement, "my power is made perfect in weakness" means that *the power of God or Christ is fully present and effective, in the various forms or manifestations of human frailty.* Here, the preposition '*in*' has to be understood temporally and not instrumentally. That is, the power is present or becomes active whenever the weakness steps in and not in the sense of weakness becoming an instrument or a precondition for power to become active.

5.   Significance of the Text 2 Cor 12:1-10

Four moments of this text are relevant for our purposes here. First, contrary to the self-boasting indulged in both by the false apostles and Paul himself—in which they remain the subjects of the referred to activities (11:1-29)—in the subsequent two incidents, namely, the paradise experience and the reception of the thorn in the flesh, the subject of activity is no more Paul, but the Lord. It becomes clear from the fact that in both the cases the 'impersonal passive' (with no specification as to the subject of the action) form is used to describe the respective activities. In the description of the Paradise experience it is said that Paul 'was caught up' (*harpagenta*) to the third heaven and in the reception of the thorn in the flesh it is said that a thorn 'was given' (*edothe*) to him in the flesh. In the New Testament Greek tradition, such impersonal passive forms are used to circumscribe the 'divine passive,' that is, that God is the agent of such action(s). Thus, the Lord remains the one who quasi 'caught up' Paul into heaven and who 'gave' him a thorn in the flesh.

The second moment is the prohibition about which we have already spoken. Here Paul is prohibited from speaking about the things which he heard. That he heard something gets thereby affirmed. It means that Paul, though only a human being, could and did perceive and receive a diving communication which is supposed to be spiritual. Thus, we find here a positive affirmation of humanity or materiality in relation to the spiritual world. At the same time such an experience also implies that Paul has only received this communication and therefore he is not the author of it and cannot proclaim it as if it were his achievement.

The third and most important moment for us is the one in which Paul receives an assurance from the Lord who tells him, "My grace is sufficient for you, for my power is made perfect in weakness." This assurance is in response to his treble appeal to the Lord to remove the "thorn in the flesh" (12:8). On the one hand, it illustrates the continued accompaniment of God's grace in the life of Paul, and, on the one other hand it describes God's grace as God's power, which is present and effective in the various forms or manifestations of human frailty. Then we have the fourth moment in vv.9b-10 which describes Paul's consequent ability to boast about his weakness. He says: "*I will boast all the more gladly of my weaknesses, so that the power of Christ may dwell in me.*[10] *Therefore I am content with weaknesses, insults, hardships, persecutions, and calamities for the sake of Christ; for whenever I am weak, then I am strong*" (vv.9b-10).

The key to understanding the whole text is the term 'grace'. Here grace is understood primarily as that power by which Paul has been commissioned to and constantly supported in his apostolic ministry. The Cynic and Stoic philosophers of Paul's day taught that one should be 'content' with whatever one has and thus promoted the ideal of self-sufficiency. However, the meaning here is more similar to *Midraash Tannaim* on Deut 3:26 interpreting God's refusal to let Moses cross over the Jordan: "Be content that the evil impulse has no power over thee, yea rather that I will not deliver thee into the hand of the angel of death, but will Myself be with thee."[29]

The Greek word for grace is *charis*,[30] meaning, 'favour', 'free gift' or 'grace'. The word is derived from the Greek root '*char-*' referring to something that produces wellbeing. In classical Greek it is used in three senses: "a charming quality that wins favour, a quality of benevolence that gives favour to inferiors, and a response of thankfulness to the favour given."[31] In the New Testament *charis* has a similar sharpened meaning of God's spontaneous, unmerited gift in Jesus Christ to sinful human beings for their salvation (Rom 3:24, 5:2.17). For Paul, even his vocation and his apostolic commission for the proclamation is a grace given to him (cf. Gal 1:15; 2:9; 1 Cor 3:10; 15:10; Rom 1:5; Eph 3:2.7.8). He uses the term as a *greeting* (Rom 16:20; 1 Cor 16:23), as *thanksgiving* (Rom 16:17; 2 Cor 8:16), as *power of God* (1 Cor 15:10), as unqualified, unconditional *gift of God* (Gal 2:11; 5:4), as *divine help* (2 Cor 8:1; 12:9; Phil 1:7), as *freedom of God* (Rom 3:23; Gal 2:17-21) with which God acts, as *election* (Rom 11:5), as *office* (Gal 1:15; 1 Cor 15:9), as *endowment for ministry* (Rom 12:3; 15:15; 1 Cor 3:10; Gal 2:9) and as *salvation* (Eph 2:1-10).[32] Of all these senses, the most fitting one for our context would grace understood as divine assistance or endowment for ministry.

6.   Other Warnings against Boasting

1 Cor 3:21-23 issues a warning against boasting about human leaders. In the context of 1 Cor 1-4, this proud boasting by declaring allegiance to individual leaders has caused a great division among them; therefore, they must stop boasting in the name of such leaders.

Again, in Rom 3:27-31, while explaining the universal significance of God's righteousness, Paul declares that both the Jews and the Gentiles are justified only through faith in Jesus; therefore, there is no reason for anybody to boast.

Further, in Rom 5:1-11 the theme of boasting occurs in v.2 (in hope) and in v.11 (in God). In v.2 the reason for boasting should be the hope in the Lord and not any efforts made by human beings. In 5:3-5 this boasting is also extended to tribulations. In fact, divine grace, which is the basis of Christian hope, is capable of giving confidence in the face of hardships, afflictions and troubles. In v.11 the reason for boasting is God himself.

7.   Summary of Findings

7.1. *From the Study on 2 Cor 12:9*

With its rejection of the boasting of the super apostles as illegitimate, with its rejection of some kind of esoteric knowledge which is granted only to a select few through which they could save themselves, with its rejection of any kind of privileged position for the apostles as spiritual elite who enjoy special privileges from the Lord and with its emphasis on the role and importance of divine grace in the life and ministry of not only of the ministers of the word but of every Christian who is in need of salvation, the whole text on 'fool's speech' contradicts the Pelagian rejection of grace as a requirement for human salvation and the Gnostic teachings on esoteric knowledge which is considered higher than faith and material world, and the Gnostic distinction between the transcendent God and the creator God.

With its emphasis on 'grace' 2 Cor 12:9 specifically denies the Gnostic teaching that humans are saved through some supernatural, secret knowledge. Indeed, Paul uses the term *gnosis* quite often in his epistles but not in the sense of the esoteric knowledge of the Gnostics, which was connected with some body of salvific knowledge acquired through initiation into magical sects. While the Gnostics considered *gnosis* as a *charisma* given by God and thought of it as 'illumination' or 'ecstatic or mystical vision' through which they become immortal, Paul's understanding of knowledge is neither secret nor reserved for a few initiates. According to him, "the secret and hidden wisdom of God" (1 Cor 2:7) is to be proclaimed to all (see Rom 1:14-16).

7.2. From Other Texts of Paul

There are also a number of texts in Paul similar to the one in 2 Cor 12:1-10 which actually refute the positions of Gnosticism and Pelagianism but which create the impression of adducing the teachings of these two systems. In the following we make only mention of such texts which naturally require further detailed study:

The antithesis between flesh and spirit in Gal 5:19-25 is used by Paul in the context of ethical exhortation and not in the gnostic mythologizing.

In 1 Cor 15:45-48 Paul identifies the spiritual Adam with the risen Jesus Christ. In gnostic mythology which exploits the Jewish interpretation of Gen 1-3 this spiritual Adam is considered to be the great Seth or the Immortal Human and only secondarily identified with Christ.

According to 1 Cor 15:35-50 resurrection includes bodily aspects. Contrary to this the *Treatise on Resurrection* from the Nag Hammadi Codex 1 argues that immortality is gained through the ascent of the mind to the divine. The cross and the material world are both illusory. The suffering in the Gospel is only that of the soul trapped in matter. When the soul lays aside what is corruptible, then it attains immortality.

Against the docetic understanding that Jesus is the revealer, 1 Tim 2:5, 3:16 and 2 Tim 2:8 stress Jesus' humanity. Against the elitism of the opponents, 1 Tim 2:4 extends salvation to all people.

Against the gnostic tendency to devalue the materialistic world, 1 Tim 5:23 (*take a little wine*), 1 Tim 2:9-10 (*women should dress themselves modestly and decently*) and 1 Tim 4:1-5 (*For everything created by God is good, and nothing is to be rejected*) affirm the value of this world.

While the Gnostics considered sexuality as the curse which the lower creator used to gain control over humankind, 1 Tim 2:15 alleges that the Christian woman can be saved through childbearing.

Col 2:16-23 rejects a number of practices coming from Jewish ritualism such as food rules (v.16; cf. Ezek 46:1-12; 2 Chr 8:13; 31:3) and from human teaching (vv.21-23). These rituals attached to some form of ascetic and visionary practice aimed at inducing the worshipper into the realm of angelic worship (v.18) in order to overcome the hold of the elemental spirits or the demonic rulers (*stoicheia*) over humanity.

8. Conclusion

The presentation of Jesus as heavenly redeemer, the anthropological terminology of the Pauline tradition that speaks of humans as trapped by the flesh and the Law of the creator god, expressions of realized eschatology that speak of the believer possessing eternal or ascending into heavenly realms and the dualism of light and dark, elect and unbelievers, those who belong to heaven and those who belong to this world—are all ideas similar to both gnostic philosophy as well as to the writings of Paul.[33] However, against all Gnostic faith, it must be stated that according to Paul Jesus is a redeemer who became a human being and gave his life as a sacrifice of redemption on the cross and that in Paul the flesh refers to one aspect or status of human beings and not a trap or prison. The knowledge possessed by believers is not something secret, but can be shared with other human beings as well, particularly the knowledge of salvation, which in turn becomes the content of Christian proclamation. The distinctions made by Paul between light and dark, elect and unbelievers, those who belong to heaven and those who belong to this world are not to be conceived on the basis of some inherent dualism between matter and spirit but as experiences of the conflictual situation of one and the same humanity in which every human being tries to move from one realm to another.

Endnotes

[1] J. J. Ziegler, Pope: Ancient heresy plagues modern Church: Today's Pelagians are convinced that 'salvation is the way I do things,' *OSV Newsweekly* (2.12.2014), accessed on 21.10.2017 from https://www.osv.com/OSVNewsweekly/Story/TabId/2672/ArtMID/13567/ArticleID/14079/Pope-Ancient-heresy-plagues-modern-Church.aspx.

[2] "The Myth of Neo-Pelagianism," *Catholic Sensibility* (15-11-2006), accessed on 05.03.2018 from https://catholicsensibility.wordpress.com/2006/11/15/the-myth-of-neo-pelagianism/

[3] *Catechism of the Catholic Church*, n. 406.

[4] J. J. Ziegler, ibid.

[5] Pheme Perkins, *Gnosticism and the New Testament* (Minneapolis: Fortress Press, 1993), 1. For a detailed discussion on whether Gnosticism has a pre-Christian or a post-Christian origin, see Edwin M. Yamauchi, *Pre-Christian Gnosticism: A Study of the Proposed Evidences* (London: Tyndale Press, 1973), 20-28.

[6] Willis Barnstone and Marvin Meyer (eds.), *The Gnostic Bible* (Boston & London: Shambhala, 2003).

[7] See Yamauchi, ibid., 13.

[8] When one understands Gnosticism in this way, namely as referring to the belief that salvation is by knowledge, then even Christian theologians like Clement of Alexandria and Origen, and Hellenistic Jews like Philo and pagan writers like Hermetists would be called Gnostics. See C. H. Dodd,

The Interpretation of the Fourth Gospel (Cambridge: Cambridge University Press, 1968), 97.

[9] See T. P. van Baaren, "Towards a Definition of Gnosticism," in *The Origins of Gnosticism: The Colloquium of Messina 12*, ed. U. Bianchi (Leiden: 1967), 178-180; Michael Allen Williams, *Rethinking Gnosticism: An Argument for Dismantling a Dubious Category* (New Jersey: Princeton University Press, 1996), 26.

[10] See Wilhelm Bousset, *Kyrios Christos: A History of the Belief in Christ from the Beginnings of Christianity to Irenaeus*, trans. J. E. Steely (Nashville: Abingdon, 1970), 254.

[11] See W Schmithals, *Paulus und die Gnostiker: Untersuchungen zu den kleinen Paulusbriefen* (1965).

[12] R. Bultmann, *Theology of the New Testament* I, trans. K. Grobel (New York: Charles Scribner's Sons, 1951).

[13] Those scholars who subscribe to this view include J. B. Lightfoot, W. G. Kümmel and G. Bornkamm. See Yamauchi, ibid., 44-46. According to them behind the so-called Colossian Error stand the heretical teaching Gnosticism, secret wisdom of syncretistic sort, Jewish ritualitsm and Jewish speculation about angels and the Iranian ideas.

[14] W. Lütgert, W. Bousset, R. Reitzenstein, F. C. Bauer and U. Wilckens are some of the famous authors who subscribe to this view. The most thoroughgoing study of this hypothesis has been done by W. Schmithals. See Walter Schmithals, *Die Gnosis in Korinth: Eine Untersuchung zu den Korintherbriefen* (Göttingen: Vandenhpek & Ruprecht, 1965). For more precise views of Schmithals on Gnostic influence on the *Pauline Corpus*, see W Schmithals, "The *Corpus Paulinum* and Gnosis," in *The New Testament and Gnosis: Essays in Honour of Robert Mc L. Wilson*, ed. A. H. B. Logan & A. J. M. Wedderburn (Edinburg: T & T Clark Limited, 1983), 107-124.

[15] See Jerry L Sumney, "Studying Paul's Opponents: Advances and Challenges," in *Paul and His Opponents*, ed. S. E. Porter (Leiden: Brill, 2005), 14.

[16] See Wolfgang Schrage, *Der erste Brief an die Korinther 1,1-6,11* (EKK VII/1, Zürich: 1991), 52.

[17] Now there are a number of indicators in the text 11:1-12:13 which qualify this text as a 'fool's speech.' In 11:1 Paul makes a request to 'bear' with him 'in a little foolishness' and in 12:11 he confesses saying 'I have been a fool.' Further similar acknowledgment is made also in 11:16 and in 11:21. In this section Paul tries to clarify to the Corinthians that those 'super apostles' who indulge in self-praise and boast about their own achievements speak like fools. In as much as Paul himself lists his achievements as an apostle, he too speaks like a fool.

[18] See Murray J Harris, *The Second Epistle to the Corinthians* (NIGTC, Grand Rapids: William B Eerdmans Publishing Company, 2005), 729-730.

[19] Ibid., 730.

[20] Due to the nature of scope of this article we are skipping a systematic analysis of the structure of the whole unit in order to make our study simple and easy to follow.

[21] *Prodiorthosis* or anticipatory correction and *epidiorthosis* are figures of thought used by Paul as a rhetoric technique when he feels he is about to give offence to the readers (2 Cor 11:1-4; 16-17.21) with the purpose of maintaining most sensitive contact with them. See F. Blass and A. Debrunner, *A Greek Grammar of the New Testament and Other Early Christian Literature*, trans. R.W. Fink (Chicago: University of Chicago Press, 1961), 262.

[22] W Schmithals identifies them as 'judaizing Gnostics.' See W. Schmithals, ibid., 107-113.

[23] See Murray J Harris, *The Second Epistle to the Corinthians*, 746-747; J Paul Sampley, *The Second Letter to the Corinthians* (NIB 11), CD ROM Edition.

[24] J. Paul Sampley, *The Second Letter to the Corinthians* (NIB 11).

[25] Alfred Plummer, *A Critical and Exegetical Commentary on the Second Epistle of Paul to the Corinthians* (ICC, Edinburg: T & T Clark, 1915), 316.

[26] Ibid, 317.

[27] See Murray J Harris, *The Second Epistle to the Corinthians*, 816.

[28] This "thorn in the flesh" has been interpreted differently by different people as a physical or moral handicap or as faith-crisis, etc.

[29] Gerhard Kittel, *arkeoo, arketos, autarkeia, autarkes* in TDNT I (1964), 466.

[30] See H. H. Esser, *charis*, in: NIDNTT 2, 115; Gordon D. Fee, *Gifts of the Spirit*, in: DPL, 340; Ralph P. Martin, Gifts, Spiritual, in: ABD 2, 1016.

[31] L. B. Smedes, Grace, in: ISBE 2, 548.

[32] Luke Ndubuisi, *Paul's Concept of Charisma in 1 Corinthians 12* (Frankfurt am Main: Peter Lang, 2003), 24-30.

[33] Pheme Perkins, *Gnosticism and the New Testament*, 11-12.

Grace is God's Ennobling and Enabling Gift to You and Me

Joseph Mattam, SJ

Introduction: The Centrality and Ambiguity of Grace

Hardly anyone would deny that the word 'grace' is very central in Christian experience, theology and spirituality, as it touches every aspect of life. Words like 'grace' and 'life of grace' are so very central to Christian theology that, Fransen opines: "no Christian doctrine has met with so many heresies as the doctrine of grace, and this from the fourth century, the time of Pelagius, up to our own days."[1] Starting from the Council of Carthage in 418, various Councils and Popes have spoken on this theme. Moreover, the Reformation with its emphasis on *sola gratia* (only grace) is very closely linked to an understanding of grace. An understanding of mission and salvation, too, is closely related to a concept of grace, since it is assumed that it is in and through the sacraments, especially baptism, that God imparts God's graces. The absolute necessity of preaching the good news to bring people to baptism and salvation was generally accepted by all. In spite of its centrality, no concept is more ambiguous than the idea of grace. Once I asked a group of students what grace meant to them. The answers varied so much, that at the end no one was clear what grace was. This ambiguity is primarily due to, (a) an extrinsic orientation we imbibe in thinking that grace pours down 'from above', and, (b) a dualistic thinking which characterized the 'standard' theology of grace for centuries. Let us reflect upon some ideas we have about grace.

1.   The 'Standard' Theology of Grace

The 'standard' theology of grace may be caricatured in the following way. God is up and out there 'in heaven', who, in answer to our prayers, sacrifices and sacraments, sends us grace, help and strength. More than that, there is a continuous link initiated by baptism. With baptism we have sort of a 'pipeline' relation to God, which is called 'sanctifying grace', a permanent relationship which can be ruptured by mortal sins or clogged by venial sins but can be repaired or unclogged by confession. Other sacraments help to preserve the pipeline intact and the flow of grace is assured. Acts of mercy, charity, sacraments, sacrifices, fasting, etc., increase grace, just as mortal or venial sins lead to either a total loss or a decrease in grace. The 'state of grace' was attached to certain vocations in the Church, like Marriage and Orders, which was more like a supplementary pipeline, which enabled those in that state to fulfill the 'duties' of their state. Hence, our liturgical and other prayers are full of expressions like, "God, give us your grace, give us the grace to..., shower your grace upon us ... Let us pray for the grace...." and the like. The Church is the repository of all graces—almost like a grace bank.

Though the above is a caricature, I think most people would agree that, in spite of its centrality, the word grace is ambiguous and needs clarification. Hence, I suggest that a fresh look at this central concept and experience is necessary. I shall approach it from human experience and the biblical witness and propose a concept of grace.

2.   Human Experience as Starting-Point for a New Understanding

The basic assumption behind this approach is that the divine is in the human, which is what the Incarnation affirms. Hence, to understand divine realities we have to approach them through the human. In our experience of true friendship—loving and being loved, forgiving and being forgiven, giving and receiving of gifts, helping to build up communities of love and service—we find that something new happens; a change, a transformation takes place; relationship is deepened and strengthened. Something similar happens in helping to face sickness, handicaps, calamities of one type or another, efforts at liberating people and working for justice. These experiences lead people to growth, freedom and wholeness. The story of Zacchaeus in Lk 19:1-10 illustrates this point very well. Zacchaeus seems to be an underdeveloped person ('dwarf'), unloved and despised by many, who seemingly lives for self alone, unjustly accumulating wealth. With the entry of Jesus into his life, he becomes a totally new person with new values and attitudes. He becomes a just, caring and sharing person. He is transformed and 'saved'. Such experiences are common to all people, irrespective of religion, gender, caste and so on.

When we look into and around us we are overwhelmed by the abundance of all 'gifts' lavished upon us, from all sides, from the moment we come into the world. Our day-to-day life is surrounded by gifts that have been given, unasked. Our own life, parents, brothers, sisters, relatives, friends; the sun, the moon, the stars, the air we breathe, water, space, trees, plants, flowers, fruits, grains; birds and other animals; people who do us various services; our culture, language, art, music, science and its contributions, literature; the Christ, the Spirit, the Church, the sacraments; the beautiful earth with all its rich possibilities and blessings—all these and much more have been given to us, unasked. In comparison to these, what is supposedly received by asking is insignificant. Most importantly, all these gifts are given unasked, to everyone irrespective of religion, caste, race, gender and nationality. Above all, is the birthday gift of birth—the totally unasked and yet the most important and precious gift each one receives. So is the gift of the 'heart', the meeting point between God and the creature.

3.   Biblical Background

The Hebrew terms like *gedulah* (greatness, honour, dignity), *hen* (favour), *tobh* (goodness, favour), *roham* (sympathy), *rason* (affection, favour) are rendered in Greek by the word *charis*. *Charis* means a disposition of goodwill, favour, graciousness, charm. Hence, in the First Testament, God's attitude to people is expressed through the word *heleos*, with an overtone of something undeserved and gratuitous. In the Second Testament, *charis* denotes God's attitude of loving kindness towards people who are sinners, God's redemptive favour or mercy. The term is predominantly Pauline. It expresses God's goodwill, benevolence, and eternal plan of salvation—in one word, God's *Love*, actualized and manifested in Jesus Christ, operative through the Spirit. Hence, Paul summarizes his thought: "The grace of the Lord Jesus Christ, the love of God and the fellowship of the Holy Spirit be with you all" (2 Cor 13:13). For, the saving action of God is attributed to God's love. "For God so loved the world that he gave his only Son" (Jn 3:16; See also Rom 5:8; 2 Cor 5:18-19). Hence, in 2 Cor 13:13, Paul is talking about the saving love of God, which is effected and manifested in Jesus who is God's grace, which is continued to be experienced in the fellowship of the Spirit in the community.

The Second Testament also speaks of this saving relationship of God as divine indwelling, our divinization, salvation, redemption, justification and expiation (Rom 3:25). From our side, it is expressed as being sons and daughters of God, temples of the Spirit, the Body of Christ, divinized existence, Spirit-led life, graced life and so on. The Second Testament affirms that we have a personal relation to the Father, Son and Spirit, that is, we are daughters and sons of the Father, sisters and brothers of Jesus, and temples of the Spirit, leading us to a life of faith, hope and love.

4.   A Preliminary Definition of Grace

In the light of our reflection on our human experience, and on the basis of what we see in the Bible, we may define grace as God's ennobling and enabling gift to humanity—the *ennobling and enabling love of God* raising 'us' from nothingness (we did not exist before this ennobling) to the level of God as God's sons/daughters, enabling us to love, forgive, care as God does. The human and the divine are inseparable: the divine in the human, as revealed in Jesus. All that enhances this life,

freedom, wholeness, truth, beauty, justice, brotherhood, sharing—all
this is grace; all that diminishes these are un-grace. Hence grace is
not seen as something sporadic, but the ennobling and enabling love
of God, manifested in creation, in the making of the covenant, in
the life and death of Jesus, in the community of believers and in all
human beings, as their love-ability, their power of love. This is not
just divine life in itself. God the giver, God's continual giving, we the
'recipients', our 'receiving' and the newness that is resulted from the
giving and receiving—all this is what we call grace.

While all would agree that it is God's love that is at the source of
our existence and of our salvation, when does this self-gift of God as
love take place in our lives? The classical Catholic position is that it is
communicated in baptism, making us God's sons/daughters, relegating
the existential human reality to the background. This would mean
that the non-baptized are *essentially different human beings* as they are not
God's sons/daughters. This obviously does not make sense. The saving
love of God, spoken of in the NT as grace, is the source of creation,
and hence grace comes not primarily from baptism and sacraments,
but is a foundational reality, in the lives of everyone in history. This
self-communication of God is already given in creation. That is the
foundational self-giving of God; this cannot be pushed aside as some
imaginary "natural order." That is the grace, the primary grace, which
is empowered to receive further self-communication of God.

Pelagius (d.ca. 420) was a pious British monk who taught in Rome.
He claimed that humans can discipline themselves so effectively that
they could be saved by their own free will; he seemed to deny the
need of any divine grace. He affirmed the goodness of human nature.
Human nature is good and is capable of doing good. He spoke of the
existential reality of humans as they are. The essence of the heresy of
Pelagius is an emphasis on *the primacy of human effort* in salvation, with
divine grace providing mere assistance to what humans are capable of
accomplishing on their own, as if their nature were not wounded by
Original Sin. The problem with Pelagius was that he did not attribute
this goodness to the gift of creation. Humans are good because they

are sharers in God's life. This goodness is a free gift; it is not due to the human nature in itself but because of who they are as created by God as sharers in God's life.

In his Apostolic Exhortation *Evangelii Gaudium,* n.94, Pope Francis accuses overly tradition-minded Catholics of exhibiting the "self-absorbed promethean neo-pelagianism of those who ultimately trust only their own powers and feel superior to others because they observe certain rules or remain intransigently faithful to a particular Catholic style from the past." Who are the real "self-absorbed promethean neo-Pelagians"? They are those who look with contempt on what the Church has provided in her traditions, who think they can do better by their own lights, which they vainly imagine are 'the Spirit'. The Church is in the grip of a form of neo-pelagianism on the part of those who think they can outdo the Holy Spirit with endless human projects for 'ecclesial renewal'.

If creation is not considered as God's self-giving, then God remains an outsider intruding into the freedom of the creatures, leading to the classical unsolvable opposition between grace and freedom. If, however, creation itself is seen as God's primary and fundamental self-giving, which affirms the transcendence of God on the one hand, and the immanence of God in creation as the ongoing sustaining power and source of life, on the other, then grace will not be some extrinsic intruder into the human, but the very core reality of every person. Hence, I shall reflect briefly on creation as the foundation for understanding grace.

4.1. Creation is Grace

The Bible affirms that everything ('heaven and earth') comes from the Word of God. Our Credo begins with an affirmation of our faith in God, the Creator of all. The Bible in its present form begins with the story of creation, and John and Paul give importance to it. However, Christian theology has not given much importance to this truth of our faith. One of the major failures of Catholic theology has been its neglect of creation, relegating it to the periphery, considering it as inferior to the so-called 'supernatural order'. This has had disastrous consequences for theology and spirituality. Since God is spoken of as a potter (see Isa 64:8; Jer 18) emphasizing the total dependence of creation on the creator and God's freedom in creating, normally one talks of creation as *making* something. A carpenter makes a table but it has no future except to be in that way. If creation is an act of love, then it cannot be spoken of in terms of making the ready-made. Perhaps the example or image that can help us to grasp creation best is the image of an educator. A teacher of mathematics, for example, shares with a child something of what she is (as mathematician) and the child in its turn becomes a knower of mathematics and can grow to be like the teacher. The teacher has started another centre of mathematics, without herself ceasing to be a mathematician. The seed of knowledge she imparts becomes a seed of growth in the pupil.

We may now apply this example of the educator to creation. God, we say, is love, freedom and creator. This is what God shares; God shares God's life, love-ability, creative power and freedom—that is what we are. God starts other centres of love, freedom and creativity. God expresses self in God's creation. The problem with the past understanding was that we used to say "God *gives us* life, God shares God's life *with us*," as if we were there to receive this gift. This is not accurate, as it affirmed our existence independently of God's self-gift. Then God's life was seen as an added something. God is not sharing something "with us" as we do not exist before God shares; we come into being only through God's sharing, the self-giving of God—we are what God shares, gives, not that God gives us something—we *are* God's gift.[2] We come into being only by God's sharing.

Only love is truly creative. That is to say, God does not make something when God creates, but shares God's life, God 'exists contagiously', so to say. Creation is the burning contagion of existence. God's creation can be compared to a tree giving itself in the seed. The seed is the potentiality the tree shares—the seed is precisely this potentiality to grow into the likeness of the tree. In the same way God shares God's love-ability, freedom and creative power. Creation, then, is this shared existence, participation in God's life, power of loving, creating. The capacity of the shared existence is precisely to grow unto the likeness of the original sharer—as a student becomes like the teacher, as a seed grows into a tree. The God-ward growth is our very nature, given to us with the breath that keeps us alive. Since we are created in the image of God the creator what God creates are creators. We are creators of ourselves, of our world and our history. The creature's way of being a creator is in total dependence on the creator. It is through total dependence on God that we are, and we become creators of ourselves and of the world.

A God of love who creates by sharing God's love-ability does not manipulate the God-given love. God does not force or coerce the created love, but respects our freedom to love, to build up or destroy ourselves. In sharing God's power of love and creativity, God risks seeing creation turning away from God and thus destroying itself. A love that is creative and which respects the other's freedom cannot but be a suffering love. This is the mystery of compassionate love. The world as we have it today is not a matter of God 'allowing' or 'not allowing' it to be such. If God has created creators who may not be coerced into something they do not want to be and to do, then it is 'natural' for the world to be what humankind makes it.

Creation is a matter of relationship. It is like the relation of a stream to the fountain and of the rays to the sun. By creating, God establishes a relation with the world. God brings into existence. From the part of creation, it is a relation of total dependence, not just for certain things and at certain times. Often the language we use betrays a mentality of partial or part-time dependence, as if God and we were equal partners, like two bulls pulling a cart, each contributing half. But in fact, God and we are hundred percent agents, the earthly depending totally on the divine for its very existence. It is a foundational dependence. Hence, they are not of the same order. As this is the dependence of those who are sharers in God's own power of creativity and love-ability, this makes them totally responsible for themselves and their world.

Human beings are from the earth and from the breath of God—there is continuity and otherness between the earth and the divine. Humans are the earth, but more than the earth; they are divine but not divine as God is, for they are absolutely from God and hence totally dependent on God. But at the same time, one cannot deny the divinity of human beings.

4.2. A Further Definition of Grace

In the light of the above reflections, now we may define grace as the self-gift of God, as *the love-ability which constitutes our being as creatures and children of God*. Grace means God has always loved us, God has given God-self to us, and God's saving will in our favour and all God's gifts. God loves us is a fundamental assertion of theology and spirituality. When we say that God loves us, does it not refer primarily to God's self-gift, sharing God's life, love-ability, creative power, freedom, etc? The most important expression of this truth, "God loves us" is our love-ability, which is a share in God's love. It is God's relation to us as our source, like a fountain and the stream. God loves us means above all that we are persons capable of loving and being compassionate like God (Mt 5:43-48; Jn 14:12; 15:12; Mt 6:12,14; Lk 6:32-36). This 'love-ability', we may say, is the very dynamic divine presence within us, is the deepest reality of ourselves, the very mystery of ourselves.

This love-ability, which I speak of, is not some psychological feeling or changing sentiments, but the very reality of our being humans—this is what God shares when God creates us. This love-ability is God's gift and our task; as the great Indian poet Tagore says: "My songs are the same as the spring flowers, they come from you. Yet I bring them to you as my own. You smile and accept them, and you are glad at my joy of pride." So too, while the source continues to be God and its actualization is thanks to its own inner power, yet when I do love, it is *I* who loves, or it is *I* who refuses to love. Hence, grace is not some extrinsic reality imposing itself on us, but our very true self, as love-ability manifesting itself in bearing fruit in love, forgiveness, concern, sharing, caring and building up.

This is another way of speaking about the indwelling of God in us. When we speak of God dwelling in us, the Father, Son and Spirit are not in us as an object in a container, like water in a tumbler, but they are the very depth dimension of our being and life, and since God is love, the pre-eminent expression of that presence is our love-ability. God is not outside us giving grace every now and then, but God lives in us, empowering us to love as God loves, but without forcing us. We do not get graces; we are grace, we are through and through graced beings.

Grace refers primarily to a relationship and not to something, not a heavenly insurance or banking system. Precisely because it is a relationship founded on our love-ability that it ennobles us, makes us sons and daughters of God, temples of the Spirit, carriers of God, the body of Christ and givers of the Spirit. It challenges us to live Spirit-filled lives, led by the Spirit as Jesus was. In Jesus we see this love-ability fully lived out. He loved, not according to the world, but loved all, even when he opposed their actions. (Jn 8:11, Lk 7:35ff). His table-fellowship with the outcasts, prostitutes, adulterers, women, tax collectors and sinners of society is the expression of his universal, unlimited love-ability that we all possess, or rather, that we are. The structure and content of grace is revealed in Jesus: God's love-ability shared, to be actualised in our loving even the unlovable, the enemy, those who do harm to us. On the Cross Jesus revealed this love even to the end.

Are we justified in reducing the rich biblical tradition to just the gift of 'love-ability'? I do not claim that the definition given above is an exhaustive description of the reality of grace. Grace is God's continual ever mysterious ways of reaching out to us in and through all created realities, in the secret of our hearts, through joys and sorrows, calamities, celebrations, etc. There are myriad ways in which God's loving presence in us is revealed, but the most eminent way in which it is manifested in each one is as our love-ability. I aver that the Bible is talking of the love of God in its various contexts: in relation to humanity that had ceased to live in love, to sinners the love of God is forgiveness and reconciliation. Talking to the unfaithful Jewish people, expecting God's salvation, it is spoken of as redemption and salvation. God's love is unconditional. Going back to our earlier reflection on forgiveness, gift-giving, etc., we discover that the greatest gift of God to each one is the gift of the self; the gift of the 'heart', which I have called 'love-ability'.

I believe that we have yet to understand the meaning of "love one another as I have loved you," which is the way God loves unconditionally as explained in Mt 5:43-48. Since perhaps we have not experienced the meaning of true love, we think of grace as something other. The presence of God in us, which the NT attests to, clearly means, in my way of seeing it, the empowering of us to love as God loves. We have yet to discover the miraculous power of true love; hence we imagine God intervening every now and then bringing healing to some, etc. But these supposed interventions of God have to be situated in a wider context of the world with big problems and millions of people in whose lives God has not apparently intervened specially to solve their problems.[3] It is important that we recognize each one of us as grace of God to one another, as vehicles of God's love.

Given this description of grace, how do we look at the sacraments as source of grace, and what is the relation between grace and salvation?

5. Grace and the Sacraments

Sacraments are symbolic actions of the community, actualization of what the Church is as a worshipping community. These celebrations symbolize God's saving love precisely in our human response to that love: in our acceptance and forgiveness of each other, in our concern and care for one another, in our being for and with one another. These attitudes actualize our love-ability. Hence sacraments by creating awareness and by celebrating 'increase' grace. God's love is a constant, but it reaches us through human hearts and hands. Hence the human response to this saving love, expressed in the acceptance, forgiveness, promise to care for a newcomer to the community, mutual forgiveness, concern for the community, mutual trust and surrender—all of which are manifestations of love. For example, in the sacrament of the sick, the care for the well-being of the sick person, the desire to have him/her in good health, and all that one does towards this end form the symbol of God's saving love. In every sacrament there is a human dimension calling for trust, respect, acceptance, forgiveness, care, concern and love.

6.   Grace and Salvation

I do not deny at all that salvation is God's gift to us, as is clearly mentioned in the following and other similar passages of the Bible: Rom 3:21ff; 11:5-6; Eph 3:21ff; Jn 15:1ff. I suggest that we need to understand salvation from the way Jesus spoke about it. He told Zacchaeus that "today salvation has come to this house" (Lk 19:9) because Zacchaeus had changed his pattern of relationship. Instead of living for self and for money, he opened his heart and purse and shared his wealth with the needy; he decided to be honest and just in his dealings with people. A similar picture emerges in Mt 25:31ff – when people cared for the needy, met the needs of the needy people, Jesus said they were saved. They had not performed any specifically religious acts.

For Jesus, salvation did not seem to be a matter of saving one's soul for a life after death nor even a matter of religion, nor religious practices, but a matter of proper relationships. Jesus did not seem to think of salvation as something we 'get' from God through any agents or religions, but what we become through our loving, our caring for the needy brothers and sisters, in response to God's love in our hearts. In other words, salvation is actualizing our love-ability, the gift of grace.

Therefore, based on Jesus' way of speaking, salvation is freedom from internal and external constraints like greed, ambition, lust, hatred, fear, attachment, legalism and ritualism, and freedom for loving, building up communities of love, which in our present sinful world would mean opposing injustice and working for justice. Hence, salvation is having the proper relationship to God as our loving Father/Mother, to one another as brothers and sisters, and to the earth as something not to be hoarded for self but to be shared with all God's children. See also Mt 5:23-24—the proper interpersonal relationship is prior to, and more important than offering sacrifices.

7.   Conclusion: Grace enables us to be Co-workers with God

What Jesus says makes eminent sense: "the truth will make you free;" truth, not truths (Jn 8.32). The saving truth is God's love as the ground, foundation of our life, the ennobling and enabling self-gift of God, in us as our love-ability. The Holy Spirit, the bond of love in the Mystery is the source of our own love-ability. Once seen as this power of love, then no one is in a privileged position—God has no favourites. A theology of creation affirming our inter-dependence and inter-relatedness and our radical dependence on God makes us co-workers with God for the building up of a new social order, with all God's children, whatever be their religion, race or gender.

Endnotes

[1] Peter F. Fransen, "Treatise of Grace," in *Hermeneutics of the Councils and Other Studies*, ed. H.E. Mertens and F. de Graeve (Leuven: Leuven University Press,1985). My views on grace are partly influenced by Fransen.

[2] Fransen says, "What we receive from God, we do not exactly possess, but we are it", "in God *we are* what we receive." The receiver is the gift, we are not *given something*, but *we are the given*, given to ourselves: we are grace. Fransen, ibid., 460.

[3] Joseph Mattam, "Honest to God: Moving towards an Adult Faith/ Christianity," *Indian Theological Studies* 44/3 (2007): 275-290.

Formation of Conscience as the Core of Christian Ethics

Paulachan Kochappilly, CMI

Understanding the ethos sets the ethical horizon of a community. The Liturgy of the Church is a blueprint of Christian ethos, as this text from the liturgy of the Eucharist indicates:

> O Christ, Our Lord! Enlighten us in Your laws, inflame our minds with Your knowledge, and sanctify our souls with Your truth so that we may be faithful to Your words and obedient to Your commandments.[1]

The above prayer offers the celebrants a horizon of the Way of the Lord. To walk the Way of the Lord, the celebrants implore Christ to enlighten them in the laws, to inflame their minds with the knowledge, to sanctify their souls with the truth of the Lord, to always to be faithful to the words and obedient to the commandments of the Lord. The scene is rightly set and direct: people would like to walk the Way of the Lord rather than their own way and such a walk is envisaged by the grace of the Lord. This prayer directs our attention to the process and phenomenon of the formation of conscience, the core of Christian ethics. As the programme of Christian life, so also the formation of conscience is an ongoing dialogue, involving an enlightenment of the mind with the laws and knowledge of God and the sanctification of the hearts through the truth of the Lord. Evidently, the walking the Way of the Lord and the formation of one's conscience have a common ground and goal: the celebration of life in Christ guided by the grace and wisdom of God. Living true to one's conscience is becoming more and more demanding. These days the discussion of freedom of choice and responsibility is gaining more attention than ever before.

Often on the basis of the majority, laws—national and international—are legislated, without paying sufficient attention to the truth and goodness of the reality and the relationships in question. As a result, ethical issues are sidelined, if not ignored, in political decision-making bodies. An overall liberal approach to personal, familial, and religious matters is the sign of the times. These fundamental areas of human and societal life drop their significance in the public arena and are considered to be matters for one's private life.

We live in a world marked by lawlessness with different forces at work. On the one hand we see the bulldozing legal and political systems that silence differences and dissent, and on the other, the judicial system that strongly sides political, powerful and influential giants, leading to logical conclusions. In such a conflicting context, what is the way forward? How to go about reinventing and restoring a sense of purpose and harmony? Though the ambience seems a little gloomy, there is a ray of hope for the future, if we take it as a privileged moment to embrace the challenge to form right consciences that comply with the ethical precepts and moral obligations springing from the wellspring of fundamental principles of life and its flourishing. So, the formation of conscience is the way forward amidst the encircling confusions and conflicting situations.

The future is secure and prosperous in the hands of people who take the trouble to form their conscience in line with objective norms of morality, that is, with the truth, goodness and beauty of life. In this journey, the Church has a responsibility to help the faithful discover the laws written by God and to listen to God's voice echoing in the abyss of one's heart. Since Jesus is the author and splendor of truth, in his encyclical *Veritatis Splendor* John Paul II exhorted the faithful "to turn to Christ" for finding answers to moral questions of our times. The urgent need of our day is to encounter Christ, "the Way, the Truth and the Life," who sets the path for moral imagination, orientation and action. In what follows, we shall have a brief discussion on some of the important aspects and areas of conscience formation, which can take us forward on the path of human dignity and solidarity towards the human flourishing within the ambit of divine design.

1.   Conscience as the Creative Response to the Context

Conscience is the inner voice echoing in the depths of one's being, which, "ever calling one to love and to do what is good and to avoid evil, tells one inwardly at the right moment: do this, shun that."[2] It is the law written on the human heart by God, and "in a wonderful way, that law is made known which is fulfilled in the love of God and of one's neighbour."[3] Conscience, whether it is the voice or the law in the heart of a person, responds to the contextual realities and demands. In its interaction with the context—person, thought, word or act—conscience passes judgment and directs the person to do good and avoid evil. Dialogue is the soul of conscience. Conscience sees, knows, and judges events and moments—as heart speaks to heart—in a concrete, real, and particular context. In fact, conscience may be seen as a creative and critical response to the changes and challenges a person has to confront in life. There is an engagement and involvement of a pure heart—which sees God—in perceiving the will of God for the world and for the welfare of all, resulting in the walking of the way of the Lord for the glory of God, for peace on earth, and to give hope to human beings.

Vatican Council II (hereafter VC II) envisages and exhorts the necessity of a response to the current developments and challenges, "Through loyalty to conscience Christians are joined to other men (*sic*) in the search for truth and for the right solution to so many moral problems which arise in the life of individuals from social relationships."[4] In the process of arriving at the right solution to the encircling moral problems of our times, it is vital to be aware of the fact that all of us are seekers—fellow wayfarers—of truth. The assurance of the Lord, "the truth will make you free" (Jn 8:32), should guide our steps in finding solutions, certainly, under the guidance of the Spirit and in faithfulness to reality. This sets the scene of a call and response, which may be both creative and critical. Reality invites us to relationality—a call to be related and integrated—and morality is a response to this reality on the foundation of relationality. There is a well-knit connectivity established among the areas of reality, relationality and morality. Morality is not something imposed from outside, but it is established on account of the reality and its relationality, which is searched for and nurtured by human reason, an endowment of the divine in the human. In fact, it is conscience—the subjective norm of morality—that listens to the silent and vibrant voices that echo in the depth of our beings and enables us to accept or reject them in light of the truth, goodness, and beauty enshrined in the law of Christ and in accordance with the teachings of the Church. Obviously, there is a search one undertakes, and there is a stand one takes in and for truth at the end of the journey, which is a creative response to the concrete and contextual needs and demands.

Conscience in-conversation with the reality—thought-word-act of the agent—communicates its verdict on the matter for moral perusal. Theoretically speaking, it is the objective norm – moral law – that governs ethical decision-making; practically and concretely speaking, it is the conscience which appropriates the moral law and makes alignments necessary and acts accordingly in particular cases. An act proceeding from necessary knowledge and performed in the context of freedom is worthy of moral scrutiny. Truth and freedom have a beautiful blending in the moral agent. This integration happens in the heart of a person, where God and person are mutually present and the human person is enlightened and empowered to make a right decision. Interaction of the agent with the reality – both internal and external – takes place, and conscience responds fittingly to the various urgencies of the context. Conscience consciously and creatively engages with the challenges of the situation and comes forth freely and faithfully in matters of moral issues, provided the conscience is in congruence with the objective standards of moral life.

1.1. Conscience as the Sanctuary of the Human Being

VC II characterizes conscience beautifully as "man's (*sic*) most secret core, and his sanctuary. There he is alone with God whose voice echoes in his depths."[5] Conscience is sacred, for it is one with God, who is holy, and conscience is secret, for no one can know what is transpiring in the cave of the heart, except the agent and God. *Veritatis Splendor* exalts conscience, "The relationship between man's freedom and God's law is most deeply lived out in the 'heart' of the person, in his conscience."[6] The Lord God says, "I will put my law within them, and I will write it on their hearts" (Jer 31:33). The Book of Ezekiel says: "A new heart I will give you, and a new spirit I will put within you; and I will remove from your body the heart of stone and give you a heart of flesh. I will put my spirit within you, and make you follow my statutes and be careful to observe my ordinances" (Ezek 36:26-27). So, God's spirit is within everyone and one needs simply to follow the promptings of God's spirit. Referring to people of other faiths, St Paul observes, "They show that what the law requires is written on their hearts, to which their own conscience also bears witness" (Rom 2:15). These classical passages on conscience speak of its sacredness and the reason for its holiness. God who is holy is the author of the law written on the human heart, or the voice that echoes in the depths of the human being.

Sanctuaries are considered to be holy places where people may go to encounter God, for these are special abodes of God. In a similar way, a person, as a result of one's pilgrimage, may encounter the Lord God in the sanctuary of the heart where God dwells. In one's heart, one encounters God, knows the law, and judges matters in the presence of God and the divine law. The prayer of the Holy Qurbana, prior to the proclamation of the Gospel, alludes to this wonderful phenomenon, "Christ, Our Lord! Enlighten us in Your laws, inflame our minds with Your knowledge, and sanctify our souls with Your truth so that we may be faithful to Your words and obedient to

Your commandments."[7] Sanctification of the heart happens through the word and the truth of the Lord. And the heart is cleansed and the conscience is purified and made holy. *As the being, so the behavior.* Christian morality is in "following Christ"[8] which is nothing short of Christian spirituality, the essence of which is following one's right conscience, well informed by the gospel of Jesus and conformed to the likeness of Christ.

1.2. *Conscience as the Creative Response to Reality*

Conscience responds to reality creatively simply because its response springs from the spirit of the law of the Lord. The morality of a person shines in and through the creative and responsible response of one's conscience to the demands of reality. Being in live connectivity with the abiding presence of the Lord, conscience acts faithfully, truthfully, and freely. Jesus illuminates this liberty marvelously in his teaching on "love your enemies" (Mt 5:44). Moved by his faithfulness to his Father, and being conscious of his mission as the Messiah, Jesus taught a profound new truth, in this case, love for one's enemies, which brought in a new era of freedom and newness. We notice the same newness in the teaching of Jesus on the Sabbath, "The Sabbath was made for humankind and not humankind for the Sabbath" (Mk 2:27). This mindset of Jesus comes to the fore when he defends the act of his disciples, "Have you not read what David did when he and his companions were hungry? He entered the house of God and ate the bread of the Presence, which it was not lawful for him or his companions to eat, but only for the priests. Or have you not read in the law that on the Sabbath the priests in the temple break the Sabbath and yet are guiltless?" (Mt 12:5-6). Jesus seems to be revolutionary in this context. He was taking the risk of revealing the will and the way of God in his creative response to the context—through a slight twist to the tradition-bound practices. Though such a decision invited life-threatening consequences, it was carried out faithfully in view of fulfilling the will of God. Similar situations and questions arise in the minds of the people following Christ today. A person in communion with God will address such difficult questions and circumstances humbly and firmly, bearing witness to a right conscience, which "on the day when, according to my gospel, God, through Jesus Christ, will judge the secret thoughts of all" (Rom 2:16).

Jesus challenged the rigid interpretation of the law, without compromising with the spirit of the law of the time. He was creative, innovative, and liberative in interpreting the otherwise static and archaic laws. In his new teaching, he did not undermine the law, but at the same time, he made a breakthrough in its practice, always demanding a deeper, broader, and higher application of the law, whereby exhibiting a creative response to a challenging and changing context. The moral law assumes its dynamic and creative nature through the operation of one's conscience when it acts in alignment with the latter. That is, conscience in communion with the Lord – the author of the moral law – passes true, good, and beautiful discernment and a corresponding decision on contemporary realities.

1.3. Conscience as the Character of Human Beings

Conscience, imbued with God's Spirit, decides to follow the Lord in all things and everywhere. A conscience formed after the mind of Christ and in the law of Christ will reveal its mettle through its moral imagination, vision, and action. As the face is the mirror of the heart of a person, so the actions speak of the values and virtues of a person well-tuned by a finely formed conscience. The character of a person is accessible and credible through one's practical and concrete acts. Conscience decides what to do and what not to do. Hence, the discernment is made in the conscience in light of the law of the Lord, and, if need be, against the signs of the time.

VC II attaches great significance to conscience, "His dignity lies in observing this law, and by it he will be judged."[9] St Paul indicated this truth in his letter, "their conflicting thoughts will accuse or perhaps excuse them" (Rom 2:15-16). Jesus taught, "The good person out of the good treasure of the heart produces good, and the evil person out of evil treasure produces evil; for it is out the abundance of the heart that the mouth speaks" (Lk 6:45). The role of conscience in contributing to one's character is further reiterated in the *Catechism of the Catholic Church,*

> The dignity of the human person implies and requires uprightness of moral conscience. Conscience includes the perception of the principles of morality (*synderisis*), their application in the given circumstances by practical discernment of reasons and goods; and finally, judgment about concrete acts yet to be performed or already performed.[10]

One's character depends on one's prudent judgment of conscience.[11] Formation of conscience, thus, is fundamental in discerning God's will in each situation. With regard to the formation of conscience, the teaching is clear: "The Word of God is the light for our path; we must assimilate it in faith and prayer and put it into practice."[12] Above all, being in communion with God, the character of the disciple is shaped. John Henry Cardinal Newman presents a beautiful image: "Conscience is a messenger of him, who, both in nature and in grace, speaks to us behind a veil, and teaches and rules us by his representatives. Conscience is the aboriginal Vicar of Christ."[13]

2.   Conscience as the Core of Christian Ethics

Christian ethics is in the following of Christ.[14] Following Christ does not mean "an outward imitation, since it touches man at the very depths of his being. Being a follower of Christ means *becoming conformed to him* who became a servant even to giving himself on the Cross (cf. Phil 2:5-8)."[15] Christian ethics, seen from this perspective, requires and enables people to be conformed to Christ or transformed into the image of God as revealed in Christ and supported by human reason.[16] In other words, the goal of Christian ethics is to have the transformation of one's life in Christ through the grace of the Holy Spirit. Christian ethics supports and promotes people to celebrate their life in Christ in the context of the given community. In this process of supporting and promoting the members of the Christian community to live a life in Christ, there is the need to examine revelation enlightened by human reason. John Paul II describes moral theology as "a science which accepts and examines Divine Revelation while at the same time responding to the demands of human reason."[17] No doubt, Christian ethics is in following Christ; but it is not a blind following. Instead – being conformed to Christ – must be undertaken within the framework of human reason, the divine endowment of the human being. So proper scrutiny of the perspectives of the journey is a must and it should be carried out in the light of human reason. Providentially, revelation and reason meet in conscience: the human being, the image of God endowed with reason, encounters the Lord of revelation in the cave of the heart. Such an encounter helps the person to follow Christ faithfully, truthfully, and freely and in conformity with the objective standards of morality.

Conscience is the core of Christian ethics; for there is nothing moral in a person without being referred to or discovered by conscience. *Amoris Laetitia* invites us "to form consciences, not to replace them."[18] Both the subjective and objective norms of morality work in people's hearts; conformity between the two is envisaged in conscience. The Apostolic Exhortation recognizes the responses of the faithful in their valid discernment, "who very often respond as best they can to the Gospel amid their limitation and are capable of carrying out their own discernment in complex situations."[19] Conscience is decisive in discerning God's will and deciding on the true, good and beautiful. "The judgment of conscience states 'in an ultimate way' whether a certain kind of behavior is in conformity with the law; it formulates the proximate norm of the morality of a voluntary act, 'applying the objective law to a particular case'."[20]

2.1. *Conscience as the Subjective Norm of Morality*

While moral law is understood as the objective norm, conscience is the subjective norm of morality. Conscience discovers the law written on the heart by God. God being the author of both the moral law and the law written on one's heart, there should be no conflict or confusion, but a perfect agreement between the objective and subjective norms of morality. This is the ideal for human beings. However, due to various reasons, persons have different perceptions regarding right and wrong, good and evil. St Paul assures justification to all those who obey the promptings of their conscience, for according to him, people who attend to the dictates of conscience "do instinctively what the law requires" (Rom 2:14).

As conscience is the immediate or proximate norm of morality, it passes judgment on whether an action is good or evil, right or false. Conscience exercises in light of the acquired knowledge and freedom which truth bestows on it. An act is moral in so far as it is known to and performed by the agent in freedom. Human acts and moral acts presuppose an awareness of and a choice for something already known and desired. Seen from this perspective, every moral act is a conscious and conscientious act of conscience at one stage or other. All moral acts, thus, presuppose a subjective involvement and project to be in conformity with the objective standard of morality. Personal choice is the core of a moral act; a conscience, well-informed of and conformed to the moral law, judges an action rightly and freely. One is obliged to follow one's certain conscience, though it might be objectively wrong. The mistake of this kind cannot be attributed to the agent, because "conscience goes astray through ignorance which it is unable to avoid, without thereby losing its dignity."[21] Hence, conscience—the subjective norm—is the core of morality.

2.2. Conscience Requires the Following of Christ

"Following Christ is the essential and primordial foundation of Christian morality," wrote John Paul II. If this is true, and which is uncontested and uncontestable as far as faith in Christ is central to Christianity, conscience is to be formed by following Christ. This means people need not only to turn to Christ for answers to the moral questions of our times, but also to listen to the Lord who abides in the sanctuary of the human being and respond to the commandments of the Lord in addressing the issues of the day. Conscience, being the core of Christian ethics and being creative in nature, has to be informed by following Christ. The patterns, perspectives, and precepts of Jesus need to be obeyed. The Beatitudes, the self-portrait of Jesus, have to become the hallmark of a Christian as a sign of one's following of the Lord. Life-in-Christ and life-like-Christ should be the mindset of the disciple of Christ and one must be possessed by the Spirit of Christ. In other words, following Christ means a transformation of life in Christ; the projects, priorities, and praxis of Jesus should shape the orientations and dispositions of Christians and shine forth in the life of a disciple.

This process means to follow Christ in daily life and consequently, to follow one's responsive and responsible conscience. There is always a communication and correspondence between following the Lord and following one's conscience; it is a lifelong exercise to be celebrated. Addressing moral issues, namely, dialogue, discernment, and decision, requires a certain degree of moral development as found in the person of Jesus: namely, fidelity to God, identity with one's mission, and liberty in the Holy Spirit.

2.3. Conscience as the Judgment for Love and Life, the Fulfillment of the Law

As the subjective norm of morality, conscience has to pass judgment on every moment and event of human activity. And the judgment should be in concurrence with the ultimate norm of morality, which, in a broader brushstroke, could be identified as supporting and promoting the celebration of life, both temporal and eternal. Jesus alluded to this truth, when he said, "I came that they may have life, and have it abundantly" (Jn 10:10). Life is the fundamental good; in the absence of life there is no ethical discussion or decision possible or imaginable. So, the judgment of conscience should be in recognition of, respect for, and response to the fullness, wholeness, and holiness of life. Love is the fulfillment of all law, and, therefore, the judgment of conscience should pay attention to the flourishing of love. The overarching image of God revealed in sacred Scripture is one of love. The teaching of John is compelling: "Let us love one another because love is from God; everyone who loves is born of God and knows God. Whoever does not love does not know God, for God is love" (1 Jn 4:7-8). Jesus' commandment, "Love one another as I have loved you" (Jn 15:12) is the horizon of human love. Biblical revelation and the theological tradition of the Church have to form the

Christian conscience in the love of Jesus—the self-giving love for the life of the world (Jn 3:16; 12:22-24). Conscience, in conversation with, communion in, and commitment to the law of Jesus – the celebration of love and life – will be passing judgments in the support of the cultivation of love and the culture of life. The principle of love and life has to be seen as the fulfillment of every law and the words of the prophets, preeminently revealed in the person and mission of Jesus Christ. Hence, conscience trained in the school of Jesus will always decide for love and life. The post-synodal apostolic exhortation draws our attention to such an approach; while it outlines the integrity of the Church's moral teaching, it advocates "special care should always be shown to emphasize and encourage the highest and most central values of the gospel, particularly the primacy of charity as a response to the completely gratuitous offer of God's love."[22]

Conscience deciding for love and life is not without troubles and tribulations. The lot of a disciple is not different from that of the Master, culminating in death on the cross. When confronted with different possibilities addressing a moral issue, and none of them agreeing with the norms or measures of conventional moral principles, a person with an upright conscience undergoes difficulty and agony. In such circumstances, *what should one do? Keeping in view a responsive and responsible conscie*nce, here are some steps which might guide the person in arriving at a moral decision and empowering her or him to make moral decisions on their own, while accompanying them in their discernment, and encouraging an atmosphere of responsible moral choice. The focus of this approach or method is to help people to celebrate their life in Christ in the given context of their community on the basis of a well-informed and well-formed conscience. This approach may be called a celebrative approach or method, since celebration of life in Christ is the fountain, force, and focus of this approach. It seems that *Amoris Laetitia* teaches along the same pattern and disposition:

> This offers us a framework and a setting which help us avoid a cold bureaucratic morality in dealing with the more sensitive issues. Instead, it sets us in the context of a pastoral discernment filled with merciful love, which is ever ready to understand, forgive, accompany, hope,

and above all integrate. This is the mindset which should prevail in the Church and lead us to 'open our hearts to those living on the outermost fringes of society'.[23]

We note that this is not an easy method or shortcut, but it is demanding and also rewarding to have decided for oneself on the basis of a conscience which is open to the principles of love and life, the final goal of which is expressed in the angelic hymn at the Nativity of Jesus, i.e., the glorification of God, establishment of peace on earth, and the rendering of hope to human beings.

A person confronted with a moral issue has to discover the different possibilities of celebrating life in Christ. First, one has to search for the possibilities springing from the ethos of the Christian community or tradition. In the event of finding a possibility at this stage, the deontological approach of morality gives one a green signal to go ahead with the following procedure of the celebrative method. If this search is not successful while being faithful to the parameters of Christian norms, then one has to search for the way in which a responsive and responsible conscience might illumine one's mind and heart. This proposal presupposes that one is moving in the right direction of celebrating one's life in Christ. Once the way is identified to be faithful to one's well-formed conscience, the next step is to verify that the response is open to the principles of love and life, which in turn leads to a celebration of life and a commitment or service in the community. Being successful in this verification, one is to celebrate life-in-Christ and life-like-Christ which necessarily will guide the person to commit to be a truthful member of the Church for the welfare of the world. In short, this is the structure of the method or approach of celebrating life in Christ. By emphasizing the well-deserved place for the formation of conscience and its consequent judgment, this procedure should be of help to people confronting conflicting situations and who lead a conscientious life. This approach may be further explained and better appreciated in light of *Amoris Laetitia*. Having underlined the importance of "the development of an enlightened conscience", Pope Francis teaches:

Yet conscience can do more than recognize that a given situation does not correspond objectively to the overall demands of the Gospel. It can also recognize with sincerity and honesty what for now is the most generous response which can be given to God, and come to see with a certain moral security that it is what God himself is asking amid concrete complexity of one's limits, while yet not fully the objective ideal.[24]

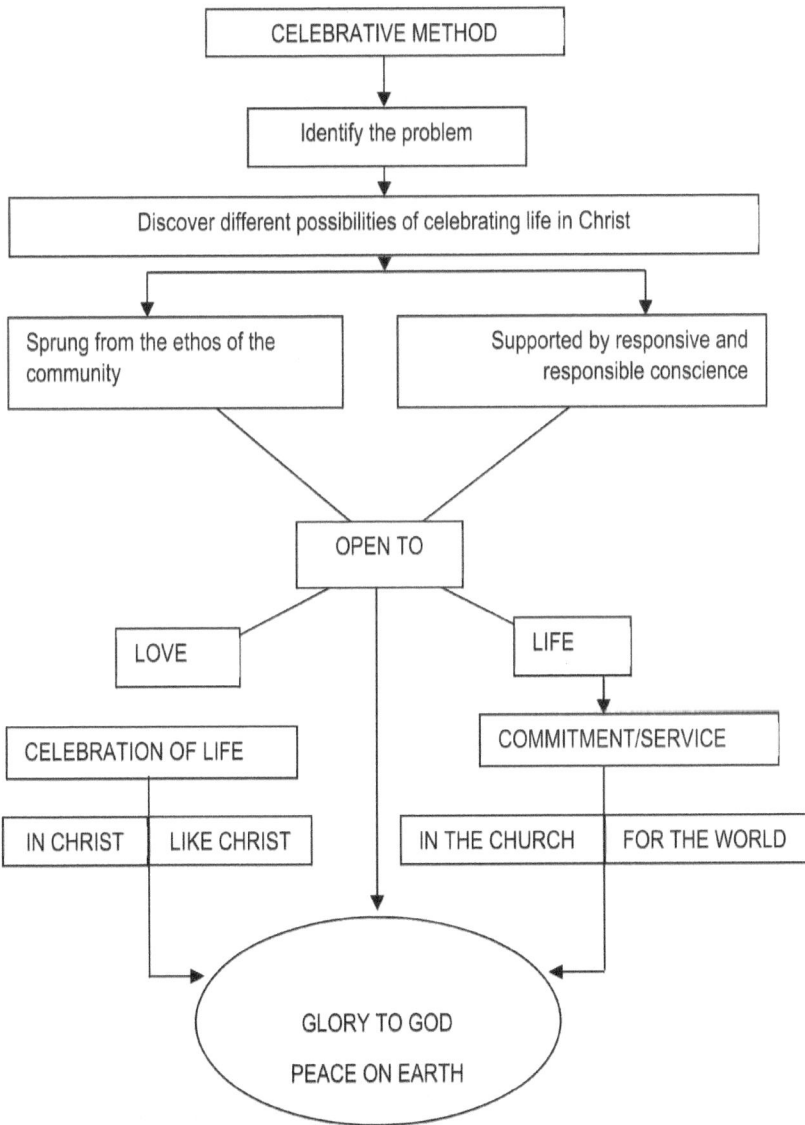

Furthermore, in a fast changing political, social and cultural environment, the mission of the Church is to illumine the heart and mind of the faithful and to empower them to hold fast the moral decisions and to follow Christ in light of the Gospel. In support of this approach, *Amoris Laetitia* exhorts, "Therefore, while upholding a general rule, it is necessary to recognize that responsibility with respect to certain actions or decisions is the same in all cases. Pastoral discernment, while taking into account a person's properly formed conscience, must take responsibility for these situations."[25]

Seen from this perspective of the celebration of life in Christ, the conscience can be faithful and free in deciding for love and life, going beyond the rigid, limiting, and legalistic boundaries of moral norms. Here, Jesus' explicit teaching on the Sabbath is worth remembering: the Sabbath is for man and not man for the Sabbath. Being the disciples of Jesus, are we not obliged to follow the path of the Lord and to attend to the voice of Francis echoed in *Amoris Laetitia*? Chapter 8, entitled "Accompanying, Discerning, and Integrating Weakness" concludes with the apostolic exhortation, "I also encourage the Church's pastors to listen to them [the laity] with sensitivity and serenity, with a sincere desire to understand their plight and their point of view, in order to help them live better lives and to recognize their proper place in the Church."[26]

3. Conscience as the Celebration of Relationships

Conscience is much more than a judgment of practical reason; rather, it is a celebration of relationships. What do I mean by the celebration of relationships? We are what our relationships are. If this is true, conscience is also formed in and through our relationships. In other words, the relationships we celebrate influence our conscience in a special way. Relationships may be summed up as threefold: namely, as my relationship with God, with creation, and with fellow beings. In other words, all these relationships have contributed to make us what we are today. Obviously, these triadic relationships influence us in forming our conscience, for we discover the divine design in and through these relationships. I am what I am because of my relationships. Relationships are built on realities. Either I engage myself with these realities and build up relationships, or the realities of life encircle me and I am in touch with them whether I love or hate them.

Depending on who, what, where, when, why, and how we celebrate, there is an explicit effect on our orientations and the level of our commitments. If we nurture and foster a radical relationship with creation, a horizontal relatedness with fellow beings, and a vertical oneness with God, these relationships will definitely shape our judgments, for they offer a horizon for self-discovery and celebration, which in turn will affect our practical judgments for better or for worse.

3.1. *Conscience Reveals oneness with God*

Conscience begins with the oneness with God, because we are created in the image of God and we have the likeness of God. Conscience discovers the will of God for our daily life, since we are one with Him. We learn to read and understand the lessons of relationship and to celebrate these relationships. Being in communion with God, we come to know the law of the Lord written on our heart. It is the spirit of the Lord who helps us to be enlightened in the school of Jesus, whom we follow faithfully and freely.

Awakened consciousness and the abiding presence with the Lord in our life are of paramount importance to form our conscience and to live an upright life. This reminds me of the necessity to develop a kind of everyday mysticism in our life. Mysticism is the heart of religious experience. Jesus did and said everything from this mystical union with the Father, "The Father is in me and I am in the Father" (Jn 10:39). While following Christ is the essence of Christian morality, we need to be rooted in the Lord and bear fruits of divine glory. As we learn to see God in everything and everything in God, there is a way forward for a better future as we collaborate with the Divine. Since we belong to God, we need to become God-like.

3.2. Conscience Discloses the Rootedness with Creation

Being created, human beings belong to the earth. This earth, as Pope Francis says, is our common home. Therefore, we need to be conscientious caretakers of the earth and everything in it. Every fiber of the human body is related to the elements of the universe. The whole universe is the creation of God, everything has a worth of its own, and all things praise the Lord our God. The cosmos reveals the love and life of God. In the beginning Yahweh saw that everything was good. God loved the world so much he sent his only Son to redeem it (Jn 3:16). Jesus sent his disciples to preach the good news to all creation. All these things mean that we need to perceive the world as belonging to God and to respect it as revealing God's beauty and glory.

The inherent interconnection of everything in the world and its radical relationship with human beings must be restored and celebrated. Unbridled exploitation of the wealth of the universe and devastation of biodiversity is detrimental for the wellbeing of all things, seen and unseen. We need to be conscious of the intricate inherent interrelationship of all things and to live in such a way that we find joy in celebrating the community of life in all its diversity and beauty. Benedict XVI observes, "The environment is God's gift to everyone, and in our use of it we have a responsibility towards the poor, towards the future generations and towards humanity as a whole."[27]

3.3. Conscience Discovers the Relatedness with Fellow Beings

As we have seen, human beings created in the image and likeness of God, have an inherent relationship among themselves as sisters and brothers. They have a solidarity and unity as children of God. Jesus taught us to behave as friends and to respect and safeguard each one's dignity. This is the basic truth we need to share with others. Therefore, there should be no discrimination on the basis of creed, caste, colour, gender, ethnicity, master or servant. We are all the members of the mystical body of Christ. We are called to love our enemies and pray for those who persecute us. Universal sisterhood and brotherhood is to be joyfully celebrated. The universe as one family has to recapture our imagination and moral action. Hence, injustice of any kind to anyone should not be tolerated; we need to find ways to bridge the gap between the haves and have-nots. Social justice must be delivered to all, especially to those who are underprivileged and marginalized. All persons of society need to be our focus as we move toward the goal of integral development.

The issue of migration is a growing phenomenon of the present day. Benedict XVI says, "Every migrant is a human person who, as such, possesses fundamental, inalienable rights that must be respected by everyone and in every circumstance."[28] Conscience must be formed in such a way that people welcome the migrants with human dignity and help them to feel at home. The Rohingya migrants from Myanmar are a typical case for our consideration as a nation.

With a new understanding and urgency regarding environmental ecology, no less attention should be given to human ecology. Benedict XVI articulates the close-knit connection between the two:

> The Church has a responsibility towards creation and she must assert this responsibility in the public sphere. In so doing, she must defend not only earth, water and air as gifts of creation that belong to everyone. She must above all protect mankind from self-destruction. There is need for what might be called a human ecology, correctly understood. The deterioration of nature is in fact closely connected to the culture that shapes human coexistence: when "human ecology" is respected within society, environmental ecology also benefits.[29]

In the same paragraph, Benedict XVI reflects on the interdependence of environmental ecology and human ecology: "The way humanity treats the environment influences the way it treats itself, and vice versa."[30] What is recommended in the present is to continue the search for "truth, beauty, and goodness and communion with others for the sake of common growth."[31] The search for *satyam, shivam, sundaram* should go on and the conscience should be formed according to the discovery of truth, goodness, and beauty.

4.   Conclusion

In light of the above discussion, we understand that conscience is central to the Christian ethical dialogue, discernment and decision-making, which, in turn, determines the character of the people and helps them follow Christ, the hallmark of Christian morality. "Many people feel that the Church's message on marriage and the family does not clearly reflect the preaching and attitudes of Jesus, who set forth a demanding ideal yet never failed to show compassion and closeness to the frailty of individuals like the Samaritan woman or the woman caught in adultery."[32] Pope Francis urges us to be "proactive in proposing ways of finding true happiness."[33] Since conscience is dynamic and operative in every moral action, the formation of conscience is vital and essential in making moral judgments. In his exhortation, he underlines the fact that "this discernment is dynamic; it must remain ever open to new stages of growth and to new decisions which can enable the ideal to be more fully realized."[34] Being the sanctuary of the human being, conscience engages creatively with reality and reveals the character of the person. Being at the core of Christian ethics, conscience acts as the subjective norm of morality. The formation of conscience is envisaged through the following of Christ, and, as such, fulfills the law of love and life. Being the celebration of relationships, conscience reveals the oneness with God, the rootedness with creation, and the relatedness with fellow beings.

As one's morality highly depends on the kind of formation one's conscience has undergone, every decision worthy to be called moral presupposes knowledge and freedom. In communion with the Lord, in the heart, conscience discovers the law of the Lord and listens to the voice of the Spirit echoing in the depths, urging and enabling the person to do good and avoid evil, and to love God, the neighbour and nature. Attending to a responsive and responsible conscience, a person may go beyond the boundaries of sheer rigid and legal interpretations of the law to be creative, liberative and celebrative, thus ensuring the glorification of God, the establishment of peace on earth and extending hope to human beings. This amounts to walking the way of the Lord. Walking the way of the Lord is to walk the way of a right conscience. In order to walk with a right conscience, on the one hand, connectivity with the context, the community, and Jesus Christ is a requirement, and on the other, in all humility, we need to learn to walk before the Lord, work for the world, and worship the Lord always and everywhere.

Endnotes

[1] Syro-Malabar Bishop's Synod, *The Order of the Syro-Malabar Qurbana* (Kochi: Commission for Liturgy, 2005), 33.

[2] VC II, *Gaudium et Spes*, 1965, n.16.

[3] Ibid.

[4] Ibid.

[5] Ibid.

[6] John Paul II, *Veritatis Splendor*, 1993, n.54.

[7] Syro-Malabar Bishop's Synod, ibid.

[8] John Paul II, *Veritatis Splendor*, 1993, n.19.

[9] Ibid.

[10] *Catechism of the Catholic Church*, 1994, n.1780.

[11] Ibid.

[12] Ibid., n.1785.

[13] John Henry Cardinal Newman, "Letter to the Duke of Norfolk," V, quoted from *Catechism of the Catholic Church*, 1994, n.1778.

[14] John Paul II, *Veritatis Splendor*, 1993, n.19.

[15] Ibid., n. 21.

[16] Paulachan Kochappilly, *Life in Christ: Essays on Eastern Christian Ethics* (Bangalore: Dharmaram Publications, 2010).

[17] John Paul II, *Veritatis Splendor*, 1993, n.29.

[18] Francis, *Amoris Laetitia*, 2016, n.37.

[19] Ibid.

[20] John Paul II, *Veritatis Splendor*,1993, n. 59.

[21] VC II, *Gaudium et Spes*, 1965, n.16.

[22] Francis, *Amoris Laetitia*, 2016, n.311.

[23] Ibid., n.312.

[24] Ibid., n.303.

[25] Ibid., n.302.

[26] Ibid., n.312.

[27] Benedict XVI, *Caritas in Veritate*, 2009, n.48.

[28] Ibid., n.62.

[29] Ibid., n.51.

[30] Ibid.

[31] Ibid.

[32] Francis, *Amoris Laetitia*, 2016, n.38.

[33] Ibid.

[34] Ibid., n.303.

12

Gnostic-Pelagian Ethics vs. Ethics of Mercy in *Amoris Laetitia*

Shaji George Kochuthara, CMI

Pope Francis has repeatedly criticised the gnostic and neo-pelagian tendencies in the Church. This paper attempts to reflect on such tendencies in Catholic moral theology. Beginning with an overview of gnostic and pelagian ethics, we shall consider God's grace manifested in mercy and forgiveness as the foundation of Christian ethics. Following this, we shall discuss how *Amoris Laetitia* (hereafter AL) is an excellent example of an ethics of mercy.

1.   Gnosticism and Pelagianism: An Overview

In the first centuries, Gnosticism and Pelagianism were among the most serious threats to Christianity. These movements, with implications for ethical life, challenged the very basic doctrines of Christianity. Hence the Fathers had to defend the Christian doctrine against these ideologies. However, we have to remember that Gnosticism and Pelagianism did not have any unified doctrine or central teaching authority, and consequently, it may not be easy to clearly define these movements or ideologies. Besides, among researchers there are differences of opinion regarding what exactly can be called 'gnostic' or 'pelagian'. The implication is that some of the ideas presented as 'gnostic' and 'pelagian' were perhaps attributed to these by their interpreters and critics, or as understood by them.

In general, we can say that Gnosticism followed a dualistic philosophy, denying the goodness of creation and human body, and advocating an alienation from the world; they claimed to have a secret/private revelation, which was the right knowledge (gnosis) that would bring about true liberation. They had constructed a philosophical system which had its own views regarding cosmology, problem of evil, anthropology, revelation, true knowledge, ethics, eschatology, etc.[1] Some of the Gnostic groups had categorized people into different classes—for example, the pneumatics/spirituals, the psychic, and the hylics.[2] Even within the same group/sect, true knowledge was attainable only to those in the higher class, or the élite, or it was available in grades. Besides, the demands of ethical life were so varied in different groups—ranging from extreme abstinence, fasting and other ascetical practices to over-indulgence. Since the body was considered immaterial, some held that whatever one did with the body was insignificant. Or, in some groups, the pneumatics were considered free from the moral law, and hence that also led to libertinism. Based on their sexual ethics, Noonan identifies as many as nine different Gnostic approaches/groups. In ethical life, in general, they claimed superiority, based on their special ascetical practices and discipline. Such practices were considered necessary for true liberation.[3] Besides the denial of the goodness of human body and the created world, Gnosticism considered salvation as something to be achieved through one's own effort, through ethical practices that they recommended, and not as something gratuitously given by God.

Pelagianism, named after Pelagius (A.D. 354-420/440), is the (erroneous) doctrine that original sin did not taint the human nature and human ability to choose between good and evil. It held that 'ability is the measure of responsibility,' and that even after Adam's fall humans possessed an unimpaired ability to perform whatever God requires.[4] That is, the humans have full control and responsibility and hence are sinners or virtuous by choice. Denying original sin,

Pelagianism denied the sinfulness of humanity and the need of grace. Jesus' only achievement, according to Pelagianism, was 'setting a good example' as against the 'bad example of Adam.' Augustine's refutation of Pelagianism led to the condemnation of Pelagius, and the Christian tradition, in general emphasised the weakness of the human will due to original sin and the redemption brought about by the death and resurrection of Jesus. Pelagianism could not accept any laxity from the human person, since the human person was conceived as possessing the strength to decide without any influence of sin, to do good. Thus, an ethics based on rigorous standards and ideals, and the human ability to achieve it, was upheld. This would imply that a successful moral life and the consequent attainment of salvation is a human achievement, and failure to achieve the ethical standard is a wilful failure. God's grace and human fragility (due to sin) would not be considered as important factors in ethical life. Though Pelagianism was rejected, its resurgence can be seen in Christian history in different forms. For example, the controversy over 'work' or 'grace' during the Protestant revolution had some shades of the resurgence of the age-old theological debate. Attempts to give importance to human achievement over the gratuitous nature of God's gift or to achieve heaven through self-efforts and self-righteousness ignoring the graciousness of God can be called as Pelagian tendencies.

Although Gnosticism had its roots in Greek philosophy, and that too prior to the advent of Christianity, later Christian and Jewish Gnostic groups, that is, those which incorporated Jewish or Christian elements became more prominent. Pelagianism, on the other hand, can be called a Christian sect. As mentioned above, both Gnosticism and Pelagianism appeared in different forms in different periods of Christian history, though only sometimes they may be denoted with these names. The ideologies, movements and theological positions which call for an opposition between the body and soul or the spiritual world and the material world, or those which call for an extreme ascetical practice seeing salvation as a human achievement, or those which would take an extreme rigorous position in ethical and spiritual life ignoring grace and human fragility were sometimes considered as containing gnostic or pelagian elements or as being influenced by them.

2.   Gnostic and Neo-Pelagian Trends in the Church Today: Pope Francis's Teaching

Gnosticism and Pelagianism in their classical form may not be visible any more. But, their new incarnations and influences can be seen in different forms today. In his Apostolic Exhortation, *Evangelii Gaudium*, Pope Francis calls some of the tendencies in the Church as gnostic and neo-pelagian. There is no attempt to give a conceptual definition of Gnosticism or Neo-Pelagianism; rather certain tendencies are described as gnostic and neo-pelagian. This criticism appears under the subheading, 'No to Spiritual Worldliness' (nn. 93-97), in section II (Temptations Faced by Pastoral Workers) of chapter two, namely, 'Amid the Crisis of Communal Commitment'. In his encyclical *Lumen Fidei* (n.47), and in various addresses, the Pope has repeated this attack on gnostic and neopelagian tendencies in the Church.[5] His criticism is more evident in his address to the Italian Church:

> Norms give Pelagianism the security of feeling superior, of having a precise bearing. This is where it finds its strength, not in the lightness of the Spirit's breath. Before the evils or problems of the Church it is useless to seek solutions in conservatism and fundamentalism, in the restoration of obsolete practices and forms that even culturally lack the capacity to be meaningful.[6]

Based on Pope Francis' critical remarks, I shall try to highlight some of the 'gnostic' and 'neo-pelagian' tendencies which are relevant for a critical reflection on moral theology: an individualistic and subjective faith that focuses on certain experiences, which keep one imprisoned in one's own thoughts and feelings; to trust only in one's powers and to feel superior to others based on one's observance of certain rules; intransigent faithfulness to a particular Catholic style from the past; a supposed soundness of doctrine or discipline that leads to a narcissistic and authoritarian elitism; instead of openness to grace, classifying others based on observance of law; ostentatious preoccupation for the liturgy and for doctrine and for the Church's prestige; lack of concern for the people and concrete needs of the times; turning the life of the Church into something which is the property of a select few; closed and elite groups; instructions without contact with the real lives and difficulties of people; unwillingness to learn from one's own sins and lack of openness to forgiveness.

3. Gnostic-Neopelagian Ethics Vs. Ethics of Mercy

In the light of the above criticism of the gnostic and neopelagian tendencies in the Church, I would like to reflect on their influence on moral theology: 1. To conceive moral life/moral theology primarily in terms of norms and rules, and adherence to them, and the lack of openness to change reading the signs of the times; 2. To build up an ethics of the élite implying particular practices, considering morality as a human achievement, and not as a loving response to the grace of God; 3. An individualistic and subjective morality excluding the community; 4. Pharisaic mentality that brands those who fail to achieve the ethical standards as sinners; 5. Unwillingness to accept the shortcomings of others.

Moral life is often conceived as guided by moral norms, which are clearly articulated, which are to be understood, assimilated and put into practice. In this approach, norms and rules become the basis of moral life, and only one who lives according to the moral norms can be considered a morally good person. The primary task of moral theology here becomes the application of norms to the concrete actions and situations. There is no doubt that any society needs some norms or code of conduct. But, seeing moral life only in terms of observing rules may lead to a legalistic and rigid morality that judges and categorises people. Not only in the past, even in the present, we can find approaches which demand such a rigid application of the law. Besides, defining moral life primarily in terms of observing norms may result in conceiving moral life as a human achievement.

In the Christian understanding, law is not the foundation or starting point of moral life and moral theology. Instead, grace of God that is manifest in his compassion, love and forgiveness is the basis of

Christian morality. It is God's grace freely given as mercy and forgiveness that empowers human beings to meet ethical demands. As Cardinal Kasper points out, "From the very beginning, God's merciful action is powerfully effective. His mercy is how God provides resistance to evil..."[7] In other words, an ethical life is a human being's response to the grace of God. Thus, as Pope Francis points out in *Misericordiae Vultus,* the Bull of Indiction of the Extraordinary Jubilee of Mercy, mercy is the basis for God-human relationships and for interpersonal relationships among humans (n.2). Underlying the Christian doctrine of original sin is the awareness that we are born into and are living in a sinful world, and hence we need redemption or the healing power of divine love and mercy.[8]

Jesus' life and message clearly show this centrality of mercy and forgiveness. The Kingdom of God is, primarily, the good news about God who loves us unconditionally. This love is revealed in Jesus Christ to lead all human beings and ultimately all of creation to participate in God's own life and love. Jesus demands that his disciples love as he loved (Jn 13:34). His love includes everyone and is totally unconditional and compassionate. We do not see any precise definition of the Kingdom of God in the gospels. Rather, its meaning is presented in symbolic actions like miracles, healings, forgiving the sinners, table fellowship and exorcism. Moreover, the Kingdom is described in parables, similes and metaphors. The parables question the present reality and open up the possibility of seeing reality in a new and different way. They call for a transformation of the present state of affairs. For example, the parable of the Prodigal Son (Lk 15:11-32) speaks about the merciful Father and asks us to be merciful like him; the parable of the Good Samaritan (Lk 10:30-37) rejects all kinds of discrimination, racism and prejudices and strongly establishes the fraternity and sorority of humanity by pointing out that everyone who is in need is one's neighbour; the parables of the Treasure and the Costly Pearl depict God's gracious gift that transforms life (Mt 13:44-46).[9] Jesus' table fellowship with the outcasts (e.g., Mt 9:10-13) reveals the compassionate God who desires to embrace all in one great community of brothers and sisters. This is the heart of the Kingdom ethics that Jesus preached: "The real content of Jesus' message of the Kingdom consists, therefore, in his image of God: God loves every human being with unconditional love."[10]

If God is the Father of all, it means that all are children of God and hence brothers and sisters. All belong to the same family. No one is a stranger; no one is an outcast; no one is inferior to me; everyone is my brother or sister. Receiving the love and compassion of God is the basis for the willingness to share his love and compassion in our relationship with others. "Be merciful, even as your Father is merciful" (Lk 6:36) is the motto of the Kingdom. In short, it can be said that the Kingdom of God is a call to be in a relationship of love and compassion with God and with others. A call to repentance and conversion is integral to the invitation to the Kingdom. This is the invitation to participate in the vision of God, to acknowledge God as Abba, Father and to accept everyone as a brother or sister. This conversion reorients our way of seeing, thinking, feeling, judging and acting. Conversion is a profound transformation of the whole person. Conversion is possible only because God loves us. The change in awareness, attitude, and conduct which we undergo through conversion is our response to accepting the offer of divine love and mercy.[11]

Jesus' special concern and preferential option for the poor is to be understood in this background. However, for him, the "poor" were not merely the economically poor. He extended his care and love especially to those who were socially marginalised, psychologically and emotionally broken and depressed and to the sinners. His compassionate love reached to them breaking borders, ignoring the social structures, surpassing many existing codes of morality construed by those in authority. That is, reaching out to the 'vulnerable' in the society was a special mark of the life and preaching of Jesus.

> During his earthly existence, Jesus did share spontaneously the lot and the joys of many excluded persons. Both, Jesus' preaching of the kingdom and his personality expressed his Father's confidence in all men and women, however vulnerable they may be. An ethics based on the kingdom's values will challenge the faith that Christians place in the most fragile.[12]

The Kingdom is all-inclusive; it extends God's love to every woman, child and man, especially to the most vulnerable. So, any attempt to divide people and to consider others as away from God's love will be diametrically opposed to the vision of the Kingdom. To accept the Kingdom or reject it will be the freedom of every person, but to consider some people as sinners and less suitable for the Kingdom and to build up castles of the elected and the 'righteous' means to follow the self-righteousness of the Pharisees. Jesus' opposition to discrimination of any kind can be seen from his strong criticism against the Pharisees and Scribes who had practically divided the society into "saints and sinners" or into those who were dear to God and those who were hated by him. Never did Jesus compromise with their self-righteousness, claim of moral superiority and arrogance towards others. Denying charity, the basic law of the Kingdom, on grounds of external observances was, according to him, a mockery of the law. Jesus' compassion made him not to see sin and guilt in his fellow human beings, but only woundedness, brokenness, sickness, confusion and fear.[13] Mercy is the central function of the Church, because Jesus the Good Shepherd made it the focal point of his ministry. An ethics based on mercy also signifies that moral life is not considered as a human achievement, but as a gracious gift of God. This will also help us understand and accept human fragility with compassion, without judging or categorising others as sinners.

4.   Ethical Approach of *Amoris Laetitia*

In this section, I would like to show how *Amoris Laetitia*, the Post-Synodal Apostolic Exhortation of Pope Francis, follows a moral methodology that rejects a gnostic-neopelagian ethics that is expressed in legalism, elitism, pharisaic mentality, subjective and relative morality. On the contrary, Pope Francis upholds a morality that is rooted in mercy, a profound awareness of human fragility and trust in God's grace, openness to change demanded by the 'signs of the times.'

4.1. An Ethics of Mercy Founded on God's Grace

Mercy is one of the foundational principles followed in this Apostolic Exhortation. As pointed out above, the starting point of the moral life is not rules and regulations, but God's grace manifested in unconditional love, mercy and forgiveness. Moral life is in fact a response to the mercy and love of God. Although the 'logic of mercy' runs throughout the document, it is more evident while discussing the difficult and irregular situations.

At the very outset, the Pope points out:

This Exhortation is especially timely in this Jubilee Year of Mercy. First, because it represents an invitation to Christian families to value the gifts of marriage and the family... Second, because it seeks to encourage everyone to be a sign of mercy and closeness wherever family life remains imperfect or lacks peace and joy (AL 5).

This is repeated later, while discussing the irregular situations:

It is providential that these reflections take place in the context of a Holy Year devoted to mercy, because also in the variety of situations affecting families 'the Church is commissioned to proclaim the mercy of God, the beating heart of the Gospel, which in its own way must penetrate the mind and heart of every person...' (AL 309).

Pope Francis is unambiguous in stating that mercy should be the central value in moral theological reflections:

The teaching of moral theology should not fail to incorporate these considerations, for although it is quite true that concern must be shown for the integrity of the Church's moral teaching, special care should always be shown to emphasize and encourage the highest and most central values of the Gospel, particularly the primacy of charity as a response to the completely gratuitous offer of God's love. At times we find it hard to make room for God's unconditional love in our pastoral activity. We put so many conditions on mercy that we empty it of its concrete meaning and real significance. That is the worst way of watering down the Gospel. It is true, for example, that mercy does not exclude justice and truth, but first and foremost we have to say that mercy is the fullness of justice and the most radiant manifestation of God's truth. For this reason, we should

always consider 'inadequate any theological conception which in
the end puts in doubt the omnipotence of God and, especially, his
mercy' (AL 311).

4.2. An Ethics that Integrates All Children of God

Elitism and Pharisaic mentality do not have any place in an ethics
of mercy. Mercy is the antidote to a legalistic, cold and bureaucratic
morality. Such a morality does not exclude anyone, does not create
classes of saints and sinners, but strives to integrate everyone:

> This offers us a framework and a setting which help us avoid a cold
> bureaucratic morality in dealing with more sensitive issues. Instead, it
> sets us in the context of a pastoral discernment filled with merciful
> love, which is ever ready to understand, forgive, accompany, hope,
> and above all integrate. That is the mindset which should prevail in
> the Church and lead us to 'open our hearts to those living on the
> outermost fringes of society' (AL 312).

The Pope calls for a Church which is the house of the merciful Father,
and which is open to everyone: "It is true that at times 'we act as
arbiters of grace rather than its facilitators. But the Church is not a
tollhouse; it is the house of the Father, where there is a place for
everyone, with all their problems'" (AL 310). This 'logic of integration'
(AL 299) is clearly recommended in dealing with those who are living
in irregular situations:

> Such persons need to feel not as excommunicated members of the
> Church, but instead as living members, able to live and grow in the
> Church and experience her as a mother who welcomes them always,
> who takes care of them with affection and encourages them along
> the path of life and the Gospel (AL 299).

This logic of integration in mercy is evident even in the reception of
sacraments by those in irregular situations, as suggested in footnote
351, which has been much debated: "In certain cases, this can include
the help of the sacraments. Hence, "I want to remind priests that the
confessional must not be a torture chamber, but rather an encounter
with the Lord's mercy" (Apostolic Exhortation *Evangelii Gaudium*
[24 November 2013], 44: AAS 105 [2013], 1038). I would also point

out that the Eucharist "is not a prize for the perfect, but a powerful medicine and nourishment for the weak" (*ibid.*, 47: 1039)" (AL 305, footnote 351).

4.3. *Mercy Fills the Gap between the Ideal and the Actual*

An ethics of mercy does not mean that there are no ideals to be followed, or anything and everything is permitted. Rather, it is based on the conviction that human fragility does not always permit the attainment of perfection or the ideal. Accepting human fragility means being open to the grace of God that is manifested in his mercy and love:

> At times we have also proposed a far too abstract and almost artificial theological ideal of marriage, far removed from the concrete situations and practical possibilities of real families. This excessive idealization, especially when we have failed to inspire trust in God's grace, has not helped to make marriage more desirable and attractive, but quite the opposite (AL 36).

Although ideals are important, we also need to remember that they may not be attainable in their fullness due to human limitations:

> We should not however confuse different levels: there is no need to lay upon two limited persons the tremendous burden of having to reproduce perfectly the union existing between Christ and his Church, for marriage as a sign entails 'a dynamic process..., one which advances gradually with the progressive integration of the gifts of God' (AL 122).

The Pope has firm trust in the goodness and sincerity of persons, though they may be fragile and limited: "We also find it hard to make room for the consciences of the faithful, who very often respond as best they can to the Gospel amid their limitations and are capable of carrying out their own discernment in complex situations" (AL 37). This trust in the goodness of the human person and the awareness of one's limitations help one not to judge human failures as 'wilful laxity,' but as weaknesses and brokenness which call for the grace of God expressed in mercy.

4.4. Communitarian Ethics

The ethics of mercy of *AL* does not call for an arbitrary, subjective and individualistic morality. Instead, it calls for a morality that is integrally related to the community. Moral discernment is to take into account one's personal and unique context, but it has to be in communion and communication with the community. In situations of conflict and in 'irregular situations,' the couples are asked to make discernment in the internal forum with the assistance of their pastor. The pastor is to facilitate the person/s to discern what is to be done in the concrete situation, in light of the moral teachings of the Church and considering the limitations present in the given situation. This presupposes that the person has a well informed and formed conscience. It is a process of encountering God in one's heart. Sharing that experience with the pastor who represents the community is an integral dimension and an additional aid in that process. "Conversation with the priest, in the internal forum, contributes to the formation of a correct judgment on what hinders the possibility of a fuller participation in the life of the Church and on what steps can foster it and make it grow" (AL 300). In short, although the unique situation of the person and the discernment by the person have an important role to play, it does not seem justified to accuse that AL is promoting individualism, subjective morality or relativism, as some of the critics have accused;[14] instead, the ethical approach of AL is profoundly communitarian.

4.5. Use of Catholic Moral Principles for an Ethics of Mercy

Though there are accusations from some quarters that *AL* is unfaithful to the Catholic tradition, and even contains heresies, it is firmly rooted in the Catholic moral tradition. In its moral theological analysis, it makes use of important and well-established principles from the Catholic moral tradition and shows how they facilitate an ethics of mercy. This may raise the question whether the accusations and disagreements with *AL*'s approach are coming from fidelity to the moral principles or from a rigidity that considers as absolute the literal obedience of the norm, without paying attention to the spirit of the law, which is mercy.

4.5.1. Mitigating Factors

AL 301-304 speak about the mitigating factors which may reduce the moral responsibility of the person and make it clear that an understanding of the Church's tradition concerning mitigating factors is necessary so that discernment in 'irregular' situations may not be understood as compromising the demands of the Gospel. The Pope, referring to the *Catechism of the Catholic Church*, lists some of the mitigating factors such as ignorance, inadvertence, duress, fear, habit, inordinate attachments, and other psychological or social factors [CCC 1735]; and affective immaturity, force of acquired habit, conditions of anxiety or other psychological or social factors that lessen or even extenuate moral culpability [CCC 2352] (AL 302). Thus, AL, referring to the Synod Fathers, makes it clear that dealing with 'irregular situations' with compassion and understanding, is not attempting to compromise the Catholic moral principles; rather, it is rooted in the rich Catholic moral tradition itself.

4.5.2. Law of Gradualness

AL 295: "Along these lines, Saint John Paul II proposed the so-called 'law of gradualness' in the knowledge that the human being 'knows, loves and accomplishes moral good by different stages of growth." However, it is rather new that the *magisterium* uses this principle to accept 'irregular situations.' For example, in the 20th century, especially following *Humanae Vitae*, we find proposals like 'Situation of Tension' (by Peter Chirico), 'Conflict Situation' solutions (proposed by Charles Robert), 'Compromise' Situation (proposed by Conrad van Ouwerkerk and later defended and elaborated by Charles Curran) and so on.[15] Often such proposals had to face criticism from the teaching authority of the Church. However, 'the law of graduality' was accepted in the official documents of the Church. In a recent lecture given at a conference at "Future Church" Curran has elaborated arguments by theologians and canonists from 1960s in favour of communion for the divorced and remarried in certain situations. He also mentions the position of Ratzinger who argued in favour of such a position, though later he changed that position.[16] In short, on the one hand, the

Catholic moral tradition has upheld the importance of moral norms, but on the other, it has been aware of human limitations in various situations and has tried to accept persons with shortcomings with understanding and mercy.

4.5.3. *Possibility of Variety Due to Cultural Differences and Uniqueness of Situations*

AL 3 reads: since "'time is greater than space,' I would make it clear that not all discussions of doctrinal, moral or pastoral issues need to be settled by interventions of the *magisterium*. Unity of teaching and practice is certainly necessary in the Church, but this does not preclude various ways of interpreting some aspects of that teaching or drawing certain consequences from it... Each country or region, moreover, can seek solutions better suited to its culture and sensitive to its traditions and local needs. For 'cultures are in fact quite diverse and every general principle... needs to be inculturated, if it is to be respected and applied.'" Here, AL makes it clear again that though principles are important, they are not to be applied blindly and arbitrarily. Cultural differences and specific nature of the context are to be taken into account. Attempts to achieve everything in the given 'space' and monolithic application of the norm may not be helpful to integrate people who are culturally and contextually different.

4.5.4. *Natural Law*

Referring to St Thomas Aquinas (AL 304) the Pope says:
I earnestly ask that we always recall the teaching of Saint Thomas Aquinas and learn to incorporate it in our pastoral discernment: 'Although there is necessity in the general principles, the more we descend to matters of detail, the more frequently we encounter defects... In matters of action, truth or practical rectitude is not the same for all, as to matters of detail, but only as to the general principles; and where there is the same rectitude in matters of detail, it is not equally known to all... The principle will be found to fail, according as we descend further into detail' (*Summa Theologiae*, I-II, q. 94, art. 4). It is true that general rules set forth a good which can never be disregarded

or neglected, but in their formulation, they cannot provide absolutely for all particular situations. At the same time, it must be said that, precisely for that reason, what is part of a practical discernment in particular circumstances cannot be elevated to the level of a rule. That would not only lead to an intolerable casuistry, but would endanger the very values which must be preserved with special care.

In his natural law theory, Thomas makes it clear that with regard to the fundamental precept of natural law, there cannot be disagreement. But, when it comes to the level of norms for concrete action, disagreements or exceptions or defects are possible. It is important that AL traces back to the natural law concept in St Thomas and highlights this important principle in the application of norms to concrete situations. Moreover, this is particularly relevant when we consider the fact that natural law ethics has been responsible, to a great extent, for the legalist and rigid approaches and positions in the Catholic moral tradition. AL shows how the natural law concept itself can be utilised for an ethics of mercy and integration.

5. Concluding Remarks

A morality that looks only to moral norms will lead to Pharisaic attitudes and elitism, which will unjustly judge others, and alienate them. Although such a morality may claim to be Christian, it will be a gnostic-pelagian morality in disguise. Christian morality is through and through rooted in compassion. AL helps us understand more profoundly this important principle in the Christian moral tradition. AL does not say that anything and everything is fine in moral life. Instead, it upholds the moral principles. At the same time, it is aware of human limitations and fragility. With this profound awareness, it is inviting us to welcome and integrate with compassion people who are broken and wounded due to human fragility. That is the real spirit of Christian ethics.

Endnotes

[1] Everett Ferguson, *Backgrounds of Early Christianity* (Grand Rapids, Michigan: William B. Eerdmans Publishing Company, 2003 [third edition; first edition 1987]), 309-311.

[2] Valentinianism, one of the major Gnostic sects, followed this classification. According to them, Pneumatics had the divine spark in them and were destined for salvation; the psychics could be saved by the ministrations of the church and good works; the hylics belonged to the material world and were hopelessly lost. Ferguson, *Background of Early Christianity*, 311.

[3] Ferguson, *Background of Early Christianity*, 311; See also, John T. Noonan, *Contraception: A History of Its Treatment by the Catholic Theologians and Canonists* (Cambridge, Massachusetts: The Belknap Press of Harvard University Press, 1986), 56-72; A.D. Nock, *Early Gentile Christianity and Its Hellenistic Background*, (New York, 1962); A.D. Nock, "Gnosticism," *Harvard Theological Review* 57 (1964): 250-274.

[4] "Pelagian Ethics," Robert F. Evans, in *Wycliffe Dictionary of Christian Ethics*, ed. C.F.H. Henry (Grand Rapids, Michigan: Hendrickson Publishers, 2000), 497.

[5] For example, see Francis, "Address to the Leadership of the Episcopal Conference of Latin America during the General Coordination Meeting," (28 July 2013), available on the website: https://w2.vatican.va/content/francesco/en/speeches/2013/july/documents/papa-francesco_20130727_gmg-episcopato-brasile.pdf; "Address at the Meeting with the Participants in the Fifth Convention of the Italian Church," (10 November 2015), https://w2.vatican.va/content/francesco/en/speeches/2015/november/documents/papa-francesco_20151110_firenze-convegno-chiesa-italiana.pdf

[6] Francis, "Address at the Meeting with the Participants in the Fifth Convention of the Italian Church."

[7] Walter Kasper, *Mercy: The Essence of the Gospel & the Key to Christian Life* (New York: Paulist Press, 2013), 45.

[8] Richard M. Gula, *Reason Informed by Faith: Foundations of Catholic Morality* (New York: Paulist Press, 1989), 106-107.

[9] John Fuellenbach, *The Kingdom of God* (New York: Orbis Books, 1995), 72-77.

[10] John Fuellenbach, *The Kingdom of God*, 177.

[11] Gula, *Reason Informed by Faith: Foundations of Catholic Morality*, 176.

[12] Vincent Leclercq, *Blessed Are the Vulnerable: Reaching out to Those with Aids* (New London: Twenty-third Publications, 2010), 64-65.

[13] George Therukattil, *Gripped by God's Mercy: Reflections for Living the Jubilee Year of Mercy* (Kochi: Karunikan Books, 2015), 133.

[14] See for example, Edward Pentin, "Moral Theology and *Amoris Laetitia*: Some Expert Assessments," *National Catholic Register*, April 22, 2016, http://www.ncregister.com/daily-news/moral-theology-and-amoris-laetitia-some-expert-assessments. Pentin reports the opinion of some of the theologians who argue that *Amoris Laetitia* encourages subjectivism, relativism and a confusion regarding subjective sin.

[15] James F. Keenan, *A History of Catholic Moral Theology in the Twentieth Century: From Confessing Sins to Liberating Consciences* (New York: Continuum, 2010), 146-151.

[16] Charles E. Curran, "*Amoris Laetitia* and Conscience," *Asian Horizons* 10/4 (December 2016): 693-706.

13

Neo-Gnosticism and Priestly Formation

George Karuvelil, SJ

Introduction: The Dangers of Neo-Gnosticism in Current Priestly Formation

Pope Francis identified neo-pelagianism and neo-gnosticism as two ills that afflict Christian faith in the contemporary world. Neo-pelagians are those who trust their own powers for attaining salvation; more specifically, they rely on the strict observance of the law to the exclusion of grace and unmerited divine mercy. Gnostics share the sense of superiority with the Pelagians, but their claim is about superior knowledge, not observance. They claim to have some secret knowledge that is suitable only for the elite, and not for the common masses. Both trends bother him, said the pope, because "they lack the Incarnation".[1]

The adherents of neo-gnosticism are "known as 'enlightened Catholics' (since they are in fact rooted in the culture of the Enlightenment".[2] The core of this new knowledge is that faith (and revelation) is not light, but an illusion of light. Only the brave elite can accept this truth; the commoners who want "peace of soul and happiness" choose faith, the illusory light.[3] The Catholic Church condemned it as a heresy ('modernism') and then in a dramatic reversal, embraced the culture of modernity with Vatican Council II (hereafter VC II), without, of course, accepting that faith is an illusion. But neither the condemnation nor its reversal addressed the basis on which faith and revelation were declared illusory. Therefore, the reversal came as an implicit acceptance of the secret knowledge. Priestly formation, then, comes to be seen as gradual initiation of the priestly candidates into this secret knowledge, with disastrous consequences; it split the intellectual life of the priest from his ministerial life, not as a moral flaw or personal human failing but as an institutional or systemic flaw in priestly formation.

Successive pontiffs have been aware of these consequences, with the last two popes tracing it to the failure in holding faith and reason together, and the present one calling it a form of Gnosticism. Naming it Gnosticism, however, only tells us that it is not in keeping with Christian faith; it does not tell us where the problem lies and how it may be addressed. Similarly seeing problem in terms of faith and reason is in danger of forgetting the message of the Incarnation, Word made flesh, that the eternal Word is enfleshed in the flux of time and history. This paper, therefore, will bring the approaches of the three pontiffs together and argue that neo-gnosticism can be countered only by recognizing the embeddedness of reason in history and culture, without making that embeddedness into an imprisonment, as the post-Enlightenment culture of postmodernism tends to do.

The paper is divided into two unequal parts. The first part provides some snippets of history to provide a sense of the theological crisis faced by the Church during the modern period, the failed solution of Vatican Council I (hereafter VC I) and the no-solution of VC II, and its aftermath. It will be seen that in the very process of combatting the modernist heresy, the Church came to adopt one of the key principles of that heresy: its antipathy towards history. This antipathy was rejected by VC II, but it only led to further erosion of faith in a culture that had no place for history. The post-conciliar period also saw some vigorous attempts to democratize and make public the so-called secret knowledge engendered by the moderns. The shorter second part of the paper examines the proposal to consider Thomas Aquinas as an exemplar for bringing faith and reason together. Examining two different ways of understanding his exemplarity, I argue that the tendency to see his doctrine as a perennial achievement must be rejected and his exemplarity must be understood in terms of his willingness to engage with the culture of his times. This would mean, in the contemporary world, the willingness to acknowledge the manifold diversity of our world without that diversity becoming the last word, if we are not to remain content with the post-truth world that enables one to come to whatever conclusion one desires.

1.   Some Snippets of History

I shall begin with two introductory snippets to bring home the said split between the academic and ministerial life and proceed to narrate how the Catholic Church responded to it before VC II, after the Council, and the more recent responses. Although the focus is on the Catholic Church, the issues, it will be seen, are not specific to it. The real issues have to do with the nature of reason engendered by the Enlightenment, undermining claims of revelation, the basis of theology. The ensuing conflict between faith and reason still continues.

1.1. The Challenge

If I remember correctly, the year was 2000. The occasion was that of spelling out the vision and mission of our institution as an Institute of Philosophy and Religion that goes by its abbreviated Indian name, JDV (for Jnana-Deepa Vidyapeeth). The resource persons were professionals from outside and they clearly distinguished the vision from mission. The vision statement was to be a single brief statement about the underlying goal of the institution, and mission was to be the concrete steps to be taken for achieving that goal.[4] The suggested vision was in terms of forming Christian leaders for contemporary India. A question arose in that context whether the philosophical and theological formation in our institution enables the students to emerge as persons with deeper Christian convictions than when they joined us or do they end up as persons who are confused and disoriented about their Christian convictions. Instances were also pointed out to show the gap between their training and the pastoral needs, where priests who were ordained after years of training in philosophy and theology were preaching either on the basis of the catechism they knew before their formation or were relying on charismatic groups. After some discussion, the dominant view was that such confusion was part of the process of their growing up. This view can be considered a good example of neo-gnosticism at work.

Gnosticism, Pope Francis reminds us, divides people into two classes, one with "a crude, imperfect faith suited to the masses" and the other "reserved to a small circle of initiates who were intellectually capable of rising above the flesh of Jesus towards the mysteries of the unknown divinity".[5] To the former belonged traditional practices like Eucharist, rosary, Lenten fasting, way of the cross, etc., to which some gave the name 'piety'. Such 'piety' was contrasted with 'spirituality' for which the so-called piety was more a hindrance than a help. The purpose of philosophical and theological formation, therefore, was to lead the priestly candidates from the "crude and imperfect faith of the masses" (fostered through 'piety') to the more mature faith of the enlightened. Some conflicts are inevitable in that process of growing up.

The conflict is not new; nor did it begin here, as my next snippet will illustrate. This is from the life of Julius Wellhausen (1844-1918), a Lutheran minister and well-known German biblical scholar. As a scholar, he studied the Bible from a scientific point of view but eventually came to the realization that his life as a scholar was incompatible with his task of preparing students for ministry. This prompted him to resign from his teaching post at the University of Greifswald. In his letter of resignation he wrote:

> I became a theologian because I was interested in the scientific treatment of the Bible; it has only gradually dawned upon me that a professor of theology likewise has the practical task of preparing students for service in the Evangelical Church, and that I was not fulfilling this practical task, but rather, in spite of all reserve on my part, was incapacitating my hearers for their office.[6]

While this incident dramatically illustrates the conflict between academic study of the bible and the pastoral goal of theological studies, Wellhausen did not bring about the problem; he was just honest enough to acknowledge it. Moreover, the problem is not with the morality or the psychology of either Wellhausen or the staff members of JDV. The problem is a deeper, systemic conflict. In the case of Wellhausen, the conflict is built into the two different ways of understanding "biblical theology".[7] One is a normative study of the bible in keeping with the faith of the Church and the other is a scientific study, which came to be known as the historical-critical method. In the case of Catholics, the conflict was felt much more widely than in the study of the bible.

1.2. The Responses

Various steps were taken by different Churches to respond to the felt conflict. Movements arose among the Protestants to safeguard the normative study of the bible. J.W. Rogerson mentions some of the institutional measures taken by the Protestants. Among these measures were the founding of a seminary in 1817 to train clergy "in accordance with traditional beliefs", the whole series of commentaries on the bible to combat its unorthodox interpretations.[8]

1.2.1. The Modernist Heresy and Neo-Scholasticism

Having inherited the seamless philosophic-theological system of Thomas Aquinas (1225-1274), the Catholic Church had no difficulty in recognizing that modern thinking was at odds with its faith. It felt a "grave pastoral urgency" to protect the faithful from its ill-effects. This was the purpose of the Dogmatic Constitution *Dei Filius* promulgated by VC I in 1870. Besides condemning a number of errors in the modern thought, it also affirmed confidently that "God ... can be known with certitude by the natural light of human reason".[9] In 1879 Pope Leo XIII issued the encyclical *Aeterni Patris*, which sought a revival of the philosophy and theology of Aquinas. Then came the encyclical of Pope Pius X in 1907 that condemned the modernist heresy, culminating in the anti-modernist oath (1910) which was binding on all seminary professors, among others.

What was the modernist heresy? Rather than a single heresy, it was called a "synthesis of all heresies" by Pius X.[10] But there are three that stand out. One concerns history, the historical study of the bible as well as "the heretical invention of the evolution of dogmas", the influence of history in the formation of the dogmas.[11] Another aspect of the modernist heresy that was strongly denounced was about religious experience. This was condemned as it would make "every religion, even that of paganism" true. "For on what ground" asked the Pope, "could falsity be predicated of any religion, whatsoever?"[12] The third error of modernism concerns reason. *Dei Filius* was "principally about reason".[13] The anti-modernist oath extolled reason, as against those modern trends that sought to base theology on faith alone (fideism) or on feeling and individual experience.[14] Besides asserting the capacity of reason to know God, it condemned the "erroneous concepts of reason held especially by seminary professors and suchlike".[15] Of these the last is the most important, as the other two arise from the third.

It might seem strange that erroneous concepts of reason are condemned rather than reasoned about. But, faced with a very different understanding of reason than that of Aquinas, the Church was at a loss as to how to counter it other than by putting the entire Church a "reason under oath"[16] scheme. Let us consider these differences in the understanding of reason.

1.2.2. Modern View of Reason

The modern understanding of reason differed from that of Aquinas in its nature, scope, and the significance. Concerning its nature of reason, Aquinas was convinced—like his ancient Greek predecessors—that "all men are forced to give their assent" to the voice of natural reason.[17] Modern thinkers would continue to hold this view. Blaise Pascal (1623-1662) was a significant exception. Although in the prevalent Scholastic atmosphere Pascal's insight about the nature of reason was ignored, history would prove him right.

Pascal was a child prodigy. Besides being a brilliant mathematician, physicist and inventor, he was also an ardent Christian, a philosopher, theologian, mystic and apologist, all rolled into one. He was the first modern thinker to realize that reasoning to God's existence does not have the kind of universally binding character that Aquinas and other Scholastics claimed. In order to understand his objection to the scholastic arguments for God's existence, we must begin with the fact that arguments for God's existence in the Thomistic tradition begin with the senses. Following Aristotle, Aquinas was very clear that "Our natural knowledge begins from sense. Hence our natural knowledge can go as far as it can be led by sensible things".[18] From this Aquinas drew two conclusions about our knowledge of God: (1) we cannot know God's essence, as God is not sensible; (2) we can know His existence as sensible things are His effects.[19] This second point is elaborated into the five arguments for the existence of God.

Pascal's insight was that arguments from the world to God can work only for those who already believe. He could have been sympathetic to such arguments, he said, if only they were addressed to believers because those "with a living faith" "see at once that all existence is none other than the work of the God whom they adore. But [as far as unbelievers are concerned], I see by reason and experience that nothing is more calculated to arouse their contempt" than such arguments.[20] Only believers see the world as an effect, not unbelievers. In effect, Pascal was saying that the obligatory nature attributed to natural reason by Aquinas is not really obligatory, at least as far as the arguments for God's existence are concerned. Besides reasoning about the limits of reason, he would go on to add that the "heart has its reasons of which reason knows not".[21]

Regarding the scope of reason, Aquinas held that natural reason is capable of leading us to some knowledge of God, though the knowledge so obtained is limited to God's existence and some attributes. His use of natural reason is elaborated into the famed Five Ways or arguments to prove the existence of God. Kerr provides a remarkably brief one sentence summary of those proofs in these words:

Beginning with features of any human experience of the (change, causation, contingency, gradation, finality), all of which are to be non-religious, the arguments conclude to the existence of an unmoved mover, a first cause, some *per se* necessary existent, something which is most fully in being, and some guiding hand in nature—which everyone takes to be 'God'.[22]

This ability of reason to establish metaphysical facts from our experience of the world (broadly, from physical facts) would be severely contested during the modern period. David Hume (1711-1776) was the key figure in this. His arguments about the impossibility of metaphysics—including the principle of causality that is taken for granted in everyday life—would affect all subsequent thinkers. Shaken by Hume's conclusions Immanuel Kant (1724-1804) set out to establish a very severely circumscribed view of metaphysics where Humean conclusions were upheld as far as knowledge of God is concerned. The impossibility of classical metaphysics became the new orthodoxy in place of Aquinas and Scholasticism. At a time when the Church needed a new Aquinas to provide a new vision to counter this view about the scope of reason, the Church retreated into the teachings of the old Aquinas.

Important as the changed views about the nature and scope of reason are, most important was the changed significance of reason. For Aquinas, God can be known in two different and complementary ways: through natural reason and through revelation. While Aquinas is very clear about ability of natural reason to lead us to the knowledge of God, he is equally clear about the many limitations of such knowledge. Natural reason can only bring us to the existence of God and some attributes like oneness, but not about God as Trinitarian, which needs revelation. Further, even what can be known about God through natural reason is deficient in three ways. Firstly, such knowledge is limited to some persons who have the ability, the interest, and the leisure for the use of reason. Secondly, even those who attain such knowledge of God arrive at it only after a great deal of time. Thirdly, truths of reason are often mixed with falsity, as can be seen from many reputed wise men, each "teaching his own brand of doctrine".[23] On account of these limitations, revelation is the best means of knowing even those truths that are accessible through reason.

This severely circumscribed view of reason is made to stand on its head by Descartes (1596-1650), the father of modern philosophy. Faced with the pervasive scepticism and his tremendous confidence that is typical of the Enlightenment, Descartes set out to question everything until he could find something that is indubitable. In other words, everything he learned from his parents and teachers can have no validity until that is shown to be based on independent grounds. This scorched earth policy of Descartes had a twofold implication. Firstly, it implies that revelation that is the foundation of theology has no standing until God's existence is proved. Proving God's existence becomes the new game in town. Thus, Aquinas' deficient means of knowing God now becomes the foundation stone without which no theology would be possible. Other modern thinkers would follow him in this matter, with some notable exceptions like Pascal. The second implication of the Cartesian revolution is that it would undermine the role of history whether in the form of oral traditions passed on from one generation to the next, or in the form of written documents. This follows from undermining the validity of everything that has been learned unless it can be independently validated.

1.2.3. Impact of the Modern View of Reason

Pascal's insight into the non-obliging character of the theistic arguments would be put on dramatic display in the life of Jean Meslier (1664-1729). Meslier was a French Catholic priest who lived and served as a parish priest for 30 long years. He is remembered today, not for his pastoral zeal but for the 'secret knowledge' he possessed that God's existence is a lie! But given the dominance of the Church at that time, he did not dare to express his inner convictions to his parishioners. Thus, torn between his pastoral duties and his inner convictions, he spent all the time he could spare in the evenings for composing proofs for the non-existence of God! In order to appease his conflicted conscience, he left his writings in the form of a manuscript addressed to his parishioners as his *Last Will and Testament*.[24] In it he bared his soul to his flock:

It was necessary that I should acquit myself as a priest of my ministry, but how often have I not suffered within myself when I was forced to preach to you those pious lies which I despised in my heart. What a disdain I had for my ministry, and particularly for that superstitious Mass, and those ridiculous administrations of sacraments, especially if I was compelled to perform them with the solemnity which awakened all your piety and all your good faith. What remorse I had for exciting your credulity! A thousand times upon the point of bursting forth publicly, I was going to open your eyes, but a fear superior to my strength restrained me and forced me to silence until my death.

As Voltaire, who popularized Meslier, would say: "A dying priest accusing himself of having professed and taught the Christian religion, made a deeper impression upon the mind than the 'Thoughts of Pascal'." It is for this reason that Voltaire described Meslier as "the most singular phenomenon ever seen among all the meteors fatal to the Christian religion".[25]

Important for our purpose is that centuries before *Dei Filius* and the anti-modernist oath reiterated the power of human reason, Meslier was already using reason to disprove God's existence, and thereby proving Pascal's point about the nature of reason. Our concern is not Meslier the individual. In the post-Cartesian culture where establishing the existence of God on the basis of reason was crucial to the very possibility of theology, Meslier set in motion a trend of thought that would be followed by others. Most notable among these would be Hume. His *Dialogues Concerning Natural Religion* is significant not only for showing the weakness of the arguments for the existence of God (especially the argument from design) but for the huge influence his critique of religion would have on subsequent thought. The impact of the trend set in motion by Meslier can be seen from the fact that two centuries after him, his secret knowledge about the non-existence of God would become so public that that Nietzsche (1844-1900) would castigate anyone who claimed ignorance of it. He said,

These days anyone with even the most modest claim to honesty has to know that every sentence pronounced by a theologian, a priest, a pope, is not only wrong, it is a *lie*—and he is not free to lie out

of 'innocence' or 'ignorance' any more. The priest knows as well
as anyone that there is no 'God' any more, that there is no such
thing as 'sin', or the 'redeemer'—that 'free will' and the 'moral world
order' are *lies*—the seriousness, the profound self-overcoming of
spirit does not *allow* people *not* to know this any more.[26]

Not only had the so-called secret knowledge of Meslier become
public by now, but also this knowledge (i.e., atheism) came to seen
as something to be proud of. This was entirely new. In the words of
Michael Buckley,

> Within what is now called the modern period ... there were men
> who judged themselves to be atheists, who called themselves atheists.
> In the ancient world, and even more in the medieval world, this
> was unheard of. 'Atheist' had been vituperative and polemic; now
> it became a signature and a boast.[27]

Atheism became a matter of boast because given the centrality of
reason in the post-Cartesian world, and a world that held on to the
idea of reason as obligating on all, atheism was seen as the only option
available for anyone who uses reason. And this goes to the heart of the
modernist crisis. It is at this point that the Church started its holding
operations with its condemnation of modernism and its promotion
of Neo-Thomism. As a result, Catholics became intellectually suspect.
Gerald Hughes, a Jesuit philosopher, describes his experience in the
University of London where most of his colleagues in philosophy
suspected the intellectual caliber of Catholics. He said: "Catholics,
especially Catholic priests, were assumed to be ill-educated, narrow
minded dogmatists, who in the last analysis were simply intellectually
dishonest. Surely, nobody could believe all that Christian stuff…"[28]

1.2.4. Surmounting Neo-Scholasticism

Walter Kasper has correctly observed that "the outstanding event in
the Catholic theology of our [twentieth] century is the surmounting
of Neo-Scholasticism".[29] Neo-Scholasticism was bound to fail because
it was basically a holding operation, which means 'a course of action
designed to maintain status quo under different circumstances'.

The circumstances of Scholasticism and Neo-Scholasticism were different in at least three different ways. One difference, Kasper tells us, was "the breakdown of metaphysics in their classic form. Metaphysics was the study of the final, all determining and cohering foundations, wisdom about the oneness and wholeness of reality".[30] At a time when Western culture as a whole had revolted against such metaphysics, mere affirmation of it could only be seen as imprisoning oneself in the past. With the epistemological turn of the modern world, it became necessary to establish the nature and limits of human knowledge before making metaphysical claims. Returning to an earlier era was not going to change that.

Secondly, when *Dei Filius* insisted on Aquinas's teaching that God "can be known with certainty from the consideration of created things, by the natural power of human reason" it ignored the whole tradition of reasoning to the non-existence of God that Meslier engaged in and was perfected by David Hume (1711-1776).[31] For the moderns, the reasoning of Meslier and Hume carried more certainty than that of Aquinas and *Dei Filius*.

A third change that was ignored by the attempted revival of Scholasticism concerned history. History, we have seen, was an unreliable source of truth, unless it can be shown to be founded on something that is more reliable. This has been the key point of the modern understanding of reason inaugurated by Descartes. History could be accepted only if it could be shown to be based on scientific facts devoid of human interpretations. This doctrine about history went along with a sharp dichotomizing of facts and values, value-neutral descriptions and value laden expressions of preferences, cognitive meaning and non-cognitive meaning, and the like. Truth had to do with the former of these pairs; modern science was supposed to epitomize this kind of value-neutral knowledge. This epistemological outlook that posits some "permanent, a-historical matrix" on the basis of which truth can judged, a matrix that is stripped of all human dimensions of culture and history has been called "objectivism".[32] Inasmuch as Gnosticism is the denial of incarnation, denial of history is the most momentous change, as it denies that the eternal Word has anything to do with the mortal flesh and flux of history.

Search for such an a-historical matrix led the Protestants—who did not have an Aquinas to fall back on—to look for a historical Jesus "as he really was"[33] without the admixture of myth and later interpretations by the Church. The same quest to escape history led to the emergence of Neo-Scholasticism as an a-historical system of philosophy and theology. Its twenty-four theses covering ontology, cosmology, psychology and theodicy made an abstract system of thought that its protagonists thought had timeless validity.

There are various factors that led to the collapse of this system. The most important was the very nature of Christianity. From the very beginning, it was a missionary religion, with a message of salvation meant for all. Inasmuch as reaching out to those outside its fold was intrinsic to its identity, the more successful the protective walls of Neo-Scholasticism became, the less successful the Church was in reaching out to its contemporaries outside the walls. The security gained by withdrawal was like training a child to swim in a bathtub, without venturing out into the open waters where it was destined to spend its life. Missionary work had become something to be done in foreign lands, not an outreach to the alienated children of modernity. As early as 1942, Henri de Lubac wrote about the weakening sense of the sacred in France. He traced this phenomenon to the inadequacy of a heresy obsessed, rationalistic Neo-Scholasticism of the period.[34] Thus, faith that was to be leaven in the dough had lost its leavening quality. If Christian theology was to carry out its mission in the changed world, it had to go beyond the neo-scholastic fortress and venture out into the new world that had emerged, especially in the traditional strongholds of the Church. This is best seen in the opening address of Pope John XXIII to the Council. He said, "our duty is not only to guard this precious treasure, as if we were concerned only with antiquity, but to dedicate ourselves with an earnest will and without fear to that work which our era demands of us, pursuing thus the path which the Church has followed for twenty centuries."[35]

Another factor that led to the collapse of the neo-scholastic system was the realization that the system of Aquinas, far from being the crown of a timeless achievement, was very much a response to the historical and cultural conditions of his time. This historical reading of Aquinas was pioneered by the, then unorthodox, Dominican Marie-Dominique Chenu (1895-1990).

1.2.5. In the Wake of Vatican Council II

Whatever the reasons for the discarding the anti-modernist moves, it left the Church with those very problems which the anti-modernist moves were supposed to remedy. In taking away the wrong solution, without providing an alternative, the Church has been left with "an agenda we still have to deal with" in the twenty-first century.[36] If it were merely an academic agenda, it could be done at leisure. Unfortunately, it is not. All the more so for Christianity, and especially Catholic Christianity, because of its condemnation of modernism, and its abrupt turnaround with VC II. Effectively, it meant accepting the very modern contentions that were condemned earlier. This created an existential crisis in the lives of its adherents where a sizable number of them, including Jesuit priests, would be blown away by the strong winds of change.[37]

I will consider only the intellectual vacuum it created, and that too, only about history. Accepting history in a culture that considered any humanly interpreted history as an invitation to falsehood merely threw the Church back to the dilemma faced by Wellhausen. This is illustrated in the publication of the *Myth of God Incarnate* (1977), and the attendant controversies that ensued. Hick, the editor of *Myth* tells us:

> The main historical thesis of the book—that Jesus himself did not teach that he was God incarnate and that this momentous idea is a creation of the church—was of course in no way new. It had long been familiar and accepted in scholarly Christian circles on both sides of the Atlantic. What was new, in Britain, was that members of the theological establishment were now saying it publicly and concluding that the incarnation doctrine, instead of continuing to be regarded as sacrosanct, should be openly reconsidered.[38]

There are two points to be noted in this passage. The first is that, as far as historical facts are concerned, the book did not say anything new; it only made public what was already known in scholarly circles. According to Hick, it "performed the necessary service of pulling down much of the curtain between what the scholars knew and what preachers have been accustomed to tell their congregations."[39] This is the democratization of the secret knowledge that the moderns claimed to possess. The second point made in the cited passage is about the significance of historical findings for the credibility of theological doctrines. Specifically, the impossibility of getting un-interpreted historical facts is said to be fatal for the doctrine of incarnation. This assumption about the status of interpreted history becomes explicit when Hick goes on to say that many readers of the *Myth* were:

> [I]ndignant that the churches had so long encouraged them to go on innocently assuming, for example, that the historical Jesus had said "I and the Father are one" (Jn 10:30), "He who has seen me has seen the Father" (Jn 14:9), rather than revealing the scholarly consensus that a writer some sixty or more years later, expressing the theology that had developed in his part of the church, put these famous words into Jesus' mouth.[40]

The sharp dichotomy between 'pure' facts and values is seen when Hick concludes that "the real point and value of the incarnational doctrine is not indicative but expressive, not to assert a metaphysical fact but to express a valuation and evoke an attitude."[41] Hick would make it his life-mission to follow up his conclusion about incarnation and extend it to other Christian doctrines like Trinity, uniqueness of Christ and so on; they were historical accretions that must be discarded.[42]

As far as the existence of God is concerned, Hick did not go as far as Meslier, but he did come to the conclusion that the universe is religiously so ambiguous that God's existence can neither be proved nor disproved.[43] Although Hick himself continued to believe that there is some mind-independent Reality to which different religions are varied culturally-conditioned responses, there was no way it could be demonstrated. If centuries earlier Pascal had questioned the value of the Thomistic proofs, Hick showed the limitations of those proofs in a different way. These, in short, were the results of Hick's adoption of 'objectivism' or the modern Gnostic understanding of reason. On the one hand, it involved a very drastic pruning of Christian faith by getting rid of (gently, if possible) such historical claims as Jesus being the Son of God, Trinity, and the like, and on the other hand, the impossibility of proving the existence of God to non-believers.

Though Hick was a Presbyterian, he was taken seriously by Catholics for two reasons. First, he had taken the call of VC II for interreligious dialogue earnestly. It is also the case that when the Catholic Church came to accept the importance of history, the Church had not yet realized the peculiar modern understanding of history. It is only with the coming of the postmoderns, especially the epoch making work of Thomas Kuhn (1922-1996) that the limits of the neo-Gnostic understanding of history would come to light.[44] Today historical-critical method in the study of the bible is widely recognized as a "product of the Enlightenment that has become as suspect as the Enlightenment project itself."[45] But for the Catholics of his time, Hick seemed to be merely following the teachings of VC II to its logical conclusion.

However, the unorthodox nature of Hick's teaching would not go unnoticed by those entrusted with the task of maintaining the orthodoxy of faith. Pope John Paul II published the *Catechism of the Catholic Church* in 1992, reaffirming the Catholic teachings. In 1997, Vatican's International Theological Commission accused Hick of relativizing Christian faith.[46] The need to proclaim the Christian truth without falling prey to "different forms of agnosticism and relativism" is also an important motif in Pope John Paul II's encyclical on faith and reason published the very next year.[47] This document is best seen as a validation of the claim about the "unfinished agenda" presented to the Church in the wake of modernity. The encyclical draws our attention to "certain fundamental truths of Catholic doctrine which, in the present circumstances, risk being distorted or denied."[48] The same concern with the "crisis of post-conciliar theology" is the moving force of the more recent *Decree on the Reform of Ecclesiastical Studies in Philosophy* promulgated by the Congregation for Catholic Education.[49]

These documents are official acknowledgements that, about half a century after VC II, the Church had begun to feel the bite of the intellectual vacuum left behind by its embrace of the modern, and later the postmodern, world.

The most fundamental problem with these latest Vatican documents is the same. They are clear about Christian faith but seem utterly lost in responding to (as opposed to condemning) the dramatic changes in the thinking patterns brought about by the modern, and later, postmodern thinking. This gap between their affirmation of Christian faith and their inability to engage others who think differently shows certain "epistemic arrogance that privileges 'our' faith"[50] If Christians can privilege their faith, why should the ISIS not privilege their version of militant Islam, or the RSS privilege their version of muscular Hinduism? Where does reason enter into the picture at all? It is in this context that the suggestion of the *Decree* that the method and the doctrine of Aquinas as "exemplary"[51] must be examined more closely.

2.   Aquinas as 'Exemplar'

Emeritus Pope Benedict XVI considered Aquinas as an exemplar for the manner in which he placed "faith in a positive relation with the dominant form of reason of his time."[52] In what sense can this thirteenth century genius be considered an exemplar for the twenty-first century? There are some hints in the *Decree* that suggest a return to Thomism. This suggestion is most clear in its advocacy of metaphysics.[53] Not only does it consider metaphysics as "the path to be taken in order to move beyond the crisis" but also goes on to specify 'metaphysics' as "first philosophy [that] deals with being and its attributes, and, in this way, raises itself up to the knowledge of spiritual realities, seeking the First Cause of all."[54] It is hard to see how this differs from the Neo-Scholastic metaphysics whose overcoming was celebrated by Kasper as the outstanding event of the twentieth century. If the exemplarity of Aquinas means such a return, it is hard to see how it can avoid the very problems that prompted VC II. A snippet from Pope Benedict's attempt to show the rationality of Christian faith to a secularized Europe will vividly show the limits of this approach.

2.1. Pope Benedict's Engagement with Faith and Reason

John Paul II's encyclical on faith and reason was addressed to the
Bishops of the Catholic Church. But his successor saw very clearly
that relating faith and reason is not an internal affair of the Church.
He was more clear-sighted than anyone else that the very aim of VC
II was to reach out to the secular world. His extensive writings (both
official and unofficial) and his engagements as Pope are pervaded
by an urgency to re-evangelize the Western world that had become
unhinged from its Christian moorings. He was anguished that, at two
crucial moments in the post-war Europe, Christianity failed to provide
an anchor to those who were in search of meaningful alternatives. The
first was the youth rebellion of 1968 and the second was the "collapse
of the socialist regimes in Europe, which left behind a sorry legacy of
ruined land and ruined souls" in 1989.[55] And from this anguish arose
his attempts to reach out to those outside the Church, and present
Christianity as a rational option to his contemporaries. The failure of
these attempts illustrates where his theological brilliance falls short in
addressing the rationality of faith in the contemporary world.

Three of his attempts to reach out to the outside world are well
known: (a) engaging with Jürgen Habermas, a leading public intellectual,
in 2004; (b) addressing the University of Regensburg in 2006; and (c)
addressing the German Parliament [Bundestag] in 2011. I shall consider
only the last, which did not have the sort of violent aftermath of his
Regensburg address,[56] but still brings out the problem of reason in
the contemporary world clearly.

Pope Benedict's address to the German Bundestag was remarkable
for its brilliance as well as its limitations. In his address, he dealt
with the foundations of law and the responsibility of politicians to
safeguard those foundations, irrespective of their political affiliations.
He observed: "Unlike other great religions, Christianity has never
proposed a revealed law to the State and to society." By this he was
making it clear that although he was the head of the Catholic Church,
he was not a theocrat; the state has its own autonomy. Then he went
on to add that the "true source of law" is "nature and reason".[57] The

erudite pope showed that this tradition goes back to pre-Christian times, especially to the Stoic philosophers and the teachers of Roman law, to the juridical developments during the Enlightenment, climaxing in the Universal Declaration of Human Rights in 1948. He did not hesitate to draw out the implication: politicians must go beyond the concern to secure a majority and do what is right and just.

The speech was highly appreciated, with one newspaper (*Frankfurter Rundschau*) even saying that the "pope could have put all his critics to shame."[58] The autonomy of the laws of state from the laws of the Church or similar laws like the Islamic Sharia is definitely good news, not only for countries that are multi-religious and multi-cultural, but also for countries with significant minority populations, even if they are of the same religion as with Shias and Sunnis or with Protestants and Catholics. The pope was showing a way forward to the whole world.

But criticism was not far behind the adulation. Some criticized the speech for what they saw as overriding the majority principle as the basis of democracy.[59] I wonder if such critics would still maintain that view even after witnessing how an unprincipled use of the majority principle can be turned into a majoritarianism that threatens the lives and livelihoods of minority populations of multi-ethnic, multi-cultural countries like India and the US. The more important criticism is that the Pope was claiming "universal acceptance of a particular worldview by declaring a specific approach to be general."[60] As a firm believer in God, it is right for him to speak of the "the harmony of objective and subjective reason, which naturally presupposes that both spheres are rooted in the creative reason of God." But what about those who do not believe in God? After all, was that not the point of acknowledging the autonomy of the laws of state? Harmony of objective and subjective reason is deeply rooted in the history of Western philosophy and Christian theology. It is a tradition that owes a lot to Stoics and the metaphysical tradition of Christian Scholasticism. Unfortunately, it was these very same things that the modern world revolted against. The Pope's outlook and his address were strong on history and tradition, but weak in reaching out to the secularized Europe that he sought to address.

2.2. *Obligating Reasons?*

At the bottom of this weakness lies a difficult question that Pope Benedict did not confront: If reason can be used to prove God's existence by Aquinas and to disprove the same by Meslier, does the word 'reason' mean any one thing? Does it have the obliging character that was given to it by Aquinas, and is usually taken for granted in Western philosophy, until recent times? Or are the postmoderns right when they say that reason is only a cultural product that reflects power structures and ideological currents of the time? There are reasons to think that the obligating character that Aquinas attributed to his arguments for God's existence is a cultural product.

First of all, Aquinas lived at a time when Aristotle's philosophy was coming to prominence, replacing the Platonic outlook.[61] Inasmuch as Aristotelian outlook was dominant at that time, and the kind of arguments that Aquinas provided for God's existence were very much a part of that outlook, it was not difficult to accept those arguments. Contrast this with contemporary world where Hume's critique of religion damaged the credibility of "religion in ways that have no philosophical antecedents and few successors."[62]

Secondly, we know that Aquinas lived in a world that was Christian (at least theist, if Muslims are also taken into account). In that world, he had to look into Scriptures (revelation) even to find any evidence for atheism.[63] Contrast this with the modern world where atheism became a "signature and a boast"! Realization of this difference enabled Pascal to see that those arguments are not binding on unbelievers; instead, they only evoke the contempt of real atheists. If the theistic culture of Aquinas gave his arguments a seeming obligatory character, the secularism, if not the atheism, of modern culture made the atheistic arguments seem compelling.

Thirdly, there is the modern shift from metaphysics to epistemology that is already mentioned. When Plato's philosophy was slowly being replaced by Aristotle's philosophy, Aquinas was insightful enough to see that his Christian faith can very well be crafted on to the Aristotelian outlook.[64] But in spite of the important differences between Plato and Aristotle, both were metaphysical in their outlook. The modern outlook, on the other hand, not only was a revolt against Aristotle,[65] but was also a revolt against the metaphysical tradition itself. In the new culture, metaphysics can enter the arena only through the epistemological route. In such a culture, then, the Humean reason is bound to have more credibility than the Scholastic one.

Fourthly, the arguments of natural theology have very different significance in the modern world that it had in Aquinas. We have already seen that knowledge of God through natural reason has very limited significance in Aquinas, unlike the pivotal place it occupied after the Cartesian revolution. Discounting the idea that Hume's use of 'natural religion' could be considered "an expanded version of natural theology" of Aquinas, Peter Byrne shows that 'natural theology' in Hume and other modern thinkers enjoy an independence from 'revealed theology' that cannot be found in Aquinas.[66] With the epistemological turn of modern philosophy the very possibility of revealed theology hung on the single thread of being able to prove God's existence. Snap that thread and the whole basis of Christian theology (faith in a revealing God and his reveled truths) would come crashing down. It is little wonder, then, that faced with the threat of modern atheism theologians busied themselves in safeguarding this single thread by finding newer and newer philosophical arguments to prove the existence of God, though without success.[67]

Finally, it must also be mentioned that as the post-conciliar Church was struggling to cope with modernity, the cultural mood changed again from the modern to the postmodern. Although the transition from the medieval to the modern marked the shift from metaphysics to epistemology, the 'objectivism' of modern thinking still maintained a permanent, a-historical matrix. This matrix was expected to function as the ultimate bulwark against falsehood and relativism. Realization of the impossibility of such a matrix marked the shift from modern to the postmodern. The characteristic feature of postmodern thinking is the recognition that we live in an inescapably pluralistic world. Thus, unlike the thirteen century when Aristotelian philosophy could be considered the "dominant form of reason", ours is a world where "the most divergent systems of thought coexist with none of them managing to dominate the others."[68] It is a world of diverse religious faiths and ideological outlooks, the world of passionate atheists and ardent theists, of militant atheists and violent religious fanatics, those who use the name of science to discredit religion and those who see it as the gateway to religious faith. It is the neglect of this cultural difference that brought Pope Benedict's passionate efforts to show the rationality of Christian faith to a secular Europe to naught.

In the light of these vast cultural differences between the time of Aquinas and ours, the argumentative route to the metaphysics of a 'First Cause' that the *Decree* advocates must remain a chimera. But these considerations do not show, nor are they meant to show, the impossibility of truly obligating natural reasons; these are not meant to be an invitation to write obituaries of epistemology, as postmoderns do.[69] The present claim is limited: the seemingly obligatory nature of Aquinas's arguments for God's existence arose from the particular cultural setting of his time. This is equally true of the arguments against God's existence, though I have not focused on it.

2.3. *The Genius of Aquinas*

If the exemplarity of Aquinas in relating faith and reason does not consist in his arguments for a First Cause, how else could he be an exemplar for our times? In this section, I shall suggest that he can be an exemplar in a very profound sense that responds to the problem of neo-gnosticism. In order to do that we need to see his real achievement not in terms of his arguments for God's existence, but in terms of his rebooting of Christian faith into a newly emerging culture. Though the terminology of booting is new, the idea is as old as Christianity itself. Just as a computer becomes operational only when it is booted up, so too Christians have found, from the very beginning, that they have to prepare the ground before their message can be communicated in a given culture. The first booting was done by early Fathers of the Church like Clement of Alexandria, Origen, and others.[70] The culture onto which they did the booting was that of the ancient Greco-Roman world, and the 'Operating System' (OS) they used for the purpose was Platonic philosophy, suitably tweaked for their purpose. This was the original or the first booting. This initial booting was so successful that it functioned very well for the next twelve centuries, with minor tweaks to the original OS.

After twelve centuries of glorious functioning on the basis of the initial booting, the cultural outlook of Europe took a decisive turn from the other-worldly, Platonic outlook to the more this-worldly Aristotelian outlook. Living in the midst of that change, it was the genius of Aquinas that recognized the compatibility of Christian faith and Aristotle's philosophy. But it was indeed a gigantic task to rethink Christian faith in Aristotelian terms.[71] This rebooting required a new OS that was Aristotelian and not Platonic, although Aquinas did incorporate some insights from the old into the new.[72]

3.   Conclusion: The Need for Fresh Rebooting

While Pope Francis battles the manifestations of neo-gnosticism within the Church to maintain the integrity of faith, there is the wider battle outside. Unlike ancient Gnosticism that remained within secretive groups, neo-gnosticism has transformed itself into a culture that is antithetical to Christian faith. Addressing this wider issue is essential if the missionary thrust of VC II and the reasoning of emeritus-Pope Benedict XVI is to bear fruit. It is also necessary for resolving the systemic conflict built into priestly formation today. Addressing this wider issue calls for nothing short of a fresh booting of Christian faith into the contemporary culture. While Pope Francis does the prophetic work of denouncing that which is not in keeping with Christian faith, it must be complemented by a fresh intellectual vigour for rebooting faith into the contemporary culture.

For various reasons, this rebooting is even more challenging than the challenge faced by Aquinas. Two obvious reasons have already been mentioned: there is no one dominant form of reason today and contemporary culture is not enamored of the classical, unifying metaphysical scheme. Both call for reasoning about reason before rationality of Christian faith can be considered. Difficult though this task is, it cannot be avoided if the challenge of neo-Gnosticism and its impact on priestly formation are to be addressed.

Endnotes

[1] https://www.ncronline.org/blogs/distinctly-catholic/pope-francis-pelagians-gnostics-and-cdf.

[2] Pope Francis, Address to the Leadership of the Episcopal Conferences of Latin America

during the General Coordination Meeting, 4.1.c) https://w2.vatican.va/content/francesco/en/speeches/2013/july/documents/papa-francesco_20130728_gmg-celam-rio.html.

[3] http://w2.vatican.va/content/francesco/en/encyclicals/documents/papa-francesco_20130629_enciclica-lumen-fidei.html., 2

[4] The manner in which it finally got spelt out is a hotchpotch where it is impossible to distinguish the vision and mission.

[5] *Lumen Fidei*, 47.

[6] Cited in Philip Kitcher, 'The Many-Sided Conflict between Science and Religion,' in *The Blackwell Guide to the Philosophy of Religion*, ed. W. Mann, Blackwell Philosophy Guides (Oxford, UK; Malden, MA: Blackwell Pub., 2005), 272.

[7] Bernd Janowski, 'Biblical Theology,' in *The Oxford Handbook of Biblical Studies*, ed. J. W. Rogerson and J. Lieu (New York: Oxford University Press, 2006), 716.

[8] J. W. Rogerson, 'Historical Criticism and the Authority of the Bible,' in *The Oxford Handbook of Biblical Studies*, ed. J. W. Rogerson and J. Lieu (New York: Oxford University Press, 2006), 841.

[9] http://inters.org/Vatican-Council-I-Dei-Filius 2.

[10] http://w2.vatican.va/content/pius-x/en/encyclicals/documents/hf_p-x_enc_19070908_pascendi-dominici-gregis.html 39.

[11] Fergus Kerr, 'A Different World: Neoscholasticism and Its Discontents,' *International Journal of Systematic Theology* 8/2 (2006): 135, http://dx.doi.org/10.1111/j.1468-2400.2006.00187.x.

[12] http://w2.vatican.va/content/pius-x/en/encyclicals/documents/hf_p-x_enc_19070908_pascendi-dominici-gregis.html, 14.

[13] Kerr, 129.

[14] Fergus Kerr, *Twentieth-Century Catholic Theologians: From Neoscholasticism to Nuptial Mysticism* (Malden, MA: Blackwell Pub., 2007), 2.

[15] Kerr, 'A Different World: Neoscholasticism and Its Discontents,' 130.

[16] Kerr, *Twentieth-Century Catholic Theologians : From Neoscholasticism to Nuptial Mysticism*, 1.

[17] See Thomas Aquinas, *On the Truth of the Catholic Faith Summa Contra Gentiles Book 1: God*, trans. A. C. Pegis (New York: Doubleday, 1955). Bk.1 ch.2 (hereafter SCG); *Summa Theologiae*, trans. Fathers of the English Dominican Province (hereafter ST) 1, q.1, a.8.

[18] Aquinas, *ST* I, q 12, a 12. See also SCG I: III.

[19] Ibid.

[20] Blaise Pascal, *Pensées* (Grand Rapids, MI: Christian Classics Ethereal Library, 2002), 242, http://www.ccel.org/ccel/pascal/pensees.html.

[21] Ibid., 277.

[22] Fergus Kerr, 'Theology in Philosophy: Revisiting the Five Ways,' *International Journal for Philosophy of Religion* 50, 1/3 (2001): 115, http://www.jstor.org/stable/40020986.

[23] Aquinas, SCG Bk 1, ch. 4, 5.

[24] This book is freely available at http://www.gutenberg.org/ebooks as *Superstition in All Ages* (1732).

[25] Ibid.

[26] Friedrich Wilhelm Nietzsche, Aaron Ridley, and Judith Norman, *The Anti-Christ, Ecce Homo, Twilight of the Idols, and Other Writings*, Cambridge Texts in the History of Philosophy (Cambridge: Cambridge University Press, 2005), 38.

[27] Michael Buckley, *At the Origins of Modern Atheism* (New Haven: Yale University Press, 1990). 27

[28] Gerald Hughes, 'Do we still need Jesuit Philosophers?' *Jivan*, July 2003, 4.

[29] Walter Kasper, *Theology and Church*, trans. M. Kohl (New York: Crossword, 1989), 1.

[30] Ibid., 3.

[31] His works that are entirely devoted to religion are *Dialogues Concerning Natural Religion* and *The Natural History of Religion*.

[32] Richard J. Bernstein, *Beyond Objectivism & Relativism* (Philadelphia: Univesity of Pennsylvania Press, 1983), 8.

[33] Daniel P. Fuller, 'The Resurrection of Jesus and the Historical Method,' *Journal of Bible and Religion* 34/1 (1966): 18, http://www.jstor.org/ stable/1460562. for a more detailed account of the search for historical Jesus, see James D. G. Dunn and Scot McKnight, *The Historical Jesus in Recent Research, Sources for Biblical and Theological Study* (Winona Lake, Ind.: Eisenbrauns, 2005).

[34] John McDade, 'Epilogue: '*Ressourcement*' in Retrospect,' in *Ressourcement : A Movement for Renewal in Twentieth-Century Catholic Theology*, ed. G.l Flynn and P. D. Murray (Oxford: University Press, 2012), 511-512.

[35] http://vatican2voice.org/91docs/opening_speech.htm

[36] Kerr, 'A Different World: Neoscholasticism and Its Discontents,' 129.

[37] One example is the reduced number of Jesuits. Their numbers reduced from a peak number of a little above 35,000 in 1965 to a little over 18,000 in 2010. See, Patrick Howell, 'The 'New' Jesuits, The Response of the Society of Jesus to Vatican II: Some Alacrity, Some Resistance' *Conversations in Jesuit Higher Education*, 42 (2012), 11.

[38] John Hick, *The Metaphor of God Incarnate: Christology in a Pluralistic Age*, 2nd ed. (Louisville, Kentucky: Westminster John Knox Press, 2006), 2.

[39] Ibid., 3.

[40] Ibid., 2.

[41] John Hick, 'Jesus and the World Religions,' in *The Myth of God Incarnate*, ed. idem (London: SCM Press, 1977), 178.

[42] George Karuvelil, 'Absolutism to Ultimacy: Rhetoric and Reality of Religious 'Pluralism',' *Theological Studies* 73/1 (2012): 55-81, http://search. ebscohost.com/login.aspx?direct=true&db=rlh&AN=71891797&site=eho st-live.

[43] John Hick, *An Interpretation of Religion: Human Responses to the Transcendent* (New Haven, Conn.: Yale University Press, 1989), 73-125.

[44] Thomas S. Kuhn, *The Structure of Scientific Revolutions*, 3rd ed. (Chicago: University of Chicago Press, 1996).

[45] Rogerson, in *The Oxford Handbook of Biblical Studies*, 842.

[46] http://www.vatican.va/roman_curia/congregations/cfaith/cti_ documents/rc_cti_1997_cristianesimo-religioni_en.html. Although the document does not take Hick's name, the previous year, Cardinal Ratzinger, Prefect of the Congregation for the Doctrine of Faith, had criticized Hick

by name. See http://www.ewtn.com/library/curia/ratzrela.htm. It is likely that Ratzinger criticized the non-Catholic Hick (very unusual for the Vatican) because of Hick's influence on the Catholics.

[47] http://w2.vatican.va/content/john-paul-ii/en/encyclicals/documents/hf_jp-ii_enc_14091998_fides-et-ratio.html, no. 5.

[48] Ibid., no.6.

[49] http://www.vatican.va/roman_curia/congregations/ccatheduc/documents/rc_con_ccatheduc_doc_20110128_dec-rif-filosofia_en.html, no. 9.

[50] Terrence W. Tilley, "Christianity and World Religions,' a Recent Vatican Document,' *Theological Studies* 60 (1999): 333, http://www.jstor.org/stable/1465926.

[51] *Decree*, no. 12.

[52] Benedict XVI, *Christmas Address to the Roman Curia*, 22 December 2005.

[53] *Decree*, no.3.

[54] Ibid., no. 4.

[55] John F. Thornton and Susan B. Varenne, eds., *The Essential Pope Benedict XVI: His Central Writings and Speeches*, 1st ed. (New York: HarperSanFrancisco, 2007), 1.

[56] This led to violent reactions from the Muslim world, including bombing of churches and even a killing.

[57] http://w2.vatican.va/content/benedict-xvi/en/speeches/2011/september/documents/hf_ben-xvi_spe_20110922_reichstag-berlin.html

[58] http://www.wsws.org/en/articles/2011/09/pope-s30.html

[59] Ibid.

[60] Wilhelm Guggenberger, 'Democracy and Truth: Pope Benedict's Speech in Berlin,' in *Democracy in an Age of Globalization*, ed. J. Thayil and A. Vonach (Innsbruck: Innsbruck University Press, 2015), 158.

[61] Anthony Kenny, *Medieval Philosophy*, *New History of Western Philosophy* (Oxford; New York: Clarendon Press; Oxford University Press, 2005), 54-74.

[62] J. C. A. Gaskin, 'Hume on Religion,' in *The Cambridge Companion to Hume*, ed. D. Fate Norton and J. A. Taylor (Cambridge; New York: Cambridge University Press, 2009), 480.

[63] *ST* I, q 2, a 1where he quotes Ps. 52:1 about the 'fool' who said in his heart, 'there is no God.'

[64] John F. Wippel, *Mediaeval Reactions to the Encounter between Faith and Reason, The Aquinas Lecture 1995* (Milwaukee: Marquette University Press, 1995), 8-34.

[65] Anthony Kenny, *The Rise of Modern Philosophy*, *New History of Western Philosophy* (Oxford; New York: Clarendon Press; Oxford University Press, 2006), 68.

[66] Peter Byrne, *Natural Religion and the Nature of Religion: The Legacy of Deism* (London: Routledge, 1989), 2-3.

[67] Buckley. Although Buckley is right in making this observation, he fails to recognize that given their scholastic background, they could not have done otherwise.

[68] René Latourelle, 'Introduction to the English Language Edition,' in *Dictionary of Fundamental Theology*, ed. R. Latourelle and R. Fisichella (New York: St. Paul's, 1990), xiii.

[69] Susan Haack, 'Recent Obituaries of Epistemology,' *American Philosophical Quarterly* 27/3 (1990): 199-212.

[70] Winrich Löhr, 'Christianity as Philosophy: Problems and Perspectives of an Ancient Intellectual Project,' *Vigiliae Christianae* 64/2 (2010): 160-188, http://dx.doi.org/10.1163/157007209x453331.

[71] See, Wippel.

[72] For the Platonic elements in Aquinas, see Patrick Quinn, *Aquinas, Platonism and the Knowledge of God* (Aldershot. Brookfield USA: Avebury, 1996).

14

The God-Jesus' Psyche
as Continuing Phenomenon

Konrad Noronha, SJ

Introduction: The Enigma of Expressing the God-Experience
Studying God and even expressing who God is, is extremely difficult.
Yet, much work has gone into trying to illustrate and spell out
understandings of God through an integration of theology/spirituality
with psychology, through the positivism, relativism, individualism, and
secularism that dominate modern thought (p.12).[1] The same is true
for neuroscience and evolutionary psychology which today provide
fertile ground for exploring views from ontology, anthropology, and
epistemology (p.158).[2] Religions have not arisen because of the denial
of God leading to human self-sufficiency and the alluring drive to
remake the world according to one's subjective designs, but because
of the faith of their followers. Religions have come into being because
of the personal and collective experiences of God-phenomena.

With no clear human way of understanding God, any way of
understanding is insufficient to describe something, someone invisible
and intangible. Attempts have been made to experience God variously
through art, writing, and day-to-day activities. These experiences
have been studied through different lenses, including the pure and

the social sciences. Research psychologists who have delved into the scientific study of human thought and behavior have provided some notable challenges to established religious beliefs especially with "doctrinally safe" ideas (p.41).[3] One of the ways in which God experience is described, studied and illustrated is through the science of phenomenology. Phenomenology

> ... is the study of structures of consciousness as experienced from the first-person point of view. The central structure of an experience is its intentionality, its being directed toward something, as it is an experience of or about some object. An experience is directed toward an object.[4]

The God phenomenon, the Jesus phenomenon, is obtained through scripture, even though scriptures are the writings of followers, and not the direct writings of Jesus. Another way of experiencing the God or Jesus phenomenon is through tradition. This helps in understanding the God-Jesus phenomenon better. The phenomenon then becomes a reality for the one who has experienced it.

1.   Scripture and Tradition

Scripture and/or tradition are two ways in which God is understood by religious people. Most scriptural understandings come through the Bible, while historical understandings come through tradition. "The term God or God image is found only six times in the Bible (New Revised Standard Version), three times about human beings (Gen 1:26, 27 and 9:6)[5] and three times about Jesus Christ (Col 1:15; 3:10; and 2 Cor 4:4)."[6] The Bible gives many God images, some of which are ruler, master, servant, father, spirit, warrior, destroyer, breath, fire, eternal power and divine nature, the merciful, living water, Abba Father, King, and Lord. The early Christian writers used anthropomorphisms to describe God. There are instances in the Hebrew Bible where God's manifestation in human form to individuals is mentioned:

> Abraham saw the Lord in the guise of three men (or angels) at Mamre. After wrestling with his own angel, Jacob claimed to have seen God's face and survived — a privilege denied Moses. Isaiah saw the Lord sitting on a throne, high and lofty and thought, "Woe

is me; I am a man of unclean lips and I live among a people of unclean lips and yet have seen the King the Lord of Hosts!" (Isa 6:5).[7](p. 21)

Classical theologies describe God as all-good, all-knowing, omnipresent, eternal, unchanging, deliverer, rock, always-present shepherd to his flock,[8] infinite and incorporeal, as well as impassible, immutable, ineffable, uncompounded, and indivisible. God is often depicted in Western culture as an older, white, powerful male, while more recent theologies describe God as young or black or female, or all three in combination.[9] In religious traditions, ways of worship, understandings of God, often become dogma.[10] Christ, even as God, always drew between Himself and the Father a distinction. He claimed unity and equality with the Father, but not identity. God-Jesus was God, not as the Father, but as the Son.

2.   The Psyche of God

Having looked at God images through the lens of Christian theology, we now examine the literature on God images in psychology. Most psychological theories relate God images to actions of the psyche, the mind, and early childhood influences. These include attachment theory,[11] object relations theory,[12] continuity theory,[13] narrative theory,[14] cognitive behavioral theory,[15] theistic psychotherapy,[16] faith development theory,[17] and well-being therapy.[18] Writing on God images, Rizzuto (2005, p. 40)[19] contends:

> Monotheistic religions offer very broad sources for forming representations of God and of the spiritual realm: The Hebrew Bible's imagery of God as creator and as a passionate leader of his people; Gospel narratives of Jesus as a man; the Godhead as Father, Son, and Holy Spirit; liturgical celebrations presenting God as bread and wine. God frequently comes in the company of his helpers: Abraham, Moses, the prophets, angels, Mary and Joseph, and a retinue of male and female saints. This vivid array offers the developing child and the adult an abundant assortment of possible components of the representation of God to suit any possible dynamic constellation from the moment of its early formation to its later transformations and psychic use.

Therefore, God is understood and experienced in different ways. Similarly, is the case with Jesus. Whatever be the lens through which Jesus is looked at, it is evident that it is he who becomes the object and the focus. He stirs up different emotions, especially for Christians, and those emotions reach the conscious dimension of the person's life. Whether it be theology, religious studies, psychology or any of the social sciences, Jesus affects, and there are effects on those who believe in him.

Psychology has looked at God-Jesus in various ways. His psyche has been studied, as has been his personality. There are various theoretical orientations and one of them is through the anima-animus concept of theorist Carl Jung (1875-1961). Anima is the feminine archetype in men, involving warmth, understanding, and moodiness. Anima complements male sexuality by providing an image of wholeness. Animus is the masculine archetype in women, involving reason, logic, and insensitivity.[20] For a man to be deemed well-adjusted and balanced, the feminine (anima) part of his personality must be consciously expressed, and a healthy person cannot have one without the other. Jung talks about the archetypal balance and harmony that we see in the personality of Jesus, with a predominance of the anima.

3.   The Phenomenon

The Jesus phenomenon identifies who Jesus Christ is and always will be, where he is to be found by his disciples and all others, and how he and the Father are related. In the world, today when we think of the Church and Jesus; the Church can never separate itself from Jesus' body. At the same time Jesus' body has become an extended Body. There is a movement from Jesus' humble beginnings as a child of Judaism to an understanding of him as the savior of the world. At the beginning of the Gospel we hear the words of Jesus' birth: "See—I am bringing you good news of great joy for all the [Jewish] people: to you is born this day in the city of David a Savior, who is the Messiah, the Lord" (Lk 2:10-11). At the end of the Gospel we hear in Jesus' farewell address to his disciples that they are to preach repentance for sinners "to all nations" (Lk 24:47).

Jesus often describes himself in relation to his Father. We know from the angel's message to Mary that Jesus will be the Son of God. Jesus' body belongs in the first place to God. As we hear him preach later, "My mother and my brothers are those who hear the word of God and do it" (Lk 8:21). One cannot come to God without hating one's father and mother, wife and child (Lk 14:26). Jesus said, "It is written, 'One does not live by bread alone'." He also said, "It is written, 'Worship the Lord your God, and serve only him'." In another instance, he said, "It is said, 'Do not put the Lord your God to the test'" (Lk 4:4, 7, 10). Jesus does not invoke his own strength and soul-power but invokes Scripture to respond.

In speaking about his ministry, Jesus said, "Your eye is the lamp of your body," (Lk 11:34). His ministry has much to do with seeing, with hearing, with opening the mouth, and reaching out. Jesus works among ordinary people, where his body is open, without fearing any infection from the sick, such as those with leprosy or possessed with devils or regarded as particularly sinful. Being "full of the Holy Spirit" from his baptism (Lk 4:1) and living "with the power of the Spirit" (Lk 4:14) in his ministry, we also realize that he is vulnerable to enemies.

Luke describes Jesus' actions in his parables and stories, such as the parable of the woman and the lost coin (Lk 15:8-10). The joy is equally great among God's angels over one sinner who repents, says Jesus, thereby linking the lowly to the exalted. In similar manner Jesus weeps over Jerusalem (Lk 19:41), and yet immediately afterward, in the cleansing of the temple, we see him not only angry but also impulsive in his actions (Lk 19:45-47).

While hanging on the cross, Jesus is further exposed to scorn and taunting. A separation occurs between body and spirit, with Jesus' body being surrendered to human enemies, Jews and Romans, while his spirit returns to communion with God. Of the seven last words, "Father, forgive them; for they do not know what they are doing" is the fifth (Lk 23:34), followed by "Truly I tell you, today you will be with me in Paradise" (23:43), addressed to the crucified robber who has defended him. With Jesus' final words, "Father, into your hands

I commend my spirit" (Lk 23:55), the body closes in on itself in the death process.

A final realization of who Jesus is occurs in the walk to Emmaus, where the eyes of the disciples were prepared by his words, but they do not see, until their fellowship is renewed in the breaking of bread. Jesus has broken bread before in the company of publicans and sinners, now he does so with the slow of heart and the unbelieving, before disappearing from their sight as a concrete bodily figure. Jesus as he lived his life, left behind a legacy. A better understanding of who Jesus is, can be gained by a deeper look at his psyche. Jesus' personality gives a clearer picture of the qualities and attitudes that attracted his followers. Looking at him through the lens of the psychologist Carl Jung (1875-1961) is one way.

4.   Understandings and Personality Correlates of Jesus

In trying to understand the phenomenon of Jesus we can draw from the Heideggerian understanding of faith as historical existence and ontic reality and that it must open to phenomenological analysis (p.165).[21] Psychology is one such science that seeks to understand the phenomenon of God-Jesus in his totality. Psychology today lays emphasis on the integration of inner processes and outer behavior and tries to identify the universal processes intrinsic to human life itself manifested in culturally-specific forms of behavior. There are several psychological tests that have been used to study the God-Jesus phenomenon like the Myers-Briggs Type Indicator, the Five Factor Model and the Adjective Check List. We also can understand him through the theoretical lens of Carl Jung.

4.1. The Jungian Psyche of Jesus

In the synoptics, there are 79 Jesus stories, 38 parables, 45 healings, 162 moral/spiritual teachings, and 59 prophecies. In Jungian thought, the goal in personality growth is to see and experience the interweaving of the anima and the animus in an individual. There is a significantly greater number of animus passages in the parables and moral/spiritual teachings.

> Defining animus and anima is difficult. Jung (1971) equated anima
> with vanity, helplessness, and uncertainty, while he identified animus
> with heroism, intelligence, creativity, and athletic ability. Anima is
> also identified with emotionality, sensitivity (social and otherwise),
> compassion, warmth, pathos, love, healing, and intuition, and animus
> with forceful teaching and argumentation, reason, logic, directness,
> decisive- ness, judgment, persuasiveness and social insensitivity.[22]
> (p.175)

Examples of Jesus' animus traits were generally found in the parables—
such as the parable of the merciful servant (Mt 18:23-35) or the parable
of the mustard seed (Mt 13:31-32) and moral or spiritual teachings
such as Jesus on murder (Mt 5:21-26) or the discourse on the leaven
(Mk 8:14-21). Jesus' anima predominated significantly in stories of
healings, Jesus stories, and prophecies. Examples of healings are the
healing of the dumb demoniac (Mt 9:32-34) and the man with dropsy
(Lk 14:1-6). Jesus stories include the temptation in the wilderness
(Mt 4:1-11) and the transfiguration (Lk 9:28-36). Prophecies include
the day of the Son of Man (Lk 17:22-37) and the prediction of the
destruction of Jerusalem (Lk 19:39-44).[23]

The overall portrayal of Jesus in the synoptics leads one to believe
that Jesus had an equally developed animus and anima. The individual
Gospel writers provide much the same picture of Jesus as having a
balanced animus and anima. One would expect that Jesus' animus
would be visible while the anima, as an unconscious phenomenon,
would remain below the surface of his personality. Jesus' animus was
not totally dominant; his anima emerged clearly. "The balance between
archetypes in Jesus' personality as described in the synoptics suggests
that his anima did indeed come to a conscious level"[24] (p.177).

The Jungian theoretical framework helps in understanding how
integrated Jesus was. Much research has also been conducted using the
Bible for indications about what could be an ideal personality type; a
personality type like Jesus. Various psychometric tests too have been
used to try and measure Jesus' temperament and personality. Two of
the commonest used tests are the Myers-Briggs Type Indicator[25] and
the Five Factor Model.[26]

4.2. According to the Myers-Briggs Type Indicator

Participants in a study using the Myers-Briggs Type Indicator done by Howell (2004)[27] were asked to rate Jesus according to his personality type.

> ... 25% of the participants perceived Jesus as having an ESFJ personality type; approximately 22% perceived Jesus as having an ENFP personality; approximately 20% perceived Jesus' personality as that of an ENFJ; and approximately 18% perceived Him as an ESF (p.53). 97% of participants seeing Jesus as an Extrovert, and along the Thinking/Feeling dimension, 87% perceiving Him to be a Feeler. A significant difference was also found among the four basic categories of Jesus' personality type with two of those types emerging as more common, that of the Intuitive-Feeler (43%) and the Sensing-Judger (37%), with those perceiving Jesus as a Sensing-Perceiver being fewer (18%) and those perceiving Him as an Intuitive-Thinker being the smallest in number (3%).[28] (p.53)

> Jesus could be said to be a strong Feeler due to his reputation as a healer, a comforter, and one who unselfishly sought to meet the needs of others. The perceptions of Jesus as a Judger would be among those who see him as having a very definite plan regarding their behavior. Those who view Jesus as a perceiver might be more likely to see him as flexible in his expectations for their own behavior, allowing them more spontaneity, and being less likely to have an unbending plan for the behaviors they exhibit. Jesus did meet needs for practicality and eye for detail characteristic of the Sensing types, as seen in his healing of the blind man (Jn 9:6-7), his feeding of the five thousand (Mat 14:15-21), or while on the cross his charge to John to care for his mother after his death (Jn 19:26-27). Yet Jesus also seemed to have the intuitive's flair for seeing beyond the visible when he praised those who would one day, without seeing, still believe (Jn 20:29), or in his focus away from the physical needs of the moment onto the bigger picture of spiritual needs as he gently reprimanded Martha's fretting over the details and affirmed Mary's choice to sit and listen (Lk 10:38-42)[29] (p.55).

Each of the four gospel writers exemplified one of the four basic Myers-Briggs types (Sensing-Judging, Sensing-Perceiving, Intuitive-Feeling, Intuitive-Thinking). They probably perceived Jesus' personality type differently based on his work from the perspective of the Gospel writer's own type. It has been thought that one expresses one's spirituality in a way consistent with, one's personality type and between personality and preferred interpretations of Scripture.

4.3. Personality Correlates according to the Five Factor Model

In a study using the NEO Five-Factor Inventory the profile of Jesus was compared to self-rated personality profiles to evaluate the degree to which images of Jesus are related to one's own self structure. "Jesus was perceived to be a compassionate, considerate, warmly embracing individual. Although accepting, he was perceived as having many qualities, such as being active and courageous, and not spineless or whiny. Jesus was not perceived as emotionally distressed, selfish, or slipshod (pp.367-368)."[30] Image of God (IOG) research, suggests that IOG may be like: (a) the opposite- sex parent; (b) the preferred parent; (c) the same-sex parent; or (d) both parents. Women, have an IOG more like the preferred parent.

4.4. Personality Correlates based on the Adjective Check List

Based on the Adjective Check List scales,[31] a sketch was drawn of Jesus' personality which portrayed Jesus as a caring and concerned individual who yet maintains a degree of detachment from those around him. This profile is reflective of the self-actualized person as described by Maslow (1970).

> The acceptance and compassion for others is balanced by a need for privacy. He has a concern to bring others into harmonious relationships while not always encouraging stereotypic roles and values. In many ways this profile reaffirms biblical presentations of Jesus. Perceptions of Jesus are significantly related to the needs and temperaments of the individuals themselves.[32] (p.370-371)

> From the literature, it seems reasonable that there may be a general tendency to internalize desirable characteristics of others in ourselves. It is comprehensible that Christians are more likely than non-Christians to consider the traits of Jesus Christ as exemplary and worth embodying. Furthermore, it could be that Christian ecclesial formation judge's certain traits, specifically those attributed to Christ, as desirable, and this formation instructs Christians to dutifully

exemplify the character of Christ. Said differently, it could be that as "Christians mature in their faith, they are directed to shape their lives in accordance with the life of Christ, and they are also taught the characteristics of Christ's life" (p.351).

5. Conclusion: Challenges of Treading New Paths Wedding Faith-and-Science

A science like psychology is valid to the extent that it recognizes God's presence and that there is agreement between the divine mind, the created order and the human mind (p.16).[33] With increasing openness to change comes a greater tendency to be embrace new experiences, tolerate uncertainty, and welcome diversity. There are those who appear to be motivated by a desire for the acquisition of new experiences that are novel, exciting, and diverse, which could then denigrate into new age understandings of faith (p.46)[34]

Believers must understand the human psyche in the light of faith. The human psyche can be understood or misunderstood only in the light of Church teachings of which revelation is one teaching. This can only happen by those who recognize the light of revelation as the light of revelation, and who can turn to God (p.176);[35] otherwise God, God-Jesus and faith would suffer from neo-pelagianism or neo-gnosticism leanings. The Christian psychologist is called upon to sift out ungodly speculations and prideful independence in modern psychology and understand the science of psychology with God's assumptions (p.20).[36]

Jesus, the phenomenon, whether studied psychologically or theologically has important religious implications.[37] Scholars theorize that much of our lives inhabit a middle ground between the unconscious and the conscious, the ground of the imagination. The language of the imagination and its images give rise to feelings of belonging, fundamental goodness, and control.[38] It is through the imagination that followers of Jesus assimilate and integrate him into their lives. Thus, it is this middle ground that acknowledges the importance of psychic representations, some of which may need to be challenged to expand and be transformed.[39] Therefore, the path to God is from the senses to the mind, where it becomes part of conception, imagination, and memory. The imagination is a way by which the inexpressible is made expressible and visible through and in which images, gestures, sounds, words, or actions disclose God in human experience, as it opens a realm unavailable to us.[40]

An integration of psychology and Christianity without devolving into neo-gnosticism or neo-pelagianism, means practitioners need to become immersed in Scripture and the Christian tradition. Integration within the Christian understanding would require an activation and integration of faith-beliefs and other beliefs that relate to human nature. This is true for a practicing counselor as well as for a client. Personal understandings must be considered to adequately interpret faith in its full sense and these would have to be assessed in terms of compatibility with the Scriptures. This would then help the practitioner and client make sense of original beliefs and faith understandings (pp.22-23).[41]

My own experience is that I have a strong personal faith; but it is a faith that many would consider unconventional. My work involves working to reconcile faith and reason and so I have had to forge a unique path. My faith journey is based on taking seriously the meaning of the word 'faith', which is not actual knowledge of the truth but rather the "evidence of things not seen," since if something is 'seen' we have knowledge, and then faith is no longer necessary. Also, uncertainty, ambiguity, and new ideas are not threats to be feared in faith traditions, rather they are challenges that mandate participation in an open scientific inquiry into God's truth (p.48).[42] It thus appears that for a Christian psychologist, counselor or a spiritual director to be available to a client, directee or counselee, s/he has to be able to draw from various fields, notably her/his faith along with her/his theoretical understandings.

Endnotes

[1] Johnson, E. L. (1997). Christ, The Lord of Psychology. *Journal of Psychology & Theology, 25*(1), 11-27.

[2] Garzon, F, Hall, E. L., Ripley, J. S. (2014). Teaching Christian Integration in Psychology And Counseling Courses. *Journal of Psychology & Theology, 42*(2), 131-135.

[3] Rempel, J. K. (2011). Christianity and Psychology: Living at The Intersection of Faith and Intellectual Inquiry. *Direction, 40* (1), 40-50.

[4] Smith, D. W. (Winter 2016 Edition). "Phenomenology." *The Stanford Encyclopedia of Philosophy*, Edward N. Zalta (Ed.). Retrieved from https://plato.stanford.edu/archives/win2016/entries/phenomenology/

[5] Highfield, R. (2010). Beyond the "Image of God" conundrum: A Relational View of Human Dignity. *Christian Studies, 24*, 21-32.

[6] Darton, M. (Ed.). (1976). *Image, Likeness of God, of Christ, of Adam*. In Modern Concordance to the New Testament. Garden City, NY: Doubleday & Company.

[7] Jensen, R. M. (2008). Those who see God receive life: The Icon, The Idol, And the Invisible God. *Worship, 82*(1), 19-40. Retrieved from http://www.litpress.org/

[8] Burke, R. (1977). Rahner and Dunne: A New Vision of God. *Iliff Review, 34*(3), 37-49.

[9] Popovici, A. (2011). Speakers Discuss Images of God. *National Catholic Reporter, 47*(15), 11. Retrieved from http://ncronline.org/

[10] McGrath, J. E. (2012). Jesus, Gnosis and Dogma. *Review of Biblical Literature. 14*, 268-271.

[11] Granqvist, P., & Kirkpatrick, L. A. (2004). Religious Conversion and Perceived Childhood Attachment: A Meta-analysis. *International Journal for the Psychology of Religion, 14*(4), 223-250. doi: 10.1207/s15327582ijpr1404

[12] Rizzuto, A. (1979). *The Birth of The Living God: A Psychoanalytic Study*. Chicago, IL: University of Chicago Press.

[13] Atchley, R. (1995). *The continuity of the spiritual self*. In M. S. Kimble, S. H. McFadden, J. W. Ellor & J. J. Seeber (Eds.), Aging, Spirituality, and Religions: A Handbook. *1*, 69-73. Minneapolis, MN: Fortress Press.

[14] Poll, J. B., & Smith, T. B. (2003). The Spiritual Self: Toward a Conceptualization of Spiritual Identity Development. *Journal of Psychology & Theology, 31*(2), 129. Retrieved from http://www.biola.edu/jpt/

[15] Madewell, J., & Shaughnessy, M. F. (2009). An Interview with Judith Beck About Cognitive Therapy: Judith Beck. *North American Journal of Psychology, 11*(1), 29-36. Retrieved from http://www.najp.8m.com

[16] O'Grady, K., & Richards, P. (2007). Theistic Psychotherapy and The God Image. *Journal of Spirituality in Mental Health, 9*(3/4), 183-209. doi:10.1300/J515v09n03-09.

[17] Fowler, J. W. (1981*). Stages of Faith: The Psychology of Human Development and the Quest for Meaning.* New York: Harper & Row.

[18] Sperry, Len. (2010). Psychotherapy Sensitive to Spiritual Issues: A Postmaterialist Psychology Perspective and Developmental Approach. *Psychology of Religion and Spirituality, 2*(1), 46-56. doi:10.1037/a0018549.

[19] Rizzuto, A. (2005). *Psychoanalytic Considerations about Spiritually Oriented Psychotherapy.* In L. Sperry, & E. P. Shafranske, (Eds.), Spiritually oriented psychotherapy, 31-50. American Psychological Association. doi: 10.1037/10886-002

[20] Stahlke, P. E. (1990). "Jungian Archetypes and the Personality of Jesus in the Synoptics." *Journal of Psychology & Theology, 18*(2), 174-178.

[21] Jones, G. (1989). Phenomenology and Theology: a Note on Bultmann and Heidegger. *Modern Theology, 5*(2), 161-179.

[22] Stahlke, Paulette E. (1990). "Jungian Archetypes and the Personality of Jesus in the Synoptics." *Journal of Psychology & Theology, 18*(2), 174-178.

[23] Ibid

[24] Stahlke, Paulette E. (1990). "Jungian Archetypes and the Personality of Jesus in the Synoptics." *Journal of Psychology & Theology 18*(2), 174-178.

[25] MBTI Basics. Retrieved from http://www.myersbriggs.org/my-mbti-personality-type/mbti-basics/home.htm?bhcp=1

[26] McCrae, R. R. and John, O. P. (1992), An Introduction to the Five-Factor Model and its Applications. *Journal of Personality, 60,* 175–215. doi:10.1111/j.1467-6494.1992.tb00970.x

[27] Howell, S. H. (2004). "Students 'Perceptions of Jesus' Personality as Assessed by Jungian-Type Inventories." *Journal of Psychology & Theology 32*(1), 50-58.

[28] Ibid.

[29] Howell, S. H. (2004). "Students 'Perceptions of Jesus' Personality as Assessed by Jungian-Type Inventories." *Journal of Psychology & Theology 32*(1), 50-58.

[30] Piedmont, R. L., Williams, J. G., & Ciarrocchi, J. W. (1997). Personality Correlates on One's Image of Jesus: Historiographic Analysis Using the Five-Factor Model of Personality. *Journal of Psychology & Theology, 25*(3), 363-373.

[31] Gough, H. G., Heilbrun, A. B. *The Adjective Check List Manual.* (1983). California: Consulting Psychologists Press

[32] Piedmont, R. L., Williams, J. G., & Ciarrocchi, J. W. (1997). Personality Correlates on One's Image of Jesus: Historiographic Analysis Using the Five-Factor Model of Personality. *Journal of Psychology & Theology, 25*(3), 363-373.

[33] Johnson, E. L. (1997). Christ, The Lord of Psychology. *Journal of Psychology & Theology, 25*(1), 11-27.

[34] Rempel, J. K. (2011). Christianity and psychology: Living at the Intersection of Faith and Intellectual Inquiry. *Direction, 40*(1), 40-50.

[35] Jones, G. (1989). Phenomenology and Theology: A Note on Bultmann and Heidegger. *Modern Theology, 5*(2), 161-179.

[36] Johnson, E. L. (1997). Christ, The Lord of Psychology. *Journal of Psychology & Theology, 25*(1), 11-27.

[37] Kelsey, M T. (1970). God, Education and the Unconscious. *Religious Education, 65*(3), 227-234.

[38] Philibert, P. J. (1985). Symbolic and Diabolic Images of God. *Studies in Formative Spirituality, 6*(1), 87-101.

[39] Helsel, P. (2009). Introduction to Three Diagnoses of God. *Pastoral Psychology, 58*(2), 181-182. doi: 10.1007/s11089-008-0141-2

[40] Helsel, P. (2009). Introduction to Three Diagnoses of God. Pastoral Psychology, 58(2), 181-182. doi: 10.1007/s11089-008-0141-2

[41] Johnson, E. L. (1997). Christ, The Lord of Psychology. *Journal of Psychology & Theology, 25*(1), 11-27.

[42] Rempel, J. K. (2011). Christianity and Psychology: Living at The Intersection of Faith and Intellectual Inquiry. *Direction, 40*(1), 40-50.

15

Mastery versus
Mystery on the Path to Progress

Kuruvilla Pandikattu, SJ

Introduction: Saved by Self or by God?

The ancient Roman politician and lawyer Marcus Tullius Cicero observed of his own civilization that people thank the gods for their material prosperity, but never for their virtue, for this is their own doing. This is the beginning of Pelagianism. It answers the question, "Can we really save ourselves?" in the affirmative. Princeton theologian B. B. Warfield considers Pelagianism as "the rehabilitation of that heathen view of the world," and concluded with characteristic clarity, "There are fundamentally only two doctrines of salvation: that salvation is from God, and that salvation is from ourselves. The former is the doctrine of common Christianity; the latter is the doctrine of universal heathenism."[1] Warfield's sharp criticisms are consistent with the witness of the church ever since Pelagius and his disciples championed the heresy, writes Michael S. Horton, Professor of Theology and Apologetics at Westminster Seminary California, Editor-in-Chief of *Modern Reformation* magazine. St Jerome, the 4th century Latin Father, called it "the heresy of Pythagoras and Zeno," as, in general, paganism rested on the fundamental conviction that human beings have it within their power to save themselves. What, then, was Pelagianism and how did it get started?

First, Horton claims that this heresy originated with the first human couple. It was actually defined and labeled in the 5th century, when a British monk, Pelagius, came to Rome. He was deeply distressed with the immorality of this centre of Christendom and set out to reform the morals of clergy and laity alike. This moral campaign required a great deal of energy. Pelagius found many supporters and admirers for his cause. The only obstacle on his way was the emphasis that emanated from the influential African bishop, Augustine. Augustine taught that human beings, because they are born in original sin, are incapable of saving themselves. Apart from God's grace, it is impossible for a person to obey or even to seek God. Representing the entire race, Adam sinned against God. This resulted in the total corruption of every human being since, so that our very wills are in bondage to our sinful condition. Only God's grace, which he bestows freely as he pleases upon his elect, is credited with the salvation of human beings.

In sharp contrast, Pelagius was driven by moral concerns and his theology was calculated to provide the fuel needed for moral and social improvement. Augustine's emphasis on human helplessness and divine grace would surely paralyze the pursuit of moral improvement, since people could sin with impunity, fatalistically concluding, "I couldn't help it; I'm a sinner." So, Pelagius countered by rejecting original sin. According to Pelagius, Adam was merely a bad example, not the father of our sinful condition. According to him, we are sinners because we sin, and not the other way around! Consequently, of course, the Second Adam, Jesus Christ, was a good example. Salvation is a matter chiefly of following Christ instead of Adam, rather than being transferred from the condemnation and corruption of Adam's race and placed 'in Christ', clothed in his righteousness and made alive by his gracious gift. What men and women need is moral direction and strong will, not a new birth. Therefore, Pelagius saw salvation in purely naturalistic terms—the progress of human nature from sinful behaviour to holy behaviour, by following the example of Christ.

In his *Commentary on Romans*,[2] Pelagius thought of grace as God's revelation in the Old and New Testaments, which enlightens us and serves to promote our holiness by providing explicit instruction in godliness and many worthy examples to imitate. So, human nature is not conceived in sin. After all, the will is not bound by the sinful condition and its affections; choices determine whether one will obey God, and thus be saved. In short, Pelagius taught that the human will, as created with its abilities by God, was sufficient to live a sinless life, although he believed that God's grace assisted every good work. Pelagianism has come to be identified with the view (whether taught by Pelagius or not) that human beings can earn salvation by their own efforts.[3]

The aim of this article is to help trace out elements of Pelagianism in contemporary society. For this, we first ask the basic question: Is there real progress, including spiritual progress, today? Then we take up an example of clear Pelagian trend in the scientific quest for transhumanism. This will enable us to reflect on the mystery (or the unbidden) inherent in our life, so that we can be open totally to grace. This will enable us to trace some of the Pelagian tendencies in our own lives. Finally, following the French philosopher and theologian, Paul Ricœur, we shall look at the Christian vision of freedom and life in terms of the paradoxical consent of hope.

1.   Is Human Progress Real?

Is modern society better than that of the 18th century, or the Renaissance, or ancient Greece or Rome? The relentless 24/7 news media portray a world of conflict, disaster, and human turpitude. Was there ever a golden age, or are we living in it? I believe there is a clear answer to this question, and it is good for us to realize it.[4] I have just been re-reading a splendid essay on the subject by historians, the Pulitzer Prize winner (1968) and the Presidential Medal of Freedom (1977), Will Durant and his wife Ariel, written in 1968. Richard Koch, author, 'The 80/20

Principle,"[5] summarizes it before adding his own views, based partly on a difference of perspective and partly on hindsight from the last half century. His is a conservative capitalistic and liberal perspective.

The Durant couple gives a rather sombre view. The idea of progress, they say, finds itself in dubious shape. Maybe the Middle Ages and the Renaissance, which stressed mythology and art rather than science and power, were wiser than us. We keep increasing our technology and knowledge, yet with good comes evil. Our comforts and conveniences may have weakened our stamina and moral qualities. "We double, triple, centuple our speed, but we shatter our nerves in the process, and we are the same trousered apes at two thousand miles an hour as when we had legs." We have news from around the planet, "but at times we envy our ancestors, whose peace was only gently disturbed by the news of their village. We have laudably bettered the conditions of life for skilled workingmen and the middle class, but we have allowed our cities to fester with dark ghettos and slimy slums."[6]

You can imagine the drift. Is modern art, philosophy, or architecture superior to that of ancient Greece? Are we better people? If progress "means an increase in happiness, its case is lost almost at first sight. Our capacity for fretting is endless ... we always find an excuse for being magnificently miserable ... It seems silly to define progress in terms that would make the average child a higher, more advanced product of life than the adult or the sage—for certainly the child is the happiest of the three."[7]

But then our historians change tack. How should we define progress? The answer they come up with is a good one – "we shall define progress as the increasing control of the environment by life." Has the average person "increased his ability to control the conditions of his life?"[8]

And in a rather discursive way, they end up saying, more or less, "Yes". The tripling of life spans in the last three centuries indicates better control of the environment. "Shall we count it as trivial that famine has been eliminated in modern states, and that one country can now grow enough food to overfeed itself and yet send hundreds of millions of bushels of wheat to nations in need? Are we ready to scuttle the science that has so diminished superstition, obscurantism, and religious intolerance, or the technology that has spread food, home ownership, comfort, education, and leisure beyond any precedent?" Education, they say, is the transmission of civilization, "so our finest contemporary achievement is ... the provision of higher education for all."

Koch proposes three different criteria. One is that of our historians – *the better control of our environment*. I would highlight not only the increase in prosperity and life expectancy, but also the decrease in disease and suffering, and in warfare and violence. Life is better than it has ever been for most people on the planet, and that is a stunning achievement for which science, technology, and the dedication of a huge number of physicians, scientists, and business people deserve unstinted praise.

A second criterion is political and social – *the spread of freedom and equality for all people, regardless of social class, nationality or ethnicity, gender, or sexual orientation*. Our society is far from faultless in this regard, but in acknowledging that fact we are miles ahead of any previous generation. Koch holds that next generation will be well ahead of us, and so on, because the liberal sensitivity is cumulative. He takes the examples of rights of gay and liberation of women.

Given his liberal bias, the third criterion he proposes is *the spread of free enterprise*. He acknowledges that the free market economy "will never be loved, but they bring with them not only greater prosperity, but also greater fairness and opportunity—again, far from ideal, but hugely better than under a bureaucratic society—for the majority of people. Personal creativity can be expressed in an open economy to a massively greater extent than under a closed one."

Of course, there are deep problems, Koch admits. One is that the existing trends towards greater control of the environment, greater freedom and equality, and greater economic freedom, need to be further extended. Future generations will see that we are so far only scratching the surface in all these areas. Another problem is that of the underclass and lack of upward social mobility. In some countries, this problem is severe and getting worse. We need creative solutions here, and a change in the system of education, especially for young children, is long overdue. A third problem is the lack of meaning in society. Modern secular society has brought enormous benefits, but in rejecting the importance of religion – or its equivalent for atheists and agnostics – it has thrown the baby out with the bath water. Depression and drug and alcohol dependence are symptoms of a lack of moral seriousness. No society can hang together without people of goodwill believing in a common ideology and having a sense that every day can advance the meaning of life for themselves and their fellow citizens.

So, yes, progress is real. We should not be afraid to shout that message from the rooftops. Similar to the scientific and cultural progress, we may assume that there is also moral, religious and spiritual progress, though it is debatable. I like to believe that spiritual progress is distinct and related to the scientific and cultural progress that Koch talks about. One clear example of progress—which has a distinct streak of Pelagianism—is Transhumanism, the claim that we can save ourselves through technological progress, including the merger of human beings with sophisticated machines.

2.   Transhumanism: Mastery over Ourselves

Transhumanism (abbreviated as H⁺) is the conviction that the human race can evolve beyond its current physical and mental limitations, especially by means of science and technology. It is an international intellectual movement that aims to transform the human condition by developing and making widely available sophisticated technologies to greatly enhance human intellect and physiology. With Elon Musk advocating the need for humans to merge with machines and Zoltan Istvan, a transhumanist politician, running for Governor in California, an intellectual movement that sat on the fringes throughout the 20th century is poised to hit the mainstream.[9]

Simon Young, in *Designer Evolution: A Transhumanist Manifesto*, pens a letter to Nature itself in which he declares "our intention to take over the business of Evolution."[10] He favourably quotes the novelist William Gibson, who observed that "here we are, the first species that's ever effectively taken over its own evolution," and claims that "we're going to change big time. It's like human evolution is now *designer evolution*." Further, in his book *Radical Evolution*, Joel Garreau describes what we might expect to see through future "enhancements."[11] These include some relating to our physical nature, such as longevity, accelerated healing, and greater beauty; but also changes to our psyches, including heightened cognitive abilities, photographic memory, total recall, 'vaccination' against pain, the elimination of sleep, wireless delivery of information directly to the brain, and even electronically interconnected consciousness—and thus a wholly transformed experience of selfhood. As Garreau declares, we are in the midst of "transforming no less than human nature."[12]

Michael Sandel, an eminent critique of transhumanism, is quite perceptive: "The deepest moral objection to enhancement lies less in the perfection it seeks than in the human disposition it expresses and promotes ... The problem is in the hubris of the designing parents, in their drive to master the mystery of birth ... it would disfigure the relation between parent and child, and deprive the parent of the humility and enlarged human sympathies that an openness to the unbidden can cultivate."[13] He adds further: "The deeper danger is that [enhancement] represents a kind of hyper-agency — a Promethean aspiration to remake nature, including human nature, to serve our purpose and satisfy our desires ... And what the drive to mastery misses and may even destroy is an appreciation of the gifted character of human powers and achievements."[14]

Many thinkers, including atheist philosophers like Ronald Dworkin and Jürgen Habermas, comment: "Recent philosophy has neglected important questions about value — questions that are not about wellbeing, autonomy or justice but about what attitude we should have to the world and our place in it." These are questions we must ask even if we are not religious believers. But if the science proves to be correct—if the transhumanist project really does succeed in remaking our nature—then we are talking about a subject (*post*-human nature) with which we as yet do not have any knowledge or experience.

3. Mystery and the Unbidden

If transhumanism claims to give us full mastery or control, can we go to the other extreme and surrender ourselves to the truly mysterious or unbidden? Can we think of a "religious sentiment without religion"? Can we truly give up both the "unpredictable element" or "deeper design" in our lives and in the universe? Rather, should we not look for "Invisible hand" (Adam Smith) or "Inner voice" (Mahatma Gandhi) and still be open to surprises? Between the bidden and unbidden, or, put differently, between what we have mastered, and what we have not, or cannot, there remains an area of creative tension.

For a convinced believer, if God exists, then *nothing* is absolutely unbidden. *Nothing* happens that doesn't have its source in some agency. There is *always* some agent that is ultimately responsible for everything that happens. The absolutely, unqualifiedly unbidden exists *only* in a naturalist, Godless universe. Indeed, in such a universe nearly everything that happens is absolutely unbidden.[15] It simply occurs, without meaning or purpose. Its nature cannot be known and it itself becomes unknowable. Theist religions may encourage humility and submission to God's will. But they do not encourage openness to what is *absolutely* unbidden, notes Kahane.[16]

Our attitude to total mystery (unbidden) *directly* depends on whether we believe that God exists. For if God *doesn't* exist, then there is no master plan, and what we leave to chance we *really* leave to purposeless chance. So, why should we just let things happen, when it's in our power to make them better? To leave things to chance would suggest that they don't really *matter* to us. So, at least for naturalists, there is a clear rational presumption in favour of mastery. because it expresses God's good will and accepting it *simply because it happens*— between accepting a providential plan that is unbidden only *relative* to us and accepting what is *absolutely* unbidden.

4.   The Christian Response: Salvation as Gratuitous Gift

Pelagianism tends to belittle the role of grace and the divine action in human life. It asserts our own inner capabilities. This may be closely related to the fragile tension between necessity and human freedom that we experience in our daily situations. The way we respond to freedom, following the French thinker Paul Ricœur, can help us perceive our Pelagian tendencies. Ricoeur raises the issue: How do we human act freely when responding to the involuntary aspects of our nature? [17] Our different responses correspond to different mythological types:

- Human beings can rebel against their own basic limited constitution or deny their own finiteness. This corresponds to the *Promethean* Denial.

- One identifies oneself with the one's limited constitution, and attempts to accept the inevitable, which would be equated with *Orphic* Identification.

- One can distance oneself from one's own constitution and try to be an indifferent and passive observer then one would be modeled on *Stoic* Duality.

- Finally, one can with reservations consent to a future in hope, which would correspond to an *Eschatological* Hope.[18]

The analysis of the human will, according to Ricœur, leads to a paradox of tension between the willing and non-willing, and to a *freedom* which is at the same time *bound* by its very nature. This double character of the human will lets itself be shown at every level of Ricœurian enquiry. This paradox, which concretises itself in this way, cannot be eliminated. A freedom in which *creativity* and *necessity* are fully reconciled in itself, would not anymore be a *creative* freedom. Such a freedom, though imaginable, cannot be realized. It is actually a *limit-idea*.

The types of consent and corresponding freedom may be elaborated, based on Ricœur's analysis of human will with relation to the given dimensions of life. The reciprocity of the voluntary and involuntary is maintained throughout Ricœur's description of the structure of the will. In relation to human freedom, the will could be studied in its two basic aspects, which are ultimately seen as existence as *received* and existence as *task,* and that is a way of saying that the involuntary is *for* the will just as the will is *by reason of* the involuntary. This tension between the voluntary and involuntary reaches its limit in relation to that which is absolutely involuntary. It is in this context that Ricœur develops and points to the "secret conciliation" in a paradoxical philosophy. Thus, the study of the will could also be undertaken with reference to the tension between *Decision, Consent* and *Necessity.* Ricœur does this by using the following categories:

4.1. Promethean Rebellion

Consent to necessity is, after all, not the only possible movement of the will confronting necessity. Freedom can here appear as a negation or as a refusal to accept necessity. Moreover, freedom has a privileged position, since it is through freedom that necessity is recognised. If the will makes the movement of refusal in relation to necessity [involuntary], freedom appears as: (a) the sorrow of finitude, (b) the sorrow of the unformed and (c) the sorrow of contingency. Desire, then, which is expressed in the refusal of necessity, is the desire for the subject, and that is precisely closed to freedom and bound to the necessity of a finite situation. Ultimately, the final act of refusal, like Promethean rebellion, (as rebellion against the substitution of finite being) might well be self-annihilation.

Promethean myth represents the human will's potential for heroic defiance against arbitrary authority and the capacity of human reason to obtain knowledge from the natural world. Fire symbolizes knowledge and reason—the divine spark of human thought and creativity. Prometheus is the archetypal revolutionary who helps to transform the human condition from one at the mercy of outside forces to one that is master of its own destiny.

4.2. Imperfect Consent

After having arrived at the juncture of freedom and necessity, Ricœur maintains that it is in this junction that the "secret reconciliation" could occur. This secret reconciliation and hidden relationship is to be uncovered by an understanding of the movement of consent. Ricœur hopes to transcend necessity, without negating it, through consent. Again, it is at this very juncture of freedom and necessity that the limit of *descriptions* is arrived at. Here, phenomenology may be transcended. "In any case it is clear that the unity of man with himself and with his world cannot be integrally included within the limits of a description of the *cogito*. For this to be the case phenomenology must transcend itself in metaphysics." Thus, the whole and the other had become the horizon of the *cogito*. For Ricœur, philosophical anthropology without ontology is empty. According to Ricœur, this insight is also the central Cartesian insight, and that the *cogito* has a necessary relationship to Ontology and Transcendence. But we must also be cautious to reify subjectivity into an ontology and refuse to return to the "reign of the object" which reduces the fullness of the subjective experience. It is here that the movement from the refusal to consent takes on additional significance. The way in which consent is made emerges as of extreme importance. Ricœur indicates that there are three major alternatives in the movement from refusal to consent: The *imperfect consent*, the *hyperbolic consent* and the *paradoxical consent*.

In the *Imperfect Consent* (Stoicism), as in the case of the Stoics, the relationship of subject to the Whole (Transcendence) is grasped as a relation of Part to Whole. This type of consent, or affirmation, is imperfect because this is actually a *detachment* rather than a reconciliation of freedom and necessity. In Stoicism, therefore, the body is reduced to the "already dead" and feeling to "opinion". Thus, subjectivity is reduced and the subjective recovery of incarnate existence is not made. "The whole Stoic strategy is tied to two corollaries: reduction of the body to 'already a corpse' and of affection to opinion; there are no 'passions of the soul' in the fact of the body, there are only actions of the soul: the body is inert, the soul impenetrable." The Stoic escapes the shrivelling of his scorning effort because he knows himself to be a part of the Whole." He explains: "I am not the center of being, I myself am only one being *among* beings. The whole which includes me is the parabola of being which I am not. I come from all to myself as from Transcendence to existence." Further, he will agree: "I love my misery engulfed in the grandeur of the world which Marcus Aurelius called the 'health of the universe.'" Stoicism, on the one hand, represents the pole of detachment and scorn, Orphism, on the other, the loss of the self in necessity. Stoic consent seems to destroy itself because it is not reconciliation but rather detachment. Therefore, Ricœur affirms: "The ultimate limit of Stoicism is remaining on the threshold of the poetry of adoration."

4.3. *In the Hyperbolic Consent (Orphism),*

In the Hyperbolic Consent found in the Orphic tradition (for example, in Goethe and Rilke), the relation of the subject to Transcendence is to be found in a poetic admiration of Transcendence. The Orphic act of consent is not to choose, move or act but to contemplate. Here again, consent in this sense fails to preserve the fullness of subjectivity. Here subjectivity is lost in a vague metaphor and Nature is made into an idol. Subjectivity is reduced by losing itself in the act of admiration. For in the act of admiration identity is achieved! "Contemplation and admiration are the *detour* of consent," according to Ricœur. "The poetry of adoration is the soul of Orphism." In the Orphic incantation (or intoxication), the universe travails under the hard law of "Die and become." Thus, the goodness of the world is the "Die and become," it is metamorphosis. Nature is majestic in its sheer existence. All non-willed existence is neither a catastrophe nor a prison, but an initial generosity and an initial victory.

Ricœur maintains that orphism remains a limit which one neither can nor dare reach. "It is the hyperbolic consent which *loses* me in necessity just as Stoicism was the imperfect consent which exiled me from the whole which it nonetheless strove to admire." Such orphic admiration (or contemplation) removes me from the centre and places me back among the ciphers. Consent gives me to myself and reminds me that no one can absolve me from the act of *yes*. Admiration and consent are circular: "Consent by itself remains on an ethical and prosaic level; admiration is the cutting edge of the soul, lyric and poetic." "Admiration becomes a help because it is beyond willing;

it is the incantation of poetry which delivers me from myself and purifies me." One who refuses one's foundation refuses the absolute involuntary which is also a shadow of the relative involuntary of motives and capacities. One who refuses one's motives and capacities annuls oneself as act. The *no*, like the *yes*, can only be total.

4.4. *Paradoxical Consent of Hope*

Only in the *Paradoxical Consent* can we preserve the necessary tension between the fullness of subjectivity and the sense of the Transcendent as a source of subjectivity. Although both of the above types of consent avoid the refusal to seek to affirm necessity, they do so at the cost of reducing subjectivity in its fullness. This refusal is avoided in the *Paradoxical Consent*. To refuse necessity is seen as the defiance of Transcendence—the refusal is perceived to be at the heart of the Rupture. Here, the relationship between the subject and Transcendence is paradoxical. In refusing necessity, the self reaches its limits and necessity is that which opposes freedom as the Wholly-Other, the absolute limit which breaks the possibility for the self to make a complete circle with itself. The *Paradoxical Consent* is the movement of the will which affirms necessity as the source of its being. It is the acceptance which affirms character, unconsciousness and vital organisation and in which finitude and finiteness are affirmed. Thus, it is the consent of hope. The affirmation of hopeful consent makes possible an engagement in life which does not reduce subjectivity and refuse Transcendence.

Such a hope has gone through both Exile (Denial and Stoicism) or Confusion (Orphism). If there is a narrow path between exile and confusion, it is because consent to limitations is an act which is never complete. Perhaps no one can follow consent to the end, admits Ricœur. That is because, "Evil is the scandal which always separates consent from inhuman necessity." Suffering and evil, respected in their own shocking mystery, protected against degradation into a problem, lie in our way as the impossibility of saying an unreserved *yes* to character, the unconscious, and life and of transforming the sorrow of the finite, the indefinite, and of contingence perfectly into joy. So, the Christian answer to the scandal of the cross and the need for salvation lies not in Promethean Denial (Revolt or War), nor in Stoic Detachment (Self-abnegation) nor in Total Admiration of the world (Orphic Ecstasy or Romanticism). It lies is the imperfect consent rooted in hope. It is love that knows pain and death. Incidentally, Pope Benedict XVI himself admits there isn't a full answer to suffering in rare TV interview. "I ask myself the same question," he said. "We don't have the answers, but we know that Jesus suffered as innocent children suffer."[19]

Thus, the salvation for a Christian comes not through Knowledge (Gnosticism or Jiddu Krishnamurthi), nor through Self-Control and Striving (Pelagianism or Ramana Maharshi). Not even through Self-Indulgence (Carvakas or Bhagwan Rajneesh), but through Love that suffers. Through Love that knows and experiences suffering and still hopes for the triumph of LOVE, that is Resurrection (Jesus).

5.   Conclusion

Some polls in the USA indicate that 77% of the conservative evangelical Christians believe that human beings are basically good and 84% of these conservative Protestants believe that in salvation: "God helps those who help themselves." Viewpoints like this indicate Pelagian tendencies among us. It is this heresy that lies at the bottom of much of popular psychology (human nature, basically good, is warped by its environment), political crusades (we are going to bring about salvation and revival through this campaign), and evangelism and church growth (seeing conversion as a natural process, just like changing from one brand of soap to another, and seeing the evangelist or entrepreneurial pastor as the one who actually adds to the church those to be saved).[20]

At its root, the Reformation was an attack on Pelagianism and its rising influence, as it choked out the life of Christ in the world. It asserted that "salvation is of the Lord" (Jonah 2:9), and that "it therefore does not depend on the decision or effort of man (sic), but on the mercy of God" (Rom 9:16). If that message is recovered, and Pelagianism is once more confronted with the Word of God, the glory of God will again fill the earth.[21]

Thus, our Mastery over self and nature (Transhumanism) can help us, not save us. Our submission to Mystery (Unbidden) can enable us, not liberate us. Our salvation can come only through Love lived in intense suffering and intimate joy, leading to self-emptying and Beatific Vision. It comes through life experiences of peace and sharing leading to abundance of joy of the Kingdom of God. It stems from forgiveness, reconciliation and mercy leading to physical and spiritual Wholeness.

Today, we urgently need to retain the tension between mastery and mystery (unbidden); between God's grace and human effort; between salvation in this world and next; between control and submission; between human effort and scientific progress and genuine spiritual progress; between promethean rebellion and orphic adoration! We need to work hard, strive, excel and suffer. We need to love, forgive and show mercy; for our salvation comes only from the Lord! Never from ourselves! Then, after having struggled and toiled, we can genuinely submit ourselves to the Lord, saying, "We are unworthy servants; we have only done our duty" (Lk 17:10).

Endnotes

[1] *Michael S. Horton, "Pelagianism: The Religion of Natural Man,"* www.modernreformation.org/mr94/ janfeb/mr9401pelagianism.html.

[2] Pelagius, *Pelagius's Commentary on St Paul's Epistle to the Romans*, ed. T. De Bruyn, Oxford, Clarendon Press, 2002.

[3] In 411, Paulinus of Milan came up with a list of six heretical points in the Pelagian message. (1) Adam was created mortal and would have died whether he had sinned or not; (2) the sin of Adam injured himself alone, not the whole human race; (3) newborn children are in the same state in which Adam was before his fall; (4) neither by the death and sin of Adam does the whole human race die, nor will it rise because of the resurrection of Christ; (5) the law as well as the gospel offers entrance to the Kingdom of Heaven; and (6) even before the coming of Christ, there were men wholly without sin. 2 Further, Pelagius and his followers denied unconditional predestination. It is worth noting that Pelagianism was condemned by more church councils than any other heresy in history. In 412, Pelagius's disciple Coelestius was excommunicated at the Synod of Carthage; the Councils of Carthage and Milevis condemned Pelagius's *De libero arbitrio*—On the

Freedom of the Will; Pope Innocent I excommunicated both Pelagius and Coelestius, as did Pope Zosimus. Eastern emperor Theodosius II banished the Pelagians from the East as well in AD 430. The heresy was repeatedly condemned by the Council of Ephesus in 431 and the Second Council of Orange in 529. In fact, the Council of Orange condemned even Semi-Pelagianism, which maintains that grace is necessary, but that the will is free by nature to choose whether to cooperate with the grace offered. The Council of Orange even condemned those who thought that salvation could be conferred by the saying of a prayer, affirming instead (with abundant biblical references) that God must awaken the sinner and grant the gift of faith before a person can even seek God. (From Horton)

[4] Richard Koch, "Is Progress Real," Huffpost, Jan 31, 2017, https://www.huffingtonpost.com/richard-koch/is-progress-real_b_14500590.html

[5] The Pareto principle, named after economist Vilfredo Pareto, specifies an unequal relationship between inputs and outputs. The principle states that 20% of the invested input is responsible for 80% of the results obtained.

[6] *Ibid.*

[7] Cited in Richard Koch, "Is Progress Real," Huffpost, Jan 31, 2017, https://www.huffingtonpost.com/richard-koch/is-progress-real_b_14500590.html

[8] *Ibid.*

[9] Rich Haridy, "Welcome to the era of transhumanism" *New Atlas*, February 16, 2017. https://newatlas.com/transhumanism-mainstream-era-popular/47941/

[10] Simon Young, *Designer Evolution: A Transhumanist Manifesto*, Amherst, N.Y.: Prometheus, 2005.

[11] Joel Garreau, *Radical Evolution: The Promise and Peril of Enhancing Our Minds, Our Bodies—and What It Means to Be Human*, New York, Broadway, 2006.

[12] Patrick J. Deenan, "The Science of Politics and the Conquest of Nature" in *The New Atlantis* 32 (Summer 2011): 90-102.

[13] Michael Sandel, *The Case Against Perfection*, Cambridge, MA, Harvard University Press, 2007, 57.

[14] Ibid., 54.

[15] G. Kahane, "Mastery Without Mystery: Why There Is No Promethean Sin in Enhancement," in *Journal of Applied Philosophy* 28/4 (2011): 355-368.

[16] Ibid.

[17] The involuntary dimensions "limiting" our freedom are: our physical constraints, our family, environment, temporal and cultural contexts.

[18] Kuruvilla Pandikattu, *Between Beneath, Before and Beyond: An Exploration of the Human Condition Based on Paul Ricoeur*. 2013.

[19] *Nick Squires. "Pope Benedict admits there isn't a full answer to suffering in rare TV interview" The Telegraph, 22 April 2011,* http://www.telegraph.co.uk/news /worldnews/the-pope/ 8468312/Pope-Benedict-admits-there- isnt-a- full-answer-to -suffering-in-rare-TV-interview.html. *Accessed on November 12, 2017*

[20] *Horton, ibid.*

[21] *Ibid.*

16

The Earthiness of Subaltern Religious Imagination:

A Critical Exploration into the Phenomenon of Pilgrimage to Velankanni

A. Maria Arul Raja, SJ

1.   Initial Observations on Pilgrimages to Velankanni

The number of pilgrims to the shrine of Velankanni has been ever growing, transforming it from the status of a parochial centre into a regional, national and international centre. The devotional practices of the pilgrims to Velankanni are manifest in the following activities: pilgrimage to the shrine, walking with or without footwear, pulling mini-cars with the statue of Mother Mary, witnessing flag-hoisting, participating in the car festival and wearing the rosary around their necks for forty days. Moreover, pilgrims and devotees do charitable acts of feeding the poor, offer metal replica symbols in gratitude for favours received, tonsure their heads and move on their knees towards the sacred tank of Our Lady (*Madha Kulam*) from the Shrine Basilica for almost 1 kilometre on the hot, sandy terrain. All these popular devotional practices are undergone by devotees at Velankanni irrespective of their age or health conditions.

The untold miseries, anxious dilemmas, helpless conditions and countless petitions of pilgrims seem to be expressed with hope through various symbols such as offerings, pilgrimages, penance, alms, and religious practices in Velankanni. A comprehensive study of the pilgrimage to Velankanni should look into various factors as follows: the personality fabric of the devotees, textures of the cultural patterns, anatomy of the ritual activities, nuances of the devotional communication, emotive powers operative behind myths and symbols, paradigms of mob religiosity and dynamics of the plurality of religions. Such in-depth studies could be undertaken in relation to societal transformation. However, this paper limits itself with the modest attempt at having some glimpses into some of the interior movements operative in the conflicting consciousness of the subaltern people in relation to the pilgrimage to Velankanni. With phenomenological observations and exploratory analyses leading to hermeneutical reading, let us enter the realm of the reality of pilgrimage to Velankanni,

Even through some initial phenomenological observations, the pilgrimage to Velankanni could be perceived as a 'divine initiative' or a 'human one' or 'the integration of both' with the centrality of the 'celestial virgin goddess from the high heavens carrying the godly infant'. In the context of Catholic doctrine, the same could be expressed as the divine initiative of God through Mary, the Blessed Mother of God, through the means of apparitions to the ordinary folk. Irrespective of creed or culture, a vast majority of the pilgrims and tourists to Velankanni seem to be magnetically attracted towards the miraculous statue of Mother Mary holding the Infant Jesus at the central shrine encircled by massive structures of churches, lodges, shopping complexes facing the shores of the Bay of Bengal. Quite obviously, the composition of the devotees and tourists cuts across religious, cultural, linguistic, and national boundaries.

The subaltern people grappling with their own problems of life and death are central agents in any religion-making and meaning-generating engagement. While studying phenomena about the reality of the pilgrimage to Velankanni, we focus on the aspects of the subaltern experience of the victimhood, subject-hood and community-hood in engagement with the shrine of Velankanni and with their worshipping rituals and devotional practices at once expressed as the "treat" (celebration of life) as well as "retreat" (abnegation in life). These religio-cultural expressions seem to be in constant multifaceted dialogue with the deeper self, others (both congenial as well as inimical), and global factors such as official religions (Catholicism, Hinduism, or Islam)[1] and politico-economic factors (deprivation of health, prosperity, education or employment).

2. Approaches to Human Engagement with Religious Experiences

Religions can be categorized as cosmic ones emphasizing enlightenment and immanence and meta-cosmic ones based on revelation and transcendence. People keep remaking such religions and creating new forms of religious expressions in tune with their own earthly needs and every day wants. In this dynamic engagement, the experiences of historicity and coherence are interpreted through myth and anarchy and *vice versa*. Moreover, the process of historization of myths and mythicization of history takes place quite often in the realm of popular devotions. For comprehending these nuances, researchers have to deploy the tools for handling the elements of the subjective and subjectivity beneath the so-called objective and objectivity.

By and large, the origin of religions in India is attributed to the 'nature-myth' involving the functions of sun, moon, stars, seasons of the year and movements of the planets upon the lives of people.[2] The notion of animism seeks to address the roles of trans-empirical existence of persons or souls or spirits or spiritual beings, especially through the medium of dreams and practice of ancestral worship.[3] The role of magicians functioning as healers and/or scientists were emphasized in the primitive religious explorations in the origin of gods and goddesses.[4] Religion is also counted as an emotional response to various human situations,[5] especially through the objectification of fear,[6] and through concepts of fascinating mystery and tremendous mystery.[7]

The psychological perspective helps us to explain how the religious symbols and practices aid or impede the growth or development of an individual, family, or group. Mere psychological theories analyzing only individual emotions and collective motives may not be adequate in comprehensively understanding complexities operative in the phenomenon of pilgrimage to and other devotional practices in Velankanni.[8] The sociological perspective focuses on the network of relationships binding people together in cohesive groups.[9] The historical perspective seeks to study human behaviour through sequences of events. The comparative perspective deals with how a specific religious phenomenon (like foundational stories and myths, and religious rites and agents), could be compared or contrasted with other similar phenomena. The hermeneutical approach has an eye on how the religious phenomena are meaningful to the devotees in their daily problems of life and death.

"One advantage of studying a long-term socio-cultural process such as pilgrimage is that one's attention is directed toward the dynamics of ideological change and persistence, rather than committed to analysis of static ideological patterns and cognitive structures".[10] The situation of dynamic interactions of perceptions, values, and meanings of people of the same native culture but of different religious elements taking place in the pilgrimage practices in relation to the shrine of Velankanni entails new categories of understanding.

> Religion possesses the capacity to function as a counter-symbolic factory whereby subaltern communities reject the hegemonic symbolic universe of the dominant communities and conjure up one of their own. The act of 'making' their own symbolic world view in the face of severe domination becomes the basis of hope, not just for their resistance but, more importantly, for the working out of their own subjectivity.[11]

There are subaltern suspicions about the domestication of the spontaneous outburst of the worship patterns of popular devotions by the ecclesiastical authorities, on the one hand; and on the other, there are misgivings from the official clergy about the whimsical nature of the popular discourses on apparitions, miracle narratives, statues shedding tears of blood or unofficial car processions outside the sacramental system and liturgical stipulations. Besides these points of divergence between official religious prescriptions and subaltern devotional practices, there are many points of convergence between them. Amidst these multiple aspects of transcendence- immanence, order-autonomy, and tradition-charism, one needs to undertake a systematic in-depth and interdisciplinary probe into the subaltern experiences of the popular devotions.[12]

In this context, the trans-empirical intervention of the Divine Mother overpowering the natural and satanic forces for effectively addressing the healing needs of mortals facing situations of crisis is underscored in the foundational stories and origin myths of Velankanni. The apparitions of Mother of God celebrated as the privileged moments of the beatific favours from 'the goddess from above' for attending to the needy seem to vigorously evoke a deep sense of fascinating and amazing mystery. Besides vertically enriching the personality from deep within, the Velankanni experience seems to horizontally re-create networks of family units and kinship circles along with a wider bond of union with other co-pilgrims at least temporarily. These aspects of inter-relationality in Velankanni experience encourage people to continue their devotional practices.

3. Multiple Factors in the Location of Velankanni Shrine

The essentialist meaning possessed by the shrines (holy places and buildings) and the pilgrimages (sacred events and practices) derived through formal analysis cannot be upheld. One has to get out of this formalist discourse, because such sacred shrines do not continue to exist apart from the dynamic meaning-generating systems of the pilgrims. The traditions of pilgrimages do not continue to engage the collective consciousness of the pilgrims outside their living context, social relations and affiliation to the divine. The following table is a cursory attempt at identifying some of the external and internal factors affecting their subjective realm and meaning-generating dynamics in the context of Velankanni shrine and pilgrimages.

Interior Movements beneath the Devotional Practices	Topographical Settings	From the World of the Pilgrims	From the World of the Velankanni Shrine
Fusion of the Senses of → Celebration of Life ("Treat") and → Mortification in Life ("Retreat")	Fusion of Horizons of → Vast ocean and fertile land filled with heavy throngs of pilgrims and → Rural and urban settings buzzing with heavy traffic of vehicles	→ Engagement with wide varieties of delight to the eyes, ears and palates → Participation of and contributions of large waves of people → Traversing between the horizons of sea and land, piety and entertainment, → Interior movements and exterior performances related to penances, offerings, almsgiving, and prayers	→ Shrine myths catering to the needy with privations of physiological, psychological, familial, social, and economic disasters → Healing stories with popular acclaim through mass media and social media, and personal testimonies → Young motherly statue decked with Indian saree and ornaments holding her baby in her arms evoking fertility → Direct reference to health in the name Arockia Madha (Our Lady of Good Health)

The different levels of liminal excitement and the resultant contentment experienced by the subaltern pilgrims seem to be influenced by the interplay of various internal and external factors as indicated in the table above. One has to realize that the subaltern constructs of the shrines and pilgrimages are the outcome of the complex process of their interactions with multiple variables with diverse impacts on them.

4. Interior Movements of Subalterns

Subaltern "religions are naturalistic, spontaneously materialistic and they are non-institutionalised....They are the symbolic treasure houses of the sufferings and joys of those people. They are the wailing walls of the people as well as the gorilla-war pits of the people. They are the local utopias of the people.[13] "In the pilgrimages of the historical religions the moral unit is the individual, and his goal is salvation or release from the sins and evils of the structural world"[14]

One can understand that the subaltern expectations from, perceptions on and interior movements during the pilgrimages to the shrines are quite complex with the constant interplay of multiple variables. The admixture of these variables could be generally identified under three headings: (1) Victimhood, (2) Subject-hood, and (3) Community-hood. They could be spelt out as follows:

4.1. Subaltern Victimhood

The subaltern engagement with themselves as victims may express itself in terms of fearing and blaming others, inimical or amicable. The relationship of the pilgrims with the divine, the self or nature could be intimate or distant. They may be predominantly controlled by the consciousness of helpless determinism amidst their struggles. While suffering with the cumulative effects of humiliating exclusion and social death to varying degrees, the subaltern people may undergo the ordeal of the sense of depressive resignation with the spirit of defeatism, pessimism, or nihilism. Their interior movements could be briefly enlisted as follows:

- fear of possible divine wrath for not fulfilling some promises made

- addiction to and uncritical resignation to irrational traditions of discriminatory hierarchy

- escape into a different world of spiritualism

- temporary anonymity for hiding the existing situation of anguish

- seeking outlet for pent up, unresolved and accumulated emotional baggage

- substitute to fill in the inner vacuum created by imposed humiliation or disappointment

- scrupulous moralistic outlook

- voluntarily accepting the pains of severe penances for one self

4.2. Subaltern Subject-hood

The assertive agency of the subaltern people struggling against the imposed humiliations may tend to develop certain retributive mindset while dealing with the perpetrators of violence upon them. This subaltern assertion could be expressed overtly or covertly with varying degrees. At times they could be triggered by assertive determination with historical consciousness fighting against helpless resignation with magical consciousness. The subaltern struggle for dignified life with human rights seeks to carve out its own strategies for claiming its legitimate space in all walks of life. The subaltern claim of space makes an entry into the realms of religion-making, myth-making and history-making activities. This could be expressed through the mild or wild defiance of the conventions and decorum imposed by the dominant society (often labelled as the mainstream). Through the practices of popular devotions like pilgrimage to Velankanni, the subaltern assertion may manifest itself in the following ways:

- direct endearment to the divine without any intermediary

- persuading the divine for certain favours

- act of fulfilment of the promise made to the divine

- thrill of undertaking a spiritual journey

- new status symbol by aping the spiritual practices of the dominant class/ caste/ gender

- assertion in terms of following their own religious practices different from or independent of those religious practices of the dominant group

- weapon for instilling fear of the divine in the minds of the oppressors

- expressive ways of tackling imposed inferiority or low self-image through the means of rigorous penance or easy-going practices

- stepping up the dignity of the self and family

- breaking the code of conduct expected of the pilgrims either deliberately or inadvertently

- entertainment with an all-out abandon with individual inebriation or community celebration with overeating and drinking

- excessive bodily expressions with colourful costumes, high decibels with noisy duels with emotional outbursts

- corrective measure towards rehabilitation

- restoration back to mainstream of society

4.3. Subaltern Community-hood

Fundamentally, the emancipatory ideology of every subaltern group is inclusive in nature. For instance, the new community envisaged to be built upon egalitarian values by the Tribals, Women, Dalits, Blacks, or any marginalized people do not harp on excluding and eliminating all capitalists, men, caste-people, Whites, and all other oppressors. Behind every struggle of every excluded people, we identify the subaltern agenda of incorporating the respective oppressive power-holders into the new community that celebrates the egalitarianism without any compromise. In short, the excluded communities are struggling for building inclusive communities. Besides this, the daily contributions of every subaltern community through their hard labour for building the community at large have to be seriously taken note of. The daily domestic chores of subaltern women, the hazardous labour of the subaltern labourers, and the contributions of the subaltern intellectuals keep up the rhythm, health, hygiene, economy, and harmony of the entire society. The subaltern spirit of community-building expresses itself through the following manner in the realm of pilgrimage to Velankanni:

- participation in a social event
- joining the world of people at large away from the local situation of oppression
- acquisition of a sense of equality with other pilgrims irrespective of their case or status
- reprioritising ethical choices
- rigorous disciplining oneself from drinking, smoking, or extra-marital affairs
- punishing both the body and the inner world
- deterrent to evil tendencies and sins
- prevention of committing a pattern of sins
- purification and exploration
- exemplary acts for the edification of others

4.4. Subaltern Religious Imagination

No doubt, shrines and pilgrimages as sites of religious aesthetics evoke lots of imagination in the minds and hearts of the subaltern people. But what matters is not mere passive aesthetics but active aesthetic performances. Mere propositions on aesthetic objects or religious acts by others do not evoke active and activated response from the subalterns. Performances in the body evoke chains of further acts. For the body or mind to be in a position of eliciting an effect, power, or capability from any other sources (venerable object, sacred place, holy person), it must manifest itself in a particular concrete way, which then becomes the triggering moment for generating new energies from within. This can only be done through the appropriate aesthetic performance. It is not what the object 'says' or 'expresses' by itself that is the key issue here. But what it does and what forms of action and social relations the object elicits is significant here. Hence, from the point of view of aesthetic fulfilment in the religious realm, we could identify some of the internal factors which seem to determine the various levels of contentment among the subaltern people. They are indicated in the illustration below:

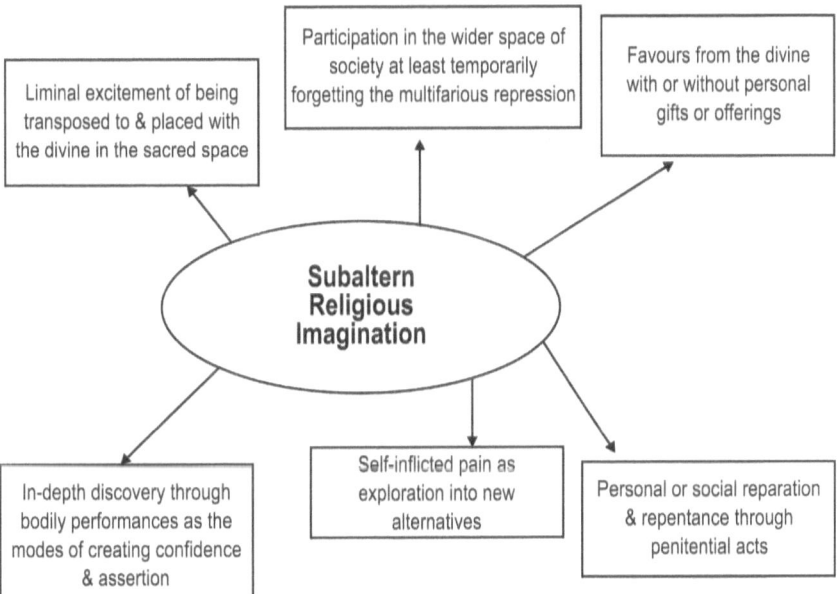

The above aspects, though not exhaustive, seem to be at play when subaltern people undertake pilgrimages to shrines. The interior processing of the negativities and deprivations experienced in their day-to-day life play a vital role in all the aspects of the above cultural representation.

5.   Analysis of the Pilgrimage to Velankanni

Various elements involved in the preparation, performance and completion of the process of pilgrimage to sacred sites can be understood through the concepts of *Syncretism, Liminoid,* and *Communitas.*

5.1. Syncretism

Popular devotional practices could be perceived from the concept of *syncretism.* On the one hand, the term *syncretism* is pejoratively interpreted as chaotic combinations of various religious factors leading to the dilution of the standard doctrines of the official religions; on the other hand, it is positively understood as spontaneous or creative amalgamation of various religious factors. By and large subaltern sensibilities tend to function as a way of resistance to the clerical hegemony of the dominant religions in view of sustaining their cultural survival or autonomy.[15] For instance, we come across Catholics who receive communion in the Eucharist also undertake 40-day penance of wearing rosary with strict discipline, tonsuring their head, undertaking the kneeling-walk towards the sacred tank from the shrine, or even performing the ritual tying *thaali* (the sacred marital thread tied around the bride's neck by the bridegroom as the sign of marital bond) during the moment of elevation of the host in the Holy Mass even without undergoing the regular sacrament of matrimony in the Catholic Church. From the viewpoint of the subalterns, the official sacrament of Eucharist is in perfect integration with such unofficial practices without any confusion.

5.2. Liminoid

The aspects of pilgrimage to Velankanni could be also viewed through the prism of the concept of *liminoid phenomenon.*[16] It could be understood as the temporary separation of the (elevated and divine) status from the (ordinary-human) space breaking away from the usual social roles. This experience of *limonoid* seems to take place in pilgrimage to Velankanni with the manifestation of intense prayers along with the abstention from alcohol and other habitual indulgences, at least temporarily. This is in the realm of the self-abnegation on the part of devotees trying to follow intense penitential practices and prayers. But on the other hand, the other people maintain certain respectful distance from the devotees seeking to undertake the pilgrimage to Velankanni by venerating them as saintly humans, addressing them as *sāmi* and even falling at their feet with reverential awe. These are the moments when both the pilgrims and others temporarily set aside the existing discriminatory practices normally operative between male-female, elevated caste-denigrated untouchable, and rich-poor. This temporary *liminoid* experience may give some respite to the subaltern people from their daily share of humiliation and may trigger the dream of permanently undoing the systemic evil of oppression.

5.3. *Communitas*

A sense of *communitas* is said to be created during the pilgrimage which is "a spontaneously generated relationship between levelled and equal human beings."[17] This *communitas* is distinguished as an existential/ spontaneous one (constructed by common social interests) and a normative one (governed by common values of life). The pilgrims usually do not mingle with each other. They come as family, remain for worship as family, and leave the site as family. While the pilgrims walk for about ten or fifteen days towards Velankanni, there might be a semblance of spontaneous or even normative *communitas*. But this is only a short-lived experience and the pilgrims join their families as soon as they reach Velankanni. Some of them walk as groups from the same village or family. It may be possible when the volunteers work in the shrine. But neither the spontaneous *communitas* nor the normative *communitas* seem to qualitatively take place with sustenance in Velankanni as in other pilgrimage centres in the caste-ridden India.[18] But the spontaneous *dialogue of action* takes place, on a temporary basis, amidst the pilgrims in the case of relief works needed during the time of crises like tsunami in the name of devotion to Mother of Velankanni. No single theoretical explanation comprehensively throws light on the complexities involved in the dynamics of the subaltern attitudes and outlooks towards the pilgrimage to Velankanni.[19]

6.   Down-to-earth Mother of Velankanni

The large number of Indian subalterns with their agrarian background seem to be at home with the divine favourable to the needs of fertility leading to human, animal and agrarian fruition. These needs could be adequately addressed only by the divine who is abundantly fertile. This is the simple anthropomorphic logic behind the construction of the icon of the divine. In other words, the subaltern iconographic construction of the divine is founded on the human-divine continuum. In Velankanni the icon of Virgin Mother holding a male baby evokes much respect from the minds and hearts of the pilgrims as the credible deity to bestow on them the boons of fertility for humans, cattle, and agricultural fields.

Though the Virgin Mother from the heavens is venerated with reverential awe, the bodily aspects of her virginity and motherhood are much celebrated as that of closest kin from among their own family members of the subaltern people. That is why the offer of the Indian costume of saree and golden jewels to the Mother of Velankanni are counted as the privileged gifts to the personal and intimate use of the female members of one's own family or kith and kin. The large numbers of the sarees thus offered to Velankanni *Madha* are then auctioned to the devotees. The women take the Velankanni *Madha* saree as a rare divine gift to be worn for securing incomparable blessings of intimate proximity with the virginhood, womanhood, and motherhood of the very Virgin Mother of God.

Accordingly, the experience of compassionate affirmation with the motherly embrace is expected and experienced from the Mother of Velankanni. Obviously, she is counted as the deity of a large family (*Kudumba Sāmi*) with a deep sense of belonging (*Namma Samy*). As the protector from the clutches of human-made or satanic dangers, she is celebrated as the protector-goddess (*Kāval Deivam*). The concept of breast goddess evokes the function of extending tender loving embrace to innocent devotees and that of tooth goddess alludes to the function of righteous intervention into the ways of the wicked. The Velankanni *Madha* is predominantly approached by the devotees as the affectionate mother with compassionate affirmation of the marginalized people.

7. Ambiguities Regarding Patriarchy

On the one hand, the dominant religious rituals and spiritual practices construct meticulous exclusion of women in their worship patterns. But, on the other hand, in the subaltern world, even with its own versions of patriarchy, does not seem to manifest such a zeal in excluding their women from the divine realm in the name of maintaining the purity of the deity. In the characteristic aspects of the Velankanni brand of religious rituals and spiritual rituals, one could identify some ambiguities regarding the critique of patriarchy.

Conspicuously, the Marian doctrines of Virginal Birth of Christ, Immaculate Conception, Mother of God, and Assumption of Mary will be emphasized in the preaching during the official liturgical and para-liturgical services headed by the official clergy of Catholicism. The prevailing patriarchal culture will be visibly operative practically in all the devotional activities in Velankanni. Access to the main statue, main altars and liturgical leadership are reserved for men, and the cleansing activities, decorating works, and choir involvement are predominantly assigned to women. Even the very image of Mother Velankanni prevailing in the collective consciousness of the devotees seem to have the blend of the heavenly and earthly aspects:

Young virgin hailing from heaven → Symbol of freedom from man's impurity. This womanly splendour is eloquently expressed against the prevailing derisive cultural idioms of the so-called impurity of women's body.	Beautiful young mother decked with coloured saree and ornaments) holding her infant boy → Symbol of fertility activating fertility with the fruit of her very womb with motherly affirmation assuring the yet-to-be-married with appropriate brides or bridegrooms and the married ones with children progeny, and the childless with fruitfulness of progeny.

The dominant discourse on Velankanni Mother tends to eloquently project the divine aspects while being inadequately sensitive to the welfare of the poor. This could be called the instrumentalization of the poor for asserting the supremacy of the divine. But on the other hand, the subaltern discourse tends to underscore the significance of the needs of the poor who have to be served by the divine aspects. This could be called the instrumentalization of the divine for affirming the marginalized. The dominant people tend to reach out to Mother of Velankanni through the medium of doctrinal discourses, and the subaltern people through the medium of earthly services to the impoverished. And the final outcome is the convenient silence regarding the naming of the evil of patriarchy to be eliminated even through the loud discourses on the womanly splendour of the Mother of Velankanni placed upon the highest pinnacle of divine glory bestowed on her by God.

Pilgrimages to Velankanni: For Status Quo or Transformation?

Popular piety "manifests a thirst for God which only the poor and the simple can know" and "it makes people capable of generosity and sacrifice even to the point of heroism, when it is a question of bearing witness to belief".[20] It is also celebrated as "a precious treasure of the Catholic Church", in which "we see the soul of the Latin American peoples".[21] The 'popular spirituality' or 'people's mysticism' is truly "a spirituality incarnated in the culture of the lowly".[22] It is "a legitimate way of living the faith, a way of feeling part of the Church and a manner of being missionaries". Furthermore, it brings with itself the grace of being a missionary, of coming out of oneself and setting out on pilgrimage: "Journeying together to shrines and taking part in other manifestations of popular piety, also by taking one's children or inviting others, is in itself an evangelizing gesture".[23] As the 'evangelizing power' of the 'popular spirituality' is the work of the Holy Spirit gathering people together, one should not stifle or control it for the sake of democratizing the Gospel from the lowly to all.[24]

To a large number of the pilgrims to Velankanni, the devotional practices including pilgrimage evoke sentiments of simple charity of almsgiving especially to the beggars and the poor moving around the sacred field of the shrine. For some of the pilgrims it inspires an imagination of sustaining the aspect of human development in terms of temporary service to the shrine, voluntary labour for building infrastructure, donations to some charitable institutions, educational bodies, or developmental projects for uplifting the downtrodden. But in terms of the long-term and short-term programmes of empowerment of the subalterns like removal of untouchability, annihilation of casteism, eradication of patriarchy, or struggling against the culture of communalism, corruption, or consumerism, what are the contributions of the Velankanni-related devotional practices? One could observe the pilgrimage to Velankanni reinforces existing social structures in the pilgrim centre's catchment area. Experiences of mere emotionalism or simplistic liminality on a temporary basis seems to be predominantly operative in the pilgrimage to Velankanni.

But the pilgrimage along with the other associated devotional practices in Velankanni have to be empowered further to comprehensively eliminate the prevailing evils like communalism, casteism, corruption, consumerism, and patriarchy. This 'prophetic approach'[25] will do justice to the celebration of the subaltern Mother Mary, the very epicentre of the shrine of Velankanni, who was attuned to the divine project of ensuring 'salvation of the rich and proud-hearted through the salvation of poor and humble-hearted' (Lk 1:46-56).

Endnotes

[1] One could identify the confluence of devotional styles of making use of objects and offerings both in Christian and Hindu worships. See Antal, *Vailankanni Varalarum Annaiyin Aruncheyalkalum: A Descriptive Analysis of Vailankanni Shrine Basilica* (Thanjavur: Tamil University, 1988), 17.

[2] See Max Friedrich Müller, *Lectures on the Origin and Growth of Religion as Illustrated by the Religions of India*. Delivered in the Chapter House, Westminster Abbey in April-June, 1878 (London: Longmans, Green & Co., 1878).

[3] See Edward Burnett Tylor, *Religion in Primitive Culture* (New York, Harper: 1958); Herbert Spencer, *The Principles of Sociology* (London: Williams and Norgate, 1882-1898); also, Blumer Herbert, *Principles of Sociology* (New York: Barnes & Noble, 1955).

[4] See James George Frazer, *The Fear of the Dead in Primitive Religion* (New York: Biblo and Tannen, 1966).

[5] See Robert Ranulph Marett, *Faith, Hope, and Charity in Primitive Religion* (New York: B. Blom, 1972).

[6] See Wilhelm Max Wundt, *Outlines of Psychology* (New York: G. E. Stechert, 1897), 67.

[7] See Rudolf Otto, *The Idea of the Holy: An Inquiry into the Non-Rational Factor in the Idea of the Divine and its Relation to the Rational*, trans. J. W. Harvey (New York: Oxford University Press, 1958).

[8] See E. Alan Morinis, *Pilgrimage in the Hindu Tradition: A Case Study of West Bengal* (New York: Oxford University Press, 1984).

[9] See W. Richard Comstock, *The Study of Religion and Primitive Religions* (New York: Harper and Row, 1972).

[10] Victor Turner and Edith L. B. Turner, *Image and Pilgrimage in Christian Culture: Anthropological Perspectives* (New York: Columbia University Press, 1978), 25.

[11] Sathianathan Clarke, *Dalits and Christianity: Subaltern Religion and Liberation Theology in India* (New Delhi: Oxford University Press, 1998), 126; also see S. Dube, "Myths, Symbols and Community: Satnampanth of Chhattisgargh," in *Subaltern Studies - Vol. VII: Writings on South Asian History and Society*, ed. P. Chatterjee & G. Pandey (Delhi: Oxford University Press, 1993), 121-158.

[12] See David Blackbourn, *Marpingen: Apparitions of the Virgin Mary in Bismarckian Germany* (New York: Knopf, 1994), 140.

[13] N. Muthu Mohan, "View Points: Reflections on Ban on Animal Sacrifice," *Satya Nilayam* 5 (Feb. 2004), 131.

[14] Victor Turner and Edith L. B. Turner, *Image and Pilgrimage in Christian Culture: Anthropological Perspectives* (New York: Columbia University Press, 1978), 8.

[15] See Charles Stewart and Rosalinde Shaw, "Introduction: Problematizing Syncretism", in *Syncretism/Anti-Syncretism: The Politics of Religious Synthesis*, ed. C. Stewart and R. Shaw (London 1994), 1-26.

[16] See Victor Turner and Edith L. B. Turner, *Image and Pilgrimage in Christian Culture: Anthropological Perspectives* (New York: Columbia University Press, 1978); also see Arnold van Gennep, *The Rites of Passage*, trans. M. B. Vizedom and G. L. Caffee (Chicago: University of Chicago Press, 1960).

[17] Victor Turner, "The Center Out There: Pilgrim's Goal," in *History of Religions* 12 (1973), 191-230.

[18] See Peter van Der Veer, *Gods on Earth: The Management of Religious Experience and Identity in a North Indian Pilgrimage Centre*, (London: The Athlone Press, 1988).

[19] See E. Alan Morinis, *Pilgrimage in the Hindu Tradition: A Case Study of West Bengal* (New York: Oxford University Press, 1984); also see John Eade, "Order and Power at Lourdes: Lay Helpers and the Organization of a Pilgrimage Shrine," in *Contesting the Sacred: The Anthropology of Christian Pilgrimage*, ed., idem and M. Sallnow (London, New York: Rutledge, 1991), 51-76.

[20] See Pope Paul VI, *Evangelii Nuntiandi*, n.48.

[21] Opening Address by Pope Benedict XVI in the Fifth General Conference of the Latin American and Caribbean Bishops (13 May 2007), n.1.

[22] Fifth General Conference of the Latin American and Caribbean Bishops, *Aparecida Document*, 29 June 2007, nn. 262-263.

[23] Ibid., n.264.

[24] See Pope Francis, *Evangelii Gaudium*, nn.123-124.

[25] See *The Shrine and The Pilgrimage*, Pontifical Council for the Pastoral Care of Migrants and Itinerant People (Vatican City, United States Catholic Conference, Washington, D.C., 1999).

17

Pseudo-Spirituality: Eclipse of God and Neighbour

Neo-gnosticism and Neo-pelagianism in the Light of *Evangelii Gaudium*

Joseph A. D'Mello, SJ

Today, the postmodern world with all its positives is also characterized by individualism and superficiality. Any spirituality, as it is lived in a particular context, is influenced by contemporary ideologies and perspectives. Christian spirituality is no exemption. With the proliferation of spiritualities, discernment becomes the key to find out whether spiritualities promote enhancement of self or truly facilitate transformation, leading to love of God and service of neighbour. The Apostolic Exhortation *Evangelii Gaudium*[1] (hereafter EG) points out the manifestations of neo-gnosticism and neo-pelagianism in Christian spirituality and calls upon the faithful to introspect into its impact on our life and mission.

1. Spiritual Worldliness: Neo-gnosticism and Neo-pelagianism

Pope Francis is seriously concerned about the spiritual worldliness unbridled in the Church today. While addressing the issue of 'spiritual worldliness' in EG 94, he indicates that it "can be fuelled in two deeply interrelated ways" – namely, neo-gnosticism and neo-pelagianism – the former being "a purely subjective faith whose only interest is a certain experience or a set of ideas and bits of information which are meant to console and enlighten, but which ultimately keep one imprisoned in his or her own thoughts and feelings." Indeed, neo-gnosticism focuses only on interiority that has nothing to do with one's relationship with others and with the created world. It presumes to liberate the human person from the body and from the material universe.[2] Cautioning Christians about what he terms a "self-absorbed promethean neo-pelagianism," Pope Francis sees it assailing "those who ultimately trust only in their own powers and feel superior to others because they observe certain rules or remain intransigently faithful to a particular Catholic style from the past."[3] One can achieve salvation through one's own strength is the root of neo-pelagianism.[4]

2. Narcissism: The Core of Spiritual Worldliness

Neo-gnosticism and neo-pelagianism are basically centered on narcissism where God and one's neighbour are not the focus. Both these boil down to deifying and worshiping one's own ego. "A supposed soundness of doctrine or discipline leads instead to a narcissistic and authoritarian elitism, whereby instead of evangelizing, one analyzes and classifies others, and instead of opening the door to grace, one exhausts his or her energies in inspecting and verifying. In neither case is one really concerned about Jesus Christ or others" (EG 94). Traces of neo-gnosticism and neo-pelagianism were found even in Jesus' times. The parable of the Pharisee and the Tax Collector (Lk 18:9-14) substantiates this view. The parable begins as follows: "He (Jesus) told this parable to some who trusted in themselves that they were righteous and regarded others with contempt" (Lk 18:9). Henri de Lubac pointed out that in spiritual worldliness, the moral and spiritual standards are based not on the glory of God but on what is to the profit of the human person. It is totally an egocentric and anthropocentric outlook.[5]

3.   Spiritual Worldliness: The Evil Spirt Posing as an 'Angel of Light'

The striking point of spiritual worldliness is that the deeds appear to be good and righteous. However, the motivation for such actions seems to be self-glory. "Since it is based on carefully cultivated appearances, it is not always linked to outward sin; from without, everything appears as it should be" (EG 93). As St Paul exhorts the Corinthians saying: "Even Satan disguises himself as an angel of light" (2 Cor 11: 14), spiritual worldliness comes with a good desire, with holy thoughts but ends up in working for one's own name and fame. In the *Spiritual Exercises*, while describing the evil spirit, Ignatius of Loyola notes: "It is characteristic of the evil angel, who takes on the appearance of an angel of light, to enter by going along the same way as the devout soul and then to exit by his own way with success for himself. That is, he brings good and holy thoughts attractive to such an upright soul and then strives little by little to get his own way, by enticing the soul over to his own hidden deceits and evil intentions."[6] The tragedy is that the activities that are supposed to lead one to God, take one away from God due to one's selfish motivation. "In some people we see an ostentatious preoccupation for the liturgy, for doctrine and for the Church's prestige, but without any concern that the Gospel have a real impact on God's faithful people and the concrete needs of the present time. In this way, the life of the Church turns into a museum piece or something which is the property of a select few" (EG 95).

4.   A Spirituality Bereft of Interior Change

Though, externally, prisoners of pseudo-spirituality are engaged in spiritual activities as they are obsessed by appearances, (EG 97) interiorly they are in want of healing as their hearts are far from God and neighbour. They are in need of interior change. A superficial spirituality evades a process of paschal mystery as there is fear of dying to one's own ego. "Their hearts are open only to the limited horizon of their own immanence and interests, and as a consequence they neither learn from their sins nor are they genuinely open to forgiveness" (EG 97). The ideal imagery is that of the elder son in the parable of the Prodigal Son (Lk 15:11-32). Though he was living in close proximity to his father and obeying all his commands, his heart was far from his father and younger brother as he failed to forgive his brother.[7] Truly, he lacked the interior change.

5. A Spirituality Devoid of Community Life and Responsibility to One's Neighbour

Today, people sometimes speak about spiritualities that are devoid of community life and concern for one's neighbor. Such shallow spiritualities end up in promoting self-love, self-will and self-interest. We observe, nowadays, a "growing attraction to various forms of a 'spirituality of wellbeing' divorced from any community life, or to a 'theology of prosperity' detached from responsibility for our brothers and sisters, or to depersonalized experiences which are nothing more than a form of self-centredness" (EG 90). Pope Francis categorically terms such spirituality as adulterated forms of Christianity. "These are manifestations of an anthropocentric immanentism. It is impossible to think that a genuine evangelizing thrust could emerge from these adulterated forms of Christianity" (EG 94). When we are caught up with ourselves, with our "own interests and concerns, there is no longer room for others, no place for the poor. God's voice is no longer heard, the quiet joy of his love is no longer felt, and the desire to do good fades" (EG 2). There is a tendency to flee, isolate, hide, refuse to share and to lock oneself in one's own comforts. Such a life is nothing less than slow suicide (EG 272).

6. A Spirituality of Mere Activism

Spirituality can also become mere activism. "Love of neighbour" is seen in terms of organizing outreach programmes, awareness sessions, self-help groups, etc. Thus, Pope Francis cautions the faithful saying that the Church is not an NGO, an organization that runs activities for the welfare of humanity, an organization that engages itself in social analysis, statistics, etc. Some Christians can be obsessed with programmes and the entire Christian life can be centered on such activities. Works of mercy organized for the needy are often pretentious, leading to enhancement of self. Hence, activities which are supposed to be means become an end in themselves.

> In others, this spiritual worldliness lurks behind a fascination with social and political gain, or pride in their ability to manage practical affairs, or an obsession with programmes of self-help and self-realization. It can also translate into a concern to be seen, into a social life full of appearances, meetings, dinners and receptions. It can also lead to a business mentality, caught up with management, statistics, plans and evaluations whose principal beneficiary is not God's people but the Church as an institution. (EG 95)

7.　Core Characteristics of an Authentic Christian Spirituality

Christian spirituality is defined as "the search to integrate life through the transforming experience of encountering God in Christ. This experience animates and gives life, meaning and direction."[8] The important element in Christian spirituality is a profound personal experience—the transforming experience of encountering God in Christ, lived out in one's daily life. Such transforming life is guided by two principles: love of God and love of neighbour (Mk 12:30-31). Some of the characteristics of a genuine Christian spirituality—as opposed to the pseudo-spirituality fostered by heretical trends like neo-gnosticism and neo-pelagianism—are as follows:

7.1.　Encounter with Jesus and Deeper Knowledge of God and Self

True Christian spirituality is a spirituality of encounter with the person of Christ. The New Testament is replete with such encounters of Jesus with people (Mk 10:46-52; Lk 19:1-10). Once they met Jesus, they were no more the same old persons. *Evangelii Gaudium* begins with the note of encounter with Jesus: "*The Joy of the Gospel* fills the hearts and lives of all who encounter Jesus" (EG 1). Pope Francis, therefore, invites all Christians for an encounter with Jesus. "I invite all Christians, everywhere, at this very moment, to a renewed personal encounter with Jesus Christ, or at least an openness to letting him encounter them" (EG 3). Recalling the words of Pope Benedict XVI, the Holy Father says: "Being a Christian is not the result of an ethical choice or a lofty idea, but the encounter with an event, a person, which gives life a new horizon and a decisive direction"[9] (EG7). The encounter is with the person of Jesus and the event is the Christ event. "But what is central to the Christ event is the incarnation, which is presupposed in the death and resurrection of Jesus. If so, encountering the event of the incarnate Word entails encountering the human and the cosmic realities along with the divine."[10] The encounter with the person of Jesus does not take place in a vacuum rather in our life situation "amidst the joy and hope, the grief and anguish of the people of our time."[11]

Any true encounter leads to a deeper relationship through the process of 'knowing'. "In biblical language to 'know' means to 'experience', 'to enter into intimate relationship with' – a relationship as intimate as that between man and woman in the closeness of the act of love (Gen 4:1)."[12] It is 'knowing' God and self. When Jesus asked Peter to cast the net into the deep (Lk 5:1-11), there was an encounter between two of them which led Peter to know Jesus in a deeper way: "Go away from me, Lord," and there was a greater realization of self for Peter: "I am a sinful man!" (Lk 5:8) A follower of Christ is one who has met Christ and has grown in the knowledge of self and Christ.

7.2. *Entering a Perennial Process of Dying and Rising*

"Unless a grain of wheat falls into the earth and dies, it remains just a single grain; but if it dies, it bears much fruit" (Jn 12:24). Dying to self-will is the most difficult part in Christian spirituality. When we fail to die to our self, then our spirituality remains shallow and superficial. As one makes a shift in focus from self to the other while one progresses in one's spiritual journey, one goes through a phase of uncertainty, confusion and insecurity. While praying in Gethsemane, Jesus passed through this stage, praying: "Abba, Father, for you all things are possible; remove this cup from me; yet, not what I want, but what you want" (Mk 14:36). This process of dying and rising is truly a grace of God; but one should desire it and be open to receive such a life transforming grace. It is the work of the Spirit. Spiritual worldliness can block this grace and make one deaf to the whisperings of the Holy Spirit. "This stifling worldliness can only be healed by breathing in the pure air of the Holy Spirit who frees us from self-centeredness cloaked in an outward religiosity bereft of God. Let us not allow ourselves to be robbed of the Gospel!" (EG 97).

Only when one passes through the process of dying to self-will will one experience freedom and liberation. Spiritual worldliness places self-love, self-will and self-interest above the Gospel, whereas authentic spirituality leads one to freedom by dying to oneself. "The Gospel offers us the chance to live life on a higher plane, but with no less intensity: 'Life grows by being given away, and it weakens in isolation and comfort. Indeed, those who enjoy life most are those who leave security on the shore and become excited by the mission of communicating life to others'"[13] (EG 10). A Christian becomes a disciple of Christ by going through the ceaseless process of the paschal mystery in one's own life. It is an on-going experience: dying and rising daily. Even the life of Jesus was a constant dying and rising from the moment of the incarnation up to the resurrection. Hence, the paschal mystery should permeate our Christian spirituality.[14]

7.3. Joy as the Fruit of Encounter

Zacchaeus had an encounter with Jesus that led him through a process of dying to his sinful life and rising to new life. Jesus, then, rightly said: "Today salvation has come to this house" (Lk 19:9). This was a moment of joy for Zacchaeus. Christian joy does not mean absence of difficulties and struggles. Rather, it is a strong hope in the Lord amidst uncertainties and suffering. True joy and consolation are signs that it is God who is the Master of our life—the One who leads our lives and in whom we have placed total, unconditional trust. "The life of the Church should always reveal clearly that God takes the initiative, that 'he has loved us first' (1 Jn 4:19) and that he alone 'gives the growth' (1 Cor 3:7). This conviction enables us to maintain a spirit of joy in the midst of a task so demanding and challenging that it engages our entire life. God asks everything of us, yet at the same time he offers everything to us" (EG 12).

7.4. Change of Heart: A New Worldview

A spirituality is authentic if it brings true conversion, a change of heart. Today conversion is spoken of as transformation of consciousness which "is a modern term used to constellate changes undergone in one's psychological, intellectual, and spiritual horizons, changes that can be as radical as embracing a wholly new worldview and a wholly new self-understanding. Consciousness, in this sense, entails one's intellectual, moral, psychic and religious understanding, and its transformation can be understood as the heart of conversion."[15] Lonergan sees conversion as "transformation of the subject and his world. (...) It is as if one's eyes were opened and one's former world faded and fell away. There emerges something new that fructifies in inter-locking, cumulative sequences of developments on all levels and in all departments of human living."[16]

In a pseudo-spirituality one puts oneself at the centre and leads a life of isolation, which is a version of immanentism (EG 89). But a true Christian God-experience leads one to open oneself to God and the other. "Every authentic experience of truth and goodness seeks by its very nature to grow within us, and any person who has experienced a profound liberation becomes more sensitive to the needs of others. As it expands, goodness takes root and develops. If we wish to lead a dignified and fulfilling life, we have to reach out to others and seek their good" (EG 9). In an authentic Christian God-experience, there is no room for considering oneself better than others, looking down upon others. In fact, through humility one counts others better (EG 271). Through this enriching relationship with God we are liberated from our narrowness and self-absorption (EG 8)

This change of heart creates a passion for Jesus (falling in love with Jesus) and passion for people (loving everyone) as the transformed heart draws its inspiration from Jesus (EG 268). This is the fruit of conversion, i.e., a new worldview inclusive of God, self, others and the cosmos. A heart of conversion, as is in union with God and others, is aware of what is primary and secondary in life and seeks God in everything, not the self. God's glory is the motivating factor for all that one does. "This is our definitive, deepest and greatest motivation, the ultimate reason and meaning behind all we do: the glory of the Father which Jesus sought at every moment of his life" (EG 267).

7.5. *Finding God in One's Neighbour*

One's encounter with God gets a deeper meaning when one finds God in one's neighbour. Pope Benedict XVI has said that "closing our eyes to our neighbour also blinds us to God."[17] Therefore, loving others is a spiritual force drawing us to union with God. The greater is the openness to others, the greater will be our openness to receive God's gifts and blessings. Finding God in the other becomes an occasion to know something more about God. Whenever our eyes are opened to acknowledge the other, we grow in the light of faith and knowledge of God (cf. 272). As we are created in the image and likeness of God, we are open to the other. This openness is inherent and it cannot be taken away from us. Pope Francis underlines it by saying: "I am a mission on this earth; that is the reason why I am here in this world. (…) But once we separate our work from our private lives, everything turns grey and we will always be seeking recognition or asserting our needs. We stop being a people" (EG 273).

In this mission of loving and serving God and others, we must realize that every person is worthy of our giving. And, in our mission we do not go according to externals, i.e., by appearances, colour, features, etc.; rather we are invited to see others as children of God, as God's handiwork. "God created that person in his image, and he or she reflects something of God's glory. Every human being is the object of God's infinite tenderness, and he himself is present in their lives. Jesus offered his precious blood on the cross for that person" (EG 274). Every person is immensely holy and deserves our love. "If I can help at least one person to have a better life, that already justifies the offering of my life" (EG 274). For us Christians, the human person is the privileged locus of God experience. We experience God first of all in Jesus of Nazareth and then in every person.[18]

7.6. *Finding God in Pain and Suffering*

A spirituality that is individualistic and privatized can ignore the pain and suffering of others and make people live in an illusory world.[19] Jon Sobrino indicates that spirituality should begin with "an act of profound honesty about the real, the recognition of things as they actually are."[20] There was a deep honesty about the real in Jesus. What is striking in the public life of Jesus is his closeness to the poor and the marginalized. "God's heart has a special place for the poor, so much so that he himself 'became poor' [2 Cor 8:9]" (EG 197). Though he was divine, he revealed his divinity by identifying himself with the least and this led him to the total offering of his self.

The Abba experience of Jesus, the love of the Father, impelled Jesus to love in return through effective compassion reaching out to those in need.[21] "The spirituality of Jesus, the love which drives him to identification with the poor and the freedom which allows him to confront the rich, both derive from this foundational experience of God as *Abba*".[22] "If Jesus' identification with the poor is anticipated by his incarnation, his confrontation with the rich, indeed the whole of his spirituality, finds its ultimate expression in the Cross."[23] A Christian spirituality should be truly incarnational, that is, involved in the life struggles of people. It is a context where both the good and evil spirits co-exist. Only a person who has a profound God experience, who has an inner freedom can withstand the forces of evil. Such an involvement will take one through a process of the paschal mystery, a process of kenosis making one realize that Christ suffers even today. This realization will inspire us to be agents of the reign of God—striving to respond to the suffering Christ in our own little way. Truly, one cannot remain indifferent towards pain and suffering.

> Sometimes we are tempted to be that kind of Christian who keeps the Lord's wounds at arm's length. Yet Jesus wants us to touch human misery, to touch the suffering flesh of others. He hopes that we will stop looking for those personal or communal niches which

shelter us from the maelstrom of human misfortune and instead enter into the reality of other people's lives and know the power of tenderness. Whenever we do so, our lives become wonderfully complicated and we experience intensely what it is to be a people, to be part of a people (EG 270).

8.   Conclusion: Integrated Spirituality—Antidote for Neo-gnosticism, Neo-pelagianism

A spirituality divorced from life can spell disaster promoting a "globalization of indifference" (EG 54). Such a pseudo-spirituality is indeed devoid of God and neighbour. Prior to Vatican Council II, spirituality was often linked to the interior life that led to view active life in a negative way. By contrast, the spirituality of Jesus was holistic where there was a harmony between prayer and work, contemplation and action. Jesus was sensitive to the presence of Abba and at the same time sensitive to the poor and the oppressed (Cf. Lk 4:18-19). His worldview included Abba, neighbour and the cosmos. Hence "spirituality for today consists in openness and commitment to the Reign/Kingdom of God which Jesus embodied in His Person, served all His life, and announced in His ministry."[24] Only an integrated spirituality can become an antidote for neo-gnosticism and neo-pelagianism. A spirituality that is integrated will uphold the relationship with God, with others and with the material universe (against neo-gnosticism) and it will treat God as absolute and all the rest as relative (against neo-pelagianism).

Endnotes

[1] Pope Francis, Apostolic Exhortation *Evangelii Gaudium* on the Proclamation of the Gospel in Today's World, 24 Nov. 2013. http://w2.vatican.va/content/francesco/en/apost_exhortations/documents/papa-francesco_esortazione-ap_20131124_evangelii-gaudium.html.

[2] Congregation for the Doctrine of Faith, *Placuit Deo*, On Certain Aspects of Christian Salvation, 22 Feb. 2018, 2-3. http://www.vatican.va/roman_curia/congregations/cfaith/documents/rc_con_cfaith_doc_20180222_placuit-deo_en.html#_ftnref3 (Vatican Site) Accessed on March 1, 2018.

[3] EG 94.

[4] *Placuit Deo*, ibid.

[5] Henri de Lubac, *The Splendor of the Church*, trans. M. Mason, (London/New York: Sheed & Ward, 1956), 287-288.

[6] *The Spiritual Exercises of Saint Ignatius*. A Translation and Commentary by G. E. Ganss, (Anand: Gujarat Sahitya Prakash, 1993), n.332.

[7] John Paul II, Post-Synodal Apostolic Exhortation *Reconciliation and Penance*, December 2, 1984, 6.

[8] Patrick J. Hartin, *Exploring the Spirituality of the Gospels* (Minnesota: Liturgical Press, 2011), 6.

[9] Encyclical Letter *Deus Caritas Est* (25 December 2005), 1: AAS 98 (2006), 217.

[10] Joseph Lobo, "A Public Property Called Priest," *Jnanadeepa: Journal of Religious Studies* 13/2 (July 2010), 30.

[11] See Vatican Council II's *'Gaudium et Spes'* n.1.

[12] George M. Soares-Prabhu, "The Dharma of Jesus," in *Collected Writings of George M. Soares-Prabhu*, vol. 3, ed. S. Kuthirakkattel (Pune: Jnana-Deepa Vidyapeeth Theology Series, 2003), 3.

[13] Fifth General Conference of The Latin American And Caribbean Bishops, Aparecida Document, 29 June 2007, 360. As quoted in EG.

[14] James L. Empereur, "Paschal Mystery," in *The New Dictionary of Theology*, ed., J. A. Komonchak et al. (Bangalore: Theological Publications in India, 2006), 746-747.

[15] Benjamin Baynham, "Transformation," in *The New Dictionary of Catholic Spirituality*, ed. M. Downey (Bangalore: Theological Publications in India, 1995), 967-968.

[16] Bernard J. F. Lonergan, *Method in Theology* (London: Darton, Longman & Todd, 1972), 130. Lonergan also speaks about conversion as religious, moral, and intellectual. "Normally it is intellectual conversion as the fruit of both religious and moral conversion; it is moral conversion as the fruit of religious conversion; and it is religious conversion as the fruit of God's gift of his grace.": See *Method in Theology*, 267-268.

[17] Benedict XVI, Encyclical Letter, *Deus Caritas Est* (25 Dec. 2005), 16: AAS 98 (2006), 230; quoted in EG 272.

[18] Kurien Kunnumpuram, *Towards the Fullness of Life. Reflections on the Daily Living of the Faith* (Mumbai: St Pauls, 2009), 38. See also C. Davis, "From Inwardness to Social Action: A Shift in the Locus of Religious Experience" in *New Blackfriars*, 67 (1986): 114-115, 122.

[19] As per Philip Sheldrake there has been a trend in our postmodern world to privatize spirituality: "Some postmodern theorists argue that it is now impossible to defend any overarching framework of meaning or values. What tends to follow is not merely the detachment of spirituality from belief systems but a privatization of spirituality and its separation from social or public ethics. "Postmodernity," in *The New SCM Dictionary of Christian Spirituality*, ed., P. Sheldrake (London: SCM Press, 2005), 498.

[20] Jon Sobrino, *Spirituality of Liberation: Toward Political Holiness*, trans. R. R. Barr (Maryknoll: Orbis Books, 1989), 15.

[21] George M. Soares-Prabhu, ibid., 4.

[22] George M. Soares-Prabhu, "The Spirituality of Jesus. A Spirituality of Solidarity and Struggle," in ibid., ed. S. Kuthirakkattel, 98.

[23] Ibid., 99.

[24] Samuel Rayan, "A Spirituality for Our Times," in *Jnanadeepa: Journal of Religious Studies* 8/1 (January 2005), 139.

Contributors

Archbishop Thomas Menamparampil, SDB was ordained a priest in 1965, as bishop of Dibrugarh in 1981, and first bishop of Guwahati in 1992. He has served in many commissions of the CBCI and Pontifical Congregations in Rome. He was the Special Secretary of the Asian Synod and served as the Chairman on the Office of Evangelization of FABC for four terms. After his retirement in 2012, he was given the responsibility of the Jowai Diocese until 2016. As a retired Archbishop he assists in pastoral work and participates in Conferences in many universities, in India, China, Africa and Eastern Europe. Email: menamabp@gmail.com

Bishop Thomas Tharayil has an M.A. in English Literature and a Ph.D. in Psychology from the Pontifical Gregorian University, Rome. He is the Auxiliary Bishop of the Archdiocese of Changanacherry in Kerala. Bishop Tharayil was formerly the Director of the Danahalaya Institute of Formation and Counselling, Alappuzha, Kerala. He has authored three books: '*Beyond Secure Attachment*', '*Psychology and Formation: Interdisciplinary Perspectives*' and '*Attachment, Intimacy and Celibacy*'. Email: tomytharayil@gmail.com

Prof. Dr Norman Tanner, SJ, belongs to the British Province of the Society of Jesus. After entering the order in 1961, he studied at Heythrop College and Oxford University in England and the Gregorian University in Rome. Since ordination to the priesthood in 1976, he has taught Church History in these three institutions as well as giving short courses – mainly on Church History and the Councils of the Church – in many theologates and universities around the world, including several in India. His publications comprise a wide range of books and articles, including Decrees of the Ecumenical Councils, 2 vols. (1990), and New Short History of the Catholic Church (2011, paperback 2014), which has been translated into seven languages. Email: tanner@unigre.it

Prof. Dr Jacob Parappally, MSFS holds a doctorate in Theology from the University of Freiburg, Germany. He taught at Jnana-Deepa Vidyapeeth (JDV) Pune for 14 years served as Dean of the Faculty of Theology. He was Rector of Tejas Vidya Peetha, Bangalore, and President of the Indian Theological Association (2005-2011). He has authored *Emerging Trends in Indian Christology; The Meaning of Jesus Christ: An Introduction to Christology; A Way of the Cross for Today*; and edited eight books on theology. He has published more than 100 theological articles and translated the second book on Jesus Christ by Pope Benedict to Malayalam. He is the chief-editor of the Journal of Indian Theology. Email: parappally@gmail.com

Prof. Dr Michael Amaladoss, SJ, born in 1936, has a Ph.D. in systematic theology from Paris (1972). He has been a professor of theology at Vidyajyoti College in Delhi and Editor of its Journal of Theological Reflection. He has also taught in many theological centres across the world: Paris, Bruxelles, Washington DC, Cincinnati, Berkeley and Manila and participated in numerous theological seminars. Currently, he is the Director of The Institute of Dialogue with Cultures and Religions, a doctoral research institute at Chennai. He has published 34 books, some of them translated into 8 other languages, edited 8 books and about 475 theological articles. Email: michamal@gmail.com.

Dr D.J. Margaret, FMA, holds a Post-Graduate Degree in Mathematics from Annamalai University, and a Diploma in Salesian Spiritual Studies from the Auxilium Pontifical University, Rome. She also holds a Master's Degree in Theology from Vidyajyoti College, Delhi, and a Ph.D. from the University of Madras. Her doctoral thesis is entitled,

"An Inquiry into the Role of Spiritual Beliefs and Practices in Post-diagnosis Care of Women Living with HIV/AIDS". Besides research articles in women studies, she has authored *Women in Mission* (2006) and *Finding God in Illness and Care-giving* (2017). She teaches theology and spirituality in many colleges, seminaries and animation centres. She also conducts retreats, seminars and workshops for diverse audiences. Email: djmagifma@gmail.com

Prof. Dr Selva Rathinam, SJ, is a Jesuit priest from the Karnataka Province. He teaches Scripture—especially Old Testament courses like Prophets and Hebrew Language at Jnana Deepa Vidyapeeth (JDV), in Pune, India. He did his Licentiate in Sacred Scripture at the Pontifical Biblical Institute, Rome, and his Doctorate at the Jesuit School of Theology, Berkeley, USA, where he applied the Postcolonial-Subaltern Method to the study of the Songs of the Suffering Servant in Isaiah. He also teaches at various theological Institutes in India. He has written numerous articles in theological periodicals and presented scholarly papers at national and international conferences. Since 2014 he is the President of JDV, Pune. Email: selvarathinamsj@gmail.com

Dr Thomas Karimundackal, SJ, is a Jesuit priest belonging to the Kerala Province. He teaches Scripture at Jana-Deepa Vidyapeeth, Pune. Email: tomksj@gmail.com

Dr M. Paul Raj is a priest from the diocese of Sivagangai, Tamil Nadu. He is currently Professor of Scripture and Head of the Biblical Department at Jnana-Deepa Vidyapeeth, Pune. Email: maprmay22@gmail.com

Prof. Dr Joseph Mattam, **SJ**, belongs to the Gujarat Jesuit Province. An emeritus professor of theology, he was the founder and first director of the Gujarat Regional Theologate and later of the Gujarat Vidya Deep, the Regional Seminary. He lectures in many theologates and seminaries in India and abroad, especially Africa. He is a member of various national and international associations and was the president of FOIM (Fellowship of Indian Missiologists, an ecumenical association). He has authored six books and has edited 13 books, and many articles in theological and missiological Journals in India, Africa, France and the US. E-mail: joemattam@jesuits.net

Prof. Dr Paulachan Kochappilly, CMI, is a native of Kalady and holds a Doctorate in Moral Theology from Accademia Alfonsiana, Rome. He is a professor of Christian Ethics at Dharmaram Vidya Kshetram (DVK), Bengaluru. He regularly contributes articles to national and international journals. He has authored many books and edited a few volumes. His publications include *Celebrative Ethics: Ecological Issues in the Light of the Syro-Malabar Qurbana* (1999), *Evangelization as Celebration* (2002), *Life in Christ: Eastern Perspectives on Christian Ethics* (2010), etc. He was Dean of the Faculty of Theology and serves as the President of the DVK. Email: paulachan.kochappilly@cmi.in

Prof. Dr Shaji George Kochuthara, CMI, is Associate Professor of Moral Theology at Dharmaram Vidya Kshetram, Bangalore, the Chief Editor of Asian Horizons, the Chairperson of the Institutional Ethical Board of St John's Medical College (Bangalore) and the head of the Asian Regional Committee of 'Catholic Theological Ethics in the World Church' (CTEWC). He is editor of the series 'Asian Theological Ethics' (CTEWC) and 'Dharmaram Moral Theology Series.' His publications include '*The Concept of Sexual Pleasure in the Catholic Moral Tradition*' (Rome 2007), and '*Revisiting Vatican II: 50 Years of Renewal*', 3 Volumes (Bangalore, 2014-2015) and over 50 articles. Email: kochuthshaji@gmail.com

Prof. Dr George Karuvelil, SJ, is a Jesuit of the Patna Province. He teaches philosophy at Jnana-Deepa Vidyapeeth (JDV), Pune. He has served as the Dean of the Faculty as well as the editor of Jnanadeepa: Pune Journal of Religious Studies. Having contributed to journals like *Journal of Indian Council of Philosophical Research*, *Theological Studies*, and *Zygon: Journal of Science & Religion*, presently he is working on a monograph on *Rethinking Fundamental Theology: An Essay on Faith and Reason*. Email: gkaruvelil@hotmail.com

Dr Konrad J. Noronha, SJ, PhD (USA), MS (USA), MTh (Delhi), BHMS (Pune), is the Director and Coordinator of the Center for Pastoral

Management at Jnana Deepa Vidyapeeth, Pune. He has a Masters in Clinical Mental Health Counseling and a Doctorate in Counselor Education and Supervision from Loyola University, Maryland. He is a licensed homoeopathic physician (BHMS). He has done extensive clinical work in the USA and India. His refereed articles have been published in *Pastoral Psychology, Journal of Religion, Spirituality & Aging, Indian Journal of Psychological Medicine, Encyclopedia of Psychology and Religion, Vidyajyoti Journal of Theological Reflection, Jnanadeepa: Pune Journal of Religious Studies* and *Counseling and Values*. Email: kjnoronha2000@gmail.com

Prof. Dr Kuruvilla Pandikattu, SJ, is a professor of Physics, Philosophy and Religion at Jnana-Deepa Vidyapeeth, Pune, India. Currently, he is the Dean, Faculty of Philosophy. He has been actively involved in dialogue between science and religion. Author of more than 42 books and 170 articles, Pandikattu is a Jesuit priest belonging to Dumka-Raiganj Province, India. He been involved in organising national and international conferences on science-religion dialogue. The main topics of his research are: anthropology, eschatology, life-management and transhumanism. Email: kuru@kuru.in (personal) or kuru@jdv.edu.in (professional).

Dr A. Maria Arul Raja, SJ, has a Ph.D. from the University of Madras. He teaches Scripture at the Arul Kadal Jesuit Regional Theology Centre, Chennai, and is also the Supervisor of Doctoral Studies at the Institute of Dialogue with Cultures and Religions (IDCR), Chennai. He has a background of Biblical Studies, Sociology, Journalism, Mass Media, Psychology, Sanskrit, Folklore, Philosophy and Religious Studies. He dialogues with subaltern groups, Dalit Movements, Women's Groups, Youth Groups and Alcoholics. He has authored 8 books and contributed over 150 research articles to various national and international journals. He was President of the *Tamil Theology Association* [from 2007-2011] and member of the Editorial Board of the Dalit Commentary Series published by the Centre of Dalit/Subaltern Studies, New Delhi. Email: amarajasj@gmail.com

Dr Joseph Antony D'Mello, SJ, is a Jesuit priest from the Karnataka Province. He has a Ph.D. in Spiritual Theology from the Universidad

Pontificia Comillas, Madrid, Spain. He is the Secretary for Ignatian Charism for the Jesuit Conference of South Asia. He is a resident staff of Jnana-Deepa Vidyapeeth (JDV), Pune, the Coordinator of the JDV Post-graduate Diploma Programme in Ignatian Spirituality, as well as the Director of the JDV Spirituality Center. E-Mail: jossiedm@ gmail.com.

www.ingramcontent.com/pod-product-compliance
Lightning Source LLC
Chambersburg PA
CBHW031959060726
47497CB00015B/495